PRAISE FOR ISABELLA MALDONADO

Praise for *The Cipher*

"A heart-pounding novel from page one, *The Cipher* checks all the boxes for a top-notch thriller: sharp plotting, big stakes, and characters—good and bad and everywhere in between—that are so richly drawn you'll swear you've met them. I read this in one sitting and I guarantee you will too. Oh, another promise: You'll absolutely love the Warrior Girl!"

—Jeffery Deaver, *New York Times* bestselling author

"Intense, harrowing, and instantly addictive, *The Cipher* took my breath away. Isabella Maldonado has created an unforgettable heroine in Nina Guerrera, a dedicated FBI agent and trauma survivor with unique insight into the mind of a predator. This riveting story is everything a thriller should be."

—Hilary Davidson, *Washington Post* bestselling author

Praise for *Phoenix Burning*

"Maldonado's a writer to watch, and she showcases her own extensive law enforcement background in this tightly plotted police procedural."

—*Publishers Weekly* (starred review)

"Maldonado, a former law enforcement officer, brings her experience and expertise to this gripping police procedural. With its gritty heroine, this action-packed mystery will attract readers who enjoy crime novels about the war on drugs."

—*Library Journal*

"Phoenix may be burning, but Maldonado's star is rising. Gritty and gripping."

—J. A. Jance, *New York Times* bestselling author

"Maldonado's writing always bristles with urgency and authority."

—*Mystery Scene Magazine*

"Delivers a brilliant and complicated heroine, accented by a take-no-prisoners plot . . . It's spicy, smart, and entertaining, definitely worth your time."

—Steve Berry, author of *The Lost Order*

Praise for *Blood's Echo*

Winner of the 2018 Mariposa Award for Best First Novel

"A highly entertaining police procedural . . . Maldonado rises to her written challenge to entertain, enthrall, and engage readers in this high-octane thriller."

—*Suspense Magazine*

"A tense thriller with a strong sense of place and an insider's look at some of the most dangerous work in law enforcement."

—Jan Burke, *New York Times* bestselling author

"The Phoenix sun isn't the only thing burning in this thrilling debut, and I look forward to more."

—Shannon Baker, bestselling author of the Kate Fox mystery series

"An ex-narc leads a war against a powerful crime family. The payoff is satisfying."

—*Kirkus Reviews*

Praise for *Death Blow*

"If you're in the mood for a nonstop exposé of every fear you've ever had about cartel crime, Veranda Cruz is the woman to follow."
—*Kirkus Reviews*

"Finally! A kick-ass female protagonist and an author who knows firsthand the world she writes about. The combination makes for an explosive read that grabs you from page one and doesn't let go."
—Alex Kava, *New York Times* and *USA Today* bestselling author of *Lost Creed*

"Red alert to all readers of police procedurals with a strong thriller bent: Isabella Maldonado's *Death Blow* delivers nonstop action with substance, grit, and surprises."
—Lisa Preston, author of *The Clincher*

"Gritty, raw, and realistic, Isabella Maldonado's *Death Blow* is the real deal."
—Bruce Robert Coffin, bestselling author of the Detective Byron mystery series

"A gritty, gut wrenching, page-turning thriller featuring a woman cop bent on bringing down a twisted cartel leader for reasons of her own, *Death Blow* grabs you from the first jaw-dropping scene to the last, and Maldonado's stellar writing weaves it all together."
—Jamie Freveletti, internationally bestselling author of *Blood Run*

THE
CIPHER

THE
CIPHER

ISABELLA
MALDONADO

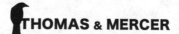
THOMAS & MERCER

Text copyright © 2020 by Isabella Maldonado
All rights reserved.

Published by Thomas & Mercer, Seattle

www.apub.com

Amazon, the Amazon logo, and Thomas & Mercer are trademarks of Amazon.com, Inc., or its affiliates.

ISBN-13: 9781542022477
ISBN-10: 1542022479

Cover design by Laywan Kwan

Printed in the United States of America

For Mike,
the other half of my heart.
I love you.

Chapter 1

Nina Esperanza gazed up at the man who held her fate in his hands. Judge Albert McIntyre perused the submitted documents in silence. She forced her foot to stop jiggling beneath the long oak table and schooled her features into what she hoped passed for a polite expression. The papers had been filed, the testimony had ended—only the ruling remained.

The judge stopped reading to eye her, taking her measure before he spoke. "I am prepared to finalize your petition to the court, but before I do, I want to be sure you are clear about the consequences of this decision. This ruling cannot be reversed. You will have full responsibility for any actions you take or agreements you enter into from now on."

Nina's guardian ad litem, Cal Withers, dug a finger into his shirt collar. "She accepts the terms, Your Honor."

Withers was the attorney appointed by the court to represent Nina's interests. At seventeen years old, she could not petition the court on her own. His silver hair, deep-set wrinkles, and calm efficiency spoke of experience. His careworn expression bore witness to years spent wrangling with an unpredictable juvenile court system that could either render or miscarry justice depending on the circumstances.

The judge flicked a glance at Withers before directing his next words to the girl whose life he was about to irrevocably change. "I understand why you are petitioning this court for emancipation. Especially given your current situation."

The few people allowed to attend the closed hearing shifted in their seats, but Nina refused to shrink down in her chair. After what had happened, she'd made a private vow never to go back into the system. If the judge didn't rule in her favor, she would run away again. And this time, no one would find her until she had passed her eighteenth birthday.

"You have demonstrated that you can support yourself," Judge McIntyre said. "But what are your plans going forward? Do you have a goal for the future?"

Withers spoke before she could answer. "Your Honor, the paperwork we filed shows an early acceptance to George Mason University. She's also been awarded a scholarship and grant money to assist with tuition. She has a part-time job and will live in a dorm on campus where she—"

The judge held up an age-spotted hand. "I would like to hear the young lady speak for herself."

Withers had tried to intervene, to spare her this moment. He and her caseworker had counseled her before the hearing. If the judge asked about her career plans, they had advised her to give a touching speech about how she had considered becoming a nurse, teaching kindergarten, or joining the Peace Corps. Technically, it wasn't a lie. She *had* contemplated those options. For about a nanosecond. Then she'd realized what she should do with the rest of her life. But would the judge accept her choice?

Under the table, Withers nudged her foot with his. She knew what he wanted her to say. Then again, she'd never done anything just because someone said she should. Probably why she'd bounced from one foster home to another.

Coming to a decision, she squared her shoulders and opted for the truth. "I'm entering the criminal justice program at GMU. After graduation, I'll join the police department, work my way to detective, and spend the rest of my career putting monsters who prey on children behind bars."

Withers scrubbed a palm over his face. The county caseworker shook her head.

Nina ignored their reactions, focusing her attention on the judge. "Is that far enough into the future, sir?"

Judge McIntyre narrowed his eyes. "You'll continue with counseling?"

"Yes, sir."

"Circumstances have made you very independent at an early age, Ms. Esperanza," Judge McIntyre said. "But you must allow others to help you when you need it. Remember that."

The courtroom fell silent. Every eye was trained on the judge. Waiting.

Her frayed nerves stretched to the breaking point. Had she just made him doubt she could deal with what had happened to her? Her breath caught.

After an eternity, his deep voice broke the silence. "I will grant the petition."

She exhaled with a long sigh.

"Now for the remaining matter." The smile died on her lips as the judge continued in a somber tone. "The petition for a name change." He held up a notarized document. "You are requesting to change your name from Nina Esperanza to Nina Guerrera. The filing indicates that you wish to choose a name rather than continue to use the one assigned to you. You could do this when you turn eighteen next year, why the rush?"

Withers found his voice. "Your Honor, my client was given her current legal name by her original caseworker when it became clear adoption would be"—he cast her an apologetic glance—"unlikely."

Her gaze drifted down to her clasped hands. As a little girl, she was not among those with bouncy blonde curls and bright blue eyes. She did not have porcelain skin or rosy cheeks. The caseworkers never referred to her as *sweet* or *shy*. Instead, she overheard snatches of conversation peppered with words like *headstrong* and *willful*. She may not have fully grasped their meaning at the time, but she knew these terms—along with her dark hair, brown eyes, and tan skin—set her apart from the other girls. The girls who got adopted.

Withers rushed to fill the awkward silence. "She had no say in the matter and believes the occasion of her emancipation from the guardianship of the Commonwealth of Virginia is the appropriate time to choose a name that reflects her new course."

The judge raised a bushy gray brow at her. "Your new course?"

She lifted her head to meet his gaze. "Do you speak Spanish, sir?"

"I do not."

She drew in a deep breath. Full disclosure was her best option. "I tracked down my very first caseworker from when I entered the system seventeen years ago."

The judge's expression darkened. "I'm aware of the . . . circumstances."

Circumstances. A detached clinical term designed to protect her feelings. The judge probably thought he was being kind, but he couldn't whitewash it.

She had been left to die in a dumpster when she was a month old.

Nina swallowed the lump in her throat and went on. "Her name is Myrna Gonzales. She told me I'd originally been called Baby Jane Doe. She wanted me to have an ethnically appropriate name, so she called me Nina, the English version of *niña*, which means 'girl' in Spanish. She also hoped I would be one of the kids who has a happy ending. That

I would be adopted by a loving family, so she named me Esperanza, which means 'hope.'" The lump in her throat expanded, straining her last words. "I didn't get that happy ending."

"No," Judge McIntyre said. "You did not."

He didn't attempt to patronize her, which she appreciated.

"But why Guerrera?" He wanted to know.

"In Spanish, *guerrero* means 'warrior' or 'fighter,' and *guerrera*—with an *a* on the end—refers to a female."

The judge took a moment to digest her words before his eyes reflected comprehension. "Warrior girl."

She inclined her head in acknowledgment. "I've given up on hope," she said quietly, then lifted her chin. "From now on, I fight."

Chapter 2

Ryan Schaeffer tamped down his excitement. He had to keep his head in the game. So much careful preparation had led to this moment. The late-afternoon sun showered down through the dense canopy of trees, dappling the running trail below. A warm fall breeze rustled through the hedgerow, the faint scent of azaleas providing momentary relief from the pungent odor of sweat clinging to his best friend.

Zippo popped his head above the shrubbery to check on the jogger. "Here she comes." He held the binoculars up to his eyes, focusing them on the winding trail near the shore of Lake Accotink. "I can make out that neon blue tank top she's wearing."

"Let me see." Ryan yanked the field glasses from Zippo's grasp, eliciting a stream of expletives. "Oh yeah." His pulse kicked up a notch as he dialed in a clearer image. "She's a hottie."

The jogger's short-cropped dark hair was sweat-damp and sexy, like the spandex that clung to her toned body. He studied the steady rhythm of the footfalls bringing her closer to his hiding place. His blood heated.

"And she's small," Zippo said. "She can't weigh more than a buck ten. How much of a fight can she put up?" He jabbed Ryan's ribs with a bony elbow. "Should be easy for you, dude."

A senior at East Springfield High, Ryan was already bigger than his father. Four years on the gridiron had taught him how to tackle a runner. Zippo was right—he could take her without breaking a sweat. They'd come to the park every day after football practice, hunting. Today they'd finally found the perfect . . . what had Zippo called her? *Prey.* They were the hunters, and she was their prey.

He glanced at Zippo. "You aren't going to wuss out, are you?"

Zippo grabbed his crotch. "Dude, I'm locked and loaded."

Ryan nodded. "You getting this?"

Zippo held up the burner phone he'd bought last week. "On it."

Ryan would take his turn first while Zippo livestreamed the whole thing. He'd sworn the cops couldn't trace anything back to them. Ryan had gotten ski masks for both of them so they could change places once he finished with her.

Ryan gave a thumbs-up. This would be epic. He peered back through the lenses. "She'll be at the spot in about thirty seconds. Better get in position."

They pulled the knit masks over their heads. Zippo crouched, poking his phone through a hole in the hedgerow.

Ryan hunkered into a three-point stance next to the thickest part of the foliage. She wouldn't see him until it was too late. He watched her approach. They had picked out a place near the end of the running trail, figuring she'd be tired if she jogged the whole way, but it didn't matter. She was tiny. Up close, her brown eyes looked huge in her small face. He would make those eyes go even wider. Body thrumming with anticipation, he focused and waited.

The instant she ran past him, he launched himself, slamming his shoulder into her back with all his weight.

She sprawled headlong, thudding facedown on the grass beside the trail. He had knocked the wind out of her, but he figured she would recover enough to scream in a few seconds.

He couldn't let that happen.

She rolled over as he threw his body forward again and slammed down on top of her, using the full force of his bulk to crush her. He heard the air rush from her lungs in a grunt and knew he'd bought another few seconds of silence.

Before he was prepared, she began to fight. One of her palms shot upward, connecting with his nose. He howled and batted her hand away. While he tried to grasp her arms, she brought her knee up into his crotch. Gritting his teeth, he managed to avoid rolling off her and doubling over.

Realization dawned. If he didn't regain control fast, this crazy chick would kick his butt. Pinning her legs with his thighs, he reached for her wrists. They were so slender he could easily hold them both in one hand. He grabbed one and fumbled for the other when he felt searing pain in the soft flesh along the back of his jawbone just under his earlobe.

He pulled his head back, lifting slightly off her, and caught a glimpse of something black in her free hand. Had she stabbed him? There was no blood. Still clutching one of her wrists, he drew his other arm back to punch her face when the agony returned to light up every nerve above his shoulders. She kept digging that black thing into him.

All thought ceased in the wake of the most excruciating pain he had ever felt. The sensation felt overwhelming, devastating, immobilizing.

Where was Zippo? A small part of his mind still able to function understood he needed help taking down a woman less than half his size. What the hell had he gotten himself into? Darting a glance to the left, he saw the back of Zippo's gray T-shirt flapping behind him as he ran away. He would murder the little weasel first chance he got. The throbbing along his nerves eased a fraction, and he became aware the woman underneath him was speaking.

Her enormous brown eyes had narrowed to slits. "What's your name?"

Intense pain had reduced his thought processes to their most primal level. His synapses only fired on one overriding subject. "You're hurting me."

"Am I?" She pressed in harder, blurring his vision around the edges. "I'm all choked up about that. Here's a thought. Don't jump women in the park."

He could only muster a feeble protest. "I didn't . . . it was just a prank. Wasn't serious."

"Save it." Her lip curled. "You're under arrest."

Everything crashed in on him as her words sent his once-bright future spiraling into darkness. Less than five minutes ago, he'd been headed for college on a full-ride football scholarship. Now he'd be playing hoops in a prison yard.

His watering eyes met her steady gaze. "C-cop?"

"Special Agent Nina Guerrera." Her voice dropped to a whisper. "FBI."

Chapter 3

Nina sat on the edge of a stiff vinyl chair in the waiting area outside Special Agent in Charge Tom Ingersoll's office. He had been holed up inside with Supervisory Special Agent Alex Conner, her immediate boss, for the past half hour.

Conner had left a message with the front desk directing her to the SAC's office as soon as she arrived for work this morning. In two years at the Washington field office, her first assignment after joining the FBI, she had never been summoned to see Ingersoll. Certain this had something to do with her off-duty jog in the park yesterday, she replayed the events in her mind for the hundredth time, unable to figure out what—if anything—she had done wrong.

She gingerly touched her side and winced. Had the oaf cracked one of her ribs when he landed on her? Every muscle ached from his crushing weight slamming down on her small frame. The local PD had called an ambulance, but she'd waved off the paramedics, who then made sure her attacker hadn't sustained lasting injuries. She'd refused transport to the hospital and spent the rest of the evening giving her statement to her former Fairfax County police colleagues. Now she wondered if an X-ray at the ER might have been a smarter move.

Conner opened the door, interrupting her ruminations. "We're ready to see you now."

She stood and strode into the office, confident facade in place. Once inside, she greeted Ingersoll with a curt nod before easing herself into one of the two seats positioned in front of his desk.

"I was concerned to hear about what happened in the park yesterday," Ingersoll began. "Glad to see you're okay."

"I'm fine, sir. Thank you."

Conner took the seat next to her. "According to the police report, you used a tactical pen on your attacker."

Agents could carry weapons off duty and were encouraged to do so, but jogging presented a challenge. She couldn't run through the park holding a handgun without someone calling the police, and there was nowhere to stash it in her spandex running outfit. Given her limited choices, a small device she could hide in her hand was the best option.

She slid the pen from her inside jacket pocket and held it out. "I always carry something for personal defense when I go for a run."

Conner took the proffered instrument, twisting the cylinder to extend the writing tip. "I agree that a lone . . . person in a heavily wooded park should take reasonable precautions."

She was sure Conner had almost said *lone woman* but managed to stop himself before his size 11 wing tip ended up in his mouth.

Ingersoll took the pen from Conner's outstretched hand to inspect it. "These aren't standard issue."

"I used to carry it as a beat cop before I came to the Bureau. Used the carbide tip on the back end to break out the window of a burning car once. Managed to get the driver out in time." She shrugged. "Handy little tool."

The black aluminum-alloy casing, slightly thicker than a normal ballpoint pen, seemed innocent enough. In trained hands, however, the gadget could be formidable.

"The police report says you used the mandibular-angle technique," Ingersoll said, handing it back to her.

The maneuver generated compliance without unnecessary force. She had pressed the tip of the pen on a specific point behind the jawline near the base of the ear, causing excruciating pain to fork like an electric current along his inferior alveolar nerve. After she'd done it, she kept her commands short and simple. His brain, overloaded by stimuli from pain receptors, wouldn't process complex instructions. When he complied, she'd used a control hold to detain him while a passerby called the police. Her cell phone had been crushed during the attack.

Ingersoll picked up a file from his desk, effectively changing the subject. "This is a copy of the Fairfax County police incident report." He opened the folder. "Have you been following the story in the news or online?"

She looked from Ingersoll to Conner and back again. "My mobile phone was pulverized, and I haven't watched television this morning. What's going on?"

Ingersoll glanced down at the papers in his hand. "Ryan Schaeffer wasn't working alone when he attacked you."

"Local PD told me he had an accomplice," she said. "They tracked him down after Schaeffer turned on him."

Ingersoll flipped to another page in the file. "Are you aware the accomplice livestreamed the entire incident before he ran away?"

She felt her jaw slacken. "No."

Ingersoll gave her a wry smile that didn't reach his eyes. "As my daughter would say, you're trending."

She had the odd sensation of walking into a theater after intermission and trying to figure out the plot. "Wait. What?"

Conner spoke up. "Someone edited the video and set it to the soundtrack for *Wonder Woman*." He gave his head a small shake. "That's when it went viral."

"You haven't seen it?" Ingersoll looked surprised.

"You ordered me straight here this morning." She spread her hands, palms up. "Never had a chance to replace my cell or go to my office and sign on."

"The guy who did the soundtrack ran a contest to see who could ID the woman in the video," Ingersoll said. "Took until early this morning, but somebody finally got it right. Public Affairs has been fielding requests from reporters asking the Director for a comment."

Her mind reeled. The Director of the FBI, a man in charge of over thirty-eight thousand federal employees, was being hounded for a statement about her. "Holy mother."

Ingersoll continued, "But that's not why we asked you to come here."

She gazed back at him, unable to fathom what else could possibly have happened.

"A killer left a note at a crime scene in an alley behind M Street last night. We have reason to believe it refers to you."

A chill swept through her. "What crime scene?"

Ingersoll forestalled her question with a raised hand. "I'd like to verify a few things first." His brow furrowed. "Did you legally change your name from Nina Esperanza to Nina Guerrera ten years ago?"

The tilt-a-whirl in her head spun off in a new direction. "It was part of my emancipation process. I was seventeen."

Ingersoll and Conner exchanged a meaningful glance. Apparently, she had just confirmed something. Beyond frustrated, she looked from one man to the other, her brows arched in a tacit demand for answers.

"I appreciate that this is highly personal," Ingersoll said. "But it has a direct bearing on what we are about to discuss."

"The juvenile court records are sealed," Conner added. "We're in the process of obtaining a subpoena, but we'd rather hear the story from you first. Did you petition the court for emancipation after you ran away from foster care?"

"I did." She licked dry lips.

"Was that after you were . . . abducted?" Ingersoll wouldn't meet her eyes.

Which meant he knew. Her hands clenched in her lap. They both knew what had happened to her.

"I was sixteen." She kept her response clinical, devoid of emotion, as she recounted the most harrowing events of her life. "I had run away from a group home and was living on the street. A man drove by in the middle of the night. He stopped and . . . grabbed me. Tied me up in the back of his van."

She didn't say what happened next. The unspoken details of the hours she'd spent with her captor hung in the air between them.

"I managed to escape in the morning." She ended the story abruptly, then directed a question at Ingersoll. "Why is this important now?"

"A sixteen-year-old girl was murdered last night in Georgetown," Ingersoll said in a low voice. "She had run away from her foster family." His final words were barely audible. "Her body was left in a dumpster."

Conner took over. "Metropolitan PD has the case. Their crime scene techs found a note stuffed into her mouth, sealed in a plastic baggie."

She pictured the scene, and the long-buried pain inside her bubbled close to the surface. A young life snuffed out. A monster prowling the street, searching for his next victim.

Ingersoll slid a sheet of paper from a folder. "The note contained a message printed on standard copy paper." He tugged a pair of reading glasses from his shirt pocket, shook them open, and slid them on. Glancing down at the paper, he cleared his throat.

Heart pounding, she listened as he read the killer's message.

"After years of seeking, I thought I would never have Hope again. But today, everything changed. She calls herself a Warrior now. But to me, she will always be . . . The One That Got Away."

Ingersoll looked up, his eyes finally meeting hers. "He spaces down three times, then adds two more words in all caps."

She waited for Ingersoll to read the end of the message.

"Until now."

Chapter 4

Numbly, Nina took the paper Ingersoll held out for her. The page trembled slightly as her eyes drifted down over the message she knew was meant for her.

In an instant, she was back in the dark, suffocating space inside the van, duct tape covering her lips, stifling her screams.

Aware her bosses were watching her closely, she worked her jaw as if loosening it from the sticky tape and forced out the only question that mattered.

"Did they catch him last night?"

"No suspect in custody," Conner said. "No leads either."

She'd dreaded this moment for years. Had tried to convince herself the monster was dead. She couldn't deceive herself any longer. He had slithered from her nightmares into her waking life.

Still reeling, she addressed Ingersoll. "How did you figure out the note was about me? It doesn't mention my name. Not exactly, anyway."

"Your name came up from BAU Three."

She held her tongue while she processed the information. The Behavioral Analysis Unit housed the FBI's famous profilers. Mind hunters. Within that unit, BAU 3 was specifically tasked with crimes against children.

"One of the special agents working there has . . . prior knowledge of your case," Ingersoll said, seeming to choose his words carefully.

"How would anyone put it together?" she said, trying to figure out which agent they were talking about. "It's an unsolved abduction from eleven years ago." The year before her emancipation hearing.

Glancing away, Ingersoll rubbed the back of his neck. "It's Jeff Wade."

Her eyes closed for a moment as she tried to block out the images gathering in her mind. Special Agent Dr. Jeffrey Wade, a name she had hoped never to hear again. "I thought he left the BAU for good."

Wade had been reassigned to the training academy after he'd bungled a profile so badly that a girl died—at least, that's what the lawsuit filed by Chandra Brown's family claimed. Chandra had reported a man stalking her to the local police, who sent the information to the FBI since the circumstances were similar to an unsolved homicide that had occurred a few months earlier in a neighboring jurisdiction. A murder Wade was working on as part of a series of killings involving teenage girls. Wade had looked into Chandra's stalking complaint, decided it had no bearing on his investigation, and punted it back to the locals. Twenty-four hours later Chandra was dead, her murder subsequently linked to the series Wade had been working on.

Because Wade had such notoriety as the FBI's premier profiler, the Bureau took a drubbing. Chandra's estranged family had appeared on camera—attorney in tow—numerous times to point the blame squarely at law enforcement. Wade took a leave of absence, turning his ongoing investigations over to another BAU member, and requested a reassignment when he returned to duty. Rumor had it the legendary Dr. Wade had finally cracked under the strain of two decades spent chasing down child predators. Apparently rumors had it wrong, because he was back.

"His transfer to the academy only lasted six months," Conner said.

Ingersoll continued with the current case after a brief pause as if he, too, was remembering Wade's very public fall from grace. "Due to the bizarre wording of the note, MPD Homicide entered the info into

ViCAP to see if any other agency had a similar murder. That's how Wade ran across the report."

"Like everyone else in the Bureau, he'd seen the viral video, so you were on his mind," Conner added.

Of course Wade would be the one to snap the pieces into place. To say he was familiar with her background was an understatement. The man had nearly prevented her from becoming an agent because of what he knew about her.

To her knowledge, no one else had ever undergone the level of scrutiny she had during her application process. After Nina's polygraph had indicated possible deception on a question about her past, Executive Assistant Director Shawna Jackson had intervened, calling in Dr. Wade to perform an assessment. The EAD was one of a handful of people who reported directly to the FBI Director. Someone in such rarified air wouldn't normally get involved in the applicant-screening process, but Shawna had a personal stake in the outcome since she had recruited Nina into the Bureau.

After reviewing the polygraph exam results and her background investigator's report, Wade had summoned Nina to an interview room, where he demanded to know why she'd become emancipated and the significance of the new surname she'd chosen, and he wasn't satisfied until he'd demolished her carefully constructed walls.

He'd forced her to relive beatings from older kids in the system who had figured her for easy prey due to her small stature. He'd made her recount the night of her abduction in excruciating detail, ripping off the protective scab that had formed in her mind so the whole story bled freely from her. Through it all, he'd stared at her, scribbling on his notepad, while she described the feel of a glowing cigarette tip against her skin.

While she had spoken in halting jerks and spasms, he'd listened in rapt silence, betrayed no emotion, judged her. Since he'd been assigned to determine whether she was trying to hide something from the polygraph examiner, she sensed him waiting for her to break down. To cry or scream or lash out at him. He laid open her soul and peered inside to scrutinize her innermost secrets.

In the end, Wade told her he had concluded she wasn't being deceptive but that the polygraph had revealed her willful repression of certain details of her trauma. There were dark voids in her recollection that he believed made her a liability, a ticking time bomb sure to detonate under the right circumstances. Only EAD Jackson's intervention had prevented his report from keeping her out of the academy. From the day Nina was hired, she had worked harder than everyone else, determined to prove that Dr. Jeffrey Wade had made the wrong call for the second time in his career. And that he was a sanctimonious ass.

"We're detailing you to work directly with Wade," Ingersoll said.

She felt an almost uncontrollable urge to leave the office, go home to bed, and hope like hell she woke up from this nightmare.

"Deep in the background," Conner was saying. "As in, so deep no one sees you. Wade drove to Georgetown from Quantico. He arrived at the crime scene about half an hour ago. You can catch up with him there."

They expected her to work with a man who had dissected her with the ruthless efficiency of a pathologist conducting an autopsy, a man who didn't believe she should be an agent. Part of her wanted to refuse. No one would blame her if she did.

She willed her expression to remain impassive. No way would she let her superiors know what this assignment would cost her. "I'll get a bu-car and head to the scene now."

Chapter 5

Nina flashed her creds at the uniform on the perimeter.

He gave her official ID a cursory inspection. "You're late to the party."

Only the remnants of a crime scene active since dawn remained in place.

"Batting cleanup today." She ducked under the yellow tape strung across the alley.

One of MPD's forensic tech vans hunkered next to a curb, its grille pointed toward a graffiti-covered dumpster. She focused on a cluster of men standing behind a four-foot-high portable privacy screen. Some wore MPD uniforms, some had on white Tyvek suits, others were in business attire.

She had no trouble spotting Special Agent Wade. The bright gold FBI lettering stood out against the dark blue raid jacket draped over his tall frame. When he turned to her, his gaze reflected the bleakness of a man who had seen too much. His steel-gray eyes trapped her, performing an assessment that felt eerily similar to their last meeting two years earlier.

She strode to him and stuck out a hand in greeting. He controlled her access to the case, but she would not let him control her. "Good morning, Dr. Wade."

She figured most people who had gone to the trouble and expense of earning a PhD wanted the official title attached to their name.

"Call me Wade." His gravelly voice matched his rugged face.

His grip was firm, the calluses on his palm surprising her. She noticed he wanted her to use his last name rather than his first, keeping a certain professional distance. Fine with her.

"Guerrera," she said.

He tipped his head toward the man a short distance to his left. "Detective Mike Stanton, MPD Homicide."

Stanton acknowledged her with a quick wave.

Wade lowered his voice. "If any of this becomes uncomfortable, I expect you to let me know."

She looked him straight in the eye and lied. "I will." She was already fifty clicks past uncomfortable.

"There's no time to be delicate," Wade said, shifting into investigative mode. "The scene's no longer fresh. We need any insight you can provide, and we need it now."

She turned to the privacy screen, as much to avoid his penetrating gaze as to survey the scene. "Then I'll get started."

Detective Stanton moved to intercept her. "Before you take a look at the body, can you describe the vehicle he used . . ." He shifted on his feet, obviously uneasy. "With you?"

Logical. Someone who had specially outfitted a van for the purpose of abducting victims might keep it for years.

"Blue Ford Econoline." At his questioning look, she elaborated. "I figured out the make and model from pictures the police showed me after the incident."

The *incident.* A banal word she chose deliberately.

He gave her a slight nod. "Anything else?"

"Plain wrapper. Nothing stood out. At least, nothing on the exterior." She swallowed to moisten her dry throat. "Inside was an empty shell, even the carpeting was yanked out. He put black vinyl flooring down to cover the metal beneath me. My wrists were taped together behind my back. Ankles too."

Wade and Stanton let the silence stretch when she finished. She realized they were waiting for her to continue.

"There were these small round windows in the back." She cupped her hands in front of her to approximate the size and shape of a dinner plate. "He blacked them out with dark spray paint."

Stanton wanted more. "How did the back open?"

"Side-by-side doors. When he locked me in, he shut the one to his left first, then the one to his right."

"That never made it into the report," Wade said.

"There are a lot of small details like that." She lifted a shoulder. "Stuff no one asked me, or no one wrote down, but I recall most of it very clearly."

One of Wade's silvery brows inched up. "Most of it?"

They exchanged silent glares. This was what had almost kept her from becoming an agent. She refused to apologize. "There are some parts I don't remember. At least, I've never tried to remember."

She turned back to Stanton, continuing with her description of the van. "The engine ran smooth. No backfiring, loud pipes, or anything else that would draw attention." She reached into the crevices in her mind, pulling out more scraps of information. "He drove me about half an hour or so before he stopped. There was a divider separating the front from the back, so he had to get out and walk around to open the doors."

"What did you see?" Wade asked.

A monster in human skin.

"It looked like we were parked in the woods somewhere," she said. "The sun hadn't come up yet, so I just saw a bunch of dark trees. Couldn't make anything else out."

Detective Stanton slid his cell phone out, pivoted away, and began speaking in a rapid undertone. She figured he was asking dispatch to put out a BOLO for a vehicle matching her description. A long shot, but worth a try.

"All right," Wade said. "Crime Scene's already finished. We were holding the body until you arrived."

He edged sideways around the screen shielding the body. Following him, she understood why they had erected a visual barrier. The girl's long dark hair spilled over the ground behind her head, the right side matted with dried blood. She lay sprawled on her back, her nude body an obscene display on the grimy pavement.

Nina bent forward to gaze into the filmy brown eyes staring sightlessly back at her. She scanned down, catching traces of silver duct tape clinging to the girl's upper lip.

Standing behind her, Wade gave a quick summary. "One of the busboys from the restaurant on the other side of the alley found her. He was dumping the night's trash after closing, at about three in the morning. He saw her in the dumpster, thought she might be alive, and pulled her out. He ripped the tape off her mouth before he caught on that she'd already taken her last breath."

Detective Stanton returned from his phone call. "The killer placed the plastic baggie with the note in her mouth before covering it with the tape. Probably wanted to be sure it wouldn't fall out."

She agreed. He was taking no chances about the note. A thought occurred to her, bringing with it a sense of dread. She addressed Stanton. "Has anyone from your Crime Scene Unit turned her over yet?"

Stanton slid his eyes to Wade before he responded. "About a half hour before you arrived. We put her back the way we found her."

Careful to school her features, she considered what she had observed so far, juxtaposing the scene with the cryptic note the killer had left for her. He had to have known the FBI would bring her into the investigation, and he was sending her a message.

"After years of seeking, I thought I would never have Hope again," she muttered to herself, cocking her head to study the girl's body from a different angle. "But today, everything changed." She finished quoting the note and glanced up at Wade. "That means he has hope again, but how? In what way?"

He eyed her speculatively. "You tell me."

He wouldn't provide her with the benefit of his analysis, no doubt preferring to hear her take on the situation first. Turning away from both men, she bent down again. What else had he done to this poor girl? A glint of metal drew her attention. She sucked in air.

"You okay, Guerrera?" Wade said, his tone changing to one of concern.

"The necklace." The two words were all she could manage. Once again, the monster had proved he could snatch control away from her anytime he wanted.

A diamond-shaped charm on a silver chain lay on the filthy pavement next to the girl's matted hair, its long chain looped around the girl's slender throat. The same necklace Nina had on when he took her. She peered at the plastic beads that formed a multicolored pattern of concentric diamonds, confirming her suspicion.

She refused to let moisture gather in her eyes. "That necklace was mine," she breathed.

"You're sure?" Stanton said.

"I made it in an art class when I was fifteen. The pattern is ancient. It's called *ojo de dios*." She straightened and pointed at the charm. "God's eye."

Stanton signaled one of the evidence techs over. "Could you get extra pictures of the necklace and send them to my phone?"

Nina turned away, feigning interest in the pavement on the other side of the body to buy time to compose herself. She did not want to look at Wade until she had a semblance of objectivity. This was much harder than she'd thought it would be.

"Do you need some water?" Wade gentled his tone. "I have an extra bottle."

"I'm fine." Another lie. She felt sure Wade could see through it, but she didn't care. Instead, she focused on the facts before her, arriving at the only conclusion that put everything into perspective. "He's re-creating his time with me."

Stanton stopped watching the tech. "What do you mean?"

She crossed her arms. "How many marks did you find on her back?"

"How did you—"

Wade cut in. "Twenty-seven."

The same number of scars striping her own back. How had the monster remembered the exact number of lashes? He hadn't been the one to inflict them on her, but he'd been fascinated by them. She suppressed a shudder as she felt the sensation of his fingertip trailing down the center of her spine, tracing the ridges of her wounds.

"And three burns on her back?" she asked him.

Wade made no response.

His silence felt like a test. He was still assessing her usefulness to the investigation. She faced him and elaborated. "A cigarette burn to mark each point in a triangle. Like the ones he gave me."

Pivoting away, she made a show of scanning every inch of ground. "I've got to keep looking. There might be something else." She wasn't consciously taking anything in until her gaze fell on the dumpster decorated with urban art. In the lower left corner of the scarred and dented metal front, four rows of numbers and letters stood out, spray-painted in fluorescent blue. The top row read "4NG," followed by a colon. Something stirred inside her, drew her in. She squatted, narrowing her eyes.

Wade's knees creaked as he crouched next to her. "Paint looks fresh."

"He wore bright blue latex gloves," she said. "Exactly this color."

He raised a skeptical brow. "You think he's communicating something in code?"

"He definitely did with the note and the necklace. And both were meant for me." She angled her head. "What if 4NG means 'for Nina

Guerrera'? There's a colon after that, indicating the rest of it is the message."

They both leaned closer. The next row down read 8, 15, 16, 5. The row below that had the numbers 9 and 19, and the final row consisted of 4, 5, 1, and 4.

"Every other communication he left behind was securely attached to the body. Like he wanted to be sure we'd find it." Wade swept a hand toward the dumpster. "This doesn't match his pattern. Except for the color, it blends in with the random graffiti all over everything in this alley. He couldn't be sure we'd find it."

"To be honest, we overlooked it," Stanton said, motioning one of the crime scene techs over again.

She hadn't heard the MPD detective approach. His tone held a note of chagrin as he ordered the tech to photograph every inch of the alley.

Wade got to his feet. "Damn," he said under his breath.

She stood as he snatched his mobile phone from his pocket. "What?"

He ignored her, thumb-typing on the device. His gray eyes darted to the painted numbers again, then back to the screen in his hand. "Sonofabitch."

She was ready to grab him by his jacket collar and shake him. "What is it, Wade?"

He finally answered her. "It's a simple substitution cipher. Very basic. But it was definitely him."

"What does it say?"

"It spells out the words *hope is dead.*"

"Holy shit," Stanton said. "I noticed something else when you first got here, Agent Guerrera, but I didn't want to say anything in case I was overreading the scene."

"Noticed what?" she said.

"Look at her." Stanton gestured toward the still form lying nearby. "She looks a lot like you."

Nina stood and tried to see the girl through unbiased eyes. She was Latina, petite, and slender. Like her. Stanton was right. Perhaps she hadn't seen it before because she was looking at someone who was much younger, a total stranger, and also deceased.

"The victim's hair is long, though," Wade said. "He would have cut it short if he wanted to match Guerrera's."

"No," Nina said quietly. "He wouldn't." She reflected on the events of that night. "When he abducted me, my hair was long like hers." Her gaze remained riveted to the girl. "He grabbed my ponytail to pull me inside his van."

After her release from the hospital that night, she'd gone back to the group home and stood in the shower until the water ran cold. Then she stepped out and stood in front of the bathroom mirror, droplets from her wet hair blending with tears. She'd clutched fistfuls of the damp locks, ruthlessly chopping with kitchen shears until her head looked shorn. To this day, she wore her hair in a pixie cut.

"Maybe he's done, then," Stanton was saying as her thoughts returned to the present. "He felt like he couldn't kill an FBI agent, so he chose another victim to take her place. He closed the circle."

"I've seen this kind of fixation before," Wade said, shaking his head. "This isn't only about murder. It's about obsession." He locked eyes with Nina. "And he's just getting started."

Chapter 6

Hermosa Vista Apartments
Springfield, Virginia

Nina pulled the enchilada casserole from the oven. She paused to check the golden-brown melted cheese bubbling at the edges before shooting a glance over her shoulder at Shawna Jackson. "You weren't there. I could tell Wade really didn't want me involved. He was totally aloof. After I spotted that spray paint, he didn't believe it had anything to do with the case until he figured out the code for himself."

"You're an investigative tool to him right now. It's up to you to change that." Shawna sat at the tiny glass-topped table in the cramped kitchen of Nina's apartment.

Situated on the top floor of a four-story building in the unofficial Latin corridor of the Springfield-Franconia district, Nina's unit was what a Realtor would call *modest* or *cozy*. Like the cleaners, cooks, and landscapers who comprised most of its tenants, Nina was willing to live in the crumbling forty-year-old building for quick access to the nation's capital.

She rested the CorningWare dish on a pot holder to cool on the counter. "Honestly, how could you work with him every day?"

For a fleeting moment, Shawna's dark brown eyes held a wistful gleam. "He wasn't always like that. There was a time when Wade was warm. Caring."

Nina sat at the other side of the table. "Before the Chandra Brown case, you mean."

"Before the Bureau hung him out to dry."

"You were an executive assistant director at the time," she said. "You could've helped him."

"An EAD is not the Director. I did what I could when he . . ." Shawna hesitated, searching for the right word.

"Imploded," Nina supplied.

Shawna frowned. "Sometimes we're harder on ourselves than the criminals are. Wade took personal responsibility when Chandra died. Blamed himself."

"From what I understand, he didn't believe her when she said a man was following her. He could've done more. Might even have prevented—"

"You sound like the media."

"Because I've also been on the receiving end of one of his bad judgment calls," Nina said. "What I don't know is why you saved him."

Shawna let out a long sigh. "There's a lot you don't know. That's why I stopped by. We need to talk." She gave Nina a significant look. "Away from prying eyes."

Nina had last seen her mentor wear that expression at this very table three years ago when she recruited her to join the FBI. They'd first met many years before that when Nina was sixteen and Shawna was assigned to the BAU.

The Fairfax County police had called the FBI to help develop a profile of the man who had abducted Nina. Quantico was only a half hour drive away, and Shawna took the unusual step of coming to speak with her in person. Nina had never met anyone as impressive as the tall, polished, self-possessed federal agent and bonded with her almost instantly.

Shawna had kept in touch with Nina when it became clear no arrest would be made in her case. Concerned that her abductor was still at large, Shawna had worked with CPS to ensure no mention of Nina's new surname or address appeared in their final report as they closed out her file. As an emancipated adult in the eyes of the law, Nina would no longer have visits from social workers or entries in a database that could be hacked. Instead, her legal name change would remain part of a sealed juvenile court hearing. Part of a past she wanted to leave behind.

Shawna's example of professionalism coupled with compassion had inspired her to seek a career in law enforcement as soon as she could. While Nina's career as a police officer blossomed, Shawna climbed the supervisory ranks in the Bureau. Throughout it all, Shawna had been her mentor and friend, spurring her evolution from victim to protector.

"You're not here for the awesome food, then?" Nina asked.

Shawna didn't take the bait. "I need to tell you something about Wade. Something I had never planned to discuss with you, but now that you're going to work with him I—"

The doorbell rang.

Anxious to fend off the unwelcome intruder, Nina padded to the door and pulled it open.

"Hola, mi'ja." Her next-door neighbor, Mrs. Gomez, stood in the doorway with a ceramic tray cradled in her hands and her seventeen-year-old foster daughter, Bianca, by her side. "I wasn't sure if you'd eaten, so I brought you some *tres leches* cake."

Perpetually worried Nina would starve, Mrs. G frequently brought homemade dishes or treats. Bianca came over whenever one of her six foster siblings got on her nerves, which amounted to at least three times a week.

Nina duly performed her end of the ritual, taking the offering. *"Gracias."*

"Oh, but I see you have company," Mrs. Gomez said. "I don't want to trouble you with my problems."

Of course she did. "What is it, Mrs. G?"

Mrs. Gomez slid her a sheepish smile. "I was going to make empanadas, but my stove is broken."

Apparently tired of her foster mother's hesitation, Bianca jutted out a hip and got to the point. "We need you to call Jaime for us." She wiggled her pierced brows. "He blows us off, but he'll come running for you."

Nina sighed, stepped back, and held the door open. "Come in."

Mrs. G went into the kitchen and put the cake on the counter, then stood with her hands clasped expectantly while Nina picked up her phone to call the super.

Jaime answered on the first ring. "*Qué pasa*, Nina?"

"*Hola*, Jaime, there's a problem with—"

Mrs. G frantically waved her arms and shook her head.

Nina switched gears on the fly. "With something that needs to be fixed. Can you come over?"

"I'll be there in two minutes, *bonita*."

Rolling her eyes, Nina disconnected and turned to her neighbor. "He'll be mad when he finds out I called for you. I won't be able to get away with that a second time."

"I called him two days ago," Mrs. G said. "We are tired of microwave food." Her lip curled as if she'd been describing toxic waste. Which perhaps she had.

"Hey," Bianca said, peering around Nina for the first time to get a better look at Shawna. "Aren't you on TV or something?"

"Shawna Jackson," she said, standing. "I was on the news last night."

When Shawna left the Bureau six months ago, Nina felt it as a palpable loss. Agents had to retire at fifty-seven years old, with a possible extension to age sixty. At fifty-two, Shawna had seen an opportunity for another career and taken it. Many members of the Bureau retired to take jobs as consultants, security experts, and pundits, their hard-won expertise a valuable commodity. A few, however, had an unusual combination of talent and charisma that made them a natural to appear on national news programs as law enforcement experts.

When a series of incidents involving white police officers shooting unarmed black men had made national headlines a few months ago, Shawna found herself besieged by requests for interviews. The highest-ranking African American female agent in the history of the Bureau, her position and her experience investigating such cases for civil rights violations gave her the chops to speak with authority. Recently, she'd been hired by a major national news outlet as a senior consultant.

Mrs. G rushed over to shake Shawna's hand. "But you are even more beautiful in person."

Before Shawna could respond, a loud knock sounded at the door. Gritting her teeth, Nina tugged it open.

"*Hola, bonita,*" Jaime said through a cloud of Old Spice. "What's the problem?"

She blinked away the tears stinging her eyes from cologne fumes. "It's the stove."

He frowned. "All four burners or just one?"

"You'll have to ask Mrs. Gomez."

She watched as Jaime scanned the kitchen, comprehension gradually tightening his features.

Bianca gave him a finger wave. "*Hola,* Jaime."

He turned back to Nina, scowling. "Not cool, *bonita.* Not cool."

Bianca got in his face. "You wouldn't fix our stove. We've been microwaving our food, Jaime. Think about it." She lowered her voice to convey the true horror and gravity of the situation. "Prepackaged burritos. In the microwave." She held up two fingers. "For two days."

Jaime grimaced. "Oh, all right."

He followed them out, muttering something that sounded like "*pinche* stove" under his breath.

Nina closed the door to find Shawna suppressing a laugh. "I like your neighbors."

"You don't know the half of it. They're like one big dysfunctional family."

"So you've told me. You could afford a swanky condo downtown, you know." Shawna's eyes widened and she added quickly, "No offense."

This time, Nina laughed. "No offense taken. I like it here. This is the kind of apartment building I usually lived in growing up."

She didn't add that she'd deliberately chosen a place in the Latin corridor to remain connected with her community. Bouncing from one family to the next during her formative years, she sometimes felt detached from her heritage. To make up for the loss of a family, she studied Spanish in school and hung out with the Guatemalans, Puerto Ricans, El Salvadorans, Peruvians, Mexicans, and Colombians that made up most of the Latino population in the DC area back then.

After Nina moved into the apartment building, Mrs. Gomez, who was from Chile, occasionally acted as a surrogate mother. She taught Nina a great deal about food and cooking, and about Chilean wine, which Mrs. G claimed put "that French stuff" to shame. Nina would have bet a month's paycheck Mrs. G had never tasted French wine.

Cutting into the casserole, Nina steered the conversation back to its previous course. "You came to talk about Jeffrey Wade?"

Shawna grew serious. "When you went through the applicant process, he'd just been detailed out of BAU."

A polite way to put it. Some said he ended up at the bottom of a bottle, others said he lost thirty pounds he couldn't spare, and a few claimed he spent some of his vacation days in an institution. She wasn't sure how much was true, but the damage to his reputation had been profound and ongoing.

Shawna stared into the distance, apparently lost in thought. Nina sensed a logjam about to burst. Knowing better than to interrupt, she silently dished the fragrant food onto two plates and carried them to the table.

Finally, Shawna continued, "There's another reason he didn't recommend you for hire. I'm one of the few people who knows the whole story."

Nina dropped heavily into her chair, a sense of foreboding overtaking her.

"He had a little sister," Shawna said. "She was taken when she was fourteen years old. The police found her after a few days. Physically, she was okay, but . . ."

Nina looked down at her hands. She had always wondered why Wade had gone into the child-crime section of BAU, a relatively new position when he took it. At least she had an answer for that now. "What happened to his sister?"

"She was twenty years old when she took a lethal overdose of her meds." Shawna shook her head. "According to Wade, she was never the same after what happened."

A puzzle piece snapped into place. "He thinks that's going to be me." Nina made it a statement. "And that my job with the Bureau will be the trigger."

Shawna raised a placating hand. "Look at it from his perspective. An applicant comes through with a history of abuse and violence worse than some of the victims he'd worked with." She drew in a breath. "Worse than what happened to his sister."

"So he holds it against me that I got my shit together and became a cop?" She pointed her fork at Shawna. "I was in law enforcement for four years without any problems before I ever applied to the FBI."

"He thought he was looking out for you." Shawna cut into the enchiladas.

"And he didn't want any blowback if he signed off on my mental fitness, and five years later, I went nuts." She let out a derisive snort. "He's worse than I thought."

"No, it's not just that." Shawna hesitated. "Your file indicated that you can be . . . difficult. You don't always work well with others. You tended to work independently, even as a cop. That's not what we do in the Bureau."

Nina couldn't argue the point, and she hated knowing there were secret files out there. Files that detailed everything about her life from the time she was a month old. Files that were kept from her when others could see them. Most children didn't have paperwork documenting every aspect of their behavior and situation throughout their lives. Foster children did. Foster children described as "difficult" had the thickest files of all.

"You know Wade was my partner when I was assigned to the BAU," Shawna said, changing the subject. "But what you don't know is that a few years after I was promoted out of the unit, we became . . . involved."

"Wait, what?" She could not imagine Shawna with Wade.

"Like I said, he was a different man back then." Shawna placed a bite in her mouth, apparently considering how much to share. "We had already broken up when you applied to the Bureau, but he knew I had encouraged you to submit an application. He felt obligated to tell me he refused to support your instatement." Her features hardened. "So I went straight to the Director."

"I know," Nina said. "And there are some in the Bureau who know you intervened and hold it against me. No doubt Wade is one of them."

Shawna laid down her fork and narrowed her eyes at Nina as the mingled scents of cumin and onion filled the air between them. "I did it because the Bureau needs you." She tapped her chest with a forefinger. "Needs us." When Nina didn't respond, she raised her voice. "The FBI is still mostly a white male agency. When I first got hired, they had barely accepted women as full agents. Think about what it took for a black woman to get through the door in those days. But like you, I decided to outwork everyone else to prove the ones who doubted me wrong. I took the shit posts, shit assignments, and shit equipment. I sucked it up and made it my mission to get into a position where I could help pave the way for others. That's what I did for you, and I won't apologize for it. Not to you. Not to anybody." She was breathing hard.

Shawna never talked about the early days in her career. The discrimination she'd faced. The glass ceilings she'd continuously shattered on her way to the top tier of US law enforcement.

"I didn't see it that way," Nina said quietly. "Thank you."

Shawna gave her a nod of acceptance before continuing. "I told the Director we shouldn't hold the fact that you were a survivor against you. I reminded him you'd been a cop for four years with nothing but commendations in your personnel file." Picking up her fork, she stabbed her enchilada like it had somehow offended her. "Then I used the nuclear option. The Director knew I'd been Wade's partner years earlier." She lowered her gaze. "I called Wade's judgment into question. Told the Director of the FBI that—as a former profiler—I thought Wade's personal issues had skewed his perspective regarding you."

"Damn, Shawna."

"I turned on my partner—a man I had once loved and still deeply cared for—because I believed in you, Nina." Her eyes moistened. "And I would do it again . . . because it was the right thing to do."

"That must have been painful." She reached out to squeeze Shawna's hand, humbled by the faith her mentor had shown in her. "What did the Director say?"

"What could he say? Wade's recent track record was against him. He'd been forced out of BAU on a temp because he was viewed as unstable. Meanwhile your performance was exemplary, and your tests were near the top percentile in every other category. Wade had concluded that your polygraph results showed no deception, only a lack of clarity on certain points due to past trauma. In addition, you had an established history of excellence in a large, well-respected police department." She shrugged. "The Director put you through."

"And Wade is treating me like I belong outside the investigation because that's what he actually thinks." Resentment settled over her. "That I have no business being in the FBI."

"I never meant to tell you any of this, but now that you're his partner, I thought you should know."

"How can I work with Wade when I can't trust him?"

"Because it's your only option," Shawna said. "It's your decision, but if you choose to be his partner, at least now you'll know where you stand."

She processed Shawna's words, fully aware that she would stand exactly where she always had. Alone.

The price of admission to the most important investigation of her life was partnering with an agent who had tried to bork her appointment to the Bureau. She didn't bother to say it wasn't fair. They both knew it.

She met Shawna's steady gaze. "If my choice is to stand by and watch or get in the ring, I'll fight. Every time."

Chapter 7

After a careful assessment of the injury, the fighter known as Odin raised the needle to pierce the edge of the ragged tear above his left eye. White-hot pain rose up to challenge him, cow him, defeat him. He beat it back, pulling the surgical thread through the swollen flesh.

"Damn," Sorrentino said from behind him. "You don't feel nothing, do you?"

Eyes on the cracked mirror, Odin pushed the needle through the other side of the wound, watching the skin tent before the tip broke through. "I feel everything." He tugged, pulling the edges together. "But I'm in charge. I decide whether or not to react." He plunged the sharp steel in again. "I master myself."

Sorrentino guffawed. "Like you mastered The Raider tonight."

Odin allowed a satisfied smile to curve his lips. Andrew "The Raider" Bennett had been the fool who had stepped into the cage with him. Now Bennett would discover the joys of a ruptured spleen.

That was the way of blood sport. Those in the crowd vented their pent-up fury in vicarious combat as the gladiators vied for glory. But Odin had a secret that gave him an edge. He was different from the others. Different from all of humanity. He had taken the genetic advantages he'd been blessed with and pushed himself harder than the rest. The combination of physical and mental superiority set him apart. The sight of flying sweat, the taste of blood in his mouth, the musky scent of fear—all of it intoxicated him.

"I had good money riding on you," Sorrentino said. "I always bet on Odin."

He ignored the flattery. Sorrentino had landed somewhere on the evolutionary scale between a cockroach and a toad, but he had an instinct for business. He knew enough to bet on a winner.

Odin finished the last suture and began to tie it off.

Sorrentino moved in closer, bushy black unibrow scrunching as he watched. "Nice straight stitches. Where'd you learn that?"

He cut his eyes to Sorrentino, resting his cold gaze on the man until he took a nervous step back. Satisfied he'd ended that line of discussion, he returned to his task.

"You available Friday night?" Sorrentino asked, switching to a safer topic.

He snipped the ends close to the skin and straightened before flicking a glance at the row of flat-screen televisions mounted in the upper corner of the wall. "I've got business Friday night. I'll text you when I'm free for another fight."

Sorrentino, apparently understanding he'd been dismissed, shuffled out of the locker room.

Odin's gaze returned to the monitors. Ignoring the ESPN and NASCAR feeds, he focused on the screen airing local news. He rammed his scissors into the med kit and spit a thin stream of blood on the cement floor. Local news. He'd damn well make national headlines if the media knew about the connection between the homeless girl in the alley and the FBI agent in the viral video. Nina had been on every channel. Everyone's hero. What if they found out their new darling had been responsible for that girl's death?

He recalled the video of her fight with that lummox who had attacked her in the park. He'd watched it a thousand times. She was still small, like he remembered, but she'd obviously been training. She had honed her skills and now wore a gun and a badge.

Nina Guerrera. Warrior girl.

He'd never known about the name change. When he tried to look up Nina Esperanza, the trail ended on her seventeenth birthday. He assumed the name change had been part of a sealed juvie court hearing, one of the few kinds of records he couldn't access. She'd slipped by him all this time. She owed him eleven years' worth of retribution.

This time, she would pay her debt in full before he finished with her.

Chapter 8

Nina hated secrets. This particular one felt like a sore festering beneath the surface, tainting every interaction she had with Wade, destined to explode in a toxic spray and shower its poison over both of them at some unknown point in the future.

No matter what Wade had done, or the reasons behind it, every personal consideration took a back seat to hunting the unsub—the FBI term for unknown subject—which is how she found herself following Wade into the BAU meeting room the next morning as if she had no idea why he'd knifed her between the shoulder blades two years ago.

She took stock of the people seated around the conference table. At its head sat Gerard Buxton, a man she knew by reputation.

"Agent Guerrera." Wade gestured in the direction of her gaze. "This is Supervisory Special Agent Buxton, unit chief for BAU Three."

Buxton acknowledged her with a nod. "I brought together a few key people for the first briefing on this case." He turned to his right where a pale woman with auburn hair spiraling into a cascade of curls halfway down her back sat upright, her sea-green eyes alight with curiosity.

"Kelly Breck," she said. "On loan from Cyber, where I landed after a stint in Video Forensics." The hint of a southern drawl softened the technical terms.

Nina chose not to question the inclusion of a cybercrime specialist at a BAU briefing. Buxton had a reputation for using unconventional approaches to investigations, and for getting results.

The man with a blond crew cut seated next to Breck looked like he was on recon from the Marine Corps base a few miles down the road. Black-rimmed glasses offered an incongruous touch to his chiseled features.

"Jake Kent," he said. "BAU Three."

Nina and Wade took chairs opposite the other two agents.

"Let's get started with victimology," Buxton said without preamble.

All eyes turned to Wade, who opened a leather-bound notebook. Everyone else had some sort of electronic device open on the table. No one seemed to be surprised by Wade's antiquated style of note taking.

"The girl's name is Sofia Garcia-Figueroa," Wade began. "Sixteen-year-old Hispanic female. Mother's currently in rehab trying to kick a meth addiction. Father's two years into a ten-year stretch for drug charges. Sofia has been in foster care since she was five years old. She'd been living in a group home for the last six months and ran away for the third time two weeks ago. The group home supervisor reported it after a missed bed check, but no further action was taken to locate her. According to MPD detectives, she began supporting herself through prostitution." He looked up from his notes. "Like her mom."

Listening to the recitation of Sofia's story tore at Nina. In a few brief sentences, Wade had summed up a lifetime of pain, rejection, and trauma. Sofia might have turned her life around, but she would never have the chance now.

Wade flipped to the next page. "Last place anyone saw her was a few blocks down on M Street at nineteen hundred hours the night before she was found."

"Was she with a john?" Kent asked.

Before Wade could answer, Buxton gave Breck a significant look.

She took the cue. "I've been working with Video Forensics. We got her on a bodega's surveillance camera walking in to buy cigarettes," Breck said. "She was alone."

"Did she use a fake ID to buy the smokes?" Nina asked.

"Didn't have to," Wade cut in. "The clerk who works that shift apparently doesn't put a lot of stock in tobacco sales laws. Metropolitan police are dealing with him now."

"Who found the body?" Kent wanted to know, apparently just getting looped in on the case.

"Joaquin Ochoa," Wade said, glancing down again. "A busboy at the Triple Threat nightclub. He went through the rear service door to take out the trash around three in the morning, after closing time. Saw her foot sticking up. We're lucky the dumpster was fairly full, or she would have been down near the bottom and he never would've seen her."

Nina hadn't heard that detail before. "The unsub didn't want to dispose of her. He wanted to be sure I went to the scene. He must have known ahead of time the dumpster would be full." She turned to Wade. "Was it close to the time the garbage is normally collected?"

Wade flipped a few more pages. "Trash is picked up weekly. Scheduled for the following morning at six." He gave her a nod of agreement. "He wanted her found."

"And he wanted her found in a dumpster," Nina said. She was certain of it. Nothing this killer did seemed random.

"That's been bothering me," Wade said. "Why did he place her in the bin? If he merely wanted to delay discovery, he could have hidden her on the pavement behind it. She wouldn't have been spotted until trash collection time when a garbage truck with a hydraulic lift picked up the dumpster to empty it. In fact, that would have made more sense if he wanted to be certain someone saw her." He looked at Nina. "Makes me wonder if he knew your history."

He made the comment with the clinical objectivity of a seasoned investigator, but his words fell on her with the force of a physical blow. He'd posed the idea that the unsub had staged Sofia's body in a grisly parody of Nina's as an infant, which meant he suspected the unsub might be aware someone had thrown her in the trash.

She recovered as quickly as she could, striving to hide her reaction. "I don't see how he could have known. I certainly didn't tell him about it when he had me."

"But there were some people who knew?" Wade continued.

"The circumstances of my entry into the foster system were in my file, but I never spoke about it to anyone." Her eyes slid away from Wade's. "Ever."

"What a killer does with his victim postmortem speaks volumes," Kent said, saving her from further explanation. "Someone who arranges the body carefully, or covers it up, indicates that he knew the victim or experienced a modicum of remorse for his actions. On the other hand, someone who treats the body with contempt demonstrates total dehumanization of the victim." He tapped his notebook. "This killer felt no regard for Sofia and did not believe she deserved any consideration whatsoever. That could be the extent of his reasoning for dumping her where he did."

"True," Wade said. "But there's more here. What about the note he left in her mouth and the coded message spray-painted at the scene? Both mentioned 'hope' in a way that made it clear he knew Agent Guerrera's former surname." He turned back to her. "How would he know that about you?"

She hesitated a beat before responding. "Because I told him." The statement hung in the air a moment before she elaborated. "He forced it out of me. At first, I gave him a fake name, but he could tell I was lying." She straightened in her chair. Damned if she would let anyone judge her sixteen-year-old self. "He kept hurting me until I told the truth." He had broken her that day. A part of her would always remain broken.

Undeterred by her obvious discomfort, Wade delved deeper. "Did he seem to understand that 'esperanza' meant 'hope' at the time? Did he make a comment about it?"

She thought back, forcing her mind to compartmentalize, sifting through the detritus of memory fragments. "No. He must have figured that out later."

Everyone seemed to mull this over a moment before Buxton pushed the discussion forward, diverting them from the awkward turn the conversation had taken. "Was Sofia Garcia-Figueroa sexually assaulted in any way?"

"Raped," Wade said, pulling his eyes from Nina to scan his notebook again. "There are also twenty-seven horizontal lacerations across her back as well as three burns from what looks to be a cigarette and ligature marks around her throat. We won't know in what order everything happened until we hear more from the ME."

Nina's stomach gave a nasty lurch. "You mean the sex assault could have been postmortem?"

"The full autopsy will give us a better idea," Wade said. "We're also waiting on a tox screen and a DNA report."

"I've got a rush on it," Buxton said.

"Any idea where the murder occurred?" Kent asked.

"We only know it wasn't at the scene where the body was found," Wade said. "Forensic analysis of trace evidence may help determine that too."

Nina focused on the girl's life for clues about her death. How would she have managed to live on the street? Working as a prostitute was risky on many levels. She would have needed protection, and she had likely fallen prey to the narcotics trade that sucked so many in.

"Is she affiliated with any gang?" she asked. When Wade raised his brows, she elaborated. "Did she have a pimp? A supplier?"

"MPD is working that angle," he said. "They have boots on the ground in the neighborhood right now. I should hear from Stanton today or tomorrow. That's all I have."

Buxton immediately turned to Breck. "Let's hear about the video."

Apparently caught off guard, Breck jumped and grabbed the laptop in front of her. Nina sympathized with her. Buxton was running the meeting at a fast clip.

"We analyzed video from multiple city cams and businesses along M Street," Breck said. "None of them were angled to show the alley behind the nightclub."

"I'll bet he knew that too," Nina said. "He planned everything else, it would be logical for him to scope out the site in advance."

"We focused on a ten-hour window beginning two hours before she was seen alive in the bodega and the time she was found in the dumpster," Breck said. "But we can do another search with an expanded time frame."

"You get anything?" Wade asked.

Breck's face split into a grin. "Watch this."

She spun her laptop, facing the screen outward. They all leaned in, focusing on a video of M Street cast in the eerie glow of streetlights and neon signs. The late-night party zone, bordering on seedy, bustled with a mixture of motorized and foot traffic, many in various states of inebriation.

Breck clicked a key, and each vehicle vanished, along with its floating time stamp. Pedestrians strolled along sidewalks or darted across the busy thoroughfare, serpentining between now-invisible cars beneath the circles of light cascading down from streetlamps, everyone shadowed by a unique time stamp.

Breck narrated as they watched, her southern accent growing stronger with excitement. "We used a face-rec filter to spot the victim, but she never appeared in any footage along this street in the ten-hour window we checked."

"She didn't walk into the alley, then," Nina said. "Someone *took* her there."

"We've already established that the trash hadn't been emptied for several days prior," Wade said. "So she couldn't have been transported into the alley in a garbage truck. How else would he have gotten her there?"

Nina considered the possibilities. "Can you narrow the visual parameters to people carrying boxes or carts? Anyone making deliveries."

"Not only can I do it, I can make it look easy." Breck typed a command. "Check it out."

Men with dollies or boxes wended their way down the strangely empty sidewalk. One of them stopped short, waving his arms and shouting before crossing the street. Nina chuckled as the man spun to jab his middle finger in the air, the commonplace behavior made comical by the digital subtraction of the vehicle that must have almost hit him.

Kent leaned forward, eyes locked on the screen. "Can you eliminate everyone except people going into the Triple Threat club?"

Breck's pale fingers flashed on the keys. More images vaporized. They watched in rapt silence.

"There." Nina pointed. A heavyset man in a dark uniform with a pronounced limp wheeled a handcart with a large, bulky cardboard box into the nightclub. The bill of his ball cap hid the upper half of his face and a dense beard blurred the lower half. Time sped by, then slowed again as he pushed the empty cart out, unhurried steps meandering down M Street until he left the frame.

"Where's his truck?" Nina said.

"Let me tag him." Breck entered another command. "Okay, I'm picking him up here."

The man sauntered toward a Ford Econoline van, hauled open the rear doors, and thrust the dolly inside.

Nina's blood chilled when she saw the vehicle.

He limped around to the driver's door, hoisted himself inside with obvious effort, and drove off.

"License plate?" Kent said.

Breck zoomed in. "Van doesn't have one."

"Traffic cams," Buxton said, agitated. "Follow him."

"We only pulled video from a two-mile radius around the scene." A hint of pink flushed Breck's porcelain skin. "I'll expand the search parameters. Now that we have a suspect vehicle, I can go back and track it."

Nina concentrated on their remaining option. "Can you search databases for face-rec on the delivery man too?"

"Let me see if I can get a better look at his face," Breck said. "It's dark, but we can probably lighten the image enough to clear it up."

"Something's not right," Nina said. "The man who attacked me was physically fit and muscular." She pointed at Kent. "Built like him. This guy looks obese, and he limps on his right foot."

"You haven't seen him in eleven years." Wade gestured up and down his body. "Take it from me, a lot can go south on a man's physique in that amount of time. Especially if he injured his leg and couldn't work out."

Breck swiveled the laptop back toward herself and began typing. "I'll map his gait and enter it into the system. If a suspect candidate shows up on video, we can compare his limp to this one."

Kent slid off his glasses. "If I wanted to defeat face-rec . . . could I put on a fake nose, a beard, or glasses to confuse the system?"

Breck shook her head. "Facial recognition works off your overall facial bone structure, so stuff like that won't matter. You'd have to go a lot farther to fool the kind of tech we have now."

"But it could be done with cosmetic implants or surgery?"

She gave him a dubious frown. "Theoretically."

"Either way, we have our first viable lead now." Buxton interrupted the ancillary discussion. "Agent Breck will follow up on it. In the meantime, let's get to the profiling."

Nina perked up. This is what she had been most anxious to hear. Though his reputation had taken a hit, Dr. Jeffrey Wade was still the Bureau's most experienced mind hunter. How would he mentally dissect the psyche of the monster?

"It all comes down to motive," Wade said. "The unsub's behavior reflects his personality, which will conform to certain patterns. These patterns provide insight into what makes him tick." He steepled his fingers, tapping them against his chin. "This killer is methodical. He chose Sofia as his victim specifically to draw Guerrera into the investigation. His note makes it clear he's connecting this crime to the one he attempted to complete eleven years ago. It's wish fulfillment. We can reasonably conclude that he acted out after seeing Guerrera in the viral video."

Kent furrowed his brows. "You're saying the video was the precipitating stressor?"

"That's the most logical assumption," Wade said. He glanced at Nina. "Killers may fantasize about their crimes for quite some time before acting on them. Usually a series of circumstances or events converge in a way that spurs action. Seeing you again—especially where you are in a position of authority, decisively taking down a predator—could certainly set him off."

She assumed Wade was providing more background for her benefit and possibly Breck's. As the two people in the room with no background in profiling, they would benefit from more information.

She took advantage of the opportunity. "What kind of predator hits twice in eleven years?"

"A truly obsessed stalker who found another victim to take your place," Wade said. "Someone who had repressed his urges until they were triggered by a stressor."

Kent pushed his glasses back on. "Or a predator who's been fly-ing under the radar but has killed others during the last decade or so. We can't be sure Guerrera was his first or his last before this murder occurred."

"I would be surprised if someone with such a unique and consistent pattern wouldn't red flag in the system," Wade said.

Buxton shook his head. "There aren't any similar cases in ViCAP, and we didn't get a match in the forensics database on trace material at the scene. That includes hair, fiber, fluids, the works. As I mentioned before, though, this was just a preliminary check. We'll have a more complete report shortly once they process everything at the lab."

Nina asked the awkward question they all seemed to be avoid-ing. "Has any of the evidence from M Street been compared with the samples collected from my case?"

"We're in touch with Fairfax County PD," Wade said. "They're pull-ing the box from archived evidence storage. Our lab wants the original material to test. In the meantime, they've sent the digital profile over. We'll know something soon."

"Hold that thought," Buxton said, looking down at his phone. "Public Affairs just sent me a text. Says to turn on the news." He picked up the remote and aimed it at the flat screen on the wall behind Nina.

She swiveled her chair to face the monitor. "What's going on?"

"The unsub put out a message." Buxton clicked on the remote. "To the public."

Chapter 9

Nina watched a distinguished silver-haired anchor in a dark gray suit on the wall-mounted television. A news banner flashed below him as he spoke into the camera.

". . . message through the Channel Six News Facebook page. Out of a sense of obligation to our viewers, we investigated before going live with this report. We also reached out to the FBI for comment. For more on this breaking story, here's Jerrod Swift."

The frame switched to a two-shot that included a reporter in his late twenties seated next to the anchor.

"Thanks, Steve." Jerrod pushed a dark lock away from his forehead and looked into the camera. "About twenty minutes ago, someone sent a direct message to our Facebook page claiming to be the person who killed sixteen-year-old Sofia Garcia-Figueroa in Georgetown two nights ago."

Jerrod's voiceover continued in the background as the screen switched to an image of the news channel's Facebook page. "The person who contacted us used a fake profile and claimed to have knowledge of the crime only the killer would have. We can exclusively share the contents of the message."

"What does it say?" the anchor asked as the screen cut back to a shot of the news desk.

"He's angry about what he refers to as a law enforcement cover-up."

"What kind of cover-up was he talking about?" The anchor swiveled his chair to face Jerrod. "And how did our news team conclude the message was legitimate?"

"We contacted the FBI and provided the image he sent us." A photo of the cryptic message found in the plastic baggie popped up. "They wouldn't comment, but sources close to the investigation confirmed it matched a note the killer left at the scene."

"Sonofabitch," Wade said, momentarily distracting Nina. She dragged her eyes back to the nightmare playing out before her as Jerrod continued his report.

"Whoever sent the direct message to our page claimed the message refers to FBI Special Agent Nina Guerrera, who recently appeared in this viral video. He called her the 'Warrior Girl,' which he says is the English translation of her name."

Nina clenched her jaw to block the stream of obscenities threatening to burst from her as Jerrod's disembodied voice narrated in the background while footage from Accotink Park filled the screen.

"We noticed something interesting when we reviewed the clip," Jerrod said. "Here's a still shot."

This time the screen split, with an isolated frame of Nina captured from the viral video next to a high school picture of Sofia Garcia-Figueroa.

"There's a definite resemblance," the anchor said when the camera cut back to him. "What is the FBI telling us?"

"They don't have an official statement yet."

"So what does the killer want?" the anchor asked Jerrod. "Did he indicate why he's speaking out through the media?"

"He said he's not going to let the FBI hide information from the public," Jerrod said. "Sounds like he wants credit for what he did."

Wade let out an exasperated groan. Nina surmised he didn't appreciate armchair profiling.

"And he shared a coded message with us," Jerrod continued.

Nina held her breath as an image of a series of letters and numbers flashed on the screen. They were different from the ones he'd painted on the dumpster at the scene.

The anchor continued to fire questions at the field reporter. "What does that mean, Jerrod?"

"We don't know yet, but we're working on it."

"So the killer contacted Channel Six News exclusively?"

"Yes. He didn't say why."

"Wait, I'm getting something from the producer." The anchor lightly touched his ear. "We've got a bunch of hits on our Facebook page. People are trying to decipher the message." He glanced at Jerrod. "We'll be sure to share possible solutions with the authorities."

Jerrod nodded, trying to cover his excitement with a somber expression, missing the mark. "Whatever else is going on, the killer appears to be focused on Special Agent Guerrera," he said. "Let's hope the FBI is hunting him down right now."

"Thank you for this report, Jerrod, and please let us know about any future developments. This guy is as much of a cipher as the clues he leaves behind." The anchor swiveled to address the camera. "After the break, we'll catch up with a pest control company in Reston that uses psychics and crystal power to keep bugs out of your home."

"Shut that damn thing off," Buxton said, then looked around the table. "Did anyone get that?"

Breck read from her laptop. "Thirty-two, eighteen, ten, and thirty-six, followed by an *F* and an *R*."

Wade glanced up from his scribbled notes. "If the first number is thirty-two, he didn't use a simple substitution cipher this time."

"I'll forward it to Cryptanalysis," Buxton said. "The game has changed. The unsub is pulling the public directly into the middle of our investigation."

"He wants to control every aspect of the case," Wade said. "Including the information we release. He's also enjoying the spectacle, as long as it concerns him. Classic narcissist."

"What's our best guess for his next move?" Buxton's pinched expression told Nina he dreaded the answer.

"He'll double down," Wade said. "Go after Guerrera personally. Prove his superiority by taking out a Fed."

Nina had no intention of letting that happen. The monster believed he had unfinished business with her, but he had no idea what she had become. Their paths seemed destined to converge again, but this time she would be ready for him. "And if he doesn't succeed?"

Wade's eyes bored into her. "Then someone else is going to die."

Chapter 10

Nina did not miss the implication. Sofia Garcia-Figueroa had died in her place and, if she couldn't stop the monster, another girl would do the same. She felt a pall of culpability descend, settling over her.

Breck broke the silence. "What kind of killer communicates in code?"

"In my experience," Wade said, "serial killers."

"But we only have one victim." Flicking a glance at Nina, Breck added, "One *deceased* victim, anyway."

"That's another problem I'm having with this case." Wade dragged a hand through his coarse gray hair. "The ones who engage in this way have killed before, but the physical evidence—or lack thereof—says he's only had one prior unsuccessful attempt."

The room fell silent again.

"Hope is dead," Nina said, mulling over the first coded message. "What the hell does that mean?"

"If the victim was a substitute for you, that means he ritually killed you," Wade said without inflection.

"Then why did you say someone else will die?" Breck said to Wade.

"Good question," Buxton cut in. "In fact, can you update your assessment of this unsub based on what we've just heard, Agent Wade?"

"The surest path inside the mind of a killer is his behavior, particularly at the scenes of his crimes, when he's acting out," Wade began.

"Between Guerrera's case and this new one in DC, he's established a definite pattern in both victimology and methodology. The fact that he wore gloves, avoided committing the crime on camera, altered his appearance, and obtained a delivery uniform tells me he's organized and disciplined. The stunt with the media indicates that he craves attention and further underscores his need for control. He wants to show the world that *he's* in charge of the investigation, not the FBI." He cut his eyes to Nina. "And he has a fascination with you."

Nina felt the spotlight shift to her. Like they all thought she was withholding some critical piece of information that would lead them to his door. "I have no idea why," she said, trying to keep any sign of defensiveness from her response.

Wade kept his gaze on her. "In the instance of a repeat offender, the most important cases to scrutinize are the earliest, which will be near the perpetrator's place of residence and reveal more about what prompted the crimes." He paused, apparently weighing his words. "If you were—as his note says—the one who got away, that could indicate you were also his very first victim. He hadn't perfected his skills, so you might have critical information about him. Things you may not even realize you know."

"You believe he's a serial killer?" She crossed her arms. "We don't have three victims."

Like all other agents, she had studied different types of murderers in the academy. Serial killers were defined as having at least three victims, with a chronological or psychological separation between each event. Mass murderers were characterized as killing at least four individuals in one incident. Finally, spree killers had two or more victims in different locations with no de-escalation period between.

Wade lifted a shoulder. "I'm not saying he's a serial killer, but he's definitely a repeat offender. It's possible that something about you sparked him initially, caused a reaction. When you escaped, that set him back, perhaps shook his confidence. He may have repressed his violent urges until he saw you in the video."

Kent nodded slowly. "And now the unsub's out to prove to the world, and to himself, that he can have her."

"It would be essential to him," Wade said.

Buxton dug a finger into his shirt collar and drew in a deep breath. "We need actionable intelligence to ID this guy. We're going to have to go over the incident involving Agent Guerrera." He hesitated, then added, "In detail."

His grim expression told her he was giving her a chance to back out gracefully. If she weren't in this room, part of this team, Wade would interview her privately and report his findings to the others. Everything would be filtered, protecting her from the scrutiny and judgment of her colleagues. If she remained here, she'd have to recount her story and answer questions as they arose. Basic training had taught her that firsthand interviews were always the best source of information. And she was the most valuable source they had right now.

This was her moment. The time had come for her to talk about what had happened and everything that led up to it. To speak about the most intimate, most humiliating hours of her life. She would either deal with it or she would sit on the sidelines while other agents worked the case.

As Nina looked around the table at her colleagues, she remembered recounting her story for investigators and counselors when she was only sixteen. If it would help catch the monster, she could do it again now as a grown woman.

Wade spoke out of the corner of his mouth in a voice only she could hear. "You don't have to do this."

What Wade didn't understand was that this was exactly what she had to do. She squared her shoulders and directed her gaze at Buxton. "What do you want to know?"

Buxton exchanged a covert glance with Wade. They must have planned for this ahead of time, designating Dr. Jeffrey Wade, forensic psychologist, to take her through the account. Buxton clearly knew Wade had already gone over the incident with her during her applicant process. He must have decided it would be easier for her to open up to him again.

As if.

Wade swiveled his chair to face her. "Nina, why don't you start with what you remember about the abduction?"

He had never used her first name before. He also referred to "the abduction," distancing her from the attack. She had used the same interview tactics with crime victims.

"It was late at night," she began. "I had run away from the group home and was crashing with some women camped out behind a strip mall in Alexandria."

He nodded, encouraging her to go on.

"The first time I saw the van, it passed by slowly, then came back a second time and stopped across the parking lot from us. One of the women got up to see if he wanted to do some business."

She remembered the woman as clearly as if it had happened yesterday, her stilted shuffle making her greasy blonde hair swing as she affected a streetwalker strut.

"I just hung out with the others," Nina said. "Didn't have a habit to feed, so I wasn't in the trade." She found herself focusing on Wade's cool gray eyes as she poured out her story. "The woman came back to us. Said he was interested in me, not her."

She could still hear the woman's bark of laughter, her blackened teeth and swollen gums making a cavernous void contrasting with pale skin in the moonlight.

"Without warning, the man threw open the driver's-side door, jumped out, and ran straight toward me." Nina steadied herself as the stark terror of that night washed through her, bringing memories of pain and anguish in its wake. "He wore a black ski mask and bright blue latex gloves. It was kind of chilly, but not cold enough for a ski mask. Once I saw his face was covered, I tried to get away, but he was already sprinting. He caught up to me in a few strides, grabbed my ponytail, and yanked me to him." She absently touched her cropped hair. "He wrapped one of his big hands around my throat and squeezed."

"What did the others do?" Wade said.

"Took off."

She had been certain they would rush to help her. They were five adult women. Together they could have fought him off. Instead, they had watched her being dragged away and had done nothing about it. Like so many others in her life, they had abandoned her. This was the moment when she had truly accepted she was alone. That she could only count on herself.

"He didn't even have a weapon, but they just scattered." She swallowed hard, forcing down the lump congealing in her throat. "Left me behind."

"What happened next?" Wade prompted gently.

"He picked me up and carried me to the van, then choked me until I blacked out."

"And when you came around?" Wade's even tone betrayed no emotion. He was in interview mode.

"I'd start to fight, and he would hit me in the head. Kept me disoriented." She continued to concentrate on Wade, who anchored her to the present as she sank deeper into the past. "I was dizzy and sluggish. I remember him pulling off my clothes and taping my wrists and ankles together. He also taped my mouth."

"Do you remember what kind of tape he used?"

She tried to dredge up a clearer picture. "No."

"What color was it?"

"It was dark. I don't remember."

No doubt sensing her agitation, Wade moved on. "Please don't take this next question the wrong way, but I have to ask to understand what personality type he is." He waited until she acknowledged him before speaking. "Did you fight him?"

"Like my life depended on it."

"How did he respond?"

"The more I struggled against him, the more violent he got. Actually, I think it turned him on."

Wade gave her a brief nod as if he'd been expecting that answer. "Okay, what happened next?"

"He opened the van's back doors. There were trees around. A lot of trees. He dragged me out, threw me over his shoulder like a bag of sand, and carried me to a shed. It looked small, but sturdy."

She stopped, gathering herself for the next part. Wade did not push her. Everyone waited for her to take up her story.

"After he got me inside, he shut the door and laid me facedown on a steel table. He used nylon rope to bind my left wrist to a pole at the upper left corner. Once I was secure, he cut the tape off, grabbed my right wrist, and tied that to the other corner. He did the same to my ankles."

"So he made sure you were restrained at all times?" Wade asked.

"I couldn't get away." It came out as a whisper.

"It's okay," Wade said, his voice low and soothing. "Then what?"

"He disappeared for a few minutes. When he came back, he was wearing a black cloak with his mask and gloves still on."

"What did his cloak look like?"

"I was on my stomach, but I could see that it was long and opened in the front. He had a rope tied around his waist."

"You're doing good. Go ahead."

She wasn't certain if anyone but Wade had read the Fairfax County police case report and knew exactly what had happened to her. She had planned to compartmentalize, shifting into her investigative role to create emotional distance. Her goal had been to recite the facts as if they had happened to someone else and she was merely reporting them, but the images from that night had assaulted her, threatening to overwhelm her. Steeling herself with thoughts of Sofia Garcia-Figueroa, she plowed on.

"He kept touching the marks on my back. Said he . . . he wished he had been the one to give them to me." She paused, rethinking her words. "Actually, he said 'bestow' them on me, like he was talking about an award."

Apparently, the fuzzy bits of memory Wade had found problematic during her application process were beginning to clear a bit.

"I'm sure this must be difficult." Wade's tone grew sympathetic. "What did he do after that?"

She rubbed damp palms against her slacks, readying herself for the next part. "He took out a cigarette and lit it. I watched him from the corner of my eye. He talked to me the whole time, asking me questions about the belt marks and whether I cried when I got them. That's also when he asked me to tell him my name."

Breck's hand went to her mouth as she listened.

"Did he specifically mention belt marks?" Wade asked.

She closed her eyes, scouring her subconscious for details. "I believe he did."

A note of urgency tinged Wade's voice. "How would he know a belt made those marks?"

She knew where Wade was going with this line of questioning. He was working on the assumption that the unsub knew her before he had taken her. She punched a hole in his theory. "The welts were fresh. I'd only gotten them a few days earlier. He could probably still see where the buckle had cut the skin. Pretty obvious what caused them."

Wade tried a more direct approach. "Can you recall seeing him before that night?"

A question the police had asked a thousand times. One she had asked herself many times more.

"I can't."

Wade studied her in silence, taking her measure. The air conditioner kicked on, its hum filling the air around them. "What did he do with the cigarette?"

He knew damn well what the monster had done with the cigarette.

"He used it on my back three times." Her pulse raced, but she held herself still, unflinching with her answer. "He made a triangle. A burn hole at each point."

She remembered the sound of her own scream drowning out the sizzle as the glowing tip seared her. The odor of burning flesh reaching her nose. Her chest heaving against the cold steel as she braced herself between each contact of the cigarette against her bare skin, once on each shoulder blade, and finally in the center of her lower back.

She didn't want to go on but knew she had to. Something she recalled could provide a clue to stop the monster, some seemingly insignificant detail that had never come up before. She owed Sofia that. And she owed whoever he undoubtedly had in his sights right now.

"After he finished, he seemed . . . excited. He untied the rope around the cloak's waist and spread the front open." Pulse pounding, she proceeded to describe all three times the monster had raped her. He had held her for hours, repositioning her between each assault.

Wade listened without interruption. When she finished, he asked, "Did he say anything to you at that time?"

"He laid on top of me. Spoke into my ear." She scrunched her eyes closed, willing his words to come to her. "Dammit, I can't remember what he said."

"It's okay," Wade said, unable to hide his disappointment.

After that, she answered every one of their questions in turn. Yes, he had worn a fresh condom each time. No, he hadn't bitten her. Yes, he had struck her repeatedly. No, he hadn't broken any bones, but she had sprained her left wrist trying to get away.

She felt spent. Mentally and physically drained. But it wasn't over yet.

"How did you escape?" Wade said, moving on with obvious reluctance.

"After he was . . . done with me, he left. I was still tied to the table, and I could only move a little. He had hurt me." She swallowed a lump in her throat. "A lot. I was soaked with sweat. My hands were so damp, they were sliding on the plastic rope. I kept pulling. My hands are small. I made them narrower like this." She raised her arm, tucking her thumb into her palm to demonstrate. "I kept pulling until my left hand slid out. After that, I managed to untie myself."

Wade's brow went up. "You didn't know when or if he was coming back, did you?"

"I had to work fast. The knot on my right ankle took the longest. I had regained my equilibrium by that point, but I had a terrible headache. I slid off the table, tiptoed to the door, and opened it. It was still dark, but the sun would be coming up soon. I didn't see anyone around. The van was gone, so I took off running through the woods."

"Still naked?" Breck spoke for the first time.

"There were no clothes in the shed, and he must have left mine in the van. Either way, my life was more important than my modesty at that point."

Wade silenced Breck with a glare. "Go on, Nina."

"I had to run a long way before I finally came out near some houses. I didn't know the area but found out later that he'd taken me to Chantilly. It's in the western part of Fairfax County, about thirty-five minutes from where he'd grabbed me."

She thought back to her frantic search for help, her terror at knocking on the door of a stranger when she was hurt and vulnerable. A stranger who could be worse than the monster she had just escaped.

"I spotted a house with a light on and rang the doorbell. A man answered, took one look at me, and hollered for his wife. She put a blanket around me while her husband called the police."

"What happened after the police arrived?"

"The usual. They questioned me while a couple of EMTs checked out my injuries. I was pretty traumatized." She had drawn from the mix of adrenaline and terror coursing through her to hold herself together through countless interviews with detectives and medical personnel over the next several hours. It was only much later, finally alone after a long shower, that she had allowed herself the luxury of tears.

"Did they transport you to a hospital?"

"You mean did they do a rape kit?" she said, her tone sharper than she'd intended. "Yes. I never saw the report, so you'd probably know more than I do about the results." Another file with information she'd never seen.

"What about the crime scene?" Wade asked.

"I was able to tell them where the shed was, but by the time they got there, it was fully engulfed. Burned to the ground in less than half an hour."

"Who owned the land it was on?" Buxton asked.

"The estate of an elderly couple who died without a will. They'd built a house on a twenty-acre parcel of land decades earlier. Their adult children, who had all moved away, were squabbling over it. The property had been in probate for over a year. The police told me my attacker had most likely constructed the shed without anyone's knowledge or consent. They processed what little evidence was left after the fire, but any prints, fiber, or DNA were destroyed."

As she finished her account, something Wade had said earlier prompted a question of her own. "You kept asking about the kind of tape he used," she asked him. "Why?"

"Might help to know if it was anything unusual. Same is true with whatever he used to cut it from your wrists and ankles. There are some military knives that can slice through parachute cords and tough fabrics."

"I don't recall seeing what he used."

"I think that's enough for now," Buxton said a little too quickly. The tension in the room eased as he made a show of looking at his watch.

She couldn't escape the feeling that the boss had rescued her when her memory failed her yet again. That she had somehow let the team down. She wanted desperately to unearth every scrap of information, but she had to admit that a small part of her had become too adept at pushing the details back into the dark recesses of her mind. In order to catch the monster, she would have to drag those pieces—and the pain that came with them—out from where she had carefully stowed them and into the light.

Chapter 11

Three hours later, Nina jumped as Kent thudded a pitcher of beer down on the scarred round table. Wade plunked four clear mugs beside it as he sat next to her.

Breck picked one up and poured. "The first one's for Guerrera."

Nina grasped the mug's chilled handle. "Buxton's not coming?"

Kent gestured around the room. "I get the feeling the higher-ups make it a point not to see what goes on in here."

After a grueling day in the confines of the BAU, they had piled into one of the Bureau Suburbans to drive the short distance to the Quantico facility, where the FBI academy had its own bar. Known as the Boardroom, the venue was a destination for everyone from new agents to senior police executives from around the world attending the FBI National Academy. Depending on the evening, there might be dancing, karaoke, or card playing among those who wanted to blow off steam.

She glanced around. "Not a big crowd tonight. No one's getting rowdy."

Wade tipped the pitcher, sloshing amber liquid into his mug. "I think Buxton wanted us to have a chance to chat among ourselves."

Made sense. They had been thrown together to work as a team. Wade and Kent were the only ones permanently assigned to the unit.

They needed to gel in order to be productive. May as well take advantage of the opportunity.

She slid an empty mug to Kent. "I saw you studying the code on the computer a couple of hours ago. Any luck?"

"I was working with the cryptanalysts on the internal server." Kent filled it from the pitcher before pushing it to Breck. "Breaking codes is their wheelhouse, but I wanted to focus on the unsub's previous phraseology to see if it might shed light on this new message."

"Kent has training in psycholinguistic analysis," Wade said, digging through a basket of pretzels in the center of the table. "Courtesy of Uncle Sam."

She raised a brow at Kent, inviting explanation.

"I was in Special Forces before joining the Bureau," he said simply. "My team needed someone to assist with interrogations." He held up a hand. "Don't ask for details. All my missions were classified. I had an undergrad degree in psychology, so they picked me for advanced training. Paid for my master's too."

Breck nudged Wade's arm. "You hunting for a peanut at the bottom of that bowl?"

Wade stopped pushing pretzels around. "I could use some protein."

"I could, too, but peanuts won't do it for me," Breck said. "I'm hungry enough to eat a horse and chase the rider."

Nina smiled. "I love the way you talk, but I can't place your accent."

"Georgia," Breck said. "Not Atlanta either. I'm from the Low Country, where sushi is still called bait." She stood. "I'll order us a pizza."

"What drew you to study linguistics?" Nina asked Kent, far more interested in his background than food.

"It was a logical progression," he said. "I can speak four languages, and I like to read. Words interest me."

"What can you tell about a person from their speech?"

"Not just speech but written communication too. I can get a feel for their education level, IQ, area where they grew up, and worldview, among other things. Sometimes idiosyncratic turns of phrase can offer insight, such as when the unsub said he wished he'd been the one to 'bestow' the wounds on your back." He put down his beer. "Sorry, didn't mean to bring that up again."

She noticed Wade watching her and jerked her thumb at him. "He took me through it three more times while you and Breck were busy." She waved Kent's concern away. "I'm getting numb to it."

Which had probably been part of Wade's plan. Inoculate her through repeated exposure while data mining her subconscious for every minuscule detail about her abduction.

"I've been thinking about the unsub's odd word choice too," Wade said. "You know who bestows things on people?"

"A king?" Breck said. She had just returned from the register at the far end of the room.

"An organization?" Kent offered.

Nina responded with the first thing that occurred to her. "A god."

Wade lifted his beer in mock salute. "Exactly."

Nina's fingertips brushed her bare throat. "The god's eye necklace. He kept it all those years. What does that mean? Does he think he's a god?"

"Don't have enough info to be certain," Wade said. "He definitely wants to exercise ultimate power and control. His comments to the media today indicated as much."

"Predators are all about control," Kent said. "Part of their personality entertains grandiose notions of superiority, but another part has to dominate everyone around them in order to cover deep-seated feelings of inadequacy."

"That's a total contradiction," Nina said.

"One of many reasons they're not what you'd call well-adjusted folks." Kent picked up a pretzel and examined it. "I believe the technical term is *loony*."

"Some have childhoods involving parental abuse." Wade's brow furrowed thoughtfully. "With this guy's personality, I would suspect a father or father figure."

"You dig through their skulls, and I dig through their hard drives," Breck said. "I like my job better."

"Speaking of which." Nina turned to her. "I saw you in a huddle with the Cyber team this afternoon. You guys make any progress?"

"I need another beer for this." Breck refilled her mug. "Apparently, the unsub loved that comment from the news anchor—you know, the one about how he's as much of a cipher as the clues he leaves?" When they nodded, she curled her lip. "Now he's calling himself the Cipher."

"Plays into his ego," Wade said. "He's beyond understanding. A mystery."

"Mystery." Breck let out a derisive snort. "He's nuttier than a squirrel turd." She took a swig. "He set up social media accounts with an image of an ancient cipher scroll. It's like he's branding himself."

"Which means he intends to keep this going," Nina said.

"He's getting a ton of followers," Breck said. "Mostly they troll him, but there are also a few fans."

Nina almost choked on her beer. "Fans?"

"He posted an image of the clue on his Facebook page and challenged people to solve it." Breck took another sip. "Got a bunch of likes. In fact, people are forming teams and competing to see who can crack the code first. There's a group from MIT that claims to have come up with several possible answers."

Wade shook his head. "So now he's got all kinds of people playing his game. Talking about him."

"Can't we subpoena the social media platforms to turn over his information?" Nina asked.

"We've already filed emergency subpoenas," Breck said. "They'll give us the data, but I'm not optimistic. He seems fairly tech savvy. No way he used his real name to set up his profile, and he probably found a way to hide his IP and location too."

Kent cursed. "Then let's shut him down."

"No." Wade's voice was surprisingly sharp. "Every scrap of information we get about him, everything he posts, gives us a clearer picture of who he is."

"He's getting the public to interfere in our investigation," Kent said. "What if someone solves that clue before we do? Our Crypto team is still working on it."

"The last messages were aimed at Guerrera," Wade said. "The next one will probably be more of the same. Past behavior is the best predictor of future behavior."

The table grew quiet. They were clearly waiting for her to weigh in. She had been the subject of the Cipher's previous messages and the target of his threats. How did she feel about thousands, perhaps millions, of people playing a game with a man who wanted her dead?

She downed the rest of her beer. "If it will help catch him, I vote to leave the sites up and active."

"This will continue to put more public attention on you," Kent said. "And on the Bureau too."

She understood the underlying message. Depending on how the case went, it might not go down well at the executive level. From its inception in the days of J. Edgar, all agents held one rule sacrosanct.

Don't embarrass the Bureau.

Would that include having her name and her new nickname splashed all over the internet?

"We'll need to present a united front to Buxton," Breck said, obviously thinking along the same lines. "I gave him a quick briefing before he left the office. We're keeping everything as it is until we hear back about the subpoenas, then he plans to shut the Cipher's social media profiles down if we don't have any investigative leads to follow. We've got everything in place to pull the plug, but I convinced him to wait.

I agree with Wade, but for different reasons. The longer the Cipher interacts, the better chance we have of untangling whatever safeguards he's installed to hide in cyberspace."

Kent ran his finger around the rim of his mug. "I don't like it, but I'm a team player. We'll go to Buxton together tomorrow." He leveled his deep-blue eyes on Nina's. "This unsub has already hurt you so much. It feels like we're giving him a lot of rope hoping he'll hang himself. Too much rope, if you ask me."

She gave him a slow nod of understanding. The Cipher was dangerous, and they had chosen to deliberately allow him access to a worldwide audience he desperately craved. Would it be worth the risk to give him extra rope, or would he take the slack and use it against them? More than anyone else alive, she knew what the monster could do with a length of rope.

Chapter 12

After precious little sleep, Nina's morning routine was interrupted by the unexpected appearance of her next-door neighbor's foster daughter. Nina opened her apartment door to find Bianca just outside, clutching a massive gray cat.

"I think you broke the internet," Bianca said by way of greeting.

She turned a bleary-eyed gaze on the girl. "That cat's starting to get a little too comfortable around here."

"Seriously, you've got to see this," Bianca said, pointedly ignoring the hint. She marched inside with the big tom draped over one shoulder and her cell phone in her free hand. "You're blowing up every platform, and you're at the top of every search engine."

A teenage social media addict, Bianca spouted a rapid-fire stream of updates on the status of the growing public fascination with the killer, his secret codes, and the Warrior Girl, as Nina was coming to be known.

Bianca held the phone out to her. "And did you know he's using a creepy serial killer nickname now?" She paused for effect. "The Cipher."

When Nina didn't react, Bianca let out an impatient huff. "Well? What do you think about the name?"

Nina closed her eyes briefly. "I'd already heard." She sipped at her coffee. "This isn't helping our investigation. Do people who respond to his posts realize they're feeding his ego?"

"I'm sure some of them do," Bianca said. "But they can't help themselves, you know?"

She did know. "Now that he's got an audience, he'll feel compelled to give them a show."

"But you'll stop him before he can do anything else. I mean, the FBI has every computer geek they've got tracking this guy down, right?"

"First, they're not geeks. They're highly trained agents and analysts." When Bianca raised a pierced brow, Nina added, "Okay, so some of them may log too many screen hours, but they're good at what they do. Which is why it's so frustrating."

"What? That the FBI's being outsmarted by a psycho or that they're being out-geeked by college students?"

She knew Bianca hid her concern under a thick layer of snark. Like many foster children, Bianca had learned to conceal her emotions with dark humor, outward hostility, or feigned indifference. Nina had done the same when she was in the system. She understood that Bianca was worried about her.

"I've got something to tell you," Bianca said, not quite meeting her eyes.

Her cop antennae went up. "What?"

"I put a team together. A select group of com-sci majors like me." She glanced down. "Gamers, coders, and hackers that could put the feeb dweebs to shame."

Bianca had graduated from high school at fourteen, winning a full-ride presidential scholarship to George Washington University. On target to receive a bachelor of science at the end of the semester, she'd set her sights on a master's degree next.

Nina didn't like where this was going. Resting her cup on the coffee table, she leaned forward and gave Bianca her best federal-agent-demanding-answers scowl. "Spill it. Now."

Bianca lifted her chin. "We're going to shut him down." When Nina simply waited, she snuggled the cat closer before elaborating. "He said he's going to post a link to a new YouTube channel once he gets it set up."

Breck hadn't mentioned the video streaming at the Boardroom last night. The Cipher could attract an even bigger audience with more visual content. She didn't want to consider what else he might decide to show the public either.

She would speak to Breck later. Right now, she had other concerns. "How do you plan to shut him down?"

"Hello? Remember when I mentioned we're com-sci?" Bianca said as if the answer was obvious. "We hack in and take him offline. Show him he can't get away with posting whatever bullshit he wants." Her eyes narrowed. "We're going to fight back."

She considered how best to put a stop to the scheme, but she knew Bianca was too much like her to back down without a good reason. It sounded like Bianca had already put the plan in motion. There was no time for a policy debate at Quantico.

She came to a decision. "I'll share a couple of things with you, but if you post a single word of this conversation, or repeat it to anyone else, I'll run over that phone of yours with my car." She watched Bianca stroke the cat's short, thick fur while the threat sank in.

"No need to go all agent badass on me," Bianca said. "I won't say shit to anyone."

Nina let out a sigh. Breck's blast text to the team thirty minutes ago had started the day on a frustrating note. Every major social media platform had responded to their emergency subpoenas, but the unsub's profiles had all been as fake and untraceable as Breck had predicted.

"Truth is, we're not making any headway tracking this guy down," she said to Bianca. "He knows what he's doing."

"He must have set up his accounts from somewhere. Can't you snag him through servers?"

"He's a cyberghost."

"Then shutting him down will stop him."

Not this again. "You can't, Bee."

"Sure we can. It's easy, we just—"

"I meant to say, we don't want you to." She pushed her fingers through her hair. "The whole reason I'm even sharing this much is to convince you and your friends to back off. Because if I don't, you'll just go ahead and do it anyway, won't you?"

They stared at each other until the cat squirmed in Bianca's arms. She bent to put him down. "Why do you want this guy putting out his crap? It's twisted."

"We discussed it at Quantico yesterday afternoon," Nina said. "We decided that—for now—it's better to let him keep posting." She lifted her palms. "He might give himself away."

Bianca tilted her head in thought, jet-black ponytail falling to one side. "You're also betting your guys can ping him somehow, aren't you?"

The girl was wicked smart. Emphasis on *wicked*. Nina jabbed a finger at her. "You and your friends leave this to us. Don't interfere with a federal investigation."

Bianca rested a hand on her hip. "News flash, Agent Guerrera, the whole country is interfering. Isn't that what you literally just told me you guys were talking about yesterday?"

Nina ignored the attitude. "I can't protect the whole country. But I can damn well protect one seventeen-year-old girl who is messing with something she doesn't understand." She grew serious. "Something . . . evil."

"Oh, I understand evil," Bianca said quietly. "I understand it just fine."

She'd met Bianca four years ago when she was a Fairfax County police officer, and Bianca was a troubled thirteen-year-old serial runaway. When Bianca had disappeared for the umpteenth time, Nina set out to find her, scouring every known teen hangout on her beat until she located the girl. Over burgers, Nina got Bianca to open up by sharing her own past. After learning why Bianca had run, she arrested the couple who had been her foster parents at the time, arranging for Bianca to stay with her for a few days until CPS could find an appropriate new situation for her. The instant Mrs. Gomez had spotted Bianca, she found new purpose. The Gomez children were all grown, and Mrs. G quickly convinced her husband to fill their empty nest with foster kids. Starting with a precocious adolescent with the intellect of an adult. A loving home environment had softened Bianca's hard edges.

Nina didn't want her to play the Cipher's game and backslide into a dark place after coming so far. She strode over to grasp the girl's slender shoulders. "Don't underestimate him, *mija*. I've looked into his eyes." She suppressed a shudder. "He has no soul."

Apparently conceding the point, Bianca tried another approach. "Maybe you guys should post on some of his social media accounts."

"Because we want to encourage him?"

"If you want him to give himself away, then get him talking," Bianca said.

Nina's mind raced through different possible outcomes. "That's not a bad idea." She paced across the room, thinking. "I'd have to convince Buxton first. He's bound to think direct interaction will introduce another variable we can't control."

She considered enlisting Wade's support and dismissed the idea. He seemed to be recalibrating his opinion of her during their after-hours discussion, but she sensed he was withholding final judgment.

"I say better you than the randos online," Bianca said. "They're making fun of him, calling him a freak or a moron. He gets pissed and snipes back at them." She shook her head. "Stupid on all sides."

Breck had mentioned the trolls. They must be getting to him. She considered what would happen if he got a direct message from the FBI. Would he engage? Would he repost for the world to see? A loud gasp drew her attention back to Bianca, who was looking down at her cell phone.

"They cracked the code." Her eyes glinted as she glanced at Nina. "The MIT team. They figured out the message and posted the answer."

Nina rushed to her side. "What does it say? How did they solve it?"

Bianca scrolled down with her finger. "They divided the numbers thirty-two, eighteen, ten, and thirty-six by two to get sixteen, nine, five, and eighteen. Swapping those numbers for letters of the alphabet, that spells P-I-E-R. The numbers were followed by the letters *F* and *R*. They figured the letters represented six and eighteen. Using the same logic, they divided those numbers by two, coming up with *C* and *I*. If you do the reverse of the first part of the message and exchange the letters for numbers, that makes three and nine. Put it all together, you get Pier Thirty-Nine."

Nina crossed the room to retrieve her phone from the coffee table. "I wonder if the analysts solved it too. Where did those MIT students post the answer?"

"They put it on the Cipher's Twitter feed in response to one of his tweets." Bianca's hand flew to her mouth. "Oh no, oh no, no, no."

"What?" Nina backtracked to peer over Bianca's trembling shoulder.

"The Cipher posted a picture after their message," Bianca said between her fingers.

Nina reached forward to tap the image, expanding it. The tiny screen showed a girl's body floating facedown in murky water, blonde hair rippling out like a golden fan. A caption below the picture read Too Late, Warrior Girl.

Nina's phone buzzed in her hand. In a state of shock, she reflexively lifted it to her ear. "Agent Guerrera."

Wade's words came out in a terse baritone. "Pack a bag. We're heading to San Francisco."

Chapter 13

Nina turned her back to the crowd clustered behind the yellow tape. She felt the unsub watching her, his presence almost palpable through the heavy air redolent with the musk of nearby sea lions basking in the sun.

"We should be at the morgue where the body is," Wade said. "I can get a lot more insight from observing what he did with the victim than I can getting gawked at by a gaggle of tourists."

She felt raw and exposed after recounting her story with Wade in front of the team yesterday. A six-hour commercial flight crammed together in the back of the plane hadn't helped. There had been no time alone with her new partner to establish the parameters of their working relationship in the field, and now a vague sense of tension permeated their interactions.

She was supposed to be there to offer her insight into the Cipher's actions. Instead, she felt like one of many tools at Wade's disposal. A useful resource. But she was more than that. She was a federal agent. He had his way of investigating and she had hers. He had clearly taken in everything he needed to see at the scene, but she hadn't finished her assessment yet.

"I'm sure one of the San Francisco field office agents would be happy to take you to the ME's office," she said to him. "I'll catch up with you later."

His mouth flattened into a thin line. "All I'm saying is we've spent enough time here."

"I'm a field agent." Without the slightest concern that anyone might overhear, she planted herself directly in front of him and swept her arm out in a wide arc that encompassed the bay and the pier. "As in, out in the damn field."

"You know that's bullshit, Guerrera. BAU agents go out on cases too. I went to the scene in DC if you recall. We're done here. If something else comes up, we can get info about it from the SFPD without continuing to make a spectacle of ourselves and feed the unsub's ego."

He might be the senior agent, but he could make mistakes like anyone else. "You missed the necklace and the spray paint on the dumpster in Georgetown. I don't want to overlook anything here." Point made, she turned away and strode to the edge of the pier where the blue-green water gently lapped against the sun-bleached planks.

The girl's body had been tied to one of the chains holding the cluster of floating platforms loosely together. Nina surveyed the thick guano-strewn boards that formed an island in the San Francisco Bay. She couldn't see an easy way to get to the pier itself, which was detached from the slips holding boats nearby to preserve a haven for the massive sunbathing sea lions. How had the Cipher done it?

She pivoted and walked back past Wade to the SFPD lieutenant who'd briefed her when she arrived twenty minutes earlier. "Lieutenant Spangler, what time did you say the victim was found?"

"About five this morning."

"None of the tourist shops or restaurants were open then?"

He shook his balding head. "The only people in the area were boaters preparing to go out later and some of the folks who sell food in the open-air market on Fisherman's Wharf. They set up their stands early." He shooed a persistent seagull away with a wave of his hand. "We're canvassing, but I doubt we'll come up with anything. Our best bet is the boaters."

"Is that how he would have had to get to the floating docks?" she asked. "There's no direct access from the pier."

"This is the most photographed pier in the country. It's on a constant video feed. He must have known that." Spangler jerked his chin at a row of yachts docked at a nearby wharf. "We figure he must've taken a dinghy from a slip and ferried that poor girl over here while it was still dark." He hooked a thumb over his duty belt. "He'd have to be nuts to swim her over, what with the current and the sea lions and all."

She followed his gaze. "Is the water always this choppy?"

"Pretty much."

She thanked the lieutenant and strolled slowly back, scanning the docks, the crowd lining the pier, and the slip. What had he been thinking? Why had he chosen such a public place? Risked exposure? Unfortunately, the man who probably had the best chance of reading the Cipher's intentions was standing a few yards away with his hands on his hips, glowering at her.

Undeterred by the resentment evident in his tense posture, she approached Wade with her next question. "In the photograph the unsub posted, the victim looked blonde. The report has her at about five eight. Way taller than me."

Wade looked down at her. "From what we've been told, she's nothing like you physically. That's why I want to get a look at her in person and hear what they've dug up about her background. She must have something else in common with you. Whatever that point of convergence is will tell us a lot about him."

She signaled Lieutenant Spangler. "Could you take us back to the wharf? I'd like to see the . . ." She stopped herself before saying *body*. Every victim deserved to be called by name. "Do we have an ID yet?"

"The girl was nude," he said. "No ID. A few families of missing teens came forward to see if it was their daughter, but so far, no luck. Some of the guys who work the area think she might be homeless." He motioned toward the downtown area. "We get a lot of that here. They're called 'urban campers.'"

She glanced at Wade. "Anything else?"

"The geographical profiling on this guy just got a hell of a lot harder."

They climbed aboard the SFPD watercraft tied to the thick wooden pylon and sat on the white vinyl cushions in back. Within five minutes, they were on the wharf, where an FBI agent from the San Francisco field office stood next to an SFPD sergeant, impatient expressions on their faces.

Wade reached them first. "What's up?"

The agent gestured toward the patrol sergeant, who held up a plastic evidence bag.

"One of my officers working the perimeter recovered this from a couple of people in the crowd," the sergeant said. "We've got them in two separate squad cars, ready for interview."

Bright blue ink caught Nina's eye, and she motioned for the bag from the sergeant. Turning it over, she saw an envelope with the words WARRIOR GIRL printed in the center.

A hot, prickly sensation crawled up her spine. "Where did this come from?"

"The people who found it said it was taped to a dumpster. They already opened it. Said there was a message written in some sort of code." He shrugged. "They couldn't understand it."

She and Wade exchanged glances. Another body. Another dumpster. Another coded message.

For her.

Chapter 14

The Cipher plopped the fast food burger on the dashboard, rolled down the window, and spat a chunk of gristle onto the ground. Disgusting.

He wiped the grease from his fingers and rotated the mobile phone in the bracket attached to the car's vent, turning it sideways. Much wider picture. He googled *clue found in trash* and tapped the first link that came up. The YouTube video began with a shot of a crowd at Fisherman's Wharf. He smiled. This would be fun. Worth pulling off the freeway to enjoy the scene he'd heard about on the radio. At least he had XM, so he didn't have to fumble through news channels as he drove from one state to the next, making his way back east.

His pulse quickened when he saw the black Suburban pull into the frame. He licked a spot of ketchup from the corner of his mouth and leaned forward to increase the volume.

"I don't get why they still won't let us near the pier." A shrill female voice spoke in the background as the scene played out. She seemed to be narrating as she shot the footage, as opposed to speaking to a companion. "They took the body away hours ago," she continued.

He detected anger and fear in her voice. His smile widened.

"Oh, wait. The FBI's here," she said in the background.

A bit of jostling, as if she had elbowed her way through the throng to get a better view. "Hey, there's the agent from that video. Nina something . . . the Warrior Girl."

He'd already spotted her, the oversize FBI raid jacket swallowing her petite frame. Her dark sunglasses hid much of her reaction. Damn. He'd wanted to watch those big brown eyes fill with dread. Instead, he caught her body momentarily stiffening. In that moment, he was certain she was thinking of him. They were connected.

Arousal strained his jeans, making him shift in his seat as he recalled his time with her. He'd suppressed his darkest impulses throughout his adolescence and young adulthood, denying himself. All of that changed the moment he laid eyes on Nina for the first time. She was the one.

He'd gathered the equipment and set up the shed that very night, but by the time he was ready, Nina had disappeared. He spent three days hunting her. He had been furious with her at the time, but the chase had added to the thrill. And given him a reason to punish her. He had bestowed one mark upon her for each day she made him wait. Then he had taken her three times, completing the triangle of retribution.

He would have her again. And he would punish her so much more for escaping. He would take everything she had, including her life. As his excitement mounted, he was grateful he'd pulled into a deserted community park. A lone man sitting in his car at a busy rest stop off the freeway could have attracted unwanted attention.

He willed his heated blood to cool as the unseen narrator in the video continued her commentary. "I hope she catches that Cipher guy."

He liked his new name. The Cipher. He was an enigma. He would continue to leave clues and invite the world to play his game. Under his rules. In his arena.

The picture wobbled. "Quit pushing!"

The Cipher dragged a finger across the bottom of the video, fast forwarding to the crucial part.

"... says Warrior Girl on the envelope," the female voice was saying. "This has got to be for that FBI lady."

The view screen angled down as a nicotine-stained female hand pulled the envelope from the side of the dumpster, taking the thick silver duct tape off with it.

He fast forwarded again as the woman fumbled with the seal, taking a maddening amount of time to open it one-handed for the camera. No one seemed to be paying any attention to her when she slid the index card out and held it up.

She read the message out loud. "Not understanding will make you sob. You have forty-eight hours to solve this." She was jostled again and stopped reading but kept the card in front of her phone.

He studied the series of numbers on the card: 75, 73, 3, 9, 101, 8, 75.

Let the MIT eggheads chew on that.

As the video continued, someone seemed to have finally noticed what the woman was doing. A tall skinny guy who looked to be in his twenties elbowed her. "Hey, what you got there?"

"It was taped to the side of that trash bin." She pulled the note away, possessive. "I think it's a clue from the Cipher."

"Yeah, right." The man's tone was pure derision. "Does it say Professor Plum did it in the study with a lead pipe?"

"Listen, asshole, it looks just like the other message he left."

"Let me see." The guy's hand shot out toward her.

"I found it." She yanked the card away. "It's mine."

"Give it here." He moved in close, red T-shirt momentarily blocking the screen.

A lot of jostling, swearing, and grunting followed.

"Score." The man stepped back, waving the tattered card.

"I'm telling the police." The woman followed this pronouncement with a string of expletives that questioned his intelligence, his manhood, and his parentage.

"If this is a legit clue, the FBI will be looking at you for messing with it anyway."

"And what about you, Einstein? Now your prints are all over it too."

The man straightened. "I was just making sure it got turned over to the proper authorities."

"What's going on over here?" A cop came into view.

Adjusting his phone to eliminate glare from the sun setting behind him, the Cipher chuckled as each of the two morons rushed to explain to the cop how the other had tampered with important evidence. This was better than he'd hoped for.

A sharp rap on the windshield jolted him upright in his seat. He snapped his head to the side to squint up at a police officer shining his flashlight into the car.

He buzzed the window down.

"Park closes at dark, pal."

Should he point out that it was still dusk? Claim a medical condition? Shoot the policeman where he stood? So many options.

The officer's gruff voice brought him up short. That sharp accusatory tone—along with the man's barrel chest, five o'clock shadow, and shock of dark hair—brought back a memory from twenty-five years ago. He had been eleven years old when his father had barged into his bedroom and caught him with that magazine.

"It's a good thing your pants are already down, boy," the old man said, unbuckling his belt. "Because I'm going to tan your backside."

He never had a bedroom door after that. He had also learned to be a lot sneakier. His father's mood swings took unpredictable and often violent turns. Adjusting to them became instinctive. He learned to read people's expressions and adapt on the fly.

Sitting in his car in the park, he assessed the cop's body language and made a quick decision. Letting his jaw hang open and adopting a vacant look, he affected the demeanor of a harmless idiot. "Sorry, lost track of time."

The cop spoke as if by rote. "License and registration."

He tugged the registration from a clip on the visor before fishing his driver's license from his wallet. "Here you go, sir." He figured the "sir" was a nice touch. Very respectful.

The cop eyed the documents under the flashlight's beam, then swiveled it around the interior of the car in a deliberate perusal. "You're a long way from Charlottesville, Mr. Stevenson."

He blinked in the glare. "I'll get there by tomorrow morning."

"Don't let the white-line fever get to you."

"Huh?"

The cop heaved a weary sigh. "That means stay awake, Mr. Stevenson."

"Oh."

The cop walked away, shaking his head.

The Cipher had planned for this, but he was still irritated that a perfectly good car and fake ID would have to be destroyed thanks to that asshole cop.

He tossed the half-eaten burger on the seat next to him and threw the car in reverse, thoughts already on his next move. He backed out of the spot and shifted into drive as he contemplated his situation. That woman's video was getting more hits than he would have believed possible. It was happening. Everyone wanted to join the hunt, solve his puzzles, step inside his world.

Those fools from MIT were probably already putting the new code through algorithms and coming up with viable permutations. That would only work for half of the message. The half he wanted them to figure out. The rest of it would require a different kind of insight. The arrogant pricks were about to learn who they were messing with.

Chapter 15

Nina gazed down at the L-shaped operating table in the autopsy suite as the fine-boned body on its surface bore silent witness to the Cipher's brutality. Bathed in the surgical light glaring from overhead, sixteen-year-old Olivia Burch lay on a sheet of cold steel. Detective Ralph Colton of SFPD Homicide, who had supplied the name of the murdered girl, stood to her right. Wade cut his eyes to her from her left.

"You need to leave?" he asked as a second shudder passed through her.

No way would she admit the young girl on the table brought back memories of the silvery metal beneath her own body years ago.

"A bit cold in here." She made a show of rubbing her hands together and fended off further questions with a touch of snark. "You'd think we were in a morgue or something."

They had been ushered into the autopsy suite after the procedure was already underway, a fact Wade had impressed upon her with no small amount of grumbling. He had wanted to be present from the start, which had been expedited due to the nature of the case. Colton had brought them up to speed, but Wade didn't seem mollified, especially when he had to view the three round burn marks found on the victim's back by scrolling through photos on the detective's phone.

Dr. Donald Fong looked up. "I can't do much about the room temperature."

The assistant ME was short and stocky, his black hair hidden under a disposable cap that matched his white lab coat. The lower half of his face was covered with a surgical mask, and his dark eyes peered out at them from behind a clear plastic shield extending down from his forehead past his chin.

Nina instantly regretted her ploy. "I'll be fine."

Fong gave her a curt nod and got back to business. "I scanned an overview of the DC autopsy before I started, and there's no sign of any note left in or on the body of this victim."

"Stomach contents?" Wade said. "Maybe she swallowed it."

"Empty," Fong said. "She hadn't eaten in a long time."

"Life on the street," Colton said. "Hard to tell when your next meal is coming. The beat cop who ID'd her said he'd seen her around for over a year. He'd refer her to CPS every time he came across her, but she'd be back on the street before long."

Her eyes met Wade's. They had found the connection.

"Each of his victims has been an adolescent female living apart from her biological family," Wade said. "He looks for the ones separated from the herd. Vulnerable girls with no one to protect them."

Is that how Wade viewed her as well? Is that why he hadn't recommended her for hire? She moved the discussion in another direction. "Did you locate Olivia's parents?"

"Closest relative is a grandmother in Oakland." Colton shook his head. "Grandma didn't know how to reach the parents, but I'm sure we'll hear from them soon with all this media coverage."

"Look at this," Fong said, drawing their attention back to the autopsy. "That tooth appears to be freshly broken."

He stepped on a hydraulic lift bar, raising the table a few inches to afford a closer view. Extending nitrile-glove-clad hands, he pried Olivia's mouth wider with gleaming metal tongs and pointed to an incisor with the tip chipped off, exposing a jagged edge.

"Maybe he punched her," Colton said.

Fong shook his head. "There's no correlating tissue damage to the inside of her upper lip. This tooth was fractured with some sort of instrument inside her mouth."

A flash of insight caught Nina off guard. She turned to Wade. "Can I have a word?"

After giving her an assessing look, he turned and strode from the room without comment.

As soon as the door closed behind them, Nina spoke in an urgent undertone. "The Cipher used something to spread my mouth. It was like a pair of scissors, but without a sharp edge. He ratcheted my jaw apart, then forced a gag past my teeth."

Yet another element of the crime had slipped into a dark crevice of her mind, only to be unearthed by a glimpse of an unrelated scene. Perhaps the steel table, the young girl, and the metal instrument Dr. Fong had used was enough to trigger the long-forgotten detail. How many other tiny mental scraps had gone missing?

She focused on the revelation and what it might mean. "Who would have something like that?"

"A dentist." Wade stroked his jaw, considering. "Or an otolaryngologist." At Nina's raised brow, he elaborated. "Ear, nose, and throat doctor."

"Obviously, a medical examiner or coroner uses them." Her mind raced. "We're talking about someone in a medical profession, but that could include a nurse or a veterinarian too."

Wade pulled his buzzing cell phone from his pocket. "It's Buxton." Glancing over his shoulder to be sure they were alone, he tapped the screen to put it on speaker.

Buxton sounded harried. "It's a five-alarm fire over here. What's your status, Agent Wade?"

"I'm at the autopsy with Agent Guerrera and Detective Colton with SFPD Homicide." He summarized Dr. Fong's findings and explained what Nina had recalled along with its implications. "What's going on at Quantico?"

Buxton grunted. "A photo of the clue left by the unsub is spreading through the internet like a computer virus."

"Who posted it?" Wade asked.

"According to our San Francisco field office, the woman who found the envelope taped to the dumpster failed to mention that she'd uploaded a video of the whole thing, including a still shot of the message, to YouTube." He heaved a sigh. "And the SFPD beat cop she spoke to didn't think to ask her either. He took down her info, bagged the envelope, and brought it straight to his sergeant."

Nina didn't blame the officer. This case would change standard procedure in policework going forward. That included how much of a perimeter they would set up around a crime scene. The dumpster was on the wharf, well away from where the body had been recovered.

Wade seemed to be thinking along the same lines. "At the DC scene, the unsub wanted to be sure we found his messages," he said. "This time, he lets someone in the public stumble across it, and it's also likely several cameras caught him taping it to the dumpster."

"We're collecting all relevant video." Buxton's voice carried through the empty corridor over the tiny phone speaker. "We've already got data search parameters set up, and our team is going through the feeds as the detectives bring them to us. We'll keep reviewing as new material comes in."

"It's performance art," Wade said. "He's feeding his growing audience."

"If that's his plan, he succeeded," Buxton said. "Julian Zarran has just inserted himself into the middle of this mess."

Nina had seen several of Zarran's movies. The action hero was one of the hottest box office draws in Hollywood.

Buxton continued in a frustrated rush, "People commented and shared the woman's video until it hit critical mass when Zarran retweeted it to his twenty million followers with an offer of half a million dollars to the first person or group who cracked the code."

Wade swore under his breath. "Zarran grew up in San Francisco. I'm sure he thought he was helping."

"Whatever his intentions were, he sparked a frenzy," Buxton said. "As if we didn't have enough to do, every armchair sleuth with a calculator has submitted potential solutions to the code, each one more improbable than the last. There are so many suggested answers that we can't vet them all. The right one could be somewhere in the mix, but it's lost in all the static."

"What about our analysts?" Nina said. "Is Crypto on it?"

"Of course." Buxton sounded irritated. "They'll let me know when they're reasonably certain they have the right answer. They've come up with several possibilities at this point, each leading to different conclusions. We can't afford to take a wrong turn by leaping on the first possible solution that comes up."

"This guy is either highly strategic or damned lucky," Wade said. "The amount of chaos this is causing hampers everything we're doing."

"In the past forty minutes since Zarran's announcement, more teams have formed to claim the prize," Buxton said. "Those students from MIT who figured out his last clue are on all the unsub's social media sites. They're calling themselves the Brew Crew now. I can guess what they'll spend the prize money on if they win."

"What are they saying to the Cipher in their posts?" she asked.

"That they'll break his kindergarten code before breakfast."

Wade grimaced. "Dammit, they're challenging his intelligence. His need for dominance will drive him to retaliate. He might move up the deadline."

That was the opening Nina had been waiting for. She pretended as if an idea had just occurred to her. "There might be a way to buy some time."

Wade gave her a wary look, but Buxton sounded curious. "What do you have in mind, Agent Guerrera?"

"Let's respond to him directly." She spoke quickly, wanting to outline her plan before Wade could interrupt. "On his Facebook page or his Twitter feed, or wherever. If he's talking to us, we might be able to convince him to delay his plans. At the very least, we could get him to say something revealing or give Cyber Crime a better shot at following any virtual bread crumbs back to him."

Wade wasted no time objecting. "Engaging him on social media directly will elevate his narcissism." He looked at Nina as he spoke to their boss. "Furthermore, we don't know enough about him yet. Any inadvertent comment from us could provoke him further if we say the wrong thing."

"Speaking of which," Buxton cut in, "Agent Breck is on standby to shut down all of his social media accounts. We would have done it already, but Cyber Crime is developing a new component to an existing program to trace his location. Unfortunately, the Cipher is living up to his name. He's led us down a lot of rabbit holes so far."

"Then this is the perfect time to keep him active online," Nina said. "Ignoring him hasn't worked. Shutting him down won't either. He'll set up new profiles as fast as we can take them offline. Another girl is dead. If this clue is like the last one, it'll lead us to another body in forty-eight"—she glanced at her watch—"make that forty-six hours. We have plenty to gain and nothing to lose by trying a different approach."

Wade glared at her. She took it as a positive. Her position made sense, and they both knew it.

Buxton's response crackled in the air between them. "I agree with Agent Guerrera. We need to try something different. I'll have someone from the team here at Quantico send him a direct message rather than posting something on his page. We'll send it from our official account, so he knows it's really us."

Nina had wedged her foot in the door. Time to kick it open. "Sir, I need to be the one who communicates with him."

"Explain." Buxton bit out the word after a brief pause.

"If he's fixated on me, he won't be able to resist. He'll—"

"He'll get inside your head," Wade said, interrupting her. "He'll use the opportunity to torment you, and we need you focused on the case."

Nina bristled. "Are you saying he'll rattle me so badly I can't think straight? Because if you are, then you may have read my files, but you still don't know me at all." She took a step toward him, invading his personal space. "People have tried to bully me my whole life, but I've managed to hold my ground pretty damn well."

Wade turned away, hiding his expression and perhaps grasping her underlying message.

"I want both of you back here ASAP," Buxton said into the silence. "I've gotten authorization for a full-time task force dedicated to this investigation. We're setting it up in one of the large conference rooms at the academy in Quantico for logistical and security reasons. We'll discuss the messaging idea when you arrive. The San Francisco field office can continue to work with the SFPD on the murder there, but our job is to prevent the next one."

"We'll be on the next direct flight," Wade said, still not meeting her eyes.

Buxton sounded fatigued. "Speaking of air travel, I've got teams coordinating forensic analysis of both scenes and checking flight manifests. We're collecting the names of every passenger who flew from Reagan, BWI, or Dulles into San Francisco in the past three days."

Nina picked up on the subtext—as well as the weariness—behind his words. There was nothing to compare the passenger lists with except the usual criminal databases, which she doubted contained the unsub's name. Buxton wanted the information ready so they would have another series of passengers for comparison when he struck again.

When another girl died.

Chapter 16

A light tap on her arm drew Nina's attention from the wall chart in front of her. She turned to see one of a cadre of the computer forensics specialists gazing down at her.

"The Cipher just responded to your DM on Twitter," he said.

In the hour since the morning briefing had ended, Nina had been waiting to see if the Cipher would bite. In the interim, she'd joined the rest of her team and a host of other agents, analysts, and support staff to convert one of the larger meeting rooms at Quantico into command central for the growing task force Buxton had established during their absence in California.

Enormous charts filled with crime scene photographs, copies of the coded messages, and maps covered the walls. Workstations grouped by assignment stood in clusters, occupying the floor space. A low hum of activity buzzed through the room, creating a sense of forward momentum as each team analyzed components of the information they had gleaned so far.

Nina put down her coffee and threaded her way across the sprawling meeting area to the computer terminal designated as the social media communications center. She perched on a chair in front of the glowing screen, Wade and Kent flanking her.

"Interact with him as long as you can," Breck called to her from her workstation a few feet away where she hunkered with two other cyber specialists. "The slippery bastard keeps rerouting, but we might be able to catch up if we have enough time."

She nodded her understanding. Breck had helped convince Buxton to let her contact the Cipher directly by pointing out that Nina had a better chance than anyone of holding the unsub's attention.

Kent had grudgingly endorsed the plan as well, provided Nina allowed him to coach her responses, no doubt planning to use his psycholinguistic analysis skills.

The lone holdout, Wade finally conceded that he could use the opportunity to flesh out his profile of the Cipher by watching his responses to Nina in real time. He stationed himself to her right, notepad and pen in hand, half-moon readers resting near the end of his nose.

Breck sent the Cipher direct messages from the FBI's official Facebook, Instagram, and Twitter accounts the previous night, but it had taken until now for him to answer. He'd chosen Twitter.

Nina reread the opening message they had all agreed to. Designed to pique his interest, the opening salvo was brief and to the point.

FBI: *NINA GUERRERA WANTS TO SPEAK WITH YOU.*

The response was equally terse.

CIPHER: *IS THIS THE WARRIOR GIRL?*

"He bit," Kent said. "Don't give him anything to work with. I want to see how quickly he believes you."

FBI: *IT'S ME.*

CIPHER: *PROVE IT. TELL ME SOMETHING ONLY THE WARRIOR GIRL WOULD KNOW. U HAVE 10 SECONDS.*

"He doesn't want you to have time to research," Wade said. "It's a test."

Kent's deep voice came from over her left shoulder. "He's also establishing control over the parameters of the communication. He has to feel like he's in charge. Give him a detail that reflects how he controlled you."

FBI: *YOU GRABBED ME BY THE PONYTAIL.*

CIPHER: *TELL ME SOMETHING THAT WOULDN'T BE IN ANY POLICE REPORT. MAKE IT GOOD OR WE'RE DONE.*

Resting her fingers on the keyboard, Nina scoured her brain for something small but specific. She had been lying facedown on the table, head turned to one side, the hard metallic surface against her tear-streaked cheek. The Cipher stepped out of her line of sight for a few moments. Her eyes raked the area in search of an exit, spotting a door on the opposite wall. To the right of the doorframe was . . .

FBI: *A MINNESOTA VIKINGS POSTER. ON THE WALL INSIDE THE SHED.*

CIPHER: *VERY GOOD, WARRIOR GIRL. I WILL GRANT U A QUESTION.*

"*Grant* you?" Kent's lip curled. "The Almighty has deigned to give us an audience. Textbook god complex." He leaned closer to Nina. "Ask him an open-ended question. A 'why' question."

FBI: *WHY ARE YOU DOING THIS?*

CIPHER: *U TELL ME.*

"He wants to see what we think of him," Kent said. "He has to assume we're analyzing everything he says. Flatter his intellect. Draw it out of him."

FBI: *I CAN'T UNDERSTAND YOU. WILL YOU EXPLAIN IT TO ME?*

CIPHER: *I'M DISAPPOINTED.*

Breck stood, calling out to them over her monitor. "Keep that fish on the hook." Her head disappeared as she sat back down again.

"Talk about his exploits," Wade said. "He's never had a chance to brag to anyone. Give him an opportunity."

Nina realized she would have to dig deeper. She had fooled herself into believing she could interact on a surface level, but that wouldn't work. The Cipher demanded his pound of flesh for access to his thoughts. She changed tactics, going with her gut.

FBI: *YOU LIKE TO WATCH SUFFERING.*

CIPHER: *WRONG. TRY AGAIN.*

"You haven't lost him," Kent said. "But another assessment he considers way off base could end the communication."

She turned to Wade. "Give me something."

Wade glanced over at the wall charts. "The victims he's chosen have all been at-risk youth. Girls who—"

"Girls who nobody wanted." She finished the thought and bent over the keyboard.

FBI: *YOU TAKE WHAT OTHERS DON'T WANT.*

CIPHER: *LIKE U.*

Direct hit. She tamped down any sign of reaction, keeping her eyes trained on the screen, and felt Kent's warm hand on her forearm.

"You're doing great," he said quietly. "Remember his mind is warped. He's a sick sonofabitch."

She forced a smile. "I've got this, thanks."

FBI: *HOW DO YOU KNOW?*

CIPHER: *I SEE ALL.*

"Interesting turn of phrase," Kent said. "He could be referring to his precrime planning."

"See if you can get him to talk about his process," Wade said. "How he targets his victims."

FBI: *SO YOU WATCH FIRST?*

CIPHER: *I AM ALWAYS WATCHING.*

"Stalking behavior," Wade muttered, scribbling furiously on his notepad. "Victim selection is important to him. Part of the game, in his mind."

"Go deeper," Kent said. "More about his methodology."

FBI: *HOW DO YOU CHOOSE?*

CIPHER: *THEY MUST BE PUNISHED.*

Sensing this phrasing was important, she stopped. Sure enough, Kent and Wade began debating potential underlying meanings of the phrase.

Kent studied the screen as if literally and figuratively reading between the lines. "His language distances himself a bit. He doesn't say 'I punish them,' but 'they must be punished.' He is either uncomfortable with what he does or he feels separate and above it all."

"It's the latter," Wade said decisively. "Like a god condemning sinners, those who are unworthy."

A thought occurred to her. "A god also sees all." She pointed at the previous messages. "And punishes."

"Go with that," Wade said, "but make it personal to you."

FBI: *WHAT ABOUT ME? WHAT DID I DO TO DESERVE PUNISHMENT?*

CIPHER: *U WERE A SPECIAL CASE.*

"We have to know how he singled you out," Kent said. "That, more than anything else, can point us toward his identity."

FBI: *HOW SO?*

CIPHER: *MY TURN TO ASK A QUESTION.*

She waited through a brief pause, then a new message appeared.

CIPHER: *R U FUCKING ANYONE?*

"Redirection," Wade said. "We got too close."

Kent's cool tone ratcheted up a notch. "He's switched to obscenities, trying to shock you. His next communication will be a highly personal attack."

She had no intention of playing his mind games.

FBI: *NONE OF YOUR DAMN BUSINESS.*

CIPHER: *I'LL TAKE THAT AS A NO. IS IT BECAUSE OF ME?*

"He feels possessive of you," Wade said. "He wants to be the only man you think about."

"I agree," Kent said. "He's jealous."

The thought made her ill. "I won't talk to him about my sex life." She stopped herself before adding *or lack thereof.*

Wade and Kent were throwing out suggestions about how to get the conversation back on track when another message popped up on the screen.

CIPHER: *UR TAKING A LONG TIME 2 RESPOND, WARRIOR GIRL. HAVE I UPSET U, OR IS THAT WASHED UP MIND HUNTER UR WORKING W/ TRYING TO COME UP W/ A RESPONSE?*

Wade reddened. "He's seen me on the news and must have googled my name."

It wouldn't have taken much searching for Dr. Jeffrey Wade's background to come up. He had been well known even before the extensive media coverage of the Chandra Brown case.

"We can use this," Kent said.

Breck's hand appeared above her screen making a twirling motion, encouraging them to continue. Nina typed in something to keep the exchange going.

FBI: *I SPEAK FOR MYSELF.*

CIPHER: *HOW MANY OTHERS R IN THE ROOM W/ U RIGHT NOW, NINA? I WANT U ALONE.*

"Now he's using your first name," Kent said. "Getting intimate. Go with it."

She had an idea about what to say next. It would probably make everyone around her, especially Wade, furious. But it might save a girl's life.

FBI: *THEN COME AND GET ME.*

Kent swore.

Wade's jaw tightened. "What the hell are you doing, Guerrera?"

CIPHER: *I WILL, WARRIOR GIRL, BUT AT A TIME & PLACE OF MY CHOOSING.*

She ignored the two men barking instructions into her ears and sent back a quick reply.

FBI: *NOW IS GOOD.*

CIPHER: *FEELING BRAVE, LITTLE ONE? I'LL HAVE U BEGGING LIKE U DID BEFORE. DO UR FBI FRIENDS KNOW HOW MUCH U CRIED & PLEADED & SCREAMED? THEY WILL SEE THE REAL U SOON.*

Wade had gone silent. Nina had the feeling he wasn't only analyzing the Cipher's responses but hers as well. She deliberately turned away from him to address Kent. "What's he talking about?"

"His language is indicative of manipulation," Kent said. "He wants you back in the state of fear where he put you before. In his mind, that connects you to him. It allows him to exert control over you without even touching you. He doesn't have to be anywhere near you to make you think about him, which is essential to him because he thinks about you all the time."

Nina gave him a humorless smile before turning back to the screen.

FBI: *FINE, LEAVE THE OTHERS ALONE. THIS IS BETWEEN US.*

CIPHER: *IT ALWAYS HAS BEEN. IT STARTS AND ENDS W/ U, NINA.*

FBI: *THEN LET'S END IT NOW. JUST THE TWO OF US. NOBODY ELSE NEEDS TO GET HURT.*

Everyone stopped talking. She knew scores of monitors were following their exchange throughout the building. Buxton's included.

CIPHER: *GOODBYE, WARRIOR GIRL . . . FOR NOW.*

He made no more responses to any of her comments.

Buxton had come out of his office. He made a beeline for Breck's workstation. "Did you locate him?"

She shook her head, eyes lowered. "He's bouncing through so many servers . . . I haven't seen anything like it outside of terrorist cell communications, and even most of them don't have that many redundancies. This guy has a tech background, or he's done a ton of research."

"You're still prepared to stop him?" Buxton asked.

Breck's head lifted, her delicate features set in determined lines. "It'll take a few minutes, but yes. We've already gotten agreements from most social media platforms. They'll shut his profiles down at our request since he's using them to publicize his murders. We've told them to hold off for investigative reasons, but I can ask them to pull the plug anytime you want."

"Let's keep that option open for the time being," Buxton said. "Right now, it's our only way to communicate with him directly." He rounded on Nina. "Speaking of which, what the hell was that?"

His conversation with Breck had bought her time to come up with a way to mitigate the damage. She gave him the most honest answer she could. "My attempt to keep him from killing another girl in the next twenty-four hours."

The reminder of their timetable and what was at stake dulled the sharp edge of his tone. "You were supposed to follow the coaching, Agent Guerrera."

Kent cleared his throat. "The Cipher's responses did provide new insight, sir."

She threw him a grateful look, but the reproach in Kent's expression told her he wasn't pleased with her tactics any more than their boss had been.

Buxton glanced at Kent. "What did you come up with?"

"I'll review a copy of the exchange again and look for any matches in our database for some of his more distinctive speech patterns. For now, I can tell you he's highly intelligent, educated, and idiosyncratic with his language. He may have some OCD tendencies in his professional or personal life. He's highly structured and methodical." He paused. "And he's got one hell of a god complex."

"I'd like your full analysis as soon as possible." Buxton switched his attention to Wade. "Your thoughts?"

"If Guerrera was trying to get him to drop his other plans and come after her, it didn't work," Wade said. "She's challenged his masculinity, which I believe is fragile to the extreme. He'll feel the need to seek retribution." He flicked a glance her way. "I predict he'll move up his deadline from his last message. He'll take out another victim and publicly taunt us. He may repeat his crime a few more times just to prove he can. Then he'll target Guerrera as the finale in whatever plan he has in mind."

"What about the Vikings poster?" Buxton asked. "I'm looking for anything that can point us to this unsub's identity."

"Could mean a lot of things," Wade said. "Might be from Minnesota, could be a pro-football fan, or maybe he thinks he's Erik the Red reincarnated." He blew out a sigh. "Not enough data to be sure."

Thoughts of the poster brought the shed back to her mind. "He was fascinated by the scars on my back," she said. "He added his own marks on top of them. Then he gave the other two girls matching burns. All in the shape of a triangle." She glanced at Wade, desperate for an answer to the question she had carried with her in silence for eleven years. "Why?"

Wade grimaced. "In a very literal sense, he was branding you, marking you as his property. He covered another man's stamp of possession with his own." He dragged a hand through his hair. "As for the other victims, he's either made that his signature now or he wanted to make them surrogates for you."

"He *bestowed* his mark on you," Kent corrected. "Like when he said he would grant you a question. These are characteristic word choices that may help us identify him when we develop a pool of suspects."

She considered Kent's observations about how the Cipher phrased things. "What about his comment that it began and will end with me? Does that mean I was his first?"

Wade answered without hesitation. "He may have had ideations for years before that, but I'm fairly certain you were the first one he acted out on. We need to figure out what it was about you that sparked him to take it from fantasy to reality." He paused, stroking his jaw. "He's now also removed all doubt that he knew you from somewhere before he abducted you. He admitted he'd been watching you."

"I agree," Kent said. "All signs point to an ongoing obsession that has strengthened since he found you again."

She imagined the Cipher seeing her for the first time in years when he watched the viral video of the Warrior Girl taking down a would-be rapist in the park. Had he gotten angry? Excited? Jealous? Did he think she was "asking for it" by jogging alone in a wooded park?

"Based on what we know about his victims, he preys on teenage girls with an unstable home life who are on their own," she said, taking a stab at profiling. "Girls who should be punished."

"He's making judgments." Kent's blond brows drew together. "Rendering verdicts and carrying out sentences."

"Like a judge," Wade said. "Or a wrathful god."

Breck had strolled over from her workstation to join them. "Do you think he's some sort of religious nut?"

"Maybe," Wade said, appearing to turn the idea over in his mind. "But not in any kind of traditional sense. He doesn't indicate he's doing his lord's bidding. This guy doesn't answer to a higher power. In his mind, he *is* the higher power."

"It goes back to his behavior," Kent said. "Everything he does is freighted with meaning. He chose the girl in DC so we would be sure to make the connection with Guerrera. He wanted her pulled into the case, so he orchestrated the scene to make that happen."

"He gave up something of great value in order to execute his plan." Wade gestured to Nina. "He left her necklace behind, a prize he has kept for more than a decade."

"A trophy," she said.

Wade gave her a curt nod. "He would never relinquish such a cherished item unless he still possesses something of greater significance, or he plans to replace it with something else of even higher value."

Her mouth went dry. The Cipher wanted her at his mercy again. He had made that abundantly clear. She had not considered that his willingness to give up his trophy demonstrated how confident he was that he would succeed.

"Me." Nina offered the only logical conclusion. "He plans to replace it with me."

Chapter 17

Hermosa Vista Apartments
Springfield, Virginia

Nina trudged up the last flight of stairs to find Bianca sitting on the top step, chewing her nails. "What's wrong, Bee?"

"Saw that YouTube video," Bianca said. "We've decided to take it on."

She sighed. "Who is 'we' and what are 'we' taking on?"

"Me and my GWU team," Bianca said. "We're going to solve the Cipher's clue."

She should have anticipated this. The Cipher wasn't just tormenting her—he was doing the same to everyone he sucked into his deadly game. Now her young neighbor felt the need to take action.

"Thanks," Nina said, offering her a weary smile, "but we've got this."

Bianca looked less than impressed. "Whatever your feeb dweebs are doing, we can do better."

This was not the first time Nina had heard Bianca's disdain of all things she perceived to be bureaucratic and governmental.

"I'm asking you to stay out of this, Bee." She twisted her key in the doorknob, then unlocked the double dead bolt. Stepping over the threshold, she deactivated the alarm before passing through the tiny foyer inside. She went straight for the refrigerator, pulled out two bottles of chilled water, and handed one to Bianca. "I don't want you to take any time away from your studies."

"I can multitask, no problem. Besides, this is important."

"Which is why the FBI is dedicating a tremendous amount of resources to the problem. You may be awesome with computers, but our team of computer forensic and cyber specialists aren't 'feeb dweebs.' Let them do their jobs."

Bianca showed every sign of launching into a debate, but the door chime cut her off before she could start.

Nina padded to the foyer and peered through the peephole. She let out a groan before opening the door to Jaime, the building superintendent.

"Hola, bonita," Jaime said by way of greeting.

She'd been fending off the super's advances since she'd moved in, but Jaime hadn't gotten the message. Probably never would.

"What's up?"

"Need to check the seals on your windows. I got a bunch of complaints from tenants about their electric bills. I might need to recaulk the whole building, but I got to show the landlord that at least half the casings are leaking air."

She had to give him credit. His pretexts were getting more creative. At least she wasn't alone this time. She stood aside. "Come in."

He sidled past her, shoulders slumping when he spotted Bianca, who gave him a finger wave.

"Come to repair the O-ring on the stove?" Bianca said. "Or is it the flux capacitor this time?"

Nina stifled a laugh while Jaime flushed a deep crimson. He looked like he wanted to argue, then thought better of it and ignored the barb, turning to Nina.

"I been watching the news, *bonita*," he said. "They're saying this Cipher guy killed that one girl in Georgetown because she looked like you."

She had no desire to start a discussion about the case with him. "That's the theory."

"I could stay here while you're gone if you have to leave town again," he said. "Keep an eye on the place."

Bianca snorted. "And sniff all her undies."

He rounded on her. "That is so wrong, *mi'jita*. You got a dirty mind for a young girl. I think you spend too much time on the internet."

Nina gave him a firm response. "Thanks for the offer, but no."

Jaime wasn't ready to give up. He stepped closer to Nina. "I know you got a gun and stuff, but that guy could sneak in here while you're away and hide. Then when you come back, he—"

"I can take care of myself just fine."

Bianca put a hand on her hip. "If he comes in here, she'll kick his ass."

"What if he surprises you?" Jaime suddenly darted behind Nina and wrapped his arms around her torso, pinning her arms to her sides. "Like this."

Instinctively, she snapped her neck back, headbutting him in the chin before spinning out of his grasp.

"Damn." Jaime rubbed his jaw.

She glared at him. "If you don't want to get hurt, don't grab me like that."

"What about like this?" Jaime reached out and circled her neck with his hands.

The feel of thick fingers around her throat sent Nina's heart racing. She was in the back of the Cipher's van. Gloved hands squeezed her windpipe, gradually increasing their relentless pressure. Cutting off her screams. Suffocating her. She struggled against the tape binding her wrists and ankles. The monster leaned in close, panting with anticipation. The world darkened around the edges, then her ears rang with the laughter that spilled from his cruel lips.

She raked the edge of her shoe down Jaime's shin and stomped on his foot, simultaneously bringing her arms up in a swift arc to break his hold. She barely managed to stop herself before palm-striking the bridge of his nose.

"Stop it, Jaime!" The fear in Bianca's voice brought Nina fully back into the present.

Jaime was hopping on one foot, cursing in two languages.

"I think you'd better go," Nina said to him as her breathing slowed to normal.

"Yeah. I can see you got this." He straightened. "Glad I could help you . . . uh . . . practice your moves." Making no mention of the leaky windowsills that had been his purported reason for coming, he shuffled stiffly, trying to hide his limp, as he left.

As soon as the door closed behind him, Bianca burst out laughing.

Nina raised a brow. "It's not funny when people get hurt, Bee."

"I know, but it's Jaime." She gave her head a small shake. "I mean, he comes in here all macho, trying to be the big bad protector, and you just totally kicked his ass."

"He means well."

"He means to get in your panties."

"Not gonna happen."

"I know that. You know that. The rest of the building knows that. But he keeps trying anyway." Bianca blew out an exaggerated sigh. "Denial is a powerful thing."

"Words of wisdom from the girl who never dates."

"I don't see you going out on Saturday nights. Or having any men over to visit." Bianca aimed a thumb at her chest. "I'm helping my professor create the next generation of implantable nanotechnology. What's your excuse?"

She had no excuse. At least none that she could admit. Stalling for time to come up with a glib retort, she glanced down at the bright colors on Bianca's T-shirt. Tilting her head, she leaned closer, taking in the design for the first time.

"Nina?" Bianca's tone held concern.

"I'm fine. I was just . . . I like your T-shirt. Where did you get it?"

Bianca looked down. "It's from the science club competition at the end of last semester. Funny, right?"

The black cotton shirt featured a color-coded depiction of the entire periodic table with the phrase WE'RE IN OUR ELEMENT beneath it.

Nina tried a laugh that came out hollow. "Gotta love science humor."

"Where have you been? Nerds are considered cool now."

Nina winked. "Good to hear, because I'm at least twenty percent nerd myself."

"Excuse me, but you are ninety percent badass," Bianca said. "Whatever makes up the other ten percent doesn't matter."

She must be better at faking than she thought. The momentary distraction was giving her space to breathe as she came down from the Jaime-induced adrenaline rush. Jet lag had slowed her normal recovery time. "I need another bottle of water. I'm dehydrated."

"That's because the air on planes is recycled." Bianca grabbed a second bottle from the fridge and passed it to her. "You probably didn't drink enough to make up for two cross-country flights."

"I hear they recycle their toilet water too," Nina said, unscrewing the top. "Do you think that's why airplane coffee tastes funny?"

Bianca laughed in midgulp. "You made me snarf my water."

Nina put her bottle on the counter. "I'll get a paper towel."

She waited as Bianca dabbed at the front of her shirt, the moisture darkening the neon design. She squinted at the neat rows of boxes, each with letters in the center and numbers in the corner.

Letters and numbers.

She grabbed Bianca's wrist and yanked her arm away.

"What the hell, Nina?" Bianca took a step back.

She released her grip and whirled, looking for her laptop. After a fruitless search through the living room, she remembered it was still packed in her suitcase. Ignoring Bianca's questions, she raced to her bedroom to retrieve the computer and brought it back, opening it on the kitchen table.

Bianca stared down at her. "Care to share?"

"Your T-shirt gave me an idea," she said as the laptop booted up. "It could be way off, but I need to check."

"Is this about the Cipher's clue?" Bianca grew excited. "Let me help. I could seriously use five hundred thousand bucks." She scooted a chair beside her. "And bragging rights."

Nina googled the periodic table. "Hand me a sheet of paper and a pencil from that drawer over there." She jerked her chin toward the junk drawer at the far corner of the kitchen counter.

Bianca dug through the contents and came back to the table moments later. "I'll pull up an image of the clue on the card he left in San Francisco. You write down the matching elements."

Nina spared Bianca a quick grin as she grabbed the paper and pencil. The girl caught on quickly. At times like these, Nina remembered Bianca had an IQ north of 160.

Bianca read the numbers, pausing between each so Nina could look for the atomic numbers and jot down the corresponding chemical names and element symbols.

"Seventy-five," Bianca said.

Nina dragged her finger across the screen to enlarge the tiny print on the chart. "Rhenium, abbreviated R-e."

Bianca continued to the next number in the series. "Seventy-three."

"Tantalum. T-a," Nina said, scribbling down the letters.

"Three."

"Lithium. L-i."

They continued until Nina had written all seven numbers in the code along with their chemical names and element symbols.

Bianca peered over her shoulder as she took in the jumble of letters. Re, Ta, Li, F, Md, O, Re.

"Are you thinking what I'm thinking?" Bianca whispered.

"Probably not."

"What if this is an anagram?" Bianca practically vibrated with excitement. "You know, a word scramble. I do them to relax after homework sometimes."

Nina felt an eye roll coming on and barely managed to suppress it. "You do realize that other teenagers doodle obscene drawings in their notebooks to unwind?"

Bianca held out a hand. "Let me see that." She slid the page in front of her and stared down at it. "There are thousands of possibilities." She glanced up at Nina. "And that's just in English. What if he switched to a different language?"

Nina shrugged. "It was a long shot."

"I'm not giving up yet. Can I borrow your laptop?"

"Help yourself."

Bianca's fingers flew across the keyboard. "Holy crap. I just typed those letters into a random word generator, and the algorithm stopped after over ten thousand possible combinations."

"No wonder the Bureau cryptanalysts haven't cracked it yet." She rubbed her forehead. "And those numbers might not have anything to do with the periodic table, but I can't shake the feeling that there's something to this. When I look at the letters we came up with, words keep jumping out at me."

"Work with it," Bianca said. "One of my favorite quotes from Einstein is 'The intuitive mind is a sacred gift and the rational mind is a faithful servant.' He favored intuition over logic, and so do I." She angled the paper so they could both see it. "What words do you see?"

Nina glanced down. "Trial. Life. Detail. Mole. Free."

Bianca followed her gaze. They sat in silence for a full minute. Then Bianca's spine stiffened. Slowly, she turned her eyes to Nina, a slow grin spreading over her face.

Nina caught her excitement. "What?"

"The last word you said was 'free.' That gave me an idea. Freedom. After I subtracted the letters for that word, the remaining letters formed the first word you mentioned, 'trial.' But if you switch the let—"

"Freedom trail," Nina said, palm slapping the table. "Does that account for every letter?"

Bianca nodded. "But how do we know that's the right answer? It's only one of many possibilities."

"For one thing, he just left a body at an iconic location in California. The MIT students have been taunting him, so he might want to hit Massachusetts. Where better than one of the most important landmarks in the state?" She glanced back to the computer screen with the image of the Cipher's puzzle. "But we need more. Maybe he left another clue hidden in the message."

Bianca tapped the screen, opening another tab. She typed in *Freedom Trail* and read aloud. "The walking tour, paved with aged red bricks, features sixteen historical sites beginning at Boston Common and concluding at the *USS Constitution* in Boston Harbor." She toggled back to the clue screen. "Look at the sentences at the top. Do you see anything that indicates Massachusetts or something else that might refer to the Freedom Trail?"

"That first line," Nina said. "I always thought it was bizarre. 'Not understanding will make you sob.' It's an odd way to phrase something, and it doesn't fit the pattern of the second sentence, which sounds normal."

Bianca nodded. "It's like he wrote it weird because he needed it to work."

"Exactly. It starts and ends with a strange word choice. The beginning is a negative, and most people would say *cry* rather than *sob* at the end."

"Starts and ends . . . ," Bianca repeated. "*Not* and *sob*. The beginning and the end." She turned wide blue eyes to Nina. "Do you see it?"

"*Not* and *sob*," Nina said. Suddenly, it clicked. "*Not sob* is *Boston* spelled backward. Boston is where the Freedom Trail is located." She leaned over to give Bianca a quick hug. "You're a genius, Bee."

"I know." Bianca picked up her mobile phone. "Let me see if I beat the Brew Crew from MIT. That would mean serious bragging rights." She laughed. "And I can get the reward from Julian Zarran. I just have to . . ." The smile slid from her face as she glanced at Nina. She grew quiet a moment, then looked down. "I can't post the answer and collect the money, can I?"

Nina reached out to gently lift Bianca's chin, meeting her eyes. "Bee, this is the first time we've been ahead of this guy. This is our chance to catch him. If we can get to Boston quickly enough, we might even save a girl's life."

Bianca paled. "Of course. I won't breathe a word." She put her phone down. "This sucks."

"I'll be your official witness if you want to contact Julian Zarran after the arrest."

"Actually, now that I think about it, you were the one who figured out the periodic table, which was the hardest part of the clue. You should get the money."

"I'm a federal agent. I can't collect reward money."

"Well, that sucks too."

"Money never motivated me. I'm about taking predators off the street."

"You're in the right profession, then. You'll never run out of bad guys, and you'll never get rich."

Nina slid her cell phone from her pocket, then paused. Should she call Buxton? She could bolster her standing with the boss, prove that she was valuable for more than just her memories.

She'd never been a blue flamer. Getting ahead with overeager striving wasn't the way to make a career. She might be an outsider at Quantico, might prefer working alone, but she needed to be a team player on this investigation. Coming to a decision, she drew in a long breath and hit her preset speed-dial button.

"What is it, Guerrera?" Wade responded in his characteristic gruff baritone.

"Pack a bag," she said, echoing his words from the previous day. "We're heading to Boston."

Chapter 18

Three hours later, somewhere in the air between Reagan National and Logan International airports, Nina batted away the hand that prodded her. "I'm awake." She heard the bleariness in her own voice.

"I'm all for team bonding," Kent said to her. "But you're drooling on my shoulder."

Mortified, she sat up to inspect his shirt. "I don't see anything." The woven golf shirt embroidered with the FBI seal looked slightly rumpled along the shoulder seam, but dry.

He grinned. "At least you're up now."

She shot him a scowl. "Hilarious."

"I asked him to wake you," Buxton said. "I let you and Agent Wade catch a quick nap, but we have things to discuss before we land."

Seated across from her next to Buxton, Wade was rubbing his eyes with the palms of his hands. After their cross-country travels with almost no downtime, the undertow of jet lag had pulled Nina down as she boarded one of the FBI's leased Gulfstream jets at Reagan National. The Director had personally authorized a dedicated jet for their team for the duration of the investigation. From this point on, they would go to each site as a unit, conveying information to the task force back at Quantico.

Kent handed them each a steaming mug of black coffee. Nina had never been aboard a Gulfstream but, given what she'd heard about them, wasn't surprised to see a steel carafe sitting on the polished surface of the table that extended from the side of the main cabin.

"I want to update you on the most recent findings from the task force," Buxton began. "We compared the manifests of flights into Logan from all major airports out of San Francisco or the DC area, in case he flew back there first. There were no matching names."

Nina took a sip, the bitter warmth of the drink seeping into her system. "So he used an alias, or he didn't fly."

"It's unlikely he used ground transportation due to the short time frame between murders, but it's possible to drive from DC to San Francisco in forty-two hours without speeding," Buxton said.

"Driving would be almost as risky as flying," Breck said. "A lot could go wrong on a cross-country road trip."

Wade stretched and stifled a yawn. "An unsub with the Cipher's character traits might consider it exciting. Might enjoy demonstrating his capability. Even if only to himself."

"He's confident in his abilities," Kent said. "He might drive, but that would mean he's either self-employed or has a job where he could be gone for four or five days in a row without drawing attention."

Nina hadn't given much thought to the Cipher's career choice. Could he possibly work in a cubicle farm in a standard corporate environment? Other killers had.

"Given his computer skills, he probably has a tech job," Nina said. "Maybe one with flexible hours where he consults online or something where he doesn't even need an office."

"A less structured occupation seems likely," Buxton said. Keeping the reports moving as usual, he turned to Kent. "Did you touch base with forensics?"

"The autopsy of the DC victim is complete," Kent said. "In layman's terms, the unsub scrubbed the girl's body with a chemical agent before rolling her around in the dumpster." He spread his hands. "Basically, we have a mountain of trace materials. It's like picking out a grain of sand on the beach. And with all that cross contamination, any evidence we get will be compromised."

"What kind of chemical agent did he use?" Nina asked. "Was it something unusual or difficult to obtain?"

"A medical-grade detergent that sterilizes, disinfects, and destroys DNA," Kent said.

"What kind of cleaner does that?" Nina had seen crime scene techs use luminol to locate DNA on floors mopped with straight bleach.

"One that incorporates oxygen into the mix," Kent said. "Degrades the samples."

"Could they identify the specific brand?" Buxton asked. "Are there a limited number of manufacturers?"

"The chemical compounds that make up the detergent are present in several brands commonly used in hospitals all over the country." Kent sighed as he slid his black glasses off and pinched the bridge of his nose. "Can't trace it that way."

"Hospitals?" Nina straightened, recalling the memory jarred loose at the autopsy in San Francisco. "That instrument the unsub used to force open my mouth was like the one the ME had. Now he uses a medical-grade cleaning agent. Could the Cipher be a doctor or a surgeon?"

"A surgeon with a god complex," Wade said. "Never heard of that before."

Kent grinned at the sarcasm. "It would match some of the behaviors we're seeing."

"Let's keep that in our back pocket," Buxton said. "We might be able to use it to narrow our search going forward."

"Well, he might be a doctor." Breck, who had been typing on her laptop, abruptly stopped. "Or he might be a busboy who knows how to do a Google search. It's not hard, look." She swiveled her laptop around on the fold-out table attached to her seat's armrest. A list of oxygenated chemical cleaning agents filled the screen.

"He's obviously comfortable with computers," Nina said. "How smart would he have to be to figure out a way to confuse forensic analysis?"

"His speech patterns indicate he's either highly educated or well read." Kent pushed his glasses back on. "Either way, an above-average IQ is likely."

Wade rested his mug on the table. "That last clue tells us he's smart. He used two forms of encryption, both of which required secondary extrapolation."

Nina was grateful Bianca had dropped by her apartment. The girl's T-shirt, and her substantial brain power, had been the keys to unlocking the unsub's code. Jaime, on the other hand, would probably think twice before coming by on another pretext. Good news all around, then.

"I agree that the unsub gives the appearance of advanced intellectual ability, but Breck has a point," Buxton said. "He could simply be adept with computers." He turned to her. "Any updates from Video Forensics on either case?"

Breck pulled the laptop back around and tapped the keys. "We were able to follow the van he used in the DC case onto the Dulles Toll Road. He exited onto Route Twenty-Eight and kept heading west until there were no more cameras."

"He drove me west from Alexandria to Chantilly when he'd kidnapped me," Nina said. "In the same van or one just like it."

Buxton opened a leather portfolio embossed with the FBI seal and made a note. "We should check the same parcel of land where he took you before, but I doubt he'd be careless enough to build a new shed there."

"We could get satellite photos of the whole area," Breck added. "Use the eye in the sky to spot any unauthorized structures on the property."

"I'll make the request," Buxton said, still scribbling.

Breck nodded. "In the meantime, I just received a file from the task force video team. We've been working with visual data from both cases to create a better suspect composite."

Nina perked up. They hadn't had enough to even attempt a sketch before. This was the kind of information that could crack the case. She put down her coffee and listened carefully.

"We cleaned up the images of him from the alley in DC as best we could, considering the ball cap and facial hair. Nothing matches any face-rec databases, but when we superimposed the images with footage from San Francisco, we got enough definition to take a stab at a computer-generated composite."

Nina stood. "Can I see?" She stepped into the aisle and padded toward Breck.

"What did he look like in San Francisco?" Wade asked.

"He wasn't hobbling around in California, so he must have altered his gait somehow in DC," Breck said. Then added, "He wasn't heavyset in California either."

Nina recalled the surveillance footage in DC of the chubby delivery man with a distinctive limp rolling the handcart with the oversize box toward the nightclub. She would never have pegged him for the muscular, athletically built man who had easily overpowered her. Now she knew why. The gut and the limp had been fake.

"There's tons of video of him at Pier Thirty-Nine." Breck's comment pulled her back from her musing. "He stole a dinghy, threw an oversize chum tank in the back, and motored out to the floating dock. He opened the lid, pulled the victim's body out—hidden in a black garbage bag—and tied it to one of the pylons in the early hours before dawn. You can see him reaching down into the water with a knife to cut the bag away. No one thought anything of it at the time." Breck tucked a curly red tendril behind her ear. "The place was deserted, and he was dressed in a gray sweat suit with a hoodie covering his head. He had a turtleneck underneath pulled up over his nose and aviator sunglasses covering his eyes."

"How did he transport the body to the pier?" Nina asked, sitting down next to her.

"Parked a pickup close to the dock nearest to the dinghy, unloaded the chum tank, which had wheels on one end and a handle on the other, and wheeled it down the gangway."

"Damn," Kent said. "Right out in the open."

"It's part of the thrill for him," Wade said. "Part of the game. Proves he's so much better than we are."

"Any video of the unsub taping the envelope to that dumpster or walking through terminals in the surrounding airports?" Buxton asked.

"Nothing so far." Breck angled the screen toward Nina. "Take a look and see if you can add anything. There's still time for me to tweak the image if it's way off."

"My memories are out of date compared to what you have," she said, giving Wade a side-eye. "And apparently patchy too."

She studied the image on the laptop. The man had a well-defined jawline and pronounced features, all regular. Breck had left the sunglasses in place. There was nothing striking about him. Nothing to set him apart except an indefinable sense that made her flesh crawl.

"I remember that his eyes were blue," Nina said after a careful inspection.

Breck reached for the mouse. "Any particular shade?"

Try as she might, she could not offer more. "Sorry."

"Easy enough." Breck dragged the computer back. "I'll give him a neutral eye shape and add in a medium blue to the irises. I'll have it ready in two shakes."

"We'll distribute it to law enforcement," Buxton said.

"Do we give it to the public?" Nina asked.

Buxton frowned. "I don't want to circulate it until we have a clearer image. With that heavy beard growth and dark ball cap, he looks like fifty percent of all white males between twenty and fifty years old in the US."

Kent nodded. "Given the publicity this case already has, we'd get tens of thousands of false leads."

"For the time being, we'll just disseminate it to the officers detailed to the Freedom Trail this morning," Breck said.

Dreading the answer, she asked the question plaguing her since Kent had prodded her awake. "Has anyone posted a solution to the Cipher's clue yet?"

"Negative," Buxton said. "We still have the advantage. If our luck holds, we'll catch this guy without a public circus."

"There are more teams forming all over the country," Breck said. "Some of them want to win the five hundred grand, some want to catch the infamous Cipher, and some are trying to do both."

Nina pulled out her cell phone. "I've been checking his social media sites. He's set up a leaderboard on his Facebook page with the names of people or teams who are after him, listing the Brew Crew in the number two slot behind Julian Zarran. He's making sure everyone knows about the reward too."

"He's fueling the rivalry," Wade said. "The public attention is enhancing the whole power dynamic for him. He's driving the national conversation right now."

"Got everyone chasing their tails." Breck nodded. "Third on the list is a group of sexual assault survivors who call themselves the Pink Wave. Fourth is a band of former Army Rangers. I can't say much for his chances of survival if they get to him before we do. In fifth position is a group of students. He only lists the top five teams."

Nina rolled her eyes. "So not only are we hunting this guy, we're in direct competition with a bunch of *Scooby-Doo* gangs from around the country who are chasing him as well?"

"I know we're watching the Cipher's social media posts, but is someone monitoring the Scoobies?" Wade said. "The Cipher is the type who might try to insert himself into the investigation by posing as someone on a team and proposing solutions to his puzzles to either throw us off or manipulate us in some other way."

"The segment of the task force monitoring social media engagement is looking into the background of every team that gets involved," Buxton said. "They send me regular updates."

Nina looked through the small cabin window at the city lights far below. Hundreds, perhaps thousands, of civilians were wading into the investigation. There was no way to control what happened when they interacted with the psychopath who called himself the Cipher. He was reveling in the chaos. Stoking it.

"The unsub is using the public to run interference," Kent said, echoing her thoughts. "So far, it's working for him. This is only going to get worse."

"Agreed," Buxton said, bringing the conversation back around to logistics. "We've got to finalize our plan for Boston before we land. I've been in touch with the local FBI field office and the Boston police commissioner. They've done a soft activation of their EOC."

Nina didn't like it. An Emergency Operations Center activation usually involved authorization from city management and pulled in multiple local agencies. "Won't that call attention to—"

Buxton held up a hand. "I emphasized that we need this operation to be as covert as possible and that if the unsub knows we're onto him, he'll switch up his plans." He glanced at the lined notebook paper inside his portfolio. "They've reassigned all available plainclothes personnel to deploy along the Freedom Trail. They'll be augmented by uniformed officers on bikes, motorcycles, and on foot beats, but they'll be scattered around so it doesn't look like increased patrol." He flipped a page. "That's a total of roughly two hundred police to cover the length of the Trail, which is about two and a half miles long."

"Wall-to-wall coverage." Kent gave Buxton an appreciative nod. "The bastard won't be able to squeak out a fart without us smelling it."

"Where does the Trail start?" Breck asked.

"First stop is Boston Common," Buxton said. "It ends at Boston Harbor."

Kent let out a groan. "Another harbor. This guy likes the water. What's the BPD doing about that?"

"They have a Harbor Unit," Buxton said. "The harbormaster is deploying everything that floats. They've also coordinated with the Massachusetts Port Authority. Massport has its own police, who work in conjunction with state patrol. They've been looped into the EOC to keep an eye on the marine terminals and everything else near the water."

"What about air support?" Nina said.

Buxton glanced at his notes. "BPD doesn't have helicopters. They rely on the Massachusetts State Police air fleet." He looked back at Nina. "Another reason for the EOC. We're coordinating air support there."

"Does the BPD have drones?" Breck asked.

"They'll be circulating over the area around the clock, and they also have a substantial net of cameras all over downtown, especially at historic landmarks along the Trail." He allowed a rare smile. "Boston is sealed up tighter than a frog's ass. We're going to catch this guy."

Her supervisor's enthusiasm was contagious. For the first time since the case began, Nina felt hopeful. "What are our orders when we land?"

"We'll meet up with our local field agents at the EOC."

She had no intention of sitting in a room full of video monitors watching the takedown. "I want to go out with the plainclothes BPD cops on the Trail."

"Thanks to that viral video, you're famous, Agent Guerrera," Buxton said, shaking his head. "You'd blow the whole operation."

She'd come prepared. "I packed an oversize hoodie. I'll wear my Jackie-O sunglasses. No one will know who I am."

She noticed Wade giving her an assessing look and shot him a hard stare. He'd better not try to sideline her.

"Actually," Wade said slowly, "I think Guerrera could be useful in the field. She can pair up with a local plainclothes detective, and they would look totally natural strolling the Trail like a couple of tourists."

"I want to go out too," Kent said. "Nobody knows who I am. I could take a different spot on the Trail."

"Fine." Buxton raised his hands in mock surrender. "All of you can team up with a local and take a position."

The door to the cockpit opened and the copilot stepped into the main cabin. "Excuse me, sir, you have an urgent call from Public Affairs." He held a satellite phone out to Buxton.

Silence gathered around them as he held the device to his ear. "Buxton."

His face grew tense. "How long ago?" He nodded. "Let the EOC in Boston know about this. Tell them we'll be on the ground in ten minutes."

Buxton handed the phone back to the copilot and turned to them. "The crew from MIT just posted the solution online," he said. "Every damn Scooby east of the Mississippi and north of the Mason-Dixon is heading to the Freedom Trail."

Chapter 19

Nina had to crane her neck to meet Detective Joe Delaney's eyes. "How long have you been in Narcotics?"

"'Bout four years," he replied in a Boston accent as thick as his ginger beard.

She had trouble picturing the big Irish cop in uniform. His red hair fell past his shoulders in a shaggy ponytail, and his beard reached the middle of his broad chest.

"Must have thrown your razor in the trash the day you got your assignment."

He might have smiled. Hard to tell through the forest of whiskers.

"Don't like shaving," he said. "That's true enough."

They'd walked the Trail together, pretending to be a couple enjoying the sights, for the past two hours. Her hoodie compromised her peripheral vision somewhat, but she was certain no one had escaped their notice.

They fell into conversation as they strolled. Delaney was a talker and filled her in on the city's secrets as only a cop could. They ambled toward Faneuil Hall, renowned for its bustling shops and eateries.

It was early, but restaurants were already in food-prep mode. "Something smells good," she said.

Delaney scented the air like a bloodhound. "That'll be the famous Boston baked beans. They start early and slow cook them all day." He glanced down at her. "But you need to be careful if you're not used to eating them. They can make you fat."

She smoothed a hand over her flat belly. "Between the running and the workouts, I stay pretty lean."

"No," Delaney said. "They make you fat. F-a-r-t. *Fat.*"

She grinned. "Is that what passes for humor in Boston?"

"It's actually true either way," he said, chuckling. "Beans are pure carbs."

It sounded like he said *pure cabs.*

"Remember when we were introduced, and I asked about your current assignment? You told me you were a knack. I thought maybe it was BPD jargon for some specialty unit I hadn't heard of. Took me a few seconds to realize you meant you were a narc."

He sent her a wry grin. "Is that what passes for humor in the FBI?"

Touché.

They walked between a bistro and a café toward the outskirts surrounding Faneuil Hall. The streets were becoming crowded, and Nina spotted people darting between pedestrians and jostling sightseers, their heads swiveling in every direction.

"Scoobies," she muttered.

"Come again?"

She blew out an exasperated breath. "The internet has brought out wannabe detectives. Everyone's after the reward money or the bragging rights."

"Ah, the *Scooby-Doo* gang." He gave her an understanding nod. "They'll end up getting themselves hurt or screwing up the investigation."

She scanned the sights around her again. Was the Cipher here? Had he already come and gone? Was another girl fighting for her life at this very moment? Her hands bunched into fists. She knew all too well what he would be doing if they didn't find a way to stop him.

Delaney tapped the side of his head where his mic was hidden under a mass of hair. "I'm getting nothing. You?"

"Nothing on our end either. I'm sure the EOC will hear about it first if anything happens."

They turned to start back toward the end of the Trail.

"I usually like to see a city worker dedicated to the job, but not today," Delaney said.

She followed his gaze. A Latino man in a neon yellow Public Works vest was grasping a city trash can a block away from the Trail. She frowned. "I thought you guys requested no trash removal today."

"We did." Delaney started toward the worker. "This guy obviously didn't get the memo."

Buxton had asked the police commissioner to ensure every trash receptacle within three city blocks of the Freedom Trail remained untouched. The unsub had established a pattern of using dumpsters to deliver clues or dispose of bodies in the past. If he did it today, he would be on camera and under surveillance.

She had to jog to keep up with Delaney's ground-eating strides as they crossed the street.

"Yo," Delaney called out to the man. "Leave the garbage can alone."

Nina remained quiet. Delaney was in the awkward position of trying to intervene while maintaining his cover. She let him take the lead.

The man straightened and turned toward them, pushing a thick mop of curly black hair from his dark face. "I clean," he said in heavily accented English. "I do trash." He pointed at the can.

"You're not supposed to pick up the trash today," Delaney said, enunciating each word slowly. "Didn't your boss tell you?"

The man gave him a puzzled look. He probably wondered why a red-haired giant was telling him not to do his job. "Was at my sister house. My ride no come, so I come myself." He smiled.

"No," Delaney said. "You no come today. Understand?"

She spotted a flash of white in the man's gloved hand and addressed him in Spanish. *"Qué tiene usted?"*

His brown eyes snapped to hers, widening. "I find," he answered in English, holding up a sealed white business envelope with a piece of tape dangling from the edge. "Just now. On top of trash can." He pointed again.

Delaney snatched it from his grasp and flipped it over. He turned his back to the worker to face Nina. Without a word, he held up the envelope to show her what was printed on it.

WARRIOR GIRL

Pulse pounding, she lurched forward to grab it from Delaney. They looked at each other for a long moment.

"Should we open it?" Delaney said in a low voice.

"Hell yes."

The evidence techs wouldn't be happy, but there might be something time-sensitive inside. She would take the ass-chewing later. Right now, they needed information. She slid a finger under the flap and pulled out a white index card. Delaney peered over her shoulder as she read.

ONE IF BY LAND, TWO IF BY SEA

Nina remembered the famous phrase from history classes. "That was from the night of Paul Revere's ride, right?"

Delaney nodded. "They were supposed to light one lantern if the British were attacking by land, two lanterns if they were crossing the Charles River." He frowned. "Why would the Cipher bring that up?"

"Paul Revere," Nina said. "His house is one of the stops on the Freedom Trail. We've got to notify the EOC."

"Hold on a sec." Delaney paused with his hand halfway to his earbud. "The lanterns were lit in the steeple of the Old North Church. Another stop on the Trail."

Leave it to a Boston native. "Good point," she said. "You go ahead and advise the EOC, I'll try to get more info from the Public Works guy. He might be more chatty in Spanish."

Delaney walked away to use his comm without drawing attention. As soon as he moved, Nina saw that the Public Works employee had vanished. She had been so intent on the envelope she hadn't seen him leave. They would need his information and a formal statement.

Cursing herself for not telling him to stay, she jogged along the sidewalk, scanning the area. She spotted the man's bright vest two blocks down cleaning trash in an alley and picked up her speed. He must not have understood Delaney about not picking up trash today. Or perhaps he didn't believe him.

"*Disculpe,*" she called out to the man.

He appeared not to hear and kept moving, disappearing between two buildings.

She raced after him, rounding the corner where she'd last seen him.

A fist shot out from her left, delivering a stunning blow to the side of her head. She stumbled, trying to regain her footing. She saw the yellow Public Works vest only as a blur before the man circled behind her to wrap his arms around her, covering her mouth with his gloved hand.

When he bent his head to whisper in her ear, his English had no accent. "You won't get away this time, Nina."

Even after eleven years, she knew that voice.

Chapter 20

The Cipher drew in a deep breath, inhaling her unique scent. Nina's fear intoxicated him. Aroused him. Primed him. He tucked her tiny frame against his chest and felt her heart race like the wings of a hummingbird. The solution to his puzzle had been posted online only three hours ago. He had not expected her to arrive in Boston so quickly.

This was not how he had planned their reunion. She was making a habit of displeasing him. He would have to teach her another lesson. See to it that she learned obedience before she died.

He tightened his hand over her lush lips, silencing her and immobilizing her head at the same time. He clamped her upper body with the other arm, crushing her harder against him. She sank her teeth into his index finger. Fortunately, the thermoplastic rubber knuckle guard prevented her bite from penetrating his tactical glove. He felt her jaw working, trying to chew her way through the reinforced fabric. A chuckle escaped his lips. She struggled, exciting him again. His little Warrior Girl wanted to fight. Good.

Her arms slid behind her, inching between their bodies. Before he realized what she was doing, her hand found his crotch. She grabbed his balls through his pants, squeezed with surprising strength, and twisted with a violent jerk of her wrist.

Breath flew from his lungs in a loud blast. He tried to master himself, but his knees buckled. She didn't let go, twisting sharply in the other direction. Yielding to the pain, he shoved her away, finally breaking her grip. Doubling over, he sucked in air, his hands involuntarily clutching between his legs. She would pay dearly for this.

She spit out a piece of nylon string torn from the glove. "Down on your knees."

He lifted his head to see the muzzle of her semiautomatic aimed straight at him. The gun didn't waver.

She narrowed her eyes. "Hands behind your back."

The bitch had no way of knowing what it was like to have your nuts rearranged and clearly didn't understand that he couldn't put his hands behind his back if he wanted to. Which he didn't. He would not kneel at her command. In the end, she would kneel before him. She would pray to him, but he would not grant her salvation.

He beat back a wave of nausea as the pain threatened to overwhelm him. "Can't."

She kept her weapon trained on him with one hand and raised the other to her ear, no doubt preparing to call in the cavalry. He was out of options. She had become yet another adversary in the cage. About to defeat him.

He would not allow it.

Pushing through the agony in his loins, he planted his feet and launched himself at her. Time slowed. The instant he exploded forward, she squeezed the trigger. In a split second he felt the devastating blow of a hollow-point round thudding into the center of his chest.

He collapsed.

She rushed toward him, eyes traveling the length of his body. "Stay down. I'll get rescue." She started for her earpiece again.

Whether she contacted them or not, police would locate the source of the gunfire in less than a minute. He had studied the capabilities of the Boston PD before he made his plans. He had one final play. Nina had no way of knowing he wore body armor.

He flung out his foot, executing a perfect leg sweep. Her feet flew up in the air, and she crashed down onto the hard pavement beside him, winded. Her gun slid across the alley to clatter against the brick wall well out of reach.

Before she could recover, he rolled on top of her, his bulk preventing her from getting sufficient air to scream or fight. He brought his face so close to hers their lips nearly touched. "Not yet, little Warrior Girl, but soon. Very soon."

In that moment, he wanted her more than he had wanted anything else in his life. She was just as he remembered and yet, so much more. He wrapped his hands around her slender throat, the terror reflected in her wide eyes a thing of beauty. "You will be mine again," he whispered.

The instant his movement allowed her space, her hand shot up to claw at his gloved hands. Her short nails raked his right wrist. Cursing, he squeezed harder. He didn't want to kill her yet, only to make her pass out. A delicate maneuver.

When her thrashing ceased seconds later, he jumped up and hobbled toward the street through the far side of the alley. Uniformed police were converging from every direction. He waved to get their attention and pointed down the alley where Nina was no doubt sputtering and coughing by now.

"Man with gun," he said, laying it on thick with the Mexican accent and making sure he sounded hysterical. "He shoot lady."

The cops thundered past him in the direction he had indicated, guns drawn. They were not looking for a dark-skinned Latino Public Works employee. They were looking for a blue-eyed white man. Nina had seen his eyes and the skin around them all those years ago. She was supposed to take that information to the grave but had no doubt shared it with police, giving them a rough idea of his appearance. Today, he had found a way to turn what had been a setback to his advantage.

Gradually recovering his range of movement, he loped around a corner, prepared to disappear. Once he cleared the immediate area, fresh pain registered. He glanced down at the blood on his wrist. Panic bloomed within him.

Chapter 21

Nina blinked several times in rapid succession, bringing the red-haired giant looming over her into focus.

"She's coming around," Delaney said to the others.

Still lying on the pavement, she looked up to see a cadre of plain-clothes and uniformed Boston PD officers gazing down at her. The cobwebs cleared. "It was him," she said, her voice ragged and raw. "In disguise." She gave a brief description of the unsub in his Public Works garb.

"Pretty damn good cover," Delaney said. "We'll put out a BOLO."

"Another thing," she said, remembering. "I scratched his wrist." She sat up. "I got his DNA."

"You say he looks like a Latino male now?" one of the uniforms asked. "I ran right past that guy. I remember the yellow vest. The sono-fabitch pointed me in your direction." He mashed the transmitter on his radio to broadcast the updated lookout for the suspect she had provided, then signaled to the others, who joined the search.

She patted her waist. "Oh shit, where's my gun?" The idea that the Cipher had taken her service weapon made her head spin all over again.

Delaney slid her Glock from the back of his waistband and handed it to her, butt first. "Only one round fired."

Relief flooded through her. "Thanks. I'm sure Ballistics will want to have a look."

"Did you hit him?"

"I did. Center mass. He went down too." She scrubbed her face with her hand. "Must have been wearing Kevlar, because he got the drop on me as soon as I got close enough to check his vitals." She turned to the officer with the radio, who had remained with them. "Add that info to the lookout."

He nodded and picked up the transmitter again.

"Speaking of gunshots, what took you guys so long?" she asked Delaney. "Did ShotSpotter pick it up?"

The briefing at the Emergency Operations Center before they took positions along the Trail had included details about Boston's gunshot detection system, which sends out an alert in real time and rotates surveillance cameras in the direction of the sound of gunfire within the covered area.

"EOC got the notification about the weapon discharge, but everyone was heading in the opposite direction at the time. Apparently, while you and I were reading the note from the trash can, a girl's body turned up."

She scrambled to her feet. "Where? What happened?"

"A seafood restaurant on Salem Street near the Old North Church," he said. "They found one of those big ice chests by their rear service door earlier this morning. One of the prep cooks assumed someone must have forgotten to take it inside after signing for it. They get deliveries of fresh fish every day, so he didn't think anything of it."

Disturbing images formed in her mind, fueling her anger.

"He hauled the chest into the kitchen," Delaney went on. "They opened it to get out the fish and found a deceased teenage girl inside, tucked in a fetal position."

Nina wanted to hit something. "Any idea who she is?"

"No ID. Naked like the others. We're circulating a photo now to see if any of our officers have seen her around. We can't put the picture out to the media. She looks pretty bad."

Nina paced, dragging a hand through her short-cropped hair. "What else did I miss?"

Delaney pulled at his beard. "Media's going nuts. One of the servers at the restaurant tweeted about the body. We've got the place cordoned off now, but the whole street is crammed with news crews and lookie-loos."

The chaos had served its purpose. "I'm sure that's what he wanted."

"The paramedics are here," Delaney said. "They'll check you out."

She took a step back. "I don't want anyone to touch my hand until we get a forensic tech out here to take a scraping from my nails."

Delaney gave her a curt nod. "Already on the way."

"That's a fairly decent contusion," one of the medics said, eyeing her temple. "Let's check your pupils."

She stood still while he held each of her eyelids up in turn, flicking a small flashlight across them. Apparently satisfied, he pressed two fingers along her wrist.

While the EMT went about his business, she continued her conversation with Delaney. "I almost had him." She tilted her head to each side as instructed. "Dammit, I should have realized something was up when I spoke to him in Spanish and he answered me in English."

"Go easy on yourself," Delaney said. "I didn't think about that either. We were both kind of busy with that envelope."

The Public Works employee disguise she had just seen looked nothing like the monster who had tormented her years ago. "I was expecting an Anglo. I must have automatically discounted him because I was so damned focused on saving whatever poor girl he might have his sights on."

"He certainly didn't match the description we had," Delaney said. "Guess he put on dark makeup or something."

She had already moved on to another thought that nagged at her. "After I blacked out, he could have easily snapped my neck. Why didn't he kill me?"

Delaney shrugged, palms up. "Did he say anything to you?"

She recalled the feeling of his large frame crushing down on her, his lips close to hers. *"Not yet, little Warrior Girl, but soon. Very soon."* Her pulse quickened as she remembered his hands tightening around her throat, the feel of his hot breath fanning her face as he whispered his parting words. *"You will be mine again."*

He had made her a promise. A threat.

His words would reveal nothing about the investigation, create no new leads, offer no new insight. But they might very well get her thrown off the case if they went public. She would become the object of even more gossip and speculation, hindering her ability to work and the team's ability to focus on leads. She would confide them to her team once they were alone, but no one else.

"No." She looked away. "He didn't say a thing."

Chapter 22

Nina surveyed the pinched faces in Boston's Emergency Operations Center. Frustration suffused the room. After being treated at the scene by paramedics while an evidence tech collected nail scrapings, she'd filled out paperwork for discharging her weapon as the search for the Cipher proceeded without her.

Relegated to the sidelines as Boston police, Massachusetts state troopers, and federal agents fanned out in a citywide dragnet, she'd been more than willing to report to the EOC with Delaney after completing a preliminary statement.

The vast space was packed with state-of-the-art technology. Jumbo screens covered an entire wall, split video feeds juxtaposed in a patchwork of camera angles, offering simultaneous views of different parts of the city. Officials and civilians manned a row of terminals, taking in an assortment of information from a variety of sources.

The general buzz in the hive of activity was interrupted by a shrill voice from one of the civilians seated in front of a glowing screen along the side wall.

"I've got something."

Nina swiveled to see a statuesque woman with long brown hair scraped back into a bun.

"We pulled the SpotShotter video," she said, fairly bouncing in her chair. She slid the mouse around on a pad beside the keyboard, clicked, then pointed at the enormous wall screen. "Look at this."

Multiple feeds consolidated into a single view showing the Cipher race into the frame and direct a rushing stampede of police toward the alley where Nina lay semiconscious.

"Watch what he does next." Excitement tinged the Boston PD video tech's voice.

The Cipher sprinted down the street and darted around a corner, where another camera picked him up. The tech had spliced the footage together before presenting it, creating a timeline of the unsub's escape. Nina watched with the others as he dodged traffic crossing the street, then proceeded down the walkway on the other side at a more sedate pace, presumably to avoid drawing attention. He slowed and came to a stop in front of a manhole cover in the middle of the sidewalk. He hiked up the hem of his jacket, exposing his waistband.

Nina squinted to see his hands, which were hastily working something loose. At first, she thought he was fumbling with a bulky belt buckle, then realized that a heavy-duty chain encircled his waist, held together by a large steel hook. A moment later, he unhooked the link and pulled the chain through his belt loops.

"What the hell is he doing?" Kent put the question to the room at large.

The Cipher bent and slipped the hook through a hole near the edge of the manhole cover. He straightened and wrapped the chain around his right hand twice, then used his left to grasp the links in a two-handed grip. In one swift motion, he bent his knees and tugged the cover aside, exposing the dark round opening leading down into the sewer system.

"No way," a BPD lieutenant said. "Those covers are made of cast iron. They weigh over two hundred pounds."

Nina wasn't surprised. She knew this was well within the Cipher's abilities.

Passersby seemed to pay no attention to a Public Works employee in a yellow vest climbing down into a sewer. Seconds after his head disappeared, the chain snaked down into the hole as he pulled it inside. With a series of jerking movements, the metal cover slid closed, effectively completing the Cipher's vanishing act. Nina marveled at his ingenuity.

"Clever sonofabitch," Wade muttered. "That whole maneuver took him maybe twenty seconds."

"He came prepared," the BPD lieutenant said, then turned to his tech. "Let's see if we can catch him on video scoping out his escape route and that manhole cover ahead of time. I also want to know where he comes out."

She nodded and sat back down in front of her terminal.

"He's meticulous and strategic," Kent said. "I'll bet he had multiple escape routes planned ahead of time."

Wade spoke loudly enough for the whole room to hear. "That's important to keep in mind going forward. If we get close to cornering this guy, we should expect him to have several bolt holes. Some of them might even be booby-trapped." He directed his gaze at the BPD brass in the room. "In fact, anyone going into that sewer should be careful. The unsub might have set up a nasty surprise to slow down any pursuers."

Deputy Superintendent Tyson, who had been introduced as the ranking BPD member present in the facility, acknowledged him with a quick nod. "I'll let my officers and the city workers know."

"How far can he go in the sewage system?" Buxton asked him.

"The combined water and sewage system has over a thousand manholes and goes all over the city." Tyson shrugged. "There's no telling where he popped out, but we'll start scanning the downtown camera system."

Buxton continued to address Tyson. "In the meantime, did you get confirmation on the ID of the latest victim?"

Tyson signaled a sergeant, who moved to the video control panel as he responded. "We forwarded a crime scene photo to our Crimes Against Children Unit. One of the CACU detectives recognized the victim. Her name is Denise Glover. Goes by Neecy. Fifteen years old."

An image popped up on the screen as Tyson finished. The picture, obviously from a high school yearbook, showed a slender girl who looked young for her age. Or perhaps the oversize glasses making her brown eyes look owlish and the pink ribbons in her dark curly hair had that effect.

Buxton turned to Wade. "We've got three victims now: first Hispanic, then white, now black. What does that say about the Cipher?"

Before answering his boss, Wade glanced at Tyson. "What do we know about Neecy?"

"Comes from a broken home. Chronic runaway." Tyson checked his notes. "Last time her foster mother saw her was over a week ago."

"That's his message," Wade said to Buxton as if the information from Tyson confirmed something he'd already suspected. "The Cipher doesn't care what they look like or where they come from. He doesn't see them as individuals, as human beings—only as a type."

"And that type is?"

"Some of society's most vulnerable individuals. Teenage girls who are either temporarily or permanently without a family."

Recalling the messages she had exchanged with the Cipher online, Nina dropped her voice so only Wade could hear. "Like I was when he found me."

He gave her an almost imperceptible nod. She decided to change the subject, channel her growing anger toward hunting the Cipher.

"What about the clue in the envelope?" she asked Tyson. "What have we heard from the detectives checking out the Paul Revere House and the Old North Church?"

The reference to the signal used by the patriots had been nagging at her. One if by land, two if by sea. A real-life code. Is that what had made the Cipher mention it?

"We got zilch," Tyson said. "The investigators enlisted the help of docents and went through every square inch of both landmarks. Nothing missing, nothing left behind, no sign of any disturbance."

"Throwing us off the trail?" she said, then caught herself. "No pun intended."

"Hold on a sec," Tyson said, suddenly excited. "The restaurant where the body was found is called Silversmith's."

Nina considered the information. Paul Revere had been a famous silversmith. "So the clue was meant to lead us to the body? He's done that before."

Wade stroked his jaw. "Planting that information could also serve as a false lead or a distraction in case we solved his clue and arrived in Boston before he had a chance to leave the scene."

"Which is exactly what happened," Kent said. "Do you think he knew we were there? That he has inside information?"

"You mean, do I think he's a cop?" The room grew quiet when Wade posed the question. "Possibly, but I find it more likely he's a police buff who's monitoring the investigation any way he can."

"Why not a cop?" Nina said. She had never considered the idea but couldn't see how Wade would rule it out with such certainty.

Wade appeared to weigh his words before he spoke, no doubt aware that he was speaking to everyone present. The opinion of a profiler would impact the investigation going forward.

"He would be attracted to a position with an aura of authority, like a policeman, a military officer, a doctor, or a pilot. He's such a control freak and so narcissistic, however, that he would have trouble taking orders and—if he managed to obtain such a position—would quickly get discharged or otherwise fired."

"So you're saying he would have to be the boss?" she said.

"When you were in that alley, your counterattack didn't deter him, did it? He wasn't the least bit afraid, even when you held him at gunpoint."

She shook her head. "I think it excited him." She hesitated a moment before posing her next question in an open forum. "Speaking of guns, the unsub could have taken mine when I was unconscious, but he didn't."

"That's because he wanted the thrill of the fight. He would prefer close quarters combat followed by the intimacy of strangulation. He's a killer, but he's also a power-assertive rapist."

She needed clarification and imagined several others in the room who didn't speak fluent psychobabble did too. "What do you mean?"

"Each victim was tortured before death. The injuries were not inflicted postmortem." Wade warmed to his subject, clearly in his element. "He enjoys manipulating others. Violence excites him. He gets off on watching his victims cry and suffer."

"In other words," she said, "he's a sadist."

"More than that. He feeds on ultimate power. He makes his victims beg. He'll offer them mercy, only to refuse it after they comply with his demands. He wants to control everything they do, including when and how they die."

Sweat beaded along her hairline as she listened to Wade. Everything he described was accurate. Down to the last detail. Had those other girls been made to plead? To cry? To suffer? Only to finally realize it had all been for nothing? She was sure they had. A toxic blend of rage and humiliation burned inside her.

Deputy Superintendent Tyson broke the silence. "What else can we do now?"

For the first time, she saw how much the experience garnered from decades spent investigating depraved killers and their horrific crimes had primed Wade to answer those sorts of questions. He rattled off his response without hesitation.

"Appeal to his ego. Let the media know we've got a huge task force on the case. Give it a name that plays off his chosen nickname. Call it Operation Cipher, or something like that."

He turned to Breck, seated with a cluster of video techs. "He's following this on regular and social media, but that may not be enough stimulation for him anymore. Get crowd shots at each scene and cross-check them with what we have in our database. See if we can enhance our image."

Breck's cheeks dimpled. "Now that we have a sample of his DNA, we can generate a picture of him using predictive DNA analysis—if we don't find a match in the criminal DNA database."

Wade responded with absolute certainty. "We won't." He turned to Buxton. "And we need to check for last-minute flight bookings with quick returns."

"Already being done," Buxton said. "Speaking of flights, I want to head back to Quantico, where we have all of our resources. We can coordinate through the task force as we follow up on any leads." He glanced at his watch. "We're all going to have a long day."

Nina was sure he was right. She glanced down at her hands, reddened from her aggressive scrubbing in hot soapy water after the crime scene tech had scraped under her nails. She longed for a shower and the chance to wash away every microscopic particle of the monster that could still be on her body. The mere thought of him touching her skin repulsed her.

The trip to Boston had started with so much optimism. A sense of impending victory had buoyed them all as they boarded the jet. She had been swept up in the feeling of confidence that they would make an arrest and save a young life. Despite their best efforts, their head start, their advance preparation, they had done neither. Instead, another girl was dead, and the Cipher had slipped away.

Free to kill again.

Chapter 23

Nina pulled the foil wrapping apart and inhaled deeply. "God bless the Boston police." She tore open a packet of mustard and squirted the contents over the layers of peppers, onions, and Italian sausage before reverently lifting the roll to her watering mouth.

Delaney's lieutenant had given them a tall paper sack filled with hoagies after driving them to the airport. Buxton plopped the bag on the small table between their seats after the Gulfstream took off.

Breck cocked a brow at Nina. "Damn, girl." It came out in two syllables. *Day-um.*

Nina jerked her chin at Wade, who was already halfway through his hoagie. "We haven't had food this good since San Francisco."

The sourdough bowl of clam chowder from Boudin Bakery was a distant memory.

Kent laughed. "I like a woman with a healthy appetite. Hate it when my date orders a salad with dressing on the side. Makes me feel like a Neanderthal eating a rib eye."

"Give yourself some credit," Wade said around a mouthful. "You've at least evolved to the Cro-Magnon stage."

Buxton dug around in the bag. "Any mayo?"

Breck handed over two packets. "Have we heard anything back from Forensics?"

"We've got a rush on the DNA," Buxton said. "If there's a match in any of the databases, I'll hear about it soon." He tried to tear one of the plastic packets open. "In the meantime, did the BPD give you video of the ice chest delivery?"

Breck put down her sandwich. "They gave me a flash drive. The unsub is slick. We handed out a composite of a blue-eyed white guy and told the cops to watch for him on the Freedom Trail, and he gets past us to leave the victim's body by posing as a Latino delivery man driving a van on Salem Street." She popped open a can of soda. "He blended in with the other food service vehicles making drops behind the restaurants and cafés."

"He's a damn chameleon," Buxton said, abandoning his attempt at twisting to tear the mayo packet open with his teeth.

Nina swallowed a bite from her hoagie. "What about his getaway from the sewage system? Did city cams pick him up anywhere?"

"No luck on that front yet," Buxton said. "But the BPD did track down the delivery van he was driving. It was abandoned on a side street half a mile from the restaurant."

"A rental?" Nina said.

"He got it from a car rental place by Logan Airport," Buxton said after mutilating a corner of the packet with his teeth. "The Boston field office agents just sent a copy of the scanned rental agreement to the task force database."

"I can access the file through our server," Breck said, opening her laptop. She typed for a few seconds, then turned the screen toward them. "Looks like he rented the van under the name Guillermo Valdez. Used a Florida driver's license."

They all leaned forward to scrutinize a blown-up image of the license the unsub had used to rent the van.

Nina almost choked on a piece of sautéed onion. "That's a photo of Julian Zarran. Didn't the rental car people recognize him? He's only been in every major action movie out in the past five years."

"It's a busy airport," Kent said. "Rental places have a lot of business. They probably had a long line of angry, tired travelers and wanted to get through as quickly as possible."

"It's no accident the unsub chose to use Zarran's image on the phony license," Wade said. "He's giving us the finger."

Kent pursed his lips. "When word gets out—and it will—Zarran's going to raise the bounty to a million."

"Probably what the unsub wants," Wade said. "More Scoobies. More chaos." He swore under his breath. "Maybe we should call Zarran."

Nina kept her focus on what they had to work with. "I take it the Miami residence on the license is also bogus?"

"We sent an official request from the task force for the Miami-Dade PD to swing by and check it out," Buxton said. "Dead end. He probably chose the address at random."

"He must have some way of getting quality fake IDs," Kent said. "He's resourceful."

They all looked up as the cockpit door opened. "Call for you, sir." The copilot handed Buxton a sat phone. "It's the DNA Casework unit chief."

Buxton put the device to his ear as the copilot retreated. "Stand by. I'm putting you on speaker."

He laid the phone on the table and tapped one of the icons on the front. "I'm with the Quantico team. Go ahead."

"This is Dom Fanning," a gruff male voice said. "We've run the sample recovered from Agent Guerrera through the system."

Nina held her breath as she waited to hear if the unsub would finally have a name or if he would remain a cipher.

"No matches," Fanning said. "He's not in any criminal database. We've already initiated a request to compare it with cooperating commercial genealogical DNA services. I explained the situation personally, and they agreed to rush it. We'll know if there's a familial match within forty-eight hours."

Buxton released a frustrated groan. "At least we have his genetic profile now."

"You have more than that," Fanning said. "I received a call from the Trace Evidence Unit a few minutes ago. They've been coordinating with our Boston ERT and wanted to see if there was a nexus with the DNA we analyzed, because what they determined is . . . unexpected, to say the least."

"What did they find?" Buxton asked.

"Emmeline Baker, the unit chief, is requesting an immediate call so she can explain it to you directly."

Buxton thanked Fanning and disconnected. While he scrolled through his phone list and placed the call, Nina considered what Fanning had reported. There had been no DNA match, but apparently the Boston field office's Evidence Recovery Team had located trace evidence that offered promise.

A clipped feminine voice carried over the sat phone's speaker. "Emmeline Baker."

Buxton announced himself and got straight to the point. "I understand you have something to report from the Boston case?"

"The findings are significant. I wanted to alert you as soon as possible."

Everyone exchanged excited glances, well aware that the Trace Evidence Unit maintains a reference collection of human and animal hair, natural and man-made textile fibers and fabrics, as well as wood and other items for comparison with samples found at crime scenes. A significant lead could have come from anywhere at the Boston scene.

Buxton placed his hands on the table. "Did you get a trace evidence hit?"

Nina stared at the phone, desperate to hear of a break in the case.

"Agent Guerrera bit the unsub's glove, tearing off a few fibers. Our evidence techs collected them from the pavement where she indicated she spat them out. Those fibers come from a manufactured fabric that is an exact match for an existing sample in our database, otherwise we wouldn't have managed such a fast response."

Buxton cleared his throat. "You've verified your results through redundant examinations?"

There was no hesitation when Baker responded. "Affirmative."

"How many cases can we link?" Buxton asked.

Baker answered after a long moment. "A total of thirty-six murders."

Chapter 24

Excitement morphed to shock as they all absorbed the information.

Nina was the first to speak. "Thirty-six murders?"

Wade narrowed his eyes. "Would the fabric in your database happen to be used by Red Zone Fight Gear?"

"Correct," Baker said. "It's a patented formula. No one else uses it. It's like a fingerprint."

"No way," Kent said, looking at Wade. "Not possible."

Nina glanced back and forth between them. Why were they both visibly upset about what should be good news?

Buxton's full attention was on the phone. "The murders you connected, is the Megan Summers case one of them?"

Nina remembered the girl's name from her days as a street cop before she joined the Bureau. Every law enforcement officer in the DC metro area had been on the hunt for the so-called Beltway Stalker. It had seemed as if the entire region breathed a collective sigh of relief when his reign of terror ended. She tried, and failed, to put the puzzle together with several pieces missing.

"Yes, it is." Emmeline Baker's voice carried through the phone's speaker, cutting into her thoughts. "We're going to review the cases in DC and San Francisco, resubmit every molecule of trace evidence through our processes. Now that we know exactly what needle to look for in those respective haystacks, we might find the same fiber. No promises, though, with so much cross contamination at both of those scenes."

"And the Boston victim?" Buxton asked.

"She has microscopic matching fibers in the skin around her neck where she was strangled. He may not have had an opportunity to scrub the body before disposing of it this time."

"Keep me posted," Buxton said. "Send the complete report when it's ready. Thanks for the heads up." He disconnected and turned to the group. "What are the odds?"

"The odds of what?" Nina said, unable to stop herself.

Strain clipped Kent's words. "Of two serial killers with the same MO, wearing the same obscure brand of MMA fighting gear, operating at the same time."

"Unless they were partners," Wade said. "It's happened before, serial killers working together." He dragged a hand through his hair. "But it had all the earmarks of one perpetrator acting alone. I'm sure of it."

"So was I," Kent said. "Until now."

"I'm missing something here," Nina said. "Can someone loop me in?"

Buxton turned to her. "What do you know about the Beltway Stalker?"

She paused, remembering how the community had been terrorized by a brutal killer who preyed on teenage girls. "He was active when I was a patrol officer in Fairfax County. Because he hit multiple jurisdictions in Maryland, DC, and Virginia, we didn't catch on that his killings were related until ViCAP matched some common characteristics in his MO."

She didn't add that the at-risk girls he chose as victims didn't initially capture a lot of attention. "I think he had about twenty victims going back six or seven years before we put the pieces together, then the media went nuts. The next ten victims after that caused a shit storm of panic."

"Do you remember how the case ended?" Buxton asked.

She paused as more details came back to her. "The Beltway Stalker committed suicide. His body was found next to his last victim, who was . . ." Her eyes snapped to Wade.

All the color had drained from his face. "Chandra Brown," he finished for her.

They held each other's gaze for a long moment. She struggled to imagine what was going through his mind. Chandra Brown had been the case that had derailed him for the better part of a year. Now she understood what Buxton had meant when he asked about the odds. She turned back to their supervisor.

"So if there aren't two killers with the same MO, that can only mean one of two things." She held up a finger. "We missed a partner who was working with him." She raised a second finger. "Or we got the wrong guy, and the real killer has been at large for the past two years."

"There's more," Buxton said quietly. "Agent Wade and the Bureau were both sued by the Brown family."

"I remember that," Breck said, strawberry-blonde brows furrowing. "CPS took her from her parents and turned her over to foster care due to abuse and neglect. Her bio parents hadn't spoken to her or even asked about her welfare in seven years."

"They certainly came out of the woodwork after she died," Buxton said. "Their attorney blamed the system and everyone in it. They also sued the state for not providing better supervision."

"And Wade ended up in their crosshairs," Nina said.

"I made the wrong call," Wade said. "Chandra's death is on me. The description of the stalker didn't match the one described in the Summers case, and his behavior pattern was different enough that I didn't think it was related to the Beltway Stalker series, so I turfed it back to the Montgomery County police."

No one spoke, giving him a moment before he continued in a monotone.

"Somewhere along the line, someone dropped the ball. No one ever followed up with Chandra. She was murdered two days later."

Buxton took off his glasses and pinched the bridge of his nose. "The FBI's reputation took a major hit every time the Brown family attorney held a press conference. What the lab just uncovered throws the whole investigation into question again." He cursed under his breath.

"If it does, I'm responsible too," Kent said. "Wade transferred out of the BAU, and I took over his caseload, including final analysis and wrap-up of the Beltway Stalker investigation." His jaw hardened. "If there was an anomaly, it was up to me to spot it."

So Kent had been the one to bat cleanup. She'd just begun her application process to become an agent when Chandra was killed and had never known who took over the investigation after Wade's very public downfall.

"No," Wade said. "You came in late because I transferred out. I'd been working the case for years. I was the best one to spot a problem, and I wasn't there to do it." Sweat beaded on Wade's forehead. "Excuse me." He stood and walked down the aisle toward the bathroom.

"The cases spanned a ten-year period," Kent said after Wade was out of earshot. "The killer used a wide variety of methods. Strangulation, blunt-force trauma, cervical spinal fracture. Some victims had been beaten, others cut, but he didn't use messy options like shooting and stabbing to kill them. Took a long time to verify we had a series. He was careful. We never got any DNA."

"How did you connect the cases?" Nina asked him.

"Through trace evidence. There were unique fibers recovered at several scenes. There may be more victims out there. What we have is based on how the local police forensics units collected, processed, and preserved evidence in each case."

Nina tried to keep up. The FBI hadn't shared all their leads with the locals at the time, so she hadn't heard these details before. "How were the fibers unique?"

"After ViCAP gave us our first match on the fibers, we sent out a request to local police agencies for samples from unsolved homicides with victims that fell within the general description." Kent leaned forward, emphasizing his point. "Serial killers can change their MO, but they can't change their motive."

"How so?"

"A killer's modus operandi is *how* they commit their crimes, their methodology, which can change as they learn from experience. Their motive, however, is *why* they kill. The underlying compulsion that is unique to each killer. I call it their itch, and it never changes."

"Their itch?"

"When the brain sends a signal along a nerve that causes an itch, that impulse may be satisfied in several ways. You can pinch the skin, hit it, tap it, or scratch it. You might even be able to will it away. But as you've probably found, once you start scratching, it's very hard to stop. The itch keeps coming back."

"So what makes serial killers different from other murderers is that they have to keep scratching their itch after the first time?"

"Exactly. That's why it's critical to analyze the first murder carefully. The killer hasn't perfected his crime, or refined his MO, so his motive—the itch he was trying to scratch—is easier to pick out. Once you understand that, you have a much better chance of identifying the unsub."

"What did this have to do with the Beltway Stalker case?" Nina said.

"That's why Wade was so angry with himself. He told me that he focused too much on MO and not enough on motive or victimology. The Beltway Stalker preyed on at-risk teenage girls, but the methods of the murders varied widely. That's why it took over twenty murders in DC, Maryland, and Virginia to realize we had a series on our hands."

Kent had given her new insight. She considered what Wade had been up against. "Wade assumed the victims were similar because they were easy prey for the Beltway Stalker and were less likely to be reported or noticed missing until they'd been gone for several days."

"It took law enforcement far too long to put the pieces together and realize that the unsub's itch was the type of victim he chose and the need to torment and denigrate them. Wade blames himself. Says he should have figured it out sooner."

"How did the fibers lead to a suspect?"

"The Trace Evidence Unit processed all of the fibers collected from the various crime labs where there were samples. They tracked the chemicals used in the manufacture to a textile mill in Philadelphia. An agent from the Philly field office went to the mill and interviewed the owner, who told them the process had been developed by request from a clothing manufacturer in DC. The manufacturer had specifications for flexibility, color, and durability. He was creating a line of specialty clothing and gear for MMA fighters. He called it Red Zone Fight Gear. His uncle owned a venue in the District called Steel Cage Central Fight Club, so he figured he could market there to get his new business going."

She recalled that the Beltway Stalker had been fairly well known in the MMA community. There had been a brief uproar about such bouts causing extreme aggression in participants. The objections had died down over time when scientists and researchers were unable to conclusively link combative sports and violence.

Kent continued with his recitation. "Wade and the lead case agent went out to interview the manufacturer. He told them his products never caught on. He couldn't compete with the stuff made overseas at a fraction of the cost, and his overhead was too high. He went out of business more than ten years earlier. Said his uncle offered to buy his leftover stock—paid him pennies on the dollar."

"So that's how you traced it back to that specific fight club," Nina said.

"I went with Wade and the case agent to interview the uncle at the club. I still remember the guy. Name's Sorrentino. Turned out he sold most of the stock he bought off his nephew to the fighters at his club . . . at full retail."

"Nice guy."

"A real piece of work. Anyway, he claims he never kept any sales records or receipts and had no memory of who bought stuff from him."

"He couldn't even provide one name?"

"We threatened him with an audit from our friends at the IRS, and he almost wet himself. He'd been selling the stuff for years. Every sale was a cash deal, and he never paid any taxes on his profits. He also paid cash for the gear he bought from his nephew, so there was no money trail. I'm sure that was part of his scheme. He told us he sold various items to more than a hundred people over more than a decade."

Nina rolled her eyes. "No help at all."

"Worse than that," Kent said. "Chandra Brown was murdered right after our visit. I'm convinced Sorrentino mentioned we were asking around, or the Beltway Stalker saw us there, and he knew we were closing in. He decided to have one last kill before he ended it on his terms. At least, that's what his note said."

She'd always been curious about the contents of the note, which had never been released. "What else did it say?"

She held her breath as Kent eyed her warily. He might think she planned to second-guess his investigation. And he would be correct.

He blew out a sigh. "I never liked the fact that it was typed, but he confessed to all thirty-six murders and gave details only the killer would know, stuff we kept out of the media. We had physical evidence tying everything together, a confession, and most importantly, the deaths stopped." He folded his arms. "Case closed. Why would we look any further?"

"You wouldn't," Nina said. She could see the pain in his expression as the inevitable self-recrimination set in.

"I did the usual after-action behavioral analysis for our profiling database," Kent said. "He had a lot of issues with aggression. Had a few arrests for violence against women. Seemed to dislike authority. It fit well enough."

"But like you said, there weren't any more deaths after Chandra Brown, right?"

Kent heaved a sigh. "At this point, I'd have to say she was the last *known* case."

"It all makes sense now." Wade had quietly padded back down the aisle to rejoin them. "He's a chameleon. He changes his appearance, his vehicles, his patterns." He clenched his hands into tight fists. "And he fed us a scapegoat two years ago."

Wade's haggard face bore the desperate look of a sinner seeking absolution. He spoke as if compelled to explain his mistakes. "Most serial killers are driven by the kind of compulsion that makes them repeat behaviors. That's what forms their pattern." He raised his voice. "If anything, the Beltway Stalker's pattern seemed to be that he changed constantly. If it weren't for forensics, we would never have linked the murders. They're that different from one another."

"If the Beltway Stalker and the Cipher are the same person, he's changed his pattern again," Kent said. "He's gone from flying under the radar to attracting as much attention as possible."

"I'm still not ready to concede that we're dealing with the same killer," Buxton said. "As Agent Guerrera noted, they could have been partners and now the surviving cohort is working on his own. That would explain the change from total secrecy to maximum public engagement. We need more data before we can draw a solid conclusion."

The cabin fell silent. Nina noticed Wade studying Buxton.

Wade narrowed his eyes at his supervisor. "You're going to pull me from the case." He made it a statement.

Buxton regarded Wade a moment before he responded. "I would rather have this conversation in private, Agent Wade."

"I don't give a damn who hears," Wade said. "I need to work this case. I *need* to find him."

"It's not about what you need," Buxton said. "It's about what serves the investigation."

As the two men stared each other down, Nina considered the situation. Buxton was ready to yank Wade because he had been compromised. At some point, Buxton might decide that no one was more compromised than she was. If he saw Wade as a liability, he might see her that way as well.

Her eyes traced Wade's profile. Years of studying madmen and the horrific things they did had clearly taken their toll. Etched in the deep lines of his face was the pain of knowing he could not save everyone. That some might escape justice. That for Wade, the Cipher was the one.

The one that got away.

The thought reminded her of the note the Cipher had written to her and put in Sofia Garcia-Figueroa's mouth. Suddenly, she knew Dr. Jeffrey Wade had to stay on this case. And so did she.

She faced Buxton. "Wade studied this unsub for years. He understands him better than anyone else in the Bureau." She flicked a glance at Kent. "No offense."

"None taken," Kent said.

She turned back to Buxton. "Now that we understand what we're up against, Wade can go back through his notes and update the profile."

Buxton raised a skeptical brow. "We need a completely new profile. From scratch. Which Agent Kent could do."

Aware she was overstepping, she pressed on. "We can all work together to create a complete picture." She tapped her chest. "I'm his only surviving victim." She moved her hand to point at Wade. "He did the initial profile." She ended with Kent. "And he did the postmortem."

"You're saying you each have something to offer," Buxton said.

Everyone waited as Buxton appeared to weigh her argument. She noticed Wade's eyes cut to her, brows raised in apparent bewilderment, but he said nothing.

Buxton heaved a sigh. "All right. You'll work up a new profile as a team. And you'll respond to the scene of every case going forward." His expression grew stern. "But if I detect any sign of trouble, or if any of you become further compromised, or if I decide your continued involvement will be to the detriment of the investigation, I will not hesitate to bench any one of you."

They nodded their agreement.

Wade turned to her. Understanding passed between them. The same man had wounded both of them irrevocably. The Cipher, who had escaped both of them to torment and kill more innocent victims. They each felt responsible for every life lost, and because of that, they now shared a common goal.

Her monster was his monster too.

Chapter 25

That evening, the Cipher stood in the cage, ready for what would come. He had taken care to extend the trainer's tape he had wrapped around his knuckles and wrists a fraction higher than usual. Not enough to draw attention but enough to cover the scratches Nina had given him. He would be sure to bestow many more upon her in retribution. In the meantime, he had to pay the price for the weakness he had displayed earlier in Boston.

He held himself perfectly still, braced for the vicious uppercut coming straight at him. His opponent's fist, covered in a fingerless fighting glove, connected. The force of the blow snapped his head back. He staggered, then hit the mat.

The referee gave him a knowing look. The crowd held its collective breath. He had fought in this arena long enough to become a legend. No other fighter did what he did. No one else could. Slowly, starting like a distant drumbeat, then increasing in strength and tempo, the crowd began to chant. "Odin! Odin! Odin!"

It had been audacious to claim the name of a Norse god as his fighting moniker, but no one laughed. No one even smiled. They all feared him, as they should.

Still down on the floor, he made his decision. He had taken his punishment for allowing Nina Guerrera to get the better of him. The one who called herself Warrior Girl had no idea what a true warrior was. He would teach her.

He allowed rage to build within him as he got to his feet and walked to his corner. Opening himself to its dark power, he gathered it to him, fueling the retribution he would mete out tonight. He turned and stared into the calculating eyes of his opponent. Eyes that reminded him of his father's. As the referee paced between them, the Cipher recalled the final punishment his father had given him. He'd been a wiry seventeen-year-old when dear old Dad had ordered him into a shed at the far end of their extensive northern Virginia property.

"Take off your shirt, boy," his father said.

He obliged, tugging his T-shirt over his head.

The small dark eyes regarded him with contempt. "Why did you lose the tournament?"

He knew better than to make excuses. "He outmaneuvered me."

"You're damn right he did." The glowing cigarette tip bobbed up and down as his father spoke. "Do you know that kid was adopted from the streets of Calcutta when he was four years old?"

He made no reply.

"I spend my life's savings for a Thoroughbred who loses to a nag." His father spat at his feet. "Superior genes, we were told." He shook his head in disgust. "You weren't some mutt conceived in the back of a pickup truck. You were supposed to be exceptional in every way." His father poked a meaty finger at him. "So the only conclusion I can come to is that you didn't try hard enough. Didn't want it badly enough."

Fully aware of where this was heading, he stared straight ahead.

"Nothing to say for yourself?" His father blew a plume of smoke in his face. "Let's see what you're really made of." He pulled the cigarette from his lips. "You be still. You master yourself. Master the pain."

His father walked behind him.

The first touch of the glowing butt wrenched a scream from him. The white-hot pain hurt worse than anything his father had done with a belt. Or his fists. Or an electrical cord. He shrank away from the agony.

"Dammit, boy, I will keep this up until you learn how to stand still and take it."

The cigarette touched his other shoulder blade, searing his flesh. Sweat poured from his scalp, trickling down his face as he fought to hold his position. He clenched his teeth so hard his molars ached, but he did not cry out. Not that it would have mattered. No one could hear him at the far reaches of their property.

His father stepped back. He could hear the old man behind him taking a deep drag off the cigarette, pictured the cherry glowing hot and bright. "That's better, but you moved your shoulders. I don't want to even see you flinch."

In the silence, he heard the sizzling of his own skin, smelled the scent of burning flesh as his father pressed the blazing tip into the center of his back.

This time, he held perfectly still. A single tear slid down his cheek as he forced his mind to retreat. To find solace in the future he would create for himself. He endured. He withstood. And he planned, with intricate detail, his father's death.

The crowd's roar pulled him back to the present as the referee raised his arm in a swinging arc, signaling the fighters to resume.

The Cipher closed the distance in two rapid strides. The roar of the audience clapping, shouting, and stamping their feet quickened his pulse. Electrified him. They knew what Odin was about to do. He sensed that the man before him did too. He absorbed the fear that emanated from his opponent like steam. Let it feed his bloodlust.

The man would now receive his reckoning, as would Nina Guerrera. He operated on two levels, considering how best to destroy both opponents. What would cause the most damage? Render each incapable of fighting?

It came to him in an instant. As he used his foot to deliver a lightning strike to the man's solar plexus, he realized how he would break Nina's spirit. Like the bloodthirsty audience in the arena tonight, the world watched his cage match with the Warrior Girl.

His audience wanted a show, and he would give them one they would never forget.

Chapter 26

Nina sat beside Wade at the circular conference table inside Buxton's temporary office adjacent to the task force area. She looked around at the group and, for the first time, felt she belonged. Kent sipped black coffee from a US Navy mug, fogging his glasses. Breck closed her ever-present laptop and looked up expectantly. Wade laid his notepad on the table. All eyes turned toward their supervisor, who appeared not to have slept.

Buxton rubbed the back of his neck, then twisted his head side to side. "The task force has been working through the night," he said as soon as they settled. "I wanted to speak with the four of you directly before we go in for the first briefing of the day. The assistant director in charge caught the news last night, and he's asking for daily reports." He heaved a sigh. "I'll have to spend a lot more time in meetings and on conference calls, so I want to make sure everyone knows."

His index finger came down on the table in front of him. "*This* team has the lead. Everything will feed in and out from the four of you."

Breck's brows shot up. "But I'm in Cyber Crime," she said. "Not the BAU."

"We still have a lot of images to sort through, and Agent Guerrera may do more direct messaging with the unsub," Buxton said. "I don't want to wait while we go through channels. I spoke to your supervisor last night. With your dual background in video forensics and cyber investigations, you're a perfect fit for this assignment. She approved a temp to the Cipher task force for you."

Breck's cheeks dimpled. "I'll do whatever I can to help bring this asshole in. Someone needs to cancel his birth certificate." Her smile widened. "Sir."

"I've been checking the Cipher's social media accounts," Nina said. "He hasn't posted anything since Boston."

She had repeatedly cycled through his platforms since she woke up, dreading what he would say to the world after another murder and successful escape.

"Public Affairs is coordinating with the social media team," Buxton said. "News channels have the story on heavy rotation. I think they're hoping the Cipher contacts one of them directly again."

"Maybe he's traveling," Breck said.

Wade gave her a dark look. "Maybe he's plotting."

Kent picked up his mug again. "His past pattern was to leave a clue and a deadline at each scene." He peered down at the dark liquid inside thoughtfully. "The scene in Boston had a rhyme I now believe was designed to draw attention away from where he had dumped the body. There was no clue left behind."

"I'm sure everyone in town searched for it." Nina rolled her eyes. "Zarran just announced he's doubling the reward money, so even more people will join the hunt."

Wade nodded. "When there's a million dollars at stake, people will act irrationally."

Kent looked at Buxton. "Did we reach out to Zarran?"

"The LA field office is at his residence now trying to talk some sense into him," Buxton said, opening his leather portfolio. "Let's brainstorm our next steps in the investigation before I present them to the group."

Wade spoke first. "I'd like to talk to Sorrentino again. We never had to lean on him hard because the case closed right after we spoke to him, but I always believed he knew more than he let on."

"We should catch him at his residence," Kent said. "Last time we went to the club, a girl died very soon after. I don't want to show our faces there. The Cipher could get wind of it and act out again."

Nina had spent a fair amount of time lying awake the previous night considering what she had learned on the flight from Boston. "Our working theory is that the Cipher was at the club and saw you two interviewing Sorrentino, so he framed another fighter for all of his murders?"

"Or they were committing the crimes together," Breck said. "And he framed his partner for the whole thing."

"No." Wade's tone was sharp enough to cut. "I went over my case files again last night. I'm more convinced than ever that the Beltway Stalker was a lone operator."

Wade was staking what was left of his damaged reputation on his analysis. If he turned out to be wrong about this, too, the Bureau would be done with him.

"Let's keep an open mind," Buxton said to Wade. "I agree we shouldn't go to the fight club to interview Sorrentino. Slide by his house." He tipped his head toward Nina. "Take Agent Guerrera with you."

She caught Wade sliding her a look from the corner of his eye. Their first tag-team interview. Should be interesting.

Buxton moved on to Kent. "Review the suicide note left with the body of the Beltway Stalker. Do a linguistic analysis comparing it with the communications we've received from the Cipher. I'd like more evidence that they are one and the same person."

"Roger that," Kent said.

"I'd like to see the file on that case as well," Nina said.

"I'll see that you get a flash drive with everything on it," Buxton said before turning to Breck. "Get with Video Forensics and review—"

A knock at the conference room door interrupted him.

"Come in."

"Excuse me, sir." A tall, slender woman in a pale pink blouse poked her head in. "Public Affairs has been trying to reach you. They said it's time-sensitive." She disappeared, discreetly closing the door behind her.

Buxton rubbed bloodshot eyes. "My phone's been buzzing all damn night. I mute it for ten minutes to hold a briefing and look what happens." He slid a cell phone from his pocket and let out a long, slow breath. "Four missed calls."

He laid it on the table and tapped the screen. "This is Buxton. You're on speaker."

"Overmeyer from Public Affairs," a baritone voice responded. "We've got activity on all monitored platforms from the unsub. We believe it's legit."

"What's he saying?"

"He's teasing a video that he's getting ready to put out. Cyber Crime is trying to ping his location, but it looks like he's rerouting through a series of different servers."

"What's the video supposed to be?" Buxton asked.

"He doesn't say much, except that everyone will want to watch and that it's about Agent Guerrera."

All eyes turned to her. Her mouth went dry and her palms grew clammy. What fresh hell was the Cipher planning for her now?

"We tried to reach you sooner," Overmeyer continued. "You might want to watch the feed in real time when he airs it. He's supposed to be posting it on his Facebook page any second now."

"Thank you." Buxton disconnected.

Breck opened her laptop. She accessed Facebook and checked the unsub's page. A graphic with a video feed popped up. Breck expanded the image to cover the entire screen. Four words in a bold white font stood out in stark relief against a black background. FOR YOUR VIEWING PLEASURE.

The letters on the screen dissolved, replaced by a video feed moments later. Heart pounding, Nina leaned closer to the monitor. A fluorescent glow from above poured down over the naked form of a young girl. She lay facedown on a steel table, her wrists and ankles secured to four metal poles, one at each corner of the rectangular surface.

Horror crashed over Nina in sickening waves as she stared at the screen, transfixed. Revulsion gripped her at a sound she had desperately tried to push from her mind. A sound she had heard only yesterday.

The voice of the Cipher.

"Do you know who's coming to rescue you?" he asked the girl tied to the table.

Nina watched her sixteen-year-old self, body splayed before the camera. Naked, trembling, vulnerable. The girl she used to be.

The monster loomed just out of view, his shadow touching her calves as he bent forward to whisper, "No one."

The girl pulled against her restraints, rubbing her wrists raw.

The monster moved back, raising his voice. "Do you know who cares that you ran away?" He paused. "No one."

A howl filled with impotent fury came from the girl as she thrashed harder.

"Do you know who will cry over your grave?" He continued his relentless torment. "No one."

The girl turned her head to look at him, eyes blazing.

"And do you know why that is?" This time, he didn't wait for a response. "It's because you are trash."

At his deep chuckle, a tear slid down the girl's cheek.

Nina swallowed a hot blast of bile climbing the back of her throat. She'd had no idea the Cipher had recorded what he had done to her. No camera had been visible in her line of sight. Now millions of people were about to watch her torment. Worse than a public execution, it was public defilement. The private anguish she had hidden for years was about to be exposed for the world to see.

And everyone would surely watch.

Just as her team was riveted to the screen now. Just as she was. No one could look away from the horror unfolding in front of them.

The monster entered the screen from the left. Tall and broad shouldered, he dwarfed the slight girl lying on the table like a butterfly pinned to a board. Keeping his back to the camera, he wore a black cloak, a hood pulled over his head.

When he raised his arm, a large hand encased in a blue latex glove extended from the wide sleeve. He bent down to touch the girl's bare back.

"These are beautiful," he said. "Still fresh."

He traced a finger along rows of angry red welts and raw lacerations. "Tell me how it felt when the belt lashed your back." His voice dropped to an accusatory whisper. "Did you cry?"

The girl said nothing, trying to shrink away from his touch.

"I wish I had been the one to bestow them on you." He slowly dragged his fingertip down the length of her spine as he spoke, stopping to caress an older pale white scar running crosswise underneath the fresh marks. "But I have my own plans for you. For the rest of your life . . . even if it's only a few hours . . . you will be mine."

Nina wanted desperately to turn off the laptop. To slam it shut. But that would be like closing her eyes in the face of a gun pointed directly at her. The bullet wouldn't stop because she wasn't watching it penetrate her flesh. It would keep going. Boring into her heart. Tearing her to pieces.

"Do you want mercy?" The voice was smooth, a velvet caress. "Beg me. Perhaps I will take pity on you. You are quite pitiful, after all."

The memory of that moment flooded through Nina, pulling tears into the corners of her eyes. She knew what came next.

The monster stepped back, the click of a lighter audible in the silence. Then his other hand came into view, a lit cigarette held casually between his fingers.

"P-p-please," the girl said.

"Oh, no, little throwaway. That's not nearly enough. Maybe you don't understand your situation. You need to try harder. Perhaps this will make it clear."

The man touched the glowing tip to the center of her left shoulder blade. The girl thrashed and screamed.

The screen went blank.

Words appeared in bright white, contrasting with the inky background as before.

IF YOU WOULD LIKE TO SEE WHAT HAPPENS NEXT, CLICK THE "LIKE" BUTTON. WHEN I RECEIVE 1,000 LIKES, I WILL SHOW THE NEXT 60 SECONDS OF THIS VIDEO.

Every eye in the room swiveled from the screen to Nina. Revulsion was stamped on their shocked faces. She had seen the look before when police officers and social workers inspected her wounds, and she knew what she would see next.

Pity.

Alternating currents of rage and humiliation swept through her. The walls closed in around her. Suffocating her. She had to get out. To escape.

Breck reached out to her with a trembling hand, eyes bright with unshed tears. She opened her mouth to speak, but no words came out.

Nina halted her with a raised palm. "Stay away from me." She glared at the others, shooting to her feet. "All of you, just stay the fuck away from me."

No one moved. No one spoke.

She flung open the door and bolted from the room.

No one tried to stop her.

Chapter 27

Twelve minutes later, Nina left the locker room at a dead sprint, desperate to escape the claustrophobic confines of the building. Her feet turned toward the trail of their own volition, giving her direction and purpose.

The infamous FBI obstacle course dubbed "the Yellow Brick Road" consisted of 6.1 miles of wooded terrain through the Virginia foothills at Quantico. Anyone who successfully completed the course had to conquer physical and mental challenges along the way.

She leaped over a tree root thrusting up from the ground and kept going, her footfalls varied on the uneven ground. Along the way, she jumped through a simulated window, maneuvered across a cargo net, and splashed through standing water. Then she arrived at the rope climb and gazed up at the jagged stone cliff high above her, calculating. Wrapping her hands around the thick corded rope, she hoisted herself up until she found a toehold in the craggy rocks. She worked her way up, pulling with her arms and pushing with her legs against the sheer rock face until her shoulders and quadriceps burned. When she got close to the edge jutting overhead, she heard a shuffle. She tilted her head back to squint at a looming silhouette peering down at her.

Wade squatted. "You gonna climb up here or not?"

She did not want or need company. "How did you find me?"

"It's where I would have gone," he said. "I started at the end of the course and worked my way toward the beginning. Figured I'd run into you sooner or later."

"Go away."

"Come up here and let's talk."

She put her foot against the rock face and pushed off, using her arms to pull herself higher. "I don't know what kind of head-shrinking bullshit you're trying to pull, Wade, but I'm not in the mood." She grunted as she heaved again. "I don't need help, and I don't want company."

Wade didn't move.

Cursing, she pushed with her feet and pulled with her hands until every muscle fiber in her arms twitched. When the ridge was only inches above her, she looked into Wade's eyes again. He could easily reach down and haul her the rest of the way to the top of the outcropping, but he merely watched her.

Maybe he did understand.

She flung an arm up to grasp the ledge above her. Gritting her teeth, she flexed her unwilling biceps until her chest flopped onto the hard surface. After a moment's breath, she rolled her legs up and over as well.

Still squatting, Wade gazed down at her, an impassive expression on his lined face. "I'm not here to carry you, Guerrera."

"Leave," she said, gasping. "Go. The fuck. Away."

He pointed toward the main building. "I'll leave if you go back in there with me."

She sat up. "Why do you care what I do?"

"Because I'm the only other person who wants this guy as bad as you do."

She let out a derisive snort. "So it's about you." She got to her feet and brushed the dirt from her hands. "You're about to get dragged through the mud again over the Chandra Brown case, and you want to make sure you get the right guy this time."

When he flinched, she knew her barbed words had found their mark. In her anguish, she had lashed out at the only target that presented itself. She knew it wasn't right, knew it wasn't fair, but she had warned him to stay away.

"If that's what you need to believe." He stood to face her, a pained expression on his face.

She relented. "I want some time to myself right now. Surely someone with a PhD in psychology can understand that."

He considered her a long moment before speaking. "I know it makes me a total asshole to say this, but I can't give you that. We need you on the team. Now. Buxton thinks you're compromised. No agent has ever been shown being tortured and then gone out to investigate their torturer." He dragged a hand through his hair in what she was coming to understand as his characteristic sign of frustration. "Shit, Nina, I've been in the Bureau longer than Buxton, and I've never seen anything like this. I can't blame him for sidelining you, but I believe he's wrong."

"What did he say?"

"That you're no longer in a position to interview witnesses, suspects, or anyone else." He crossed his arms. "You'll assist the investigation from your desk back at the Washington field office. No more field work."

Buxton had made good on his threat to bench anyone on the team who proved to be more of a liability than an asset to the investigation. They stood in the middle of the forest, eyes locked. She recalled their conversation on the return flight from Boston to DC. Wade had been the one Buxton had targeted yesterday, and she'd argued to keep him on the team because he was the only other person in the Bureau who wanted to go after the unsub as much as she did.

Now Wade had used the same reasoning on her. And it was true. He had endured the public shaming and humiliation she was about to face. The unsub had irrevocably damaged both of them.

Wade was not the enemy, but her outburst had damaged the tenuous alliance forged between them aboard the jet. She continued to regard him. He hadn't stalked off when she insulted him. Hadn't retaliated with a verbal assault of his own. She'd done her best to get rid of him, yet here he stood, looking at her with those inscrutable gray eyes.

"Chandra Brown wasn't the only bad call I made two years ago," he said in a soft voice. "I was also wrong about you, and Buxton is making the same mistake now."

She asked the question that had burned in her mind since the day Shawna told her the truth about her hiring. "Why did you red-stamp my psych eval?"

He closed his eyes and rubbed the back of his neck. "I've seen so much trauma in my career. Atrocities committed by the worst humanity has to offer. I've delved deep into the minds of the most depraved predators. People who hunt children." His voice lowered to a hoarse whisper. "You do that long enough, and the darkness in their souls gets smeared all over yours."

Now that he'd started, he seemed to want to get it all out. She didn't interrupt, absorbing his words, trying to see herself from his perspective.

"I read your file in preparation for your psych eval," he said. "The applicant investigator included the case report from your abduction as well as police photographs and ER reports documenting the abuse you suffered in the system before you were kidnapped." His eyes bored into hers. "And how you came to get those scars on your back." He extended a hand as if to touch her shoulder, seemed to think better of it, and dropped his arm back to his side. "And the circumstances that forced you to run away from the group home." He shook his head. "I couldn't reconcile that with the person I saw before me in the interview room. I was hard on you. I tried to burrow down to see what was beneath that professional exterior."

"You thought I was a ticking time bomb who might explode under the right kind of pressure?"

"I'm sorry, Nina," he said. "I realize now there was something I failed to consider. A trait we psychologists don't have the luxury to study as much as we do disorders, neuroses, and coping mechanisms. You have more of it than anyone I have ever personally examined." He looked at her as if she were a rare specimen. "Resilience."

"Resilience," she said, tasting the word.

"Human beings are capable of unfathomable cruelty and immense strength. You have not only survived—you have thrived." His voice grew thick. "I've followed your career since you came on. I'll admit that I was waiting for you to snap. Go off the rails. I'm not proud that a small part of me wanted vindication. Instead, you proved me wrong. You've been an asset to the Bureau."

She glanced down, uncomfortable with accolades. Wade wasn't done yet, it seemed.

"And you've been invaluable to this investigation," he went on. "You were the one who spotted the first message on the dumpster in that alley in DC. You figured out the Boston clue before anyone else, and you could have called Buxton to take the credit, but you called me first. That's what a partner does. You stuck up for me when Buxton wanted to boot me off the case on the plane yesterday. Now it's my turn to do the same for you."

She raised her head to meet his gaze. He had confronted her with a challenge. Could she face the monster as the world watched, knowing everyone had seen her humiliation and pain? More importantly, could she face herself if she didn't?

Chapter 28

Nina pushed through the door to the task force area, Wade on her heels as she strode inside the expansive room. A hive of activity greeted her. Agents clustered in groups, bending over spreadsheets, turning pages in file folders, and tapping on keyboards. She glanced up and sucked in a breath. The oversize monitor on the far wall's screen was split into four quadrants, each with a different freeze frame from the video. One was an image of the Cipher, his large figure cloaked except for a gloved hand clutching a lit cigarette. Another was a close-up of the girl's left wrist, secured to the metal corner pole with nylon rope.

She halted, transfixed. First, one agent noticed her and elbowed the person next to him. That agent nudged another. Gradually, silence spread through the room like a virus, silencing all discussion, bringing all work to a halt.

Buxton was on his cell phone in the corner. As soon as he saw her, he muttered something into the phone and disconnected. Sliding the device into a clip on his belt, he stepped toward her. "My office."

She followed him down the corridor, Wade's steady footfalls behind her.

Buxton walked past the admin assistant, who quickly looked down at her keyboard as Nina walked by.

She'd better get used to that kind of reaction.

"Come in and close the door," Buxton said, then frowned as he looked over her shoulder. "I want to speak to Agent Guerrera alone."

She turned to see not only Wade but also Breck and Kent following her into the temporary executive office.

"We're with her," Kent said.

Breck nodded.

Buxton raised a questioning brow at Nina.

"I'd like them to stay," she said.

"Fine." Buxton treaded to the same table where they had watched the video. They each took a seat.

He addressed Nina. "Agent Guerrera, as you've probably guessed, I read your case file before taking you on a temp assignment in the BAU. I had to be aware of everything that happened in your background regarding the Cipher." He drew in a deep breath. "What I read in that file was . . . disturbing, to say the least. What you have gone through, what you have suffered, no one should have to deal with, much less a sixteen-year-old girl."

She simply nodded. What could she say?

"As your supervisor, I am concerned about your health and well-being, both emotionally and physically. Now that the public has seen the video, I would be remiss if I didn't also acknowledge the impact it will have on this investigation. How will you manage to conduct interviews and deal with media at crime scenes?"

She moved to head him off. "Sir, I—"

He held up a hand. "While you and Agent Wade were outside, I've spent the last hour dealing with the fallout from that video, which went viral." His lip curled in disgust. "Public Affairs has been bombarded with media requests. I advised Cyber Crime to contact all major social media platforms with a request to shut down the Cipher's accounts. The feed is no longer accessible through any of his profiles, but it's been downloaded and reposted so many times that it's still out there for anyone who wants to watch it." His features hardened. "At least we managed to stop the bastard before he reached the thousand likes he demanded in order to show the next sixty seconds."

Relief blossomed, then wilted in Nina's chest. She had now escaped the Cipher twice. Clearly bent on revenge, he would probably share the rest of the video anyway.

Buxton continued in a grave tone. "The Director called me personally. He made it clear that we have his full support, including unfettered access to all resources."

She was equal parts touched by the Director's interest in her and mortified to realize that he, too, had seen the video.

"I assured him you would only continue on this case in an advisory capacity," Buxton said. "And that you would no longer be out in the field."

Anger, simmering close to the surface since the video, bubbled up in a hot rush. "Did you decide to bench me out of concern for my welfare, or have I become an embarrassment?"

She recalled the mantra drummed into her from the day she joined the FBI. Don't embarrass the Bureau. Some minor transgressions could be overlooked, but not that.

Buxton's eyes widened. "Agent Guerrera, I take it that you are understandably distressed, otherwise, I might have to conclude that you are being disrespectful."

It would do no good to alienate the supervisory special agent. Nina drew in a long breath, dialing back her frustration. "Sir, what I need most right now is to continue working with my team to apprehend the Cipher." She deliberately chose not to say *the man who did this to me*, hoping to create the impression of professional detachment where there was none.

Buxton did not appear mollified. "Every interview you conduct, people will have that image in their minds. The public will focus on you personally rather than answering your questions. Agents must be perceived as objective. That's not possible for you."

She tried to portray her liability as an asset. "We have a whole team of people who can be objective. We need someone who can be completely *subj*ective. Someone who's had direct experience with the Cipher."

Wade cleared his throat. "Sir, if I may?" At Buxton's nod, he pleaded her case. "The video proves there are certain things Agent Guerrera repressed. Through no fault of her own, there are details she cannot recall, but I'm confident they will come back to her if she's involved in the investigation directly. I recommend she stay on the team."

She wasn't sure she appreciated how he'd defended her. Why had he brought up the gaps in her memory? Was he trying to help her cause or hurt it? "What did I supposedly repress?"

"You never mentioned that he called you a throwaway," he said. "That's important information."

What had been a distorted series of recollections she now saw through the Cipher's eyes because of the video. Fragments of images flooded back, a tidal wave overwhelming her, forcing her gaze down.

She recalled the police officer asking her for details after she'd escaped. Her entire body trembled as she revealed the sickening chain of events. But she'd been too ashamed to repeat the word he had called her. *Throwaway.*

After a while, the memory faded, helped by her willful desire to push it down into the dark, bottomless well that held her worst moments.

"That term has meaning for him," Wade said. "He used it several times in the video. No one who investigated your case back then knew he called you that. Do you see the significance of that word?"

She glanced up at him. "Back at the scene of the first murder in DC, you suspected the unsub knew about my background before he took me that night." She made it a statement.

"Sofia Garcia-Figueroa was found in a dumpster," he said. "I assessed the facts at hand and arrived at a logical conclusion."

And she had argued against that conclusion because she didn't want to believe it. If the Cipher knew she'd been left in a dumpster as an infant, that meant he had gotten a great deal of sensitive information about her, so much that he'd possibly played a role in her life. She groped for another explanation. "Maybe he believes girls are disposable. He uses them and throws them out like garbage." She tapped her chest lightly. "Not me personally but all girls."

"Then everything else about Sofia's murder was orchestrated specifically for you, but the site he chose for the body was a coincidence?"

She had to come to terms with the possibility that Wade had been right all along. Her mind shifted into analytical mode. "How would he know about my past?"

"Exactly." Wade stroked his jaw. "They investigated this all wrong, looking for some random stranger who grabbed you eleven years ago. What if he wasn't a stranger or random? What if he knew you? Targeted you?"

"I didn't even know I was going to run away until I did it," she murmured, lost in contemplation. "How would he know?"

"According to your statement at the time, you'd been on the street for several days when he took you," Wade said. "Maybe he was hunting for you. He was obsessed, and apparently, still is."

She didn't feel like a warrior now. A deep sense of shame had held back the word that might have made a difference. At sixteen, she hadn't understood how the police worked a case, hadn't known how seemingly insignificant details could provide a trove of useful information for a sharp detective. What if that one clue could have sent the investigation in a different direction eleven years ago? Four days ago? Would thirty-six innocent girls still be alive now?

Worst of all, she suspected she hadn't told the police what he'd called her because part of her believed he was right. No one wanted her. That much had been proven time and again. She was a throwaway, as worthless as the trash she'd been tossed into.

How would others see her from now on? Would they only see the scars she could no longer hide?

The Cipher wanted her back in that place. The terrified girl in the video. Alone, humiliated, helpless. He chose victims he thought were unworthy of life. He'd stolen a part of her, changed her forever, but he would not take any more from her. Or from anyone else. She would be the one who stopped him.

Slowly, she lifted her chin and directed her gaze at Buxton. "Sir, I have the best chance of finding this unsub. And I've got to be out in the field to do it." She spread her hands. "Sidelining me won't work. The Cipher will keep dragging me back into this."

"He's obsessed with Agent Guerrera," Kent said, speaking for the first time. "He won't just forget about her."

"I'm not going to hide behind my desk hoping he doesn't find me."

"She's right," Wade said. "Sooner or later, he'll come after her directly. Which is why she has to stay on the case."

She waited, allowing Buxton to reconsider his position.

"You've been through more than any agent I've heard of," Buxton finally said. "I have to know whether you can deal with what's coming. Because things are about to get exponentially uglier."

She straightened. "I can handle anything he throws at me."

"It's not just the Cipher." Buxton looked skeptical. "It's the other agents and the public. This kind of scrutiny is . . . unprecedented in the Bureau."

Wade cleared his throat. "I've dealt with my share of public and internal scrutiny," he said. "She's my partner." He tipped his head toward her. "I've got her six."

She had prepared to face the blowback from the video alone, the way she'd dealt with most things in her life. Now, she had Dr. Jeffrey Wade—psychologist, special agent, and self-proclaimed asshole—by her side.

"So do I," Kent said.

"Me too," Breck added.

Silence filled the room. Nina had to stop her foot from jiggling under the table as she waited for her supervisor to arrive at his decision.

Buxton blew out a long sigh. "I'll have to make another round of phone calls." He gave her an assessing look. "You can stay on the team." His gaze moved around the table. "You're dismissed."

They stood to leave. As they were filing out the door, Nina turned to see Buxton pick up the phone on his desk. For a fleeting moment, she caught the ghost of a smile on his lined face.

Chapter 29

Nina goosed the sleek black Tahoe, pulling around a slow-moving pickup truck before the road resolved into a single lane. "Can't believe Sorrentino lives this far out from the District. The commute has to be terrible."

"He's a creature of the night," Wade said from the passenger seat beside her. "Works odd hours. Mostly late afternoon until two in the morning. Rush hour isn't a factor for him."

She glanced at the clock on the dash. "He probably doesn't leave before noon, so he should still be home." Wade grunted his assent as she turned onto a side street.

They had opted not to give Sorrentino a call to set up a meeting, preferring to catch him off guard and away from his club. A calculated gamble.

She'd thanked Wade for backing her up with Buxton, including his request to proceed with the plan to interview the fight club owner with her. They had spent the next hour before heading out researching one Joseph Thomas Sorrentino, who gave every indication of being crooked enough to screw his socks on.

She knew the type. Always looking for a fast buck, always cutting corners, and most importantly, always willing to sell out a friend if the need arose.

She slowed, scanning the addresses, until she pulled in front of a modest two-story colonial-style house set behind a row of bedraggled azaleas in the middle of a patchy lawn. She turned onto the cracked cement driveway and threw the SUV into park.

"I'll follow your lead," she said. "You've interviewed him before."

"I'm not too optimistic," Wade said. "He knows a hell of a lot more than he admitted to last time."

She unbuckled her seat belt and opened the driver's door. "How much are we going to tell him? He's bound to have questions."

"As little as possible."

They traipsed over broken flagstones, ending at a stained concrete slab that passed for a front porch. Nina rang the bell, setting off a cacophony of high-pitched yapping inside.

The door creaked open about two inches. A woman in her sixties wearing a pink chenille robe and brown slippers squinted out at them. "I don't want any."

She started to close the door, but Nina stuck her foot in and held up her creds. "Special Agent Nina Guerrera, FBI. We need to speak to Joseph Sorrentino, is he home?"

The woman's watery eyes narrowed as she studied the identification, then she cracked a wide grin and let out a cackle loud enough to startle her three tiny dogs into silence. "I knew it!" She turned her head to call out behind her. "Joe, get your ass down here. It's the FBI. What the hell have you done this time?"

Nina and Wade exchanged a glance. Apparently, Joe's wife was not the type to cover for him.

"Let me put the dogs away," she said abruptly and slammed the door in their faces.

Nina turned to Wade. "You don't think he's leaving out the back door, do you?"

He gave her a wry smile. "His wife would snitch him out if he tried."

Sounds of yipping dogs and shuffling feet emanated from behind the closed door before it finally opened. She recognized Sorrentino from his driver's license photo. Heavyset, with a bulbous nose set in a fleshy face, he surveyed them from beneath bushy gray brows.

"You," he said by way of greeting, addressing Wade. "I got nothing more to say to you."

Apparently, Wade had made an impression. Or perhaps a visit from the FBI had stuck in Sorrentino's mind.

"Can we come in, Mr. Sorrentino?" Wade asked.

Sorrentino looked as if he dearly wanted to slam the door in their faces but seemed to think better of it. He stepped back. "May as well."

They followed him into a cluttered kitchen and stood by while he shoved a stack of papers and a withered houseplant aside to make room at the kitchen table. A dead spider skidded off the side, plopping into a doggy water bowl on the floor.

Sorrentino motioned for them to sit with his beefy arm but did not go so far as to offer a glass of water. Just as well. No way would she drink anything he handed her.

"You recall our conversation at your club two years ago?" Wade said, taking a seat in a dilapidated ladder-back chair.

Sorrentino grimaced. "Like I remember my last hemorrhoid."

"We'd like to discuss those items you sold."

"Not that again." Sorrentino leaned forward, the chair creaking ominously beneath his girth. "I told you, I haven't sold any more stuff since you and the other Feds came to see me, and I don't know nothin' else about it." He held up his right hand as if taking an oath, the universal gesture of liars everywhere. "I swear."

"Still, let's go over it again." Wade pulled out his notebook and opened it. "The last time we spoke, you mentioned that you obtained fighting gloves from your nephew."

"That's right, my brother's kid, Sammy Sorrentino, he went out of business a long time ago, so I did him a favor and bought his leftover stock."

Wade flicked his half-moon readers open and slid them on before consulting his notes. "You paid him five cents on the dollar for every item, then you resold them at your club." He peered over the top of the glasses. "At full price."

Sorrentino cleared his throat. "Well, there's nothing wrong with making a little money, am I right?"

"Long as you pay taxes."

"Look, we already went over this." Sorrentino hitched up the corners of his mouth in what appeared to be his best approximation of a disarming smile. "You guys gave me a pass. Are you seriously here to bust my balls for selling some sports equipment at my own establishment? It was quality stuff, everybody loved it. It wasn't like I was ripping anyone off or anything."

"Except your nephew," Nina said, unable to resist needling him. Sorrentino could have been more helpful to his own family. "How come you could sell the gloves when he couldn't?"

She must have surprised him with the question, because his eyes widened as he seemed to notice her for the first time. "Heeeey, aren't you the famous FBI chick?" He snapped his fingers. "The Warrior Girl, that's it." He gave her a speculative perusal. "You want to do a cage match? We could bill it as a special event. Guaranteed we sell out—hell, we could charge double for admission."

She narrowed her eyes. "Mr. Sorrentino, let me assure you that I have zero interest in a cage match."

"You sure? You're small but I saw that video where you kicked that guy's ass in the park. I bet you could take most of the female fighters in the circuit."

She also figured he'd seen the other video the Cipher had released and knew he could get free publicity from media coverage and make a fortune in ticket sales. He was an opportunist, but not a very bright one.

"I don't think you're hearing me." She had a strong urge to clean out his ears with the barrel of her Glock. "I will not fight in your club. Or anyone else's. Ever."

Sorrentino shrugged. "Your loss." He seemed to struggle to pick up the thread of their conversation. "Anyway, the guys all know me. I been around a long time. They trust me. Once a couple of them tried out the gloves, the word spread, and the rest came asking. What was I supposed to do, turn away business?"

"How many did you sell?" Wade asked.

"A few."

Wade glanced at his notes again. "Last time you said it was over fifty pairs."

"Well, if you include the fighting gloves and the tactical gloves, yeah, that's about right."

"Tactical gloves?"

"MMA fighting gloves are fingerless," Sorrentino said. "My nephew used the same material to make full gloves too. He was hoping to sell to the military or police as a backup plan, but that didn't work out neither."

"And you never told your nephew about all the sales you made?"

"Hey, he'd already declared the loss on his taxes. If I split it with him, it would only mess him up with the IRS, and nobody wants that."

Nina rolled her eyes. "You're a real humanitarian."

"We need the names of the people you sold them to," Wade said. "And don't tell us you don't know. A guy like you keeps records."

Sorrentino spread his hands, palms up. "Look around. Do I seem organized to you?"

He had a point.

Wade persisted. "You're a businessman, and you know about tracking money. Perhaps a search warrant would turn up more information in your files and computers."

"I don't need another rectal exam from the Feds. You guys didn't find anything last time, and you won't this time either."

Wade scowled. "Because you make sure everything's off the books."

"Because there's nothing there to find," Sorrentino said, his voice rising with the righteous indignation of the truly corrupt. "Look, I keep track of my business, but this wasn't *my* business. It was my nephew's. I figure anything I sold was making up for my original investment."

Apparently conceding defeat on that front, Wade moved on. "Do you have a copy of the club's schedule? One that shows which fighters were in a match and on what night?"

"Sure. How far back you need to go?"

"How far back can you go?"

Sorrentino opened his arms wide in a magnanimous gesture, the picture of honesty. "To when I converted the club from boxing to MMA about twelve years ago, when I started selling them gloves to the fighters."

Wade leaned forward, eager. "Do you have the schedule here?"

"I keep it on the computer at my club. I can email it to you."

"See that you do," Wade said. "Today."

"What's the hurry?" Sorrentino's entire demeanor shifted as he went from defensive to calculating. "Hey, you guys are investigating that serial killer, the Cipher. This doesn't have anything to do with that, does it?" His beady eyes darted back and forth between them. "If I provide information, I should get a reward, right? I mean, that Hollywood guy's offering a million now, so what are the Feds paying?"

"We're offering you the opportunity to continue to operate your club," Wade said. "As opposed to sharing a cell with a guy half your age who wants to show you his fighting skills in a cage match behind actual bars."

"No need for threats." Sorrentino held up placating hands. "Just asking is all."

"Now you've got your answer." Wade handed him a business card. "I'll be expecting an email from you within two hours." He stood. "Same as last time. You are not to speak about the subject of this conversation with anyone, understood?"

"Who am I going to tell?" Sorrentino struggled to his feet. "I never said a word to anyone last time and I won't now. It only makes me look bad."

"That goes for your wife too."

Sorrentino waved the notion off. "I don't tell her shit. She'll only be disappointed you two aren't taking me away in cuffs."

As they left Sorrentino to his domestic bliss and treaded out to the SUV, Nina considered the situation. They had learned precious little from the fight club owner, but perhaps his database would provide useful information. At least they could eliminate fighters who had been in the cage during the times they knew the Cipher had been active.

It wasn't much to go on, and she was growing frustrated. The unsub continued to land solid blows, damaging her reputation, thwarting the investigation, and humiliating her in the process. She, on the other hand, was shadowboxing.

Despite days of intensive investigation, he remained as much of a cipher as ever.

Chapter 30

After a long day poring over old case files from the Beltway Stalker investigation, Nina craved a long, hot shower. The shower she'd taken in the locker room at Quantico after her run had been slightly above lukewarm. She had managed to clean herself up before going out on the interview with Sorrentino, but it hadn't been a pleasant experience.

She'd come back to her apartment that evening and headed straight for the bathroom, only to be interrupted by her doorbell. Hair dripping, Nina tightened the satin belt around her short bathrobe and picked up her gun. Palming the weapon, she padded to her door and stood on tiptoe to peer out the peephole. A mussed pile of jet-black hair with an artful streak of cobalt took up most of the small portal.

Sighing, Nina ducked into the kitchen to stash her Glock in an upper cabinet. She darted back to the door and flung it open, beckoning Bianca inside. "Don't you have homework or something?"

She deliberately kept her tone brisk and playful, as if she had not been subjected to the worst public humiliation of her life a few hours earlier.

"Already done," Bianca said, playing her part without missing a beat. "Saw your car outside. Came to check on you."

"I don't need a seventeen-year-old to make sure I'm okay."

Bianca followed her into the kitchen. "Everyone in the building is talking about it."

No point in pretending she didn't understand. "I'll bet they are."

"It was all over campus too," Bianca said. "People got freaked watching the video on their phones. Once my psych professor realized no one was paying attention in class, he decided to include it in today's abnormal psychology lecture."

Great. A professor at George Washington University had incorporated her into his curriculum. She pictured a lecture hall full of coeds scribbling notes as they analyzed the unsub's mind, then decided it might be interesting to hear an academic's take.

"What did he say?"

"Basically, he took an hour of our lives we will never get back to tell us the Cipher is a complete whack-a-doo." Bianca shook her head. "Captain Obvious at the podium."

She saw through the snark. Bianca was worried. She rested a hand on the girl's slender shoulder. "We'll get him, *mija*."

Bianca wasn't the type to be comforted by platitudes. "Spoken like a true G-woman. The fan club would be proud."

Nina narrowed her eyes. "Fan club?"

Bianca moved past her, opening the refrigerator door. "You know, a group of people who admire someone or what they do."

"I know what a fan club is." She walked to the fridge, reached an arm around Bianca, and slammed the door shut. "What aren't you telling me, Bee?"

Bianca straightened. "Don't use that interrogation crap on me. It won't work."

Nina continued to stare at her.

"And don't look at me like that either." Bianca rested a hand on her hip. "I know what you're doing."

Nina didn't move. "Spill."

Bianca studied her shoes. "Man, if they could see you now, half of them would drop you for the hot guy."

"Wait, what hot guy?"

Bianca blew out a sigh redolent with all the frustration of a teenage genius forced to explain herself. Again. "Give me your laptop."

Nina fetched the computer from the coffee table where she'd put it next to the living room sofa and placed it in Bianca's outstretched hand.

"Look," Bianca said, tapping on the keyboard. "Someone created a fan page and posted a roster for Team FBI." She turned the laptop to face Nina. "People are voting for their favorite feebs."

Appalled, Nina swiped her finger down the screen. Candid shots of raid-jacketed federal agents at various crime scenes scrolled by. "What the hell is this?"

"People got pictures of you and that old guy, Agent Wade, working the cases in DC, San Francisco, and Boston, so everyone knows you two are the lead investigators."

"Old guy?"

"But in Boston, suddenly we get two other agents." Bianca went on as if Nina hadn't spoken. "A red-haired chick and a total hottie with a *G.I. Joe* haircut and glasses."

"And you refer to them as Ginger and G-man Joe?"

"Not me," Bianca said, overly innocent. "I didn't come up with those nicknames."

"I can't believe this is happening," Nina said. "Another ring added to the circus."

Bianca tapped the screen. "No one knows who the tall black guy in the dark suit is either."

"That would be Supervisory Special Agent Buxton. Our boss."

"Got it." Bianca handed her the computer and tugged a cell phone from her back pocket.

"Hold on. You'd better not be texting that out."

"Me? No."

Watching Bianca thumb-typing gave Nina a sneaking suspicion. "Who set up this FBI fan page?"

"No idea."

Bianca's tell. A reflexive knee-jerk denial with zero eye contact.

"It was you." Nina jabbed a finger at her. "You and your friends."

"Look, that psycho killer has a fan page," Bianca said, full of attitude. "He gets a cool nickname. Everyone calls him the Cipher. The good guys should have all that too."

She knew some serial killers attracted groupies but hadn't heard about this new twist in the current investigation. "Where is the Cipher's fan page?" She pushed the laptop back at Bianca. "Show me."

Bianca stowed her phone away again and pulled up a website as Nina held the computer. Images of the clues and the videos popped up. She would refer the page to Cyber Crime. They might already be monitoring it, but she had to be sure.

She closed the laptop and looked at Bianca. "Some people are fascinated by violent criminals. Notorious murderers receive love letters and marriage proposals sent to them in prison by total strangers."

"My psych professor called it *hybristophilia*." Bianca curled her lip. "People with major issues who fall for psycho killers. I don't get it."

"Could you do me a favor and shut down your FBI fan page?"

Bianca went back to checking her cell phone, avoiding both Nina's gaze and the question.

Nina crossed her arms. "Could you at least keep away from the investigation?"

"In case you hadn't noticed, everyone on the planet is involved with this investigation. I thought you might appreciate it if someone did it for the right reasons." Her voice broke. "I just can't stand . . . what he did to you . . ."

Nina took a step toward her. "Bee, it's okay, I—"

"It's not okay," Bianca said. "Nothing about this is okay. I don't care what you say, there's no way I'm going to stand by and let that asshole post more footage of him torturing you. Not if I can do something to help you guys find him."

After a long silence, Nina laid the laptop on the kitchen table and sat down. Making a calculated decision about how much to share, she motioned for Bianca to sit in the chair across from her. "Our team is dissecting the video. We've already figured some things out that we didn't know before. We're going to stop him."

"Before he carries out his promise to show more of that video?"

She swallowed the lump forming in her throat as she envisioned Bianca watching the next sixty seconds.

"Please leave it alone, Bee. I don't want you looking at his feeds, reading his posts, or doing anything else that puts his poison in your head. Leave him to us. We'll track him down."

"You have a lot more faith in those feeb techies than I do."

"They're really good at what they do."

"Yeah?" Bianca reached across the table to open the laptop. "Then how come they missed this?" She spun the screen to face her, tapped it several times, then angled it toward Nina. "I'm assuming you don't know since you haven't mentioned it."

She eyed the image. "This must be some sort of sick joke."

"It's real," Bianca said, tapping an icon to play a short video clip. "There's the proof."

Nina stood and stalked to the coffee table in the tiny living room. She snatched up her phone and pressed the first speed-dial number.

"Wade here."

She wasted no time on pleasantries. "I'm sending you a link."

"What's going on?"

"You know how we were wondering why we didn't find a clue from the unsub in Boston with a puzzle leading us to another city?"

"I'm listening." Wariness put an edge in Wade's tone.

"Some moron made a video showing where he found an envelope under a trash can about a quarter mile off the Freedom Trail. He listed it for auction on eBay. The bidding opened at twenty-five thousand. It's already past sixty grand."

Chapter 31

Traffic was a nightmare the next morning, and Nina had barely managed to get through security at both the Marine Corps and FBI Quantico checkpoints before the briefing was scheduled to begin. She had rushed to the largest meeting space in the sprawling facility, the nerve center of the growing task force.

Sliding into a chair between Wade and Kent, she sent Breck a brief smile across the long rectangular table. She deliberately trained her gaze toward the head of the table, pretending she hadn't noticed the surreptitious glances in her direction from agents and analysts she didn't know. Her colleagues, like millions of others, had obviously seen the video.

"All right, people," Buxton said, abruptly quelling all sidebar conversations. "We have a lot of ground to cover. I want to make this quick so we can get back to our respective assignments. Let's start with last night's eBay fiasco." He turned to Nina. "Agent Guerrera, can you start by telling us how you learned about the auction?"

"My next-door neighbor is fostering a seventeen-year-old girl who's finishing up her undergraduate degree at GW." A wry grin lifted the edge of her mouth. "She's got a scary-high IQ and a serious social media addiction. She showed me the link someone posted to an eBay auction."

Breck spoke up. "Our team spotted it at the same time your neighbor did." She gave her head a bewildered shake. "That girl should work for the Bureau when she graduates."

Nina grinned. "She'd end up running the place."

Apparently satisfied with her explanation, Buxton gestured toward a slender man in a slightly rumpled suit sitting a few seats down from him. "This is Supervisory Special Agent Jay Yakamura from the Boston field office. His team followed up on the clue that was listed for sale on eBay."

Nina was surprised to see him at the meeting instead of on a video call. His personal attendance spoke volumes about the emphasis the FBI had placed on the investigation.

Yakamura put down a Styrofoam cup brimming with black coffee and rubbed his eyes. "We contacted eBay as soon as we received notification from the task force about the envelope up for bid. They have a strict policy against selling illegal merchandise or any items that might encourage people to commit a crime. Once we explained that the envelope was material evidence in a murder investigation, they immediately removed the listing and provided the seller's contact information."

"Nice," Breck said.

"Turns out the seller lives in Lynn, not too far from Boston," Yakamura said. "We paid him a visit at home last night."

Kent raised his signature ceramic US Navy mug in a mock toast. "I'll bet he dropped a load in his boxers when he opened the door to two federal agents."

Yakamura tried to hide his smile without success.

"What's his story anyway?" Kent asked.

"Says he followed the case on social media all week. When he saw the Brew Crew post the solution, he drove to the nearest T station."

Nina had heard Detective Delaney refer to the Massachusetts Bay Transportation Authority's rapid-transit system as "the T" when he told her that one of the stops came out a short walk from the beginning of the Freedom Trail.

"He got off at the Park Street station," Yakamura went on. "Then he decides to stop for a blueberry muffin at one of the local bakeries on his way to the Trail. He eats his muffin, then strolls to the nearest trash can to toss the wrapper. He drops it on the ground because he's a putz but stoops to pick it up because he's an environmentally conscious putz. That's when he sees the envelope taped to the bottom of the receptacle. Says it was dangling down, so the bright blue lettering jumped out at him."

Along with everyone else in the room, Nina was riveted. Listening to this story was like watching a train wreck.

"He figures it's one of the Cipher's clues," Yakamura said. "So naturally, he snaps it up and stashes it in his pocket, taking care no one sees him. Then he follows the story on the news. Once he hears the Cipher escaped, he hightails it back to his place in Lynn rather than contacting the police."

A few groans could be heard around the table.

"He opens the envelope and spends the next twenty-four hours trying to get his few functioning brain cells to kick in. He finally realizes he has no hope of solving the clue, so he comes up with plan B."

Nina stole a glance at Buxton, who looked even more exhausted than Yakamura. He was pressing a finger against his left eye to stop it from twitching.

"Our guy figures he can't win the million bucks Zarran is offering up for solving clues," Yakamura said. "But he can still cash in by selling it to someone who thinks they can."

Wade gave his head a disgusted shake. "So he lists it on eBay." He cut his eyes to Nina. "I guess there's no risk of your neighbor's foster daughter bumping into him at her next Mensa meeting."

"What was his demeanor during the interview?" Buxton wanted to know.

"He did what came naturally," Yakamura said. "He played dumb. When that didn't work, he started asking about a finder's fee."

Nina grimaced. "Not the sharpest tack on the corkboard, is he?"

Yakamura gave her a sidelong glance. "He's the tack that misses the corkboard altogether and gets stuck in the drywall." He took another swig of coffee. "After discussing the amenities available in federal prison, our guy decides to turn over the envelope . . . without a reward."

"What was in the envelope?" Kent asked.

"The message inside was another deviation from the unsub's previous pattern." Yakamura pointed to the oversize screen on the wall, which flickered briefly before a close-up of a four-by-six white index card popped up. "This time, he wants people to solve a riddle to locate the actual clue."

FIND THE CLUE.

This was followed by four lines printed in boldface.

IN SILENCE SHE WAITS, DAY AND NIGHT.

LIVING WITH THE KEEPER OF THE LIGHT.

SHE SEES THEM COME, SEES THEM GO.

WHAT LIES IN HER HEART, NO ONE CAN KNOW.

The words at the very bottom of the card laid out his timetable.

THE NEXT ONE DIES IN FOUR DAYS.

A pall descended on the room as everyone concentrated on the message. Nina's fists clenched. Another deadline. Another girl in imminent danger. And they were no closer to stopping the Cipher.

Buxton's uncharacteristically harsh tone reflected exasperation. "We need answers, dammit."

"We're working on it, sir," a woman Nina had seen on the team of cryptanalysts said.

"Any progress?"

She squirmed uncomfortably under his withering glare. "Nothing definitive yet. We believe 'the keeper of the light' may refer to a lighthouse keeper, and he was recently active in Boston, so we're checking coastal towns in New England to see what other factors in the poem match existing structures. We'll keep you apprised of any developments."

Buxton swiveled to train his gaze on another agent sitting farther down the table. "And what about the flight manifests?"

"There were no duplicate names listed as traveling between any of the three cities on the affected dates," he said. "But now we know he has access to fake documents and disguises, so he could potentially fly under different names and have different appearances to match each identity."

"Or he might not have flown at all," Nina said.

"We can't ask local law enforcement across the country to check for data on subjects or traffic stops without giving them a name or even a description," Kent said.

A short, stocky blonde woman seated next to Breck lifted her hand. "I might be able to help with that."

Buxton acknowledged her. "For those of you who haven't met her, this is Emmeline Baker. She's in charge of the Trace Evidence Unit."

A unit chief was another unexpected addition to the meeting, again marking the gravity of the situation and the highly public and time-sensitive nature of the investigation.

"We figured out how he disguised his ethnicity in Boston," Baker said. "Spray tan. Extra dark." She tipped her head toward Nina. "The residue was found in the sample collected from Agent Guerrera's nails."

"Black wig, brown contact lenses, dark skin," Wade said. "Throw in a Public Works uniform, and he's unrecognizable."

Baker nodded. "He's proven he can operate in a crowded area where everyone is looking for him. It means he can move around with impunity." She let that sink in before continuing. "I have an update on the fiber match as well. As we discussed during our last call, we resubmitted samples found at the DC and San Francisco scenes, as well as from Agent Guerrera's abduction case, this time specifically comparing them to the unique set of fibers found in the Beltway Stalker series."

"The fibers from the gloves?" Nina asked.

"It's the only consistent evidence we have," Baker said. "Once we knew what to look for, we were able to find almost microscopic filaments with enough detail to provide a conclusive match for all three crime scenes attributed to the Cipher. The Boston case gave us the break we needed. There was far less cross contamination and nowhere near as much scrubbing of the body as in the two prior murders."

"So the Cipher and the Beltway Stalker are definitely the same person?" Nina said, anxious to nail Baker down. They had debated whether the Cipher had been the Beltway Stalker's partner, laying low for a couple of years before striking out on his own. "You're saying we can bring charges against the unsub for thirty-nine murders and an abduction?"

Baker held up a hand. "I can go so far as to say identical fibers, which come from a unique source, were found at each scene. That's as far as the science will take us. I couldn't take the stand and testify that the same perpetrator was responsible for every crime based on the trace evidence we have at this point."

No matter what Baker said, how precisely she couched her summary of the findings, she had just confirmed what Nina had already accepted as fact. First, the man who now called himself the Cipher was also the Beltway Stalker. Second, the FBI had mistakenly identified a man who died two years ago as the Beltway Stalker. Third, the same man had abducted her eleven years ago.

Buxton's jaw muscles bunched. "Nothing about that leaves this room, understood?"

She sympathized. Despite his previous refusal to make the leap, Buxton had clearly come to the same conclusions she had. He was the supervisory special agent for BAU 3. The unit chief who oversaw the profilers who worked with field agents and local law enforcement during the Beltway Stalker investigation. The BAU's reputation had taken a hit when Chandra Brown died, and soon the public would learn that her killer was still at large, continuing his murderous rampage on a bigger stage. Buxton would be front and center for the inevitable backlash.

His dark eyes traversed the length of the table before stopping on Wade. "Anything to add to your 302?"

Wade would have submitted a 302, the FBI's official form for documenting investigations, after their interview with Sorrentino.

"Nothing," Wade said. "Did you get the attachment with the club's fight schedule?"

Buxton nodded. "Forwarded it to Breck last night."

All eyes swiveled to Breck, who appeared to have been waiting for her cue. "I have a graphic." Computer keys clacked under her fingers as the projected image of a chart appeared on the wall across from her. "We generated a program and populated the data points to find a nexus between fighters and victims."

A red pinpoint of light swept up and down the left side of the graph with a list of fighters on the vertical axis. Names of victims ran along a horizontal timeline on the bottom. Green dots marked the boxes where some intersected. Nina could see that Breck had compared the times when fighters were unaccounted for with the times of death for the Beltway Stalker victims.

"We attempted to cross-reference the names with the times of each murder," Breck said. "The ones in green represent victims of the Beltway Stalker." She clicked another key, and a new chart popped up. "Here are the same fighters' schedules matched with the times of disappearance for the Cipher's victims." This time, the dots were blue. Even without overlaying the two graphs, Nina could tell there would be hundreds of data points containing both colored dots.

"I'll combine them on a new chart." Breck hesitated before adding, "Using only blue dots."

Breck had made it clear that anyone who felt the cases should be kept separate should speak up now. The team exchanged glances, but no one objected. In that moment, the investigation turned a corner. Nina knew Kent harbored doubts, but they had all tacitly agreed to move forward on the premise that the Beltway Stalker and the Cipher were the same person.

Nina gazed at the graphic. The lives of young girls, lives that had held so much promise and so much suffering, had been reduced to data points on a chart. Anger coursed through her as she witnessed the swath of destruction left by a monster who thought he could use human beings and throw them away like trash.

"Some of the older murders have a possible time of death that spans a few days or weeks," Breck said. "So we could only use the ones with a more precise window for the purpose of narrowing down the list." She moved the dot to the bottom of the screen. "Given those restrictions, we can definitively eliminate seventeen men from the list. That leaves more than two hundred potential suspects. And that's if we only consider fighters as opposed to other people working at the club."

"He's a fighter," Nina said. She wasn't sure how she knew, but the feeling was strong. "The way he moved. He had some serious experience behind him."

"I agree," Wade said. "Some serial killers are sexually inadequate milquetoast types in their regular lives. They seek power over their victims because they feel they have none in other areas." He stroked his jaw. "Not this guy. He doesn't use a gun, because he prefers direct contact. His personality type relishes physical combat, especially if he has enough skill to dominate and punish his opponents. He feeds off the raw power and violence of blood sport. He's probably stimulated by the crowd too. He certainly seems to enjoy a spectacle."

"But that's a radically different behavior pattern," Kent said, joining the discussion. "He flew under the radar before. Didn't want to draw attention to himself. Never taunted law enforcement." His brow creased in consideration. "Are we rushing to judgment here? Can we be sure the Cipher is also the Beltway Stalker? That they weren't partners?"

"He's changed." Wade grew animated, leaning forward in his chair. "That's another part of his profile. He seems to have an unusual ability to adapt."

"What was the impetus for change, then?" Kent asked. "It would have to be something strong."

"Me," Nina said before stopping to consider the reaction such a declaration would have. At a roomful of puzzled expressions, she began to explain something that had been in the back of her mind since the DC case.

"We've just gotten confirmation of a trace evidence link between my abduction and all of the murders." She glanced around the table as she spoke. "The Cipher began engaging with us after that video of the attack in the park went viral. He must have seen it and recognized me. If he's not the Beltway Stalker, then something about seeing me again triggered him to strike after holding off for eleven years. If he *is* the Stalker, then that video provoked him to change his MO dramatically. Either way, I'm the common denominator."

No one argued the point. Their silence a tacit acknowledgment that Nina was at the center of it all.

"How can we use this to our advantage?" Buxton directed the question to Wade. "There must be a way to throw him off his game, or at least to delay this next deadline of his."

Wade regarded Nina thoughtfully before answering. "His obsession with Guerrera is evident, yet he released prized mementos of his time with her." He raised two fingers to indicate the items. "The god's eye necklace and the video. He may have digital footage of every murder he committed, which would not be unusual. Many serial killers save trophies, photographs, or video of their victims to . . . enjoy later."

He didn't need to spell it out. Nina suppressed a shudder at the thought of the Cipher masturbating while he watched her in the throes of agony. Did he wear her necklace when he indulged his fantasies? The very idea filled her with disgust. She kept her face a mask of detached professional interest as Wade continued his analysis.

"I agree with Guerrera's assessment that she's a trigger for the Cipher, and I haven't changed my opinion that he and the Beltway Stalker are one and the same and that he fed us a convenient scapegoat two years ago when we were closing in at the fight club."

Kent showed signs of wanting to argue, but Buxton silenced him with a raised hand. "Go on, Agent Wade."

"He began by directing his threats to Nina with the note and the clue at the scene in DC. Then he went on the news and got an extreme reaction from regular and social media, so he changed his MO again and went straight to the public. Each time he expands his audience. We had Guerrera engage him directly via DM, but he went back to his public platforms. He now has millions of people around the world talking about him, trying to solve his arcane puzzles, paying attention to him. It's a heady experience for anyone." He drew in a deep breath. "I want to pull him back in close. Divert his attention from the public frenzy that feeds his ego."

"How are we going to do that?" Breck said. "He's the object of so much social media attention even though his profiles are down. People are still posting about him, and I'm sure he's reading the comments."

Instead of answering her directly, Wade addressed Buxton. "The only thing that could possibly entice him to give all that up is to offer him something he wants more." He cut his eyes to Nina. "I believe Guerrera should try communicating directly with him again. If she's amenable."

"That's a big ask," Buxton said. "And a big risk."

"It's my risk to take," Nina said. "I know the kinds of things he's going to say, and I'm willing to do it. I'll do whatever it takes."

"We would need to release the hold on his social media platforms," Breck said quietly. "All of them cooperated fully with taking them down, but they may not want to put them back up knowing he's fixing to put out more video."

"If we don't release the hold soon, he'll find another outlet that we can't control at all," Wade said. "He craves attention. He's becoming addicted to his own game."

Buxton glanced at his cell phone vibrating on the table's smooth surface. "Let's keep that option in our back pocket for now. I've got to take this. It's Dom Fanning from the DCU."

Nina didn't think her nerves could stretch any tighter, but an incoming call from the DNA Casework unit chief did the trick. The fact that he had reached out to Buxton indicated he had news about the commercial genealogical database search.

"I'm putting you on speaker," Buxton said after exchanging greetings. "I'm with the task force leaders."

Fanning's voice carried through the cell phone's speaker. "We got an early result from both companies. The good news is we obtained several close familial matches. Several appear to be half siblings, and one is a full sibling. A sister."

Everyone exchanged excited glances. Everyone, that is, except Buxton. "What's the bad news?" he said.

"Both genealogy companies have agreement forms for sharing DNA that include contact information for investigative purposes. This led us to an unexpected conclusion."

Nina wasn't surprised the companies required permission from participants to turn over their data. A lot of questions had been raised when law enforcement obtained familial matches from a commercial DNA database to identify a suspect in the Golden State Killer case. After the headlines, some companies had opted to have participants sign agreements declaring their willingness or refusal to share their DNA profiles with law enforcement.

"There are twenty-seven half siblings spread all over the country," Fanning said. "Not including the full sister, who lives in Maryland." He paused a beat. "And those are just the ones who submitted their DNA to the two companies. Statistically, there should be a lot more out there who didn't."

Buxton looked nonplussed. "Twenty-eight siblings total?"

"The only times I've seen results like that are when a sperm donor is involved. But in this case, many of the half siblings are related through mitochondrial DNA, which means they have a common *mother*."

"Egg donation?" Buxton said.

"To get this outcome, there would have to be both egg and sperm donation, which means—"

"A fertility clinic," Buxton finished for him.

"That would be my guess," Fanning said. "At least you should be able to track down the biological parents through the clinic's implantation records and learn the identity of their offspring. I recommend starting with the full sister."

"We'll get right on it," Buxton said.

"I have something else for your team as well." The eagerness in Fanning's voice promised another juicy lead.

"Which is?" Buxton prompted, allowing the DCU chief his moment.

"While we were waiting on the results, we used DNA phenotyping to generate a composite image of the unsub. I'll email it to you with the rest of our report."

This kept getting better. Nina knew the phenotyping process didn't create a perfect picture of the person in question, but she had seen it come close in several cases. Special software could analyze a person's DNA to predict characteristics such as hair color, eye color, facial shape, skin tone, freckling, and stature, among other things. At last, they would have an idea of what the Cipher really looked like.

Buxton thanked him and disconnected. For the first time in days, he smiled. "Ladies and gentlemen, we finally have a break in this investigation."

Chapter 32

"Do you need help with your bag, sir?" the cabbie asked.

The Cipher was always surprised at how accommodating people were to the elderly. A useful human failing. He leaned heavily on his cane. "Thank you, sonny."

The heavyset man hoisted the duffel into the taxi's roomy trunk. "Where you headed?"

"Downtown." The Cipher slowed his movements, getting awkwardly into the back of the yellow sedan.

The driver stood next to the open door as the Cipher fumbled with the seat belt. "Which hotel, sir?"

He considered how to capitalize on this opportunity. "Is there a homeless shelter downtown?"

The driver eyed him with overt wariness. "You need a place to stay?"

"No, no. Not for me." He dismissed the idea with a nonchalant wave. "I donate to homeless shelters."

The cabbie looked relieved. His fare money was not in jeopardy after all. "There's a few shelters. Some food banks and soup kitchens too." He sighed. "Seems like there's always people who need a hand."

"Especially women and children," the Cipher said. "Any shelters just for homeless women and girls?"

"Sure, there's one right in the heart of the city."

"Then take me to the hotel closest to that, please."

The cabbie closed the door and trotted around to wedge his pudgy frame into the driver's seat. He glanced at his passenger in the rearview mirror. "You one of those folks who gives money to causes and stuff?"

"A philanthropist," the Cipher said, deliberately rasping his voice. "Yes, that's what I am."

"That's real nice. You're a good man."

The Cipher smiled. People believed what they wanted to believe. Saw what they wanted to see.

As the taxi pulled away from the busy airport terminal, he sat in the back seat, going over his plans. There was another piece of information he needed, but he wasn't sure if he should risk asking the cabbie. He did not want to be memorable in any way. On the other hand, the man was a font of information. "Have you lived here a long time?" he asked, deciding to chance it.

"Born and raised."

Perfect. He cleared his throat. "I might decide to stay here awhile," he said. "Is there a part of the city that still has open spaces?"

"Everything close to downtown is packed in. If you want space, you should look on the north or south side."

"Thank you, sonny."

He had no intention of checking into any hotel. After the cabbie dropped him off, he would take the bus to the nearest hardware store to buy supplies. Then he would rent an RV and drive it to the outskirts of town to prepare it for his needs. The old man getting off the plane at the airport would morph into someone else, and he would come back into the city tonight to start hunting.

His pulse quickened at the thought. Everyone in the country was looking for him. He'd given them the perfect distraction. As he'd done so often in his cage fights, he feinted left and jabbed right.

And no one would see his next punch coming.

Chapter 33

One of the cryptanalysts bumped Nina as he scurried past, jolting her coffee from its Styrofoam cup onto Kent's sleeve.

She used the tiny napkin from under her cup to dab at his forearm and gave him a sheepish grin. "Everyone's running around like crazy in here."

"No worries," Kent said, flashing her a smile. "I'm just pleased we all have something to work with for a change. A little chaos is a price I don't mind paying."

The moment Buxton ended the meeting, every team had rushed to separate areas in the task force room to chase down various aspects of the fresh leads they'd just received. The cavernous workspace had been sectioned into areas of specialty. Agents and analysts clustered around tables, charts, and computers as they delved into their respective investigative assignments. The FBI's substantial resources were being brought to bear on each of the individuals named in the document Fanning had sent them. By the end of the day, they would know everything about each of their backgrounds, down to the names of their kindergarten teachers, their SAT scores, and every place they'd ever lived or held a job.

In a station set up in a corner of the room, the cryptanalysts were poring over the Cipher's poem, determined to solve its meaning before he posted it for one of the Scoobies to figure out and snatch the clue before they could. Nina had read the rhyme several times but couldn't make any headway. Finally, she decided she'd rather spend her time proactively hunting the Cipher instead of playing his games. She walked toward the opposite corner, where a group of agents were running through Breck's chart with the names of MMA fighters from Sorrentino's list. Wade and Kent stood with them, using their profiling skills to help whittle the list down to a manageable number for follow-up.

Of course, once they interviewed the Cipher's siblings and learned the name of the fertility clinic where they had been conceived, none of this would be necessary. Everything would be in the clinic's database.

Breck motioned Nina over to her table. "Come look at this." She pointed at her monitor. "I took the image we got from Fanning and tweaked it to include some of the facial data points we got from surveillance footage."

Nina stepped closer, anxious to finally put a face to the monster from her past. Breck had insisted Nina wait until she fiddled with it, wanting her first impression to be as accurate as possible.

"Most of his face was covered in every still shot we were able to grab," Breck said. "I did manage to capture a bit of his jawline in one frame and an idea of cheekbone height in another. Put it all together with the predicted characteristics, and voilà." She clicked her mouse with a flourish, and a close-up of a man's face materialized.

Nina bent to examine the screen closely. A muscular blond man with eyes an indeterminate shade of blue and a chiseled face stared back at her. Her blood chilled. Had she imagined the flatness in his expression, or was that an artifact of the computer generated–imaging process? Either way, the effect was an accurate depiction of the soulless eyes that had gazed down at her through the holes in the mask.

For the span of a moment that lasted an eternity, she fell into the depths of those pitiless eyes. Her pulse pounded in her ears. Cracks spiderwebbed across her carefully constructed inner walls as she struggled to hide her reaction. Transfixed, she stared at the Cipher. Her monster.

The man who had nearly destroyed her. The beast who had wrenched her apart and exposed her torment to the world.

Kent rested a hand on her shoulder. "You okay?"

She whirled to face him. "Fine."

She took a step back, creating emotional and physical distance. His piercing cobalt gaze penetrated her. Kent had a vast amount of experience in the field. He knew how to read body language. She could not afford to have him psychoanalyze her. If he suspected how much seeing the Cipher's face had disturbed her, he might say something to Buxton or—worse yet—try to comfort her. Throughout her life, she had contended with abuse, neglect, and rejection. These she could handle, but warmth and compassion would undo her.

She deliberately turned away from Kent to address Breck. "From the little I saw of him, that looks right."

Nina felt the weight of Kent's scrutiny as he kept his attention on her, but he made no further comment.

Breck bent closer to the monitor and studied the image of the Cipher. "It's hard to capture evil in a picture, but this guy comes as close as anybody I've ever seen. You can tell he's mean as a snake just by looking at him."

Nina didn't want to spend another moment staring into those cold, cruel eyes. "I'm getting restless. He's out there planning his next move. We need to make ours first."

"I just read the report on the sister." Wade had strolled over to join them. "Her name's Anna Grable, and she's a bit of an enigma. Received a doctorate in physics and another in astronomy, both from Johns Hopkins University in Baltimore."

Unexpected. A psycho killer's sister had a passion for studying outer space. "Where does Anna work?"

"That's part of the mystery. She hasn't held a job for fifteen years. She's never been married or had kids, and she lives alone on a ten-acre parcel in the suburbs of Baltimore that she inherited from her parents."

"What did you find out about the parents?"

"From what we can gather, the mother has no record of having given birth to any children. It's possible that the sister is a result of an in vitro fertilization of a surrogate mother, but we can't be sure at this point."

Nina was perplexed. "A legal adoption?"

"None that we can access so far. Buxton's prepped local field agents in every city where there's a subject with a familial DNA match to conduct interviews," he said. "I'm sure we'll find out more once they finish speaking to Anna."

Nina chafed at the idea of someone besides her interviewing the Cipher's only known full sibling. It would be a hard sell for her to go instead of the local field agents, but every cop instinct she possessed told her this was the fastest path to the truth about her quarry. "I want to interview Anna Grable in person. If I see her, something about her might trigger a memory. Baltimore's about a two-hour drive from here, so it will cost us the rest of the day, but I think it's worth it to put eyeballs on her."

"I want to go with," Breck said. "I can take pictures of her head from every angle. Since she's a full-blooded sister, her underlying facial structure might help refine the imaging process."

"She's the best lead we've got." Nina leveled Wade with a determined stare. "I'm going to ask Buxton to let us conduct the interview." She emphasized the word *us.* "I'll request an FBIP driver and one of our fleet vans so we can keep working on the road. Will you back me up?"

The FBI Police unit stationed at Quantico was normally tasked with facility protection but could be detailed for other assignments as needed. She was asking Wade to trust her instincts. Asking him as a partner rather than an adjunct to his investigation. His response would tell her more about the working relationship they had forged than anything else he'd said up to this point.

He regarded her for a long moment, then turned toward Buxton's office as he responded to her question over his shoulder. "Grab your briefcase."

Chapter 34

Nina had vacillated between edgy anticipation and utter boredom during the two-hour ride to Towson, Maryland. Buxton, opting to hold down the fort at Quantico, had arranged for the team to travel in a Mercedes-Benz Sprinter van outfitted with enough technical gadgetry to bring a smile to Breck's lips. Their driver, an FBI police officer Nina recognized from ID checks at the entry gate to the grounds at Quantico, was ensconced in the partitioned driver's compartment up front. He eased the van to a halt in front of a midcentury rambler on a spacious chunk of land, waiting with the vehicle as the team traversed the gravel driveway to the front porch.

Nina lifted her hand to knock when the door flew open. A slender woman with pale eyes and stringy blonde hair stood on the threshold. She wore a floppy knit cap, an oversize cotton top that fell to her knees, and Birkenstocks on her brightly stockinged feet.

Nina held up her creds. "Special Agent Nina Guerrera, FBI." She gestured to the group standing behind her. "Special Agents Wade, Kent, and Breck. Are you Anna Grable?"

The team had agreed that Nina would initiate contact this time. Judging by the woman's fearful reaction, it had been a good call. The sight of Kent standing directly in front of her might have made her faint.

Her wide, anxious eyes darted to each of them in turn. "I'm Anna, and I know why you're here." She stood aside and motioned them in.

After exchanging bewildered glances, they trooped through the foyer into the living room. A mustard-yellow sofa with the backrest covered in a crocheted throw and two mismatched armchairs surrounded a burled wood coffee table that was the height of stylish good taste. In 1967.

Nina sandwiched herself between Kent and Wade on the sofa while Breck perched on one of the wingbacks.

"You say you know why we're here?" Nina asked. If an interviewee volunteered information, she made it a practice to let them talk.

Anna took the remaining armchair. "You don't have to pretend. I've been expecting you." She gave them each another perusal, this time much slower. "I have to admit you all have done a good job. The dark suits give you away, though, if you don't mind my saying."

"Suits?" Wade asked.

Anna gave him a knowing wink. "You should try blue jeans and a button-down shirt next time. Maybe plaid or paisley. You'd blend right in."

Nina had the feeling they were speaking at cross purposes. "Ms. Grable, exactly who do you believe we are?"

"You might as well call me Anna. No sense in pretending you don't know everything about me."

"Anna," Nina tried again, "why don't you go ahead and spell it out for us? Pretend like we really don't know what you mean."

Anna blew out a long sigh. "I get it. This is some sort of test. You want to know if I've figured it out." She leaned forward, carefully enunciating her words. "You are from the Pleiades. We have met before on at least twelve occasions, but this is the first time you've visited while I'm awake." She sat back in her chair and gave each of them a satisfied smile.

Nina shot Wade a look. He and Kent were the headshrinkers, not her.

Wade took the hint, adopting a patient tone. "Anna, we are FBI agents. We do not come from the Pleiades, we are from Earth. We need to ask you some important questions."

Anna frowned. "There's only one way to be sure." She stood. "Follow me into the kitchen. I can sterilize a knife and—"

"No," Wade said firmly. "You cannot cut us. We need your cooperation for an investigation."

"An investigation," Anna said, sitting back down. "Is that what you're calling it these days?" She let out a huff. "I won't believe you unless I can perform a few experiments of my own. Let's see how you like being probed."

Anna had managed to obtain two doctorates but had come loose from her moorings and gone adrift somewhere along the way. Nina wondered about the Cipher. Did crazy run in the family?

Wade tried again. "Anna, we need to know about your background. Were you adopted?"

Anna's cackle was derisive. "As if you didn't know."

Kent, who was sitting closest, leaned toward her. "Please, Anna, this is very important. Tell us what you know about your parents and where you were born."

She turned to him with a conspiratorial smile. "You're here because you're in my bloodline. I'm descended from the Nordics, you know." She clasped her hands neatly in her lap. "The Grays had nothing to do with it."

Nina was lost. "Anna, what are you talking about?"

She pointed to Kent. "He can tell you."

If Anna thought that would clear things up, she was badly mistaken. Nina had been excited to interview the Cipher's only known full-blooded relative, certain she would garner exactly what she needed to track him down. Instead, she was listening to a crazy woman babble while the clock ticked down. She shot Kent a questioning glance.

He appeared to be stifling a massive eye roll. "I've run across this before due to my . . . appearance." He pinched the bridge of his nose under the thick black frames of his glasses. "There are people who believe in a race of humanoid extraterrestrials from the Pleiades star cluster who resemble Scandinavians. They are referred to by UFOlogists as 'Nordics.'" He grimaced. "This is as opposed to the 'Grays,' who are small and gray skinned, with large dark eyes."

Nina would have laughed if the situation weren't so serious. How would they get actionable information out of Anna? She had been trained at the academy not to indulge people's delusions, which was the course Wade and Kent had taken. She decided on a slightly different approach.

Adopting an expression of utmost sincerity, she faced Anna. "There might be something in your DNA that is very helpful to us. In order to get that information, we need to know about your origins. All of the files we have are gone."

"Well, why the hell didn't you just say so?" Anna said. "My parents— not biological, obviously—went to the Borr Clinic when they found out they couldn't have children. They didn't want to adopt, and they had heard about Dr. Borr's lab through friends in DC." She glanced up at the ceiling, trying to recollect. "I don't remember their names, but I'm pretty sure they worked for the government."

Surprised she had gotten Anna to talk, Nina kept to the relevant details. "Who is Dr. Borr?"

"You know, the famous geneticist. He pioneered genetically engineered offspring. Told my parents I would be special." She dropped her voice to a conspiratorial whisper. "But of course he didn't tell them the baby would be half extraterrestrial." Her eyes flitted to Kent.

"Do you know where his clinic is?" Nina asked, trying to keep her on track.

"About an hour from here, right next to—" She jabbed a finger at Breck. "Hey, what the hell are you doing?"

Breck hastily tucked her cell phone away. "Nothing."

"You were taking pictures of me. I saw you."

"I just wanted to, you know, get some photos of your head and facial features."

Nina inwardly groaned. Breck should never, under any circumstances, work undercover. She had to be the worst liar ever.

Anna shot to her feet, pointing at the front door, stiff armed. "Get out. All of you."

Despite their repeated assurances that there was nothing to fear, Anna remained adamant. In her mind, they had crossed the line by taking secret measurements of her body without her permission. She told them she'd been abducted too many times, suffered from PTSD because of it, and would no longer tolerate any probes, examinations, or hours of lost time.

A barrage of accusations peppered with obscenities followed them as they clambered into the sleek black van and instructed the driver to head back to Quantico. Nina looked out the darkly tinted side window to see Anna standing on her front porch, both middle fingers in the air.

The van maneuvered onto the main road as she glanced at Kent, who had taken the bench seat opposite her. "I didn't know you had relatives in the Pleiades."

Wade chuckled. "It certainly explains a few things."

"I'll have to report this to the home world," Kent said, deadpan. "And I'm afraid I'll also have to wipe your memories."

"I don't know about alien-hybrid babies," Breck said, typing on her cell phone. "But Dr. Borr ran a fertility clinic in Bethesda."

"I guess we know where we're going next," Wade said. "That's exactly what Fanning was talking about. We should be able to get a search warrant for medical records if they don't grant us access."

Breck frowned down at her screen. "Except that the clinic burned to the ground about thirty years ago."

"What happened?" Nina asked.

"According to this news article, the clinic was founded by Dr. Wayland Borr, who advertised his services to couples who wanted to raise superior offspring." Breck made air quotes around the last two words. "He called it the Borr Project."

A chill crept down Nina's spine. "Superior offspring?"

Breck pursed her lips. "He collected eggs and sperm exclusively from Caucasian donors screened for optimal genetic health and a genius-level IQ."

"Unbelievable," Kent said.

"Local media did a report about the clinic." Breck continued reading as the van maneuvered onto the freeway. "Described the Borr Project as a modern-day eugenics experiment. The day after the story went out, someone torched the whole building."

"Did the clinic reopen?" Nina asked.

"According to this news report, Dr. Borr committed suicide a short time later. The clinic never reopened."

"We need access to his files, any records he kept," Wade said.

"Hold on a sec." Breck swiped her finger down the screen. "The obituary mentions a surviving son. He would probably be in his forties by now. If he inherited the family estate, he would be within an hour's drive in Potomac, Maryland. It's on our way back to Virginia. We could stop by and talk to him, see if he has any of his father's paperwork."

"I'll call Buxton," Wade said to her. "Tell the driver to head toward Potomac."

Chapter 35

As Nina sat on the bench seat next to Wade, the driver pulled the van onto a circular cobblestone driveway. Breck snapped her laptop shut and Kent unbuckled his safety belt as they trundled to a stop. A dark-haired man in a black golf shirt and tactical pants stood on the front steps of a sprawling mansion, apparently ready to greet them.

"Looks like Mr. Borr doesn't get too many visitors," Wade said. "And doesn't want them."

They'd been granted access at the front gate via the intercom, denying them the opportunity of an unannounced visit but confirming that Gavin Borr was at home.

Too young to be Dr. Borr's forty-five-year-old son, the knuckle dragger standing at parade rest under the portico had to be private security.

"Why does Borr think he needs a commando to guard his estate?" Nina asked. "This is Potomac. What does he think is going to happen to him in one of the wealthiest suburbs in the metro area?"

Kent looked through the window, narrowing his eyes at the man. "He's no commando, he's a poser."

She figured Kent's background in Special Forces gave him the ability to spot the real thing.

"Still," she said, opening her door, "Gavin Borr must feel threatened."

They got out and allowed the hired muscle to inspect their creds before following him inside, leaving the driver to wait for them in the van as they had before. After ushering Nina and her team into what she assumed was the study, he closed the heavy wooden double doors behind him.

A slight, pale man with receding platinum hair greeted them. "Please have a seat. Would you like a drink?"

They declined, glancing around the well-appointed room. Nina peered at the tall wooden shelves lined with books. Even to her untrained eye, some looked very old and very expensive. A globe the size of a beach ball rested in a wooden frame in the far corner. Did people still have globes? With constant wars all over the world, it seemed to her they would be obsolete before they were even finished, much less years later sitting in someone's private library.

Borr's scratchy voice pulled her out of her reverie. "To what do I owe the pleasure of a visit from the FBI?"

Seated in an overstuffed armchair, he did not rise to greet them. His words were casual, but his repeated lip licking and the twisting of his hands in his lap betrayed anxiety. The appearance of four federal agents at his door would tend to have that effect, but Nina got the impression the man was nervous most of the time. His unnaturally pallid features, red-rimmed eyes, and slightly hunched shoulders gave him the general demeanor of a laboratory rat cringing in the corner of a cage as the scientist approached.

"We're here to talk about your father, Dr. Wayland Borr, and his work," Nina began. "Can you tell us about his clinic?"

Borr's thin lips turned down. "That damnable clinic." He motioned for them to take a seat on the plush sofa and chairs surrounding the ornate coffee table in the center of the room. "It's like I can never get away from it."

The reaction was unexpected. And intriguing. Based on what Breck had uncovered on the drive over, Nina took a gamble. "Is that why you have private security?"

His small eyes sharpened as he watched them sit. "Some people still call us Nazis. It's outrageous. We're not even of German descent." He lifted his chin. "My ancestors are from Holland. The name Borr is also prevalent in Norse mythology. Borr is the father of the one-eyed god Odin, who is Thor's father."

She had to get him back on track or this interview would devolve as badly as Anna Grable's had. "Mr. Borr, can you explain why your father's clinic made you concerned for your safety?"

"It all started because my father wanted to help infertile couples. Only he figured that, instead of taking random donors, he would screen for healthy men and women of superior intelligence." Borr shrugged. "What's the harm in that?"

The question took Nina back to her days in foster care, watching prospective parents pass her by to fawn over the other little girls. "Apparently, some people took offense to the fact that the donors were exclusively Caucasian."

"You sound like that reporter," Borr said. "The one who wrote that story and started the whole scandal. Some troglodyte burned down the clinic right after the story ran, then our whole family started getting death threats. I was in high school when it happened. My father couldn't take it, so he . . ." His eyes hardened. "After all these years, we're still harassed. I'll never forgive that damned reporter. He twisted everything my father tried to do. Painted him as some sort of racist zealot. My father was a visionary. A man of science. He was trying to advance humankind by selecting for genetically advantaged progeny."

She felt her jaw slacken. Borr, a product of his upbringing, believed he was making perfect sense. Reluctant to alienate him this early in the interview process, she swallowed the retort trying to force its way out of her mouth and redirected her line of questioning. "Were any records saved after the clinic burned down?"

"You're not the first to ask about that. Grown children of some of his clients have contacted me over the years looking for information about their biological parents." Borr waved a dismissive hand. "I remind them that this was more than thirty years ago, before there was a digital cloud. My father kept his paper records in file boxes. He backed them up on five-inch floppy disks. Unfortunately, he stored those files and disks on-site." He slumped in his chair. "Thanks to those arsonists, there's nothing left of his records."

Her mind rebelled at the thought of another dead end after having come so far. "Don't you have anything at all? Any stray notebooks he might have taken home?"

"Nothing."

"What about a business partner or an investor in his clinic?"

"My father was an unusual scientist in that he had independent means. When no one wanted to partner with him, he simply founded the clinic on his own."

"Did he have employees? An attorney? An accountant?"

"Yes to all three, but they have no information whatsoever about the identities of my father's clients. Believe me, I've tried. It seems my father went to a great deal of trouble to ensure the anonymity of donors and prospective parents. Things were different back then. There was a lot more latitude for such arrangements to be kept confidential."

Nina tried to wrap her mind around the enormity of the problem. "How long was the clinic operating? Do you at least know how many babies were born?"

"The clinic was open for about three years. I'm not sure how many successful pregnancies there were, but from the comments he occasionally made around the dinner table, I figure somewhere between fifty and a hundred. The couples who raised the children had no biological link to their babies," Borr went on. "The embryos were created from donor sperm and eggs, then implanted into the mother, or in some cases, a surrogate."

"Is there anything else you can tell us that might help?"

"I believe I've been most helpful, especially since you haven't told me what this is all about. It's my turn to ask questions now."

She braced herself for the inevitable.

Borr's pale eyes grew calculating. "I've seen the four of you on the news. You're investigating that serial killer, the Cipher." He paused as if waiting for a reaction. Getting none, he continued, "I am not a stupid man, Agent Guerrera. Given who you are pursuing, and given your urgent and unannounced visit to my home to ask about my father's records, I can only conclude that you have developed a suspect. Someone who was conceived as part of the Borr Project."

Wade cut in before Nina could respond. "We can neither confirm nor deny that, Mr. Borr."

Borr let out a wheezy chuckle. "Which I will take as absolute confirmation." The smile died on his lips. "I have only one request. Keep the clinic out of it. If word spreads that my father's experiments had anything to do with this, our whole family will become pariahs again."

"We don't share our investigative leads with anyone," Wade assured him.

"Sooner or later, the truth will out, as the saying goes. It always does." Borr pointed a bony finger at them. "I want you to understand something. This will be a hardship for everyone who was born as a result of the clinic. If one of them turns out to be a psychotic murderer, the rest will fall under suspicion. Their lives will be disrupted. They will be accused of being the products of a eugenics experiment conducted by a mad scientist. Those are the kinds of things I've been forced to hear all my life."

Something about the way he spoke perked up Nina's antennae. "Why you?"

He flinched. "I didn't mean to say that." He said it a little too quickly.

"Were you one of the children conceived in the clinic?"

Borr stared at them with such venom, she thought he might order them out of the house as Anna Grable had. She held her position, waiting him out. Finally, he seemed to deflate. "My mother was barren. It was one of the reasons my father began to study fertility."

This kept getting more interesting. "So Dr. Borr is not your biological father?"

Borr shook his head adamantly. "He used his own sperm, but he found an egg donor who was a NASA scientist. She had no interest in becoming a mother but was willing to contribute her eggs." He swallowed. "I was the first prototype. My father successfully implanted the embryo in my mother. Unfortunately, she died shortly after giving birth to me."

"I'm sorry."

He waved off the sentiment. "The point is that a few people found out about how I was born, and some have been extremely unkind. My father always expected great things of me. He thought I would become the president, cure cancer, or design cities. Instead, he got a son with an above-average IQ, but who was unremarkable in many ways and suffered from poor health. I believe I was a disappointment to him."

She felt a tingle run through her body. Her senses went on high alert, signaling that she was onto something. "Did he mistreat you?"

She recalled Wade's earlier profile, in which he surmised the Cipher had been abused by a father figure. She knew Borr wasn't her suspect, but she wondered if they had more in common than the way they had come into the world.

"He mostly failed to notice me," Borr said. "I'm only telling you this because I have a kind of kinship with the other people who came from the clinic. They are all adults now and should be allowed to lead normal lives, free of expectations of greatness or, if the Cipher turns out to be one of them, suspicions of evil or mental illness."

"I agree with you, Mr. Borr. Biology is not destiny," Wade said. "Perhaps that's something your father should have considered when screening potential donors."

Borr stiffened. "I believe it's time for you all to leave." His words were coated in ice. "You have trespassed on my hospitality long enough."

"We appreciate your—"

"Gregory will show you out. Don't come back unless you have a search warrant in hand."

They followed Gregory through the house to the front door. Ramrod straight in his black tactical garb, he wordlessly ushered them to the waiting van.

As they all got in the back and buckled up, Nina reflected that they had left both residences on a sour note, and empty handed to boot. Not a good day for the FBI.

The driver eased the van through the elaborate front gates and back into traffic.

"That didn't end well," Nina said to no one in particular.

"We got everything we could," Wade said. "I watched him closely. He wasn't holding out on us."

"I watched him too," Kent said. "And I'm convinced he's totally on board with his father's prejudice. He can lie to himself all he wants, but that's exactly what it is when you only select candidates from your own race for the program." He let out a disgusted snort. "Genetically advantaged progeny, my ass."

Nina slid Kent a covert smile. He was exactly the type Dr. Borr would have chosen, yet he would have had nothing to do with the man or his so-called project.

Kent grinned back, acknowledging their shared sentiment. She noticed Wade watching the unspoken communication with an expression of frank appraisal.

"I sent Buxton a text," Breck said, oblivious to the byplay. "He's calling us now."

She held her phone out so everyone could hear.

"Can you speak freely?" Buxton asked.

"We're secure," Wade said. "Go ahead."

"Give me what you've got." As usual, Buxton wasted no time on niceties.

Wade, as lead agent on their team, provided an overview of what they had learned from Dr. Borr's son. Buxton was infuriated to hear the clinic's records were destroyed in the fire, rendering their only promising lead to identifying the Cipher useless.

This time, he had slipped through the dragnet without even trying.

"Have any of the other people on Fanning's list been interviewed?" Breck wanted to know. "What were they like?"

The sound of shuffling paper preceded Buxton's answer. "Local field agents contacted all of them in person. Some knew about the Borr Project and some did not. The parents who raised them apparently made their own decisions about how much to tell them."

Nina grimaced. "I'll bet that made for some awkward family discussions for the ones who didn't know."

"No doubt," Buxton said. "After you called us, we researched Dr. Borr and his clinic. The children were supposed to represent some great leap forward for humankind according to Dr. Borr, but our field interviews and background checks revealed nothing unusual about the ones who were born through his program. Some were extremely bright and accomplished, but others lived ordinary lives and seemed to be . . . average."

Nina was fascinated by the implications. "Then Dr. Borr's project didn't guarantee anything. In fact, his own son admitted he hadn't lived up to his father's expectations."

"By the law of averages, a certain percentage of the population will fall above and below the mean IQ of one hundred," Buxton said. "Among those who were interviewed, there was an artist, a dentist, some stay-at-home moms, a couple of professors, one actual rocket scientist, and a janitor."

Nina leaned against the headrest, processing the information as the van sped through the thickening traffic. "So now we have a killer, possibly with a high IQ, who believes he's superior to everyone else?"

Wade answered her. "If his parents told him about the clinic, then yes."

"Which makes him all the more dangerous," Buxton said, putting words to the thoughts swirling in her mind. "Let's meet first thing tomorrow in the briefing room."

"How are the other teams progressing, sir?" Nina asked, hopeful the task force had made progress on other fronts during their absence.

"Crypto is still working on the poem," Buxton said. "No breakthroughs yet. This isn't a mathematical equation, an anagram, or a code, so it's really not their bailiwick. You all should put your heads together on the drive back. Maybe you'll come up with something."

She would make it her mission to figure out that stupid rhyme before they passed through the checkpoint at Quantico.

"Did you get any photographs of Anna Grable, Agent Breck?" Buxton asked.

"I got six before she caught me," Breck said. "I'll work them into the computer image we have, using predictive algorithms to further enhance it. By the time we arrive, we'll have a better image to go with."

"Should we show it to Sorrentino?" Nina asked, anxious for progress.

Wade answered immediately. "Not a good idea. I don't trust him not to talk. He's not above blackmailing someone if he recognizes the image or taking a bribe to lead us down the wrong path. I also don't recommend showing it around the fight club. We all know what happened the last time we started sniffing around over there."

He didn't have to mention Chandra Brown by name for everyone to get the message.

Breck nodded her understanding. "The image should be good enough to help the team reviewing the fight club leads to eliminate some of them. I'll shoot it over to them as soon as I've finalized it. I think this is the best we're going to get."

Guilt swamped her. She had been so determined to pursue these leads, and now they had lost a whole day. She had to make up for it. "Sir, I'd like to DM him again."

She cringed inwardly at the thought of what he would say to her. His last messages had been crude and provocative. Now that he had shown the first minute of the video, he would taunt her relentlessly. But she had made up her mind that she would take whatever he dished out, as long as it got her one step closer to putting him behind bars for the rest of his miserable life.

To her surprise, Buxton readily agreed. "I'll have Cyber get him back online," he said. "It's been radio silence from him since the video, which is disturbing because it means he's likely busy doing other things or he's created new profiles we don't know about yet."

"Unlikely," Breck said. "If he created a new profile, he wouldn't have his audience. His followers couldn't find him unless he made it clear he had migrated over, and in that case, we'd find him too."

Kent weighed in. "I think he's been active offline, which is not good for us. I say let Guerrera reach out, but go ahead and reactivate him tonight. He may do something to tip us off."

"Let's hope something breaks," Buxton said. "His deadline is coming at us like a freight train. We need something to throw him off track before it hits us square in the face."

Chapter 36

Nina sank back in the van's cushioned seat, grateful for Buxton's generosity. Arranging for a driver and one of the Bureau's nicest fleet vans provided the space and privacy they needed to move the investigation forward while in transit.

"Let's flesh out the profile," Kent said to Wade. "We'll have more to give the team working on the MMA fighters."

"We can be more definitive about his age now," Wade said. "Based on the years the clinic was open for business, he's between thirty-two and thirty-four years old."

Which meant the Cipher had been anywhere from twenty-one to twenty-three years old when he had attacked her eleven years ago. Had she really been his first victim? She kept her thoughts to herself, listening to the two profilers bounce ideas off each other.

Kent flicked a glance at Breck, who was sitting beside him. "The computer-generated image from his DNA profile and Guerrera's memory also tells us he's a white male, approximately six feet tall, with fair skin and blue eyes. That would match his sister's coloring."

"What's the fastest way to narrow down Sorrentino's list?" Nina cut in, anxious to move the discussion from theory to actionable information. "Any red meat for the task force to chew on?"

Wade spoke quickly. "Once they eliminate everyone who's not in the correct age range, doesn't match the physical description, and wasn't fighting during the attacks, they should look for a man who's not in a stable relationship, is a loner, and has a job well below his capabilities despite his IQ."

Kent nodded. "His temper would prevent career advancement."

"He will be aggressive toward others in the club," Wade continued. "Even in the locker room. He's arrogant and lets everyone know he's superior. He'll also really get off on the crowd's reactions. They should look up fan favorites."

"He had to keep a low profile when he was the Beltway Stalker," Kent said. "So he probably fed off the spectators during his matches, but now that he's changed his MO, he doesn't have to hide anymore. The need for adulation has always been a part of his character, though."

"He needs adulation?" Nina said, curious about this aspect of her adversary. He had always seemed supremely confident to her.

"Despite his arrogance and feeling of superiority, he's deeply inse-cure," Wade said. "Which makes him want to dominate everyone around him. Violence in the cage matches is a way for him to assert control over other men, but there is no socially acceptable way for him to physically dominate women." He raised his brows. "And he feels a lot of anger toward females."

"Why?" She wondered what could have driven him to such rage.

"He might have been rejected by girls beginning at a fairly young age, he may have watched his father abuse his mother and came to believe that's how women should be treated, or his mother could have mistreated him." Kent lifted a shoulder. "Whatever the family dynamics were, it's safe to assume he had a dysfunctional relationship with either one or both adoptive parents."

Unable and unwilling to delve deep enough to empathize with a sadistic killer, she left the profilers to their skull digging. She sidled onto the bench seat next to Breck, who had already sent the updated computer-generated image to the task force and was munching her way through a bag of mixed nuts.

She remembered her vow to get to the bottom of the rhyming clue before they arrived. "Can you pull up that poem? I'd like to see if anything we discovered today jars something loose."

"Sure." Breck seemed happiest with her laptop up and running. She propped it open so Nina could see and clicked an icon on the desktop.

Nina read the verses again.

IN SILENCE SHE WAITS, DAY AND NIGHT.

LIVING WITH THE KEEPER OF THE LIGHT.

SHE SEES THEM COME, SEES THEM GO.

WHAT LIES IN HER HEART, NO ONE CAN KNOW.

"Not exactly iambic pentameter," Breck said.

"The Crypto team said they thought the second line might refer to a lighthouse keeper," Nina said, recalling their previous meeting. "Why don't you google famous US lighthouses?"

They both scanned a long list of structures from Washington's Puget Sound to Florida's Key West. The number of options was daunting.

"Let's start with the East Coast," Nina suggested.

A few more clicks still left them with scores of lighthouses to consider.

Breck shook her head. "I feel like a bloodhound with a sinus infection trying to follow this trail of clues."

Nina privately agreed but decided to keep after it. "Can you pass me some of those nuts? I'm starving."

Breck handed her the bag. "I already ate all the pecans. They're the only things in there worth having, far as I'm concerned."

"I'm not picky. Learned to eat whatever was put in front of me as a kid." Going from home to home, sometimes not getting enough, had cured her of any fussiness about food.

"Not me. I'd rather go hungry."

Nina figured only someone who had never experienced true hunger would say that.

"Take this for example." Breck held up a peanut. "People think I love peanuts because I'm from Georgia. One peanut farmer is elected president, and suddenly everyone from our state must be crazy for the damn things." She let out a derisive snort. "Real southerners know the only way a peanut's any good is if it's boiled in the shell in salt water. Otherwise, eat the pecans first."

"I tried pecan pie once," Nina said. "Can't say I cared for it."

"Bless your heart," Breck said. "You must have gotten your teeth into something from the freezer section at the grocery store." She shuddered. "And it couldn't have been a real pecan pie unless it came fresh from the oven and there was bourbon in it."

"Bourbon?"

"That's how they make it in Savannah, where I'm from. In fact, if you want to taste the best bourbon pecan pie, you've got to go to the Pirate's House Restaurant next to the Savannah River, it's . . ." Breck trailed off, mouth open, eyes wide. "Oh. My. Gawd."

Nina grabbed her arm. "What?"

"Hold on a sec." She typed furiously, then a huge smile crept across her rosy cheeks as she pushed the computer closer to Nina.

A picture of a statue filled the screen. Nina studied the young lady and dog memorialized in bronze. The girl's arms were above her head, holding something that looked like a flag billowing in the wind.

"This has to be it," Breck whispered. "Damn. My mama would never have forgiven me if I hadn't come up with this."

"Come up with what?" Wade said. He and Kent had no doubt heard the excitement and were eager to hear what was going on.

Breck looked up at them, green eyes bright. "This is a statue of Florence Martus, the *Waving Girl*."

Kent crossed his arms. "Pretend we've never heard of Florence Martus and loop us in."

Breck pointed at the first line of the poem as she explained. "For over forty years, Florence greeted every ship that came into the port of Savannah. In the day she waved a cloth in greeting, at night, she used a lantern."

Nina reread the opening.

IN SILENCE SHE WAITS, DAY AND NIGHT.

Breck's finger moved to the second line. "She never married, and lived with her brother, who was the Elba Island lighthouse keeper."

LIVING WITH THE KEEPER OF THE LIGHT.

Nina caught Breck's enthusiasm as she skipped to the next part.

SHE SEES THEM COME, SEES THEM GO.

"Florence waved at ships whether they were coming into the harbor or setting out to sea," Breck continued. "'See' is a homonym for sea."

"And the last line?" Nina asked as she read.

WHAT LIES IN HER HEART, NO ONE CAN KNOW.

Breck's smile grew wider. "Legend has it that Florence never married because she fell in love with a sailor who promised to come back for her someday, but never did. No one knows if there's any truth to that, though."

"What lies in her heart, no one can know," Nina said. "It all fits."

"Let's contact the task force," Wade said. "We need someone from the Savannah field office to get over to that statue pronto." He tugged his phone from his pocket and handed it to Breck, allowing her to take the credit.

"I'll call Savannah now," Buxton said over the phone's speaker after hearing her rapid-fire explanation. "We'll have an answer shortly. I'll get back to you right away."

They batted ideas back and forth while they waited, trying to figure out how the Cipher could have gotten from Boston to Savannah so quickly. They concluded that he would have had to fly. As they were debating the best way to track down possible flights and airports, the phone buzzed.

"Wade here."

Buxton's voice betrayed his excitement. "Bingo."

The single word gave Nina more hope than she'd felt in days. "What did they find?"

"I sent a JPEG to Agent Breck's email," Buxton said. "It was on a sheet of standard office paper sealed in an envelope taped underneath the statue's platform. The local ERT is processing it for forensic evidence as we speak. In the meantime, they made a copy for us to examine."

Breck clicked open the FBI's private server and opened the file in her email. "Got it." She zoomed in.

Nina took in the magnified image. A square consisting of a frag-mented mosaic of jagged lines with sharp angles filled the top portion of the card. Each segmented space contained printed numbers.

"The cryptanalysts think it contains a hidden picture," Buxton said. "They're working on it now, but you're welcome to try your luck on the rest of the drive."

"Unlike the poem, this looks like it involves math, so they'll likely be quicker at solving it," Breck said, disappointment evident in her tone. "Every shape inside the lines has a different number in it."

"And there are hundreds of numbers," Buxton said.

"We'll work on it until we get there, which will be in about another hour," Nina said.

"As Agent Breck pointed out, this looks like more of a problem for the cryptanalysts." Buxton's tone brooked no argument. "You all have done enough for one day. I'll see you at the morning briefing tomorrow. I want all of you rested and on your game." He paused. "And one more thing. Pack a fresh go-bag before you come in. You'll be wheels up or on the road again the moment we crack the new code."

Chapter 37

Nina had scaled the last flight of stairs to find Bianca waiting for her. Again. The girl must have a camera set up to monitor her assigned parking space in the lot. Nothing Bianca did would surprise her.

She went through her usual routine of unlocking the door and deactivating the alarm before tossing her briefcase in the minuscule foyer, where it leaned against the wall. Bianca followed her inside.

"All of the Cipher's social media sites are back up again," Bianca said without preamble. "Not smart, if you ask me."

Nina raised a brow. "I know you don't like it, Bee, but we need the Cipher back online. Cyber Crime can shut him down again if they need to."

She'd checked the Cipher's social media sites on the way to her apartment. He hadn't posted the clue that would lead to the *Waving Girl* statue in Savannah yet. At least they were still ahead of the Scoobies so far.

"Well, don't blame me." Bianca pushed the open laptop across Nina's kitchen table to face her. "His Facebook leaderboard is getting more views than ever."

"Hold on." Nina leaned forward, spotting something she hadn't noticed before. "Why is the FBI on this list?"

She remembered when Breck had first shown her the unsub's ranking of the top five people or groups participating in his "game." Julian

Zarran still held the top spot, followed by Team FBI in second place and the Brew Crew in third. The Pink Wave had been replaced by the team that had previously been at the bottom.

"I guess he wanted to include the feebs, so he gave you guys a name and slotted you in," Bianca said.

"And who is this in fourth place? A group of college students from GW. They call themselves the Dork Side."

Bianca glanced away. "No idea."

"Sounds like a name you and your friends would come up with." Nina narrowed her eyes. "And, last time I checked, you go to George Washington University."

"Okay, fine." Bianca threw up her hands. "It's us."

"How did you get on his leaderboard?"

"The Brew Crew did it by solving a clue, and Zarran did it by offering a reward," Bianca said. "Everyone else on the list basically posted in his thread and retweeted with comments about how they were going to nail his ass."

Bianca might have an IQ in the vicinity of Einstein's, but she was no match for a psychopath. "Leave him alone," Nina said. "He's—"

A knock at the door interrupted before she could get into full rant mode. Cursing, Nina stood to open it.

Mrs. Gomez held out a glass casserole dish filled with empanadas. "For you," she said and marched inside past Nina.

"Mrs. G, you really shouldn't have. I'm not that hungry." She glanced at the dish Mrs. Gomez had now placed in the center of the table. The aroma of meat marinated in adobo sauce was intoxicating. "And even if I were, that's enough food for a family of ten."

"She cooks when she's upset," Bianca said. "She hasn't left the kitchen since the video came out."

Mrs. Gomez gave Bianca a dark look but said nothing.

"You may as well take it," Bianca said. "She's made something for everyone in the building."

"You need to eat," Mrs. Gomez said. "Keep up your strength."

As Mrs. Gomez pointed at the steaming tray piled with half-moon-shaped pastries, Nina noticed her puffy red-rimmed eyes and the dark circles underneath them.

Nina reached out to touch her arm. "Don't worry about me, Mrs. G."

"*Ay, mi'ja,*" Mrs. Gomez said, voice trembling. "I cannot stand to see what that *cabrón* did to you."

"Why don't you sit with us?" Nina said.

Mrs. G fished out a tissue from the pocket of her apron and blew her nose. "I have food in the oven." She headed for the door, paused, and turned back to Nina. "If the empanadas do not make you feel better"—she pulled a pint of tequila from the other apron pocket and plunked the bottle on the table next to the casserole—"try this." She burst into tears and left.

Nina turned to Bianca. "What the hell?"

"That's what I've been dealing with since that video came out." Bianca gave her a wry smile. "She thinks you're her foster daughter, too, you know."

Nina quickly shut down the warmth spreading through her, switching to suspect interrogation, which felt far more familiar to her than motherly concern.

She leveled her best no-nonsense glare on Bianca. "We were discussing how you and your team are going to drop out of this investigation."

"Um . . . no," Bianca said. "We were talking about how much I've already helped. Seriously, I should be on the FBI's payroll. How else would you know about the latest in Cipherdom?"

Nina rolled her eyes. Great, a new word added to the internet lexicon. "What now?"

"You know that doofus in Boston who tried to sell the envelope he found taped to a trash can by putting it up for auction on eBay?"

She nodded. "You showed me the listing."

"The Cipher just posted the clue on his wall," Bianca said. "With a comment that the FBI shouldn't be allowed to keep it secret. Says it's not fair play."

Nina groaned. All the effort that went into tracking down the eBay seller and recovering the envelope had only bought them a twenty-hour head start. They'd used the time to locate the picture puzzle the Cipher had placed in Savannah, but how long would he wait before posting that online as well?

Chapter 38

Nina sat in the corner of the crowded task force room at the monitor beside the Cyber team, the morning's first cup of coffee resting on the table beside the mouse pad. She glowered at the screen as she read the message.

CIPHER: *DID U THINK U COULD CHEAT AND HIDE IT FROM MY FANS? I DECIDE WHAT TO RELEASE AND WHEN TO RELEASE IT. NOT U, WARRIOR GIRL.*

Four hours earlier, before dawn, a team of Scoobies had figured out the Cipher's poem referred to the *Waving Girl* statue and promptly went online to complain that no additional clue was planted there. Within minutes, the Cipher had responded by posting the picture puzzle on Facebook, Instagram, Twitter, and Pinterest.

"Every time we get ahead, the sonofabitch levels the playing field," Kent said.

"Because he wants the chaos," Wade said. "He needs cover for what he's doing, and that means a crowd. If someone in the public doesn't figure it out soon, he'll post the solution to the picture puzzle right before or after he strikes again to cause maximum confusion."

"Which means we need to solve the damn thing first so we can get the jump on him," Kent said.

"Crypto's been on it all night." She glanced over to the opposite corner. "I hope they're getting close."

Kent followed her gaze. "In the meantime, we need to keep him occupied."

Nina began typing. "How about this?"

FBI: *WE HAVE AN ENTIRE TASK FORCE ON YOUR TRAIL. WE WILL CATCH YOU.*

CIPHER: *NOT IF I CATCH U FIRST, WARRIOR GIRL.*

"He's trying to rattle you," Kent said. "Stay on message."

FBI: *YOU CAN TURN YOURSELF IN WITH YOUR ATTORNEY. NO HARM WILL COME TO YOU.*

CIPHER: *U THINK I'M SCARED OF U? OF THE FBI? DR. JEFFREY WADE HAS LEARNED NOTHING FROM HIS MISTAKE.*

Frowning, Wade stepped closer. "Type exactly what I say."

Nina obliged.

FBI: *THIS IS DR. WADE. WHAT MISTAKE ARE YOU REFERRING TO?*

CIPHER: *TWO WORDS: CHANDRA BROWN.*

Wade swore. "He's taunting me now."

Kent nudged her shoulder. "Go ahead and ask him about Chandra."

After giving both profilers a long look, she made her next message short and to the point.

FBI: *DID YOU KILL HER?*

CIPHER: *I HAVE ARRANGEMENTS TO MAKE. NO MORE TIME 4 TALK.*

He would not respond to any further messages.

Nina pushed away from the keyboard. "He's toying with us and wasting our time. He said the next one would die in four days. It's already been three."

"Which makes me wonder," Kent said. "Why this new break in pattern? In the past, his clues have always led directly to a body."

"It was a distraction," Wade said. "He must need extra time to get the next victim lined up."

Nina pictured the Cipher out in the streets, hunting. He had them chasing their tails while he was stalking another girl. Frustration gnawed at her.

"Each clue gets progressively more difficult," Wade said. "The first was a rudimentary substitution cipher. The next operated on the same principle but added an extra layer of calculation and flipped part of the code. After that, we get a rhyming couplet, a complete departure for him. This time, he gives us something that seems to combine art and mathematics."

"He's showing off," Kent said.

"I agree," Buxton said. He had come up behind them. "I was following the direct messages. He's jerking us around while he stages his next kill. We have all the manpower we need, what we are running out of is time. I'd like to brainstorm some ideas about how to proceed with the investigation now that we have a better handle on who we're dealing with." He swept his arm toward the massive space and the scores of personnel at their workstations. "We have resources, let's use them."

"Can we try another search for the Cipher's biological parents?" Nina asked. "Did the Borr Project include prospective donors from around the world, throughout the US, or just in the DC area?"

"We don't know," Kent said. "There's no way to continue the search."

"We might get some new leads if we told the public about the Borr Project connection," Breck said, joining their discussion. "But how much do we tell the public at this point in the investigation, if anything?"

Buxton looked like he needed an antacid. "I don't want to release information about the Borr Project unless we absolutely have to." He raised his eyes to the ceiling. "Imagine how the bloggers and tweeters and conspiracy theorists would react. Rumors would run rampant about superpredators stalking young girls." He shook his head. "And the other grown children from the project who are now perfectly normal adults could get a lot of blowback they don't deserve."

It was similar to what Dr. Borr's son had told them, and she agreed but privately felt they were on borrowed time until the information leaked, especially now that various field office agents around the country had interviewed children of the Borr Project.

She was preparing to discuss this with the group when the lead cryptanalyst, Otto Goldstein, charged over to them, practically vibrating with intensity.

"Give me some good news about that picture puzzle," Buxton said, a hint of desperation in his voice.

Goldstein beamed, his thick wire-rimmed glasses glinting under the fluorescent lights. "We solved it."

Chapter 39

Nina sat next to Wade at the small table across from Kent and Buxton. Breck sat across the aisle, her laptop propped on a tray table unfolded from her armrest.

Buxton was pressing buttons on the in-flight television's remote. "National news," he mumbled, flicking through the channels until he found the one he wanted.

Nina recognized Amy Chen, the senior anchor. The crawl below her stated BREAKING NEWS. SCIENTIST CLAIMS MILLION DOLLAR REWARD.

"Next, we'll hear from the scientist who cracked the code," Chen said into the camera. "With me in studio is retired FBI Executive Assistant Director Shawna Jackson for an insider's take on the progress of this high-stakes investigation. All this and more as we bring you continuing coverage, right after the break."

"Shawna cleared everything with me before she agreed to go on," Buxton said over the drone of a dishwashing detergent commercial. "Given what she did for us, I could hardly ask her not to talk."

The network had contacted Shawna for comment an hour before when a scientist in California agreed to provide his solution to the Savannah puzzle in an exclusive live interview. Shawna had brokered a deal in which she agreed to discuss some of the particulars of the investigation in exchange for sitting on the story for an hour so Buxton and the Quantico team could get a head start toward the next destination. Buxton had asked Shawna to negotiate a twenty-four-hour hold, but the news channel had balked.

Chen was back on screen, Shawna sitting next to her.

"Before we speak to the former executive assistant director," Chen began, "let's hear from Dr. Charles Farnsworth, who studies spectroscopy in his California research lab." The screen split to reveal a heavyset man with a receding hairline and bushy mustache. "Tell us, Dr. Farnsworth, how did you discover the meaning behind the clue, and what is the answer?"

Farnsworth's cheeks grew ruddy as he stared blankly at the camera.

"Dr. Farnsworth?"

Nina recognized the signs of stage fright. The man had obviously just realized his fifteen minutes of fame were upon him, and he was nowhere near prepared.

Chen threw him a lifeline. "Perhaps you could tell us about your work first?"

Chen hadn't made it to the top of her profession without learning how to coax a nervous interviewee.

Farnsworth appeared relieved. "I study the interaction between matter and electromagnetic radiation," he said.

Chen looked like she was fighting a massive eye roll. "Can you put that in layman's terms, Doctor?"

"I study the light spectrum."

"Okay, and how did that help you with the clue?"

Farnsworth, now started, warmed to his subject. "The three-digit numbers inside the lines represent the electromagnetic waves, as expressed in terahertz, of the frequency interval of colors detectable by the human eye."

Chen blinked, then spoke with exaggerated patience. "Doctor, most of our viewers don't study light. Could you say it more directly?"

Farnsworth thought a moment. "Each number represents a shade of color."

"Thank you, Doctor." Chen smiled, apparently finished with the scientist's technobabble and ready to drop her bombshell on a waiting audience. "We used Dr. Farnsworth's findings to fill in the spaces on the diagram," she said, facing the audience again as the split screen went momentarily dark. "Here's what the picture reveals."

Nina leaned forward along with the rest of her team as the stylized image of a bright orange-red bird against a backdrop of blue and green filled the screen. Yellow flames blazed out from its wings and tail feathers.

"Looks like a phoenix bird to me," Chen said, turning to Shawna. "Retired Executive Assistant Director Jackson is close to Nina Guerrera and has been in touch with the team from Quantico. What do they think about the picture?"

"They're operating under the assumption that it's a phoenix," Shawna said.

"What will they do now?"

"First, they need to determine what location this refers to. There are cities named Phoenix in Arizona, Illinois, Louisiana, Maryland, Michigan, New York, and Oregon. And that's only in the US."

"Surely he's referring to Arizona," Chen said, frowning. "It's the only big city in the group."

"It seems likely," Shawna said. "But we're covering all bases."

Nina tore her eyes from the monitor to look at Wade, who had been the one to recommend Arizona as the most likely location. He had studied the Cipher's past patterns and—like Chen—had concluded that he seemed to prefer large cities where he could blend in. Nina thought she caught a wistful smile on Wade's face as he focused on Shawna.

"I also see this clue doesn't provide specifics about where the killer will strike," Chen said.

"In the past, he named the exact spot where a body was recovered," Shawna said. "This time, it's a whole city, and—if it turns out to be Phoenix, Arizona—that means over five hundred square miles of urban and desert terrain."

"Seems like he's being more deceptive. There's no way to cover that kind of area." Chen gestured toward the camera. "What can the public do to help the FBI?"

"Report any suspicious behavior," Shawna said. "We have an eight-hundred number set up."

"Here we go," Kent said. "Twenty thousand calls from cranks, conspiracy theorists, and psychics communing with the dead girls' spirits . . . and maybe—just maybe—one valid lead somewhere in the mix."

Chen touched her ear, eyes widening. "Our social media team is reporting a new post on the Cipher's Facebook page." Chen gave a curt nod, then turned back to the camera. "We're putting it up now. Some people may find this image disturbing. We advise viewer discretion."

Nina looked at the picture that had suddenly filled the screen. A young girl clutching a large poster board had been photographed from the neck down to her waist, only her bare hands and a thin section of her stomach visible to the camera. On the white surface of the board, bold block letters scrawled in black marker conveyed a message.

COME AND GET ME, WARRIOR GIRL.

I HAVE SIX HOURS TO LIVE.

Nina felt the weight of everyone's gaze upon her in the confines of the plane. As Wade and Kent had said, the Cipher's obsession with her was driving him. He had begun with her and he would keep going until he ended with her. He did not want to merely kill her—he wanted to possess her, control her, and finally, utterly destroy her.

Her. Nina Guerrera. Warrior Girl.

She glanced up to see Kent narrow his eyes at her, no doubt reading the resolve in her expression and interpreting it correctly. He mouthed the word *no*, slowly shaking his head.

But she had already made up her mind. Girls had been killed in DC, San Francisco, and Boston. This time, there was a live victim. Someone who could be saved. Whatever it took, Phoenix would not become another killing ground for the Cipher.

Chapter 40

Nina scanned the high-tech EOC. Colocated with the fire department's training academy, the new facility featured state-of-the-art technology. FBI agents from the Phoenix field office mingled with detectives and patrol supervisors as well as brass from the Phoenix PD. An array of civilian technical and support personnel milled throughout the expansive space—a typical war-room scenario she was becoming all too familiar with.

As in Boston, she had been paired with a local police detective, this time from the PPD Homicide unit. Her new partner, Javier Perez, had an athlete's build showcased in gray dress slacks and a navy polo shirt. His thick black hair and caramel skin matched her own. He was the polar opposite of Delaney, the burly Irish cop from Boston.

Thanks to the tip line, hundreds of calls had swamped the center as soon as the news story aired. Scores of detectives, agents, and patrol officers had been assigned to follow up on the more promising leads funneled to the EOC from call takers manning the lines.

Like the other teams, Nina and Perez had been handed a stack of lead sheets. Buxton had flagged her down before she headed out. She'd quickly scanned the sheet he handed her. The caller had identified herself as a sixteen-year-old girl living in a shelter, checking off two of the Cipher's criteria for victims. Then she'd indicated her friend had gone missing after getting into an RV with a stranger. Finally, she'd said she thought she recognized a tribal tattoo around the ankle of the girl who was holding the sign. Her missing friend had the same body art. The hairs had gone up on the back of Nina's neck when she read it.

"My ride's in the lot," Perez said. "You need anything else before we head out?"

She picked up a leather portfolio from the table. "I'm good."

As she followed him toward the door, Kent stepped in front of her. He lowered his voice. "Don't do it."

"Do what?"

"Whatever you were thinking of on the airplane. I saw the look on your face."

"Don't know what you're talking about."

"The unsub wants you to do something reckless. To make a mistake."

"Perez and I are going to check out our leads. Same as you and your partner."

He shot a glare in Perez's direction. "I don't like the look of him."

"Good thing you're not assigned with him, then."

Perez joined them. "Is there a problem?"

The two men gave each other appraising looks.

She rolled her eyes. "When you two are done thumping your chests, I'll be in the parking lot."

Perez caught up to her in the hallway. She noticed him eyeing her speculatively, but he said nothing until he stopped beside a black Tahoe in the first row of parking spaces.

"The shelter isn't far from here," he said as he walked around to the driver's door.

After buckling herself in, she opened her portfolio to pull out the call-in sheet Buxton had given her. "Interview subject is Emma Fisher, a sixteen-year-old currently staying at the downtown shelter for women and girls with her mother."

Perez pulled onto the street. "Does Emma's mother know she called in the tip?"

Nina scanned down the page. "Don't think so. Says Emma saw the story on the news and asked to use the phone at the front desk." She glanced over at Perez. "I'll bet she doesn't want her mother to know she was out last night."

Perez nodded. "How do you want to handle the interview?"

"I'll take the lead. She might feel more comfortable talking to a woman."

"Got it," he said, grinning. "I'll be the strong, silent type."

Within ten minutes, they arrived at a one-story mission-style adobe building on one of the smaller side streets. After parking in a space reserved for law enforcement, they pushed through the glass doors of a vestibule and walked to the front desk.

"Are you with the police?" a birdlike older woman with a short gray bob asked.

Nina flipped open her creds. "I'm Special Agent Guerrera, and this is Detective Perez."

The woman's eyes widened over rectangular spectacles. "Guerrera . . . you're Nina Guerrera?" Her slender hand fluttered to her chest. "Oh my."

Nina felt a hot flush burn through her. Like so many others, this woman had been following the story. Which meant she'd probably seen the video. She cut her eyes to Perez, and the heat intensified as she realized that he had as well. This was her new reality.

She straightened. "Where can we speak privately with Emma Fisher?"

The woman recovered. "I'll have one of the staff escort her to an interview room. We have several." She picked up a portable radio from the desk.

Nina stood silently by, refusing to make eye contact with Perez.

"Go ahead to room three," the woman said, pointing to her left. "Emma will be there shortly."

They headed down a wide corridor to a row of small rooms lining the interior wall. Room three was unlocked, and Perez trailed her inside. The room was Spartan, with a threadbare love seat on one side and two thinly upholstered chairs on the other.

"Hello?" A timid female voice sounded from the open doorway.

Nina turned to see a girl whose kohl-rimmed eyes added a hardened look to her otherwise youthful face. "Emma?"

The girl nodded, and Nina gestured toward the love seat. "I'm—"

"I know who you are," Emma said.

Nina fought the rising heat again and gestured to her side. "This is Detective Perez. We'd like to ask you a few questions about your phone call. Is your mother around?"

Emma sat down. "Mom's passed out in bed."

"Okay," Nina said. "Do you mind if we record this interview?"

Emma shrugged.

"I need you to answer out loud," Nina said as Perez put a digital recorder on the scarred oak coffee table between them. "For the record."

"Yeah, you can record this."

"Why don't you start by telling me what happened yesterday evening?"

"Trina got into this huge fight with her mom."

"Who is Trina?"

"Trina Davidson. I just met her about a week ago, and we kind of started hanging out because we're, like, the only girls here who aren't in diapers."

Nina nodded. "What time was this argument last night?"

"About nine or so. After the blowout, Trina and me decided to go outside to um . . . hang."

Nina flicked a glance at the nicotine stains yellowing Emma's chipped nails. "You wanted to smoke."

"Whatever." She waved the comment away. "Anyway, we go around the corner, but Trina only has one cig left, so I go to the Circle K across the street to buy another pack. I'm waiting in line at the counter, and I look out the window and see this guy walk up to Trina."

"What did he look like?"

"Biker dude." Emma slid her hands up and down her arms. "He was tatted up, like from his shoulders to his wrists. His head was shaved, and he had a black goatee."

Nina slid her eyes to Perez. This was nothing like any of the previous descriptions. But then again . . .

"How big was he?" Nina asked.

"Tall and pretty buff." Emma jerked her chin at Perez. "Like him."

"What did he do when he approached Trina?"

"Handed her another smoke. Talked to her. She smiled a lot. I think she was kind of into him."

"What happened next?"

"The stupid woman at the counter was taking forever with my cigarettes. Couldn't find my brand. So I asked for something else."

Nina suppressed a groan. "With Trina."

"Oh, right. She went with him to this big motor home–looking thing parked in that empty lot next door."

"You say a motor home," she asked. "You mean like an RV?"

"Yeah, like the kind people live in when they drive around the country. It was all black, even the windows. Creeped me out, don't know why."

Because your survival instincts kicked in, Nina thought.

"What happened next?" she said.

"Trina went inside the RV with him, and I went back to the shelter." Her eyes grew moist. "That's the last I saw of her."

"Did you tell anyone about it last night?"

"No. I thought maybe Trina really liked this guy. I don't know."

"So when did you decide you should say something?"

"This morning." Twin black trails of eyeliner slid down Emma's cheeks as the tears began. "I was watching the TV in the dining area, and that scientist guy talked about the clue being a phoenix bird. I knew it was about this city. I just knew it." She choked back a sob. "Then I saw the picture of that girl holding the sign, and I recognized her tattoo. I mean, a lot of people have tribal tattoos around their ankles, but Trina's is exactly like the one on TV. Just to be sure, I looked around for her, and she wasn't at breakfast, so I checked with her mom."

"What did her mom say?"

"Trina never came in last night. Her mom figured she ran away for the zillionth time. I didn't say anything about it to her. I just went to the front desk and asked to use the phone. They made me tell them why, and I said I had a tip for the eight-hundred number."

"Did you see the RV drive away last night?" Nina said.

"No. I checked the parking lot this morning. It's gone."

Nina plucked a tissue from a box on the end table and held it out. "Some detectives will come by soon to follow up with you. I'm very glad you called, Emma. You did the right thing."

"No, I didn't." Emma snatched the tissue. "If I'd done the right thing, I would have called someone sooner. Like last night. Now she's probably dead. And it's my fault."

"Don't blame yourself. You called. That's what's important right now." She thought of something. "Speaking of calls, does Trina have a cell phone?"

With luck, they could ping her signal and get a location.

"Nobody here can afford a cell. That's why I had to use the phone at the front desk to call you guys."

"Can you give us any more information about the biker? Would you be able to draw any of his tattoos or describe them in detail? Were there any specific words or images you remember?"

"It was dark, and I was pretty far away. I couldn't see anything specific."

"What about a license plate or any designs on the RV?"

"Like I said, it was dark." She pursed her lips. "Look, I've told you everything I know. Shouldn't you be out looking for her?"

Nina stood. "I know you're concerned about Trina, and so are we. We've got to follow up on what you've told us. The other detectives will want to talk to you, your mom, and Trina's mom too."

"Trina's mom will kill me." Emma crossed her arms. "She's mean."

"No one will kill you. I'm sure she'll understand."

Emma looked doubtful. "Will you tell me if you find Trina?"

"We'll get word to you."

After repeated assurances that responding police would prevent Trina's mother from throttling her, they walked out together. Nina stood by as Perez called the EOC to update them and request a follow-up interview and support services for Emma and Trina's mother.

Nina heard him ask for a contact check for a black RV. "Good idea. If we get lucky, someone who illegally parked an RV in a city-owned lot might park it somewhere else they shouldn't."

"Or he could have gotten a traffic ticket," Perez said. "Worth a try."

Nina gave him an appreciative nod. "The Cipher wouldn't have any reason to suspect we'd be looking for a motor home. He doesn't know Emma saw him talking to Trina, much less taking her inside an RV."

"*If* this is our guy in another disguise," Perez said. "But it could be some other *cochino* pervert."

She agreed that any adult who lured a juvenile was filthy and disgusting, and knew that a lot of girls had ankle tattoos, but she sensed this was the Cipher. Felt it in her bones. "Is there an RV campground close by?"

"Not anywhere near downtown."

"Where would you go if you had an RV and you wanted to hold someone against their will inside? Where is there a lot of open space and privacy from prying eyes?"

"The RV grounds in the nearby cities are crowded. The vehicles are packed in tight together."

"What about parks?"

"Not allowed overnight," he said. "The parks close at dark."

"If this is the unsub, he'll have already worked something out. He planted that clue in Savannah to make sure our attention was focused on the other side of the country while he set up shop here."

Perez pulled a buzzing cell phone from his pocket. "It's the EOC." He toed a pebble on the loose, sandy ground while he listened. "Direct. Agent Guerrera and I will check it out." He disconnected and grinned at her. "Got a hit."

Perez filled her in as they drove away from downtown.

"Patrol unit in the Maryvale-Estrella precinct got a report of an illegally parked RV last night," Perez said, making his way through traffic. "Maryvale got hit hard during the recession. A lot of developers left empty lots behind when they cleared out."

"What did the patrol officer see?"

"Drove by and found the vehicle inside a fenced area. He spoke to the night watchman, who said the owner of the lot told him he'd given permission for the RV to park there for two days. So the officer wrote down the security guard's name and left."

"They're checking on the story?"

"The officer didn't enter the name of the security company. Someone in the EOC is tracking down the landowner now. Not an easy process. In the meantime, we can have a peek."

Nina grabbed the door handle as Perez took a corner a bit too fast. "Do you think the unsub got hinked out by the patrol unit and relocated?"

"The opposite," Perez said. "He probably figures the cops won't bother him again since they think he has permission to be there. It's private property, so he's more at risk from the Zoning Department than the police." He shrugged. "And by the time Zoning gets around to him, he plans to be long gone, so he's bought himself time and won't be in a hurry to leave."

Nina hoped Perez was right. During the drive to Maryvale, he told her about Phoenix and its quirky history. It was her first time in the Valley of the Sun, and she liked the city's Southwest vibe.

Perez pulled the Tahoe to a stop in front of a chain-link fence at the dead end of a deserted street. He hadn't been kidding about the recession. The area looked as if the builders had driven their backhoes and cement mixers away in the middle of the construction project. Over the years, mesquite and wiry shrubs had reclaimed the dusty lots.

An enormous black RV stood out against a backdrop of brown desertscape about twenty yards back from the fence.

Nina looked around. "You see any sign of the security guard?"

"Nope. Maybe he only works at night."

"This RV matches Emma's description," Nina said. "What do you think?"

Perez rested a hand on his hip. "We'll either find a runaway sixteen-year-old girl, or another one of the killer's victims."

She recalled her private vow to do whatever it took. Gritting her teeth, she rushed to the fence and ran her hand along the metal links. "Do you see an opening anywhere?"

"There's a gate, but it's padlocked."

She rattled the fence. "Pretty sturdy." She stuck her foot in and began to hoist herself up.

"I guess the FBI doesn't bother with minor details like search warrants," Perez said.

"Investigatory only," she said over her shoulder. "Not entering the vehicle."

He clambered over after her, his polished shoes thudding down in a cloud of dust beside her.

She crept closer to the vehicle. "The windows are all covered like Emma said. Not just curtains pulled, looks like something's blacking them out from the inside." She shook her head. "I don't like it." She started for the RV's door.

"What the hell are you doing?"

"I thought I heard something." She raised her voice. "Trina?"

A muffled bellow followed by rhythmic thumping emanated from the vehicle.

"It's got to be her," Nina said. "I think she's kicking something."

Perez grabbed his phone. "I'll call it in."

She pulled her gun from its holster. "Screw that." She had heard what sounded to her like a high-pitched, muffled cry. The sound a girl would make with a gag in her mouth. She didn't want to wait for backup.

Perez hesitated. "Agent Guerrera?"

"Now I have exigent circumstances." She marched toward the massive vehicle. "I'm going in."

"If he's in there with her, it's a hostage situation. We need tactical—"

"Cover the back window," she called over her shoulder as she reached the steps to the RV's door. As she extended a hand toward the latch, it occurred to her that this was exactly the kind of reckless action Kent had warned her about.

Chapter 41

Nina heard Perez cursing behind her as she tugged at the door's weathered latch. Locked. "FBI, open the door."

"Mmmmf!"

The response was followed by frantic thumping.

Nina raised her foot and kicked the metal door. She managed a dent, but it held. "Trina, is he inside with you?" She thought about a way to communicate. "Kick twice if you're alone."

Two kicks answered in rapid succession.

She turned to Perez. "I told you to cover the back window."

"I'm not letting you go in alone," he said. "Backup's on the way."

"I'm not waiting." She aimed another kick at the door. And another.

"Why don't you let me do that?"

Ignoring him, she delivered another kick. The door gave. Nina yanked it open and rushed up two interior steps into the main cabin. She heard a plaintive wail coming from the sleeping quarters in back.

"Go low," Perez whispered.

From the corner of her eye, she saw the barrel of his Glock slightly above her head. She crouched and edged forward, allowing him to take the higher stance and avoid a crossfire.

The divider separating the rear compartment was open, and Nina saw bare legs manacled spread-eagle on a queen-size bed that dominated the tight space. The shackles were bolted to the wall with heavy gauge steel eye hooks. Nina moved in closer, eyes darting in every direction before settling on the girl's face.

Tears streamed from beneath a black bandanna folded to cover her eyes and tied behind her head. Mucus slid down from her reddened nose to drip over two bands of silver duct tape covering her mouth. Her wrists were also shackled to eyehooks. Nina could see that one of her legs was close enough to the built-in bedside table to allow for the girl to kick it.

The girl shook her head from side to side. "Mmmmf!"

"Watch my back," Nina said over her shoulder as she holstered her weapon. "You're safe now." She offered reassurance as she approached the bed. "I'm Special Agent Nina Guerrera, FBI. I'm not going to let him hurt you anymore." She tugged the bandanna off, then grasped the tape and tore it away with a loud ripping sound.

The girl's eyes were wild with terror. "Help me!"

Nina focused on the most critical question. "Where is he?"

"He said he'd be right back," the girl said. "You've got to get me out of here."

The sound of sirens reached the vehicle.

"Tell them to cut their sirens," Nina said to Perez. "I want to get her out of here and catch him when he comes back."

"It's no good," Perez said. "Every available unit is on the way. And I saw people from another neighborhood down the street walking toward us. They'll have a tamale stand set up in twenty minutes."

The Cipher would see the crowd and slip away unseen. She closed her eyes and swore before turning back to the girl. "Where is the key to unlock the shackles?"

"He took the keys with him."

Nina heard the tinny sound of clanging metal outside as responding police officers scaled the chain-link fence.

"See if anyone has bolt cutters," she said to Perez.

After he left, she stroked the girl's cheek. She matched the description Emma had given, but Nina needed to be sure. "Are you Trina Davidson?"

She nodded. "Where's my mom?"

"She's at the shelter. The police will bring her to meet us when we leave."

"Where will you take me?"

"To the hospital. You need to be checked out."

Trina began to shiver. "Can you cover me with something?"

"Of course." She pulled off her raid jacket. She was draping it over Trina when Perez stuck his head in the door.

"Rescue's here. They have bolt cutters."

He disappeared and two EMTs tromped up the steps, filling the cramped space with their gear.

"Excuse me." One of them shouldered past her with an oversize set of shears in his hand. When he bent toward Trina's foot, she shrieked.

Nina put a hand on the EMT's forearm. "Hold on a sec."

She squeezed past him to kneel on the mattress next to Trina. "Look at me, honey."

Trina's gaze met hers.

"They're here to help you. We can't unlock the shackles, so we need to cut the metal part holding them to the wall."

Trina's eyes flicked back to the EMT and she whimpered.

"What's wrong, Trina?"

"Can you stay with me?" she whispered.

"I'll be right here. Just focus on me. Don't worry about what they're doing. I know this is not the best time, but I want to ask you some questions. Is that okay?"

It would serve the dual purpose of distracting Trina while gathering intel as quickly as possible to put out a BOLO for the Cipher.

At Trina's nod, Nina adopted a soothing tone. "What did he look like?"

257

"Like one of those biker guys. He was huge. Really strong. He had body art all down his arms, a shaved head, and a black goatee."

A loud metallic clank made Trina jump. The hook had snapped in half. One of Trina's feet was now free.

Nina asked for more details as the medic went to work on the other ankle. "What about his eyes?"

"Couldn't see them," Trina said. "He wore sunglasses."

Another loud pop of splitting metal and Trina was able to pull her legs together. The EMT moved to her wrist.

"How did he talk?" Nina asked. "What did he say?"

Trina shook her head vehemently. "I don't want to repeat the stuff he told me."

The third hook fell apart with a loud crack. Trina clutched her free hand to her chest, holding Nina's windbreaker.

"I'm sorry," the medic said. "But I have to get to her other wrist."

He leaned over Trina, who tucked her body into a ball under the jacket. Nina reached out a hand, and Trina squeezed it in a white-knuckled grip.

"Damn," the EMT said, grunting. "This one's at a bad angle. I'm sorry, but there's no other way for me to reach it." He moved his leg, straddling Trina between his knees to brace himself.

Trina thrashed hysterically.

Nina grabbed the medic's arm and hauled him off the girl. "What do you think you're doing?"

He let out an exasperated sigh. "Trying to cut her loose."

She kept her hold on his arm. "You need to find a different position."

A fragment of memory flickered in Nina's mind. The pressure of heavy masculine legs pinning her down. Trapping her. Eleven years ago, the monster had straddled her that way, keeping her still, forcing her to submit. He had probably done the same to Trina when he shackled her.

"I don't like this any more than you do," the EMT said. "But I don't see another way to cut that thing off." He held the shears out to her. "Maybe she'll do better with you."

She took the shears and looked down at Trina. The girl was wide eyed, batshit, full-on panicked. She would have to position her body over Trina's as the medic had done to get to the last manacle. Nina struggled to tamp down a distorted sense of déjà vu, reliving her own attack from both Trina's perspective and the Cipher's as she prepared to straddle the girl.

"Listen, I want to free you, but I can't do it unless you cooperate. Will you help me by lying still?"

Trina simply stared at her, unwilling or unable to speak.

Grasping the handles firmly, she leaned over the girl, lining up the sharp blades along the edge of the metal. She squeezed. After considerable effort, Nina was rewarded with a loud pop. Trina shot up, pushing Nina aside, struggling off the makeshift bed. The EMT grabbed her, feeding her hysteria, and Trina began flailing and clawing at him.

"Stop!" He grabbed the girl's wrists. "We're trying to help you."

Something deep within Nina snapped. She hauled her arm back and elbowed the paramedic in the shoulder. Hard.

He released his grip on the girl and rounded on Nina. "What the hell?"

She was way out of line but didn't care. She had reacted reflexively when she saw him grab Trina's wrists. The girl was traumatized, and his actions weren't helping. They were making things immeasurably worse.

Trina flung her arms around Nina's neck and sobbed. Nina figured she was done answering questions for the time being.

"Can you treat her in the ambulance?" Nina said to the EMT over Trina's shoulder, disregarding his outraged expression and keeping him on task. "I want to get her to the hospital before she goes into shock."

Nina urged the men to stand back and let her maneuver Trina to her feet. Supporting her with an arm around her waist, Nina took a blanket the second medic offered her and carefully arranged it to cover Trina's head like a hoodie, only leaving a small portion of her face visible.

"No one can see who you are," she said to Trina, who nodded.

They walked out to a sea of curious onlookers holding their cell phones aloft behind the yellow crime scene tape.

Nina heard them calling her name as they caught sight of her. She bustled Trina into the back of a waiting ambulance and told Perez she would ride with her to the hospital. The detective agreed to bring Trina's mother to meet them at the ER.

After the doors closed, the second medic sat in the back next to Nina. He smiled at Trina, trying to calm her as he took her vitals.

Satisfied with his care, she considered the situation. They would not catch the Cipher today, but at least he hadn't claimed another victim. Which brought another thought to mind as the ambulance bumped its way along the city streets. He would surely exact revenge for Trina's escape.

And when he saw video of Nina escorting the girl from the RV, he would know where to direct his fury.

Chapter 42

The spicy scent of carne asada mixed with sautéed onions and jalapeños wafted through the Emergency Operations Center. Nina returned Perez's grin as she sank her teeth into the juicy burrito. He'd arranged for a delivery from a restaurant called Casa Cruz Cocina, a South Phoenix place Perez had assured her had the best Mexican food in the city.

"More red sauce?" Kent asked, pulling her attention away from the handsome homicide detective.

"I'm good."

At the opposite end of the room, Buxton was deep in conversation with Steven Tobias, the Phoenix police chief. Carryout bags of Mexican food were spread down the center of the rectangular conference table. Everyone grabbed what they wanted and plopped it onto paper plates.

Buxton turned toward the group and raised his voice to carry over the conversational din. "Let's go over what we have so far. I'd like to start with the victim's statement." He gestured toward Nina. "Special Agent Guerrera took point on the interview at the hospital."

After the paramedics had pushed Trina's gurney into the ER and transferred her onto a hospital bed, nurses had descended upon them. Nina stayed through the onslaught of medical poking and prodding, noting Trina's responses to questions about various injuries on her body. She had done her best to keep the girl calm while a special nurse examiner administered the rape kit. The biggest challenge proved to be Trina's mother, who had swooped into the room like a banshee, screeching at everyone within earshot when she wasn't sobbing hysterically over her daughter's bed. Nina had been fortunate to have a few minutes alone with Trina to ask a few more questions before passing the investigatory baton to a Phoenix detective.

Conscious everyone was waiting for her report, Nina quickly swallowed and dabbed at her mouth with a paper napkin. "The victim is Trina Davidson, seventeen years old, temporarily living at the downtown women's shelter with her mother. She'd never seen the unsub before last night and had no prior contact with him on any social media platforms."

"Did she indicate why the unsub left her alone in the RV?" Buxton asked.

"She told me she tried to escape as he was shackling her to the bed. She took a swing at him, he blocked the punch, and her fist flew back and connected with a webcam clamped to a shelf above the bed. He went ballistic when it broke. She thinks he planned to livestream her murder."

She noticed Wade making notes in his tablet.

"He finished binding her to the bed and left—Trina assumes, but doesn't know—to find a replacement camera," Nina said. "She heard a motorcycle leaving but hadn't seen him riding one before."

Buxton looked around the table. "Do we have any info on the bike?"

Everyone shook their heads.

Nina continued, "The RV has a built-in minigarage. It's big enough for a bike or a Vespa, but it won't hold a car. The space was empty, but Forensics found where oil had dripped on the floor inside."

"Must have been riding a Harley," one of the Phoenix officers muttered. The detective next to him chuckled.

"He'd been gone about half an hour when Detective Perez and I showed up. Which means he probably came back to flashing lights and wailing sirens. My guess is he turned his bike around and got the hell out of there before he came anywhere near the scene."

Buxton nodded. "What else did the victim tell you about the suspect?"

"She said he wore black leather gloves the whole time. It's October, but here in Phoenix it's about eighty-five degrees out. He wouldn't wear them for the cold."

"He must know we have his DNA," Breck said, speaking up for the first time. "So why wear gloves?"

"Trying to hide his fingerprints?" Perez suggested.

Nina considered it. "Maybe they're in a criminal database somewhere."

"There are a lot of professions that require prints too," Wade said.

"When I was in the navy, they printed us," Kent said. "Maybe he's in the military."

"He used medical tape," Nina said, recalling another detail. "He taped a laceration on the girl's thigh. Guess he didn't want her to bleed out before he came back. Could he be a combat medic or a military doctor?"

"We'll get in touch with our contacts in the military to see if they can help," Buxton said. "But I'm not holding out much hope. Let's move on to the unsub's profile. How can we add to what we have?"

This question was aimed at Wade.

"I don't think this victim was preplanned like the others," Wade said. "He went to the RV rental place wearing his biker getup. Drove into the lot on a motorcycle . . . might have been a Harley." He directed a sardonic smile at the cop who had joked about the bike earlier. "Wanted to make sure it fit in the onboard minigarage. We haven't found the bike yet, so we don't know where he got it, but I'm assuming it's rented too. He's too smart to get pulled over on a stolen bike, and I doubt he rode it across the country from DC or Savannah."

"Why do you think he didn't target Trina specifically?" Buxton asked.

"My best guess is that he planned to stake out the shelter when Trina dropped into his lap," Wade said. "She was in his age range and demographic, and she just waltzes out right in front of him. When the other girl left her alone to buy cigarettes, he couldn't pass up the opportunity."

"A narcissist would probably think it was his due," Kent said. "He's so superior that he wouldn't get caught. He's smarter than the rest of us mere mortals."

Nina turned to Kent. "Where do you think that comes from?"

"He's likely been told since early childhood that he's special," Kent said. "That he's better. He begins to feel entitled. When things don't turn out the way he thinks they should, he would naturally look for someone to blame. It couldn't be that he simply didn't measure up. It must be someone else's fault. And that someone must be punished."

"What about the camera?" Buxton asked from the other end of the table.

Wade's thick gray brows drew together. "He feels like his audience is still growing, and he needs a bigger show. He hasn't got the thousand likes he demanded to air the next sixty seconds of the previous video, so he's creating a new one that he will post regardless. Only it doesn't work out."

Nina appreciated that Wade had referred to the video without mentioning her by name. Everyone in the room had no doubt seen it, but she didn't need the distraction of discussing it in front of them. Still, she took a sip of cold coffee from the paper cup in front of her to hide the flush heating her face.

"And you agree with Agent Kent that he will need to blame someone?" Buxton asked Wade.

"Blame and punish," Wade said. "A recurring theme for him. I believe he was punished severely as a child. Probably by a father figure. He vents his frustration on young girls, so something pivotal may have occurred during his adolescent years. Perhaps with a girl of that age, or perhaps with the parent who punished him. He became stuck in that phase of development and is fixated there in certain ways."

Buxton had opened his mouth to ask another question when an agent sitting next to him got his attention. "Sir, we've got activity on the unsub's Facebook page."

Chief Tobias called out to one of his computer techs. "Get it up on the screen."

The tech's fingers flashed over a keyboard, and one of the monitors mounted to the wall flickered from solid royal blue to the Cipher's page.

"Turn up the volume," Tobias said.

The silhouette of a cloaked male figure appeared in front of a plain white wall as the live-feed of a video began.

"She calls herself Warrior Girl," he said.

Icy dread spread through Nina at the sound of his voice.

"They call her a hero. But I know the truth."

The room fell completely silent. Every eye riveted to the screen.

"And now it's time for the world to know."

Nina's heart thudded. What could he be talking about?

"No one wanted her. Not even her parents. They tossed her in a dumpster. Threw her out with the garbage." He leaned forward. "Because Nina Guerrera is trash. And they knew it."

His deep chuckle shredded her nerves.

"What do you think of your hero now? Wait until you see her as I do. Nothing reveals character like pain, and, as you are about to see, she shows nothing but weakness."

Sweat prickled her scalp as she schooled her features. Aware some eyes in the room had covertly flicked in her direction, she held herself erect and kept her gaze straight ahead.

"I'm going to show you the rest of the video," the featureless dark shape said into the camera. "You will see exactly who you are holding up as an example for your daughters. You will watch her beg for mercy, grovel like a dog for her miserable life. She is no hero. She is a scared little girl." His voice dropped to a whisper. "A worthless throwaway."

The video ended, replaced by a freeze frame of Nina as a sixteen-year-old girl. The new feed began, picking up precisely where the previous one had ended. The monster pulled back the cigarette from the girl's bare flesh, leaving her gasping and sobbing on the steel table.

Nina's stomach roiled in protest. The room fell away and all she could see was the hideous spectacle playing out before her. Her breathing ticked up, matching that of her younger self, separate yet merged in agony.

"That was just the beginning," he said to the girl. "I have so much more planned for you." He bent forward and pressed the tip onto her other shoulder blade. He waited with infinite patience while she howled in pain, fighting desperately against her bonds. Then he burned her a third time, in the center of her lower back, the scorched circles of flesh forming a triangle. He dropped the cigarette to the floor and stood back, surveying his work with cold objectivity while she begged him to stop. Oblivious to her pleas, he moved closer and put his gloved hands around the girl's throat. Then he began to squeeze as he narrated for the camera.

"Breathing. A primal instinct." He spoke clinically, like an anatomy professor discussing bodily functions. "That's why waterboarding is so effective. The body becomes deprived of oxygen and fights to suck in more. But there is no air to be had. After a while, you begin to black out."

He eased his grip, and her body contorted as she struggled to fill her lungs with great heaving gulps.

"But then, you get a bit of air," he said. "Just enough to let you stay conscious . . . so you can fully experience the next time." He squeezed again. "If I keep this up, you will begin to spasm uncontrollably. Eventually, you will die." He let go and stepped away to watch her thrash. "But I don't want that. Not yet."

Without conscious thought, Nina grasped the edge of the conference table to steady herself. She felt the monster's large hands wrap around her throat, heard his voice echo in her head, sensed his evil presence surround her.

Suffocating her.

Nina staggered to her feet and lurched away from the table. She registered movement and saw Kent start to stand up. Wade grabbed his arm, pulling him back down into his chair.

"Let her go," Wade said to Kent. "Give her a moment."

The video still played on the screen. She turned away from it. Her leaden feet began to move faster, carrying her away from the ghastly show.

She pushed through the door and out into the hallway. Slumping against the wall, she slid down until her bottom met the smooth tile floor. Her head fell into her hands, tears gathering like a breaking storm.

She had promised herself she would never let him make her cry again. She had escaped from him eleven years ago, yet he had managed to torture her as if she were splayed naked in front of him again. The helplessness returned and along with it, the anguish of knowing that a monster controlled her. He decided whether she would take her next breath or not.

She began to shake. After a long moment, she realized she was no longer trembling with fear, but rage. She would not turn her power over to him. Never again. He was lashing out, trying to reclaim what had been lost to him. He blamed Nina for that loss and was meting out his punishment.

She felt that she was at a fork in the road. If her assumptions about the material from the fight club were correct, the Cipher was a fighter. He would keep hitting her, coming at her from all angles. Like the mixed martial arts combatants she had seen on television, he would constantly change his tactics, using a variety of techniques to keep her off balance.

She had been trained in judo, where a fighter uses his opponent's own momentum against him. She would have to try that approach to have any hope of defeating the Cipher. That meant allowing herself to open up, deliberately making herself vulnerable in order to find his weaknesses. For the second time that day, she recalled her silent vow.

Whatever it took.

So be it. She would defeat him. Or die trying.

Chapter 43

The Cipher stood and pulled the hooded raincoat off, letting it crumple to the carpeted floor. The Nina Guerrera show had ended, and he was aroused. He glanced at the old-fashioned mantel clock and forced his mind to the task at hand. No time to indulge himself. He walked toward the stairs to the upper floor, stepping over the body of the old man sprawled by the dining room table.

Half an hour ago, the codger had answered his knock at the front door. The old man's eyesight was better than expected, because he took one look at the man on his doorstep and tried to shut the door. The television had been blaring in the living room, and a fairly accurate composite sketch of the Cipher as a tatted-up biker dude was on the screen. A couple of sharp blows to the head had ended the old man's worries. Permanently.

He was pleased with his choice. After watching several different houses in the neighborhood, he'd found an elderly man's house. He'd been prepared to deal with a couple, but the man was apparently a widower. So much the better. No one would come home while he was still here.

He traipsed up the steps to the master bedroom, then padded into the bathroom and turned on the shower. While the water warmed, he peeled off his black leather gloves, revealing the blue nitrile pair underneath. He took off his clothes with practiced efficiency and stepped under the adjustable showerhead. The hot water sluiced down his scarred back. He wet a washcloth, wrung it out, and scrubbed his arms. The skin grew raw as all traces of the temporary tattoos swirled down the drain at his feet in a Technicolor vortex.

Why did old people always favor washcloths over loofahs? Perhaps the fabric was easier on their crepe-like skin, or maybe it was just a lack of ability to adapt. They had grown up with washcloths, and dammit, that's what they were going to use.

He slid a green-and-white bar of Irish Spring around on the wet cloth and went back to work. The warm water did not soothe him. Only one thing would placate him now.

Retribution.

He picked at his chin, peeling away the remnants of the glued-on goatee. Satisfied, he turned off the water and stepped out to examine the results in the wide bathroom mirror. He flexed, admiring the results years of hard training and fighting had wrought. His pale skin glistened with moist droplets that ran in rivulets over his well-defined muscles, powerful without unnecessary bulk. His body, now clean shaven from head to toe, was a blank canvas on which he could paint any persona he wished.

He toweled off and strode to the master closet. The old man had been stooped but tall. The brown corduroy slacks left his ankles exposed because he was even taller, all the better to show off the compression stockings stretched over his thick calves. The orthopedic shoes were a size too small but ensured he would remember to hobble slightly. Much more comfortable than the rock he had put in his shoe in Georgetown when he was disguised as a delivery man with a limp.

Thoughts of DC set his teeth on edge. The moment he saw her in that viral video, he'd planned this whole scheme. He had chosen the little Latina runaway to draw Nina into his game, where he made the rules and he decided on the outcome. For years he had thought about the girl he had known as Nina Esperanza, the one that got away.

Now, thanks to Nina, there were two. She had defied him twice, so she would have to pay twice. First, he would take someone dear to her. Then, he would take her.

She had seen what he did to the other girls, but they were strangers. No one close to her. That was about to change. But who? She had no family. Wasn't married.

That gave him pause. Had she not been with a man since him? Because of him? Had he altered her so deeply she could not bear a man's touch? He had asked her the question during their first direct message exchange, but she'd refused to answer him. He felt sure he was the only man who had ever touched her intimately. The thought threatened to reawaken his desire, and he tamped it down.

He finished buttoning the shirt and reached up for the flat cap resting on top of the dresser. Why did every old guy own one of these damn caps? Did they come in the mail with your AARP card? He pulled it onto his bald head, pleased to cover his scalp until his thick blond hair grew back in.

Next, he pushed the man's oversize blue-blocker glasses onto his nose, distorting the hue of his eyes. If the TSA wand wavers asked him to take them off, he'd rant about his glaucoma and threaten a lawsuit. He loved being a grumpy old man.

His former disguise lay on the bathroom floor, the discarded skin of a snake. He couldn't use the biker persona anymore, and he couldn't fly to DC with the same ID he'd used to get from Atlanta to Phoenix, which he'd left in the RV. Today's disguise would last a day or two, but it only took five hours to fly to Dulles airport, and then he would disappear.

He found the man's wallet on the dresser along with his car keys. Perfect. With enough orneriness, he could bluster his way through airport security as Mr. William Winchell, eighty-six-year-old curmudgeon who didn't take any guff from smart-aleck whippersnappers. He might even shake his fist at them.

He slid the wallet in his pocket along with the keys and went downstairs to collect his phone and webcam. The TV was still blaring, and he decided to catch a quick update before he drove Mr. Winchell's Buick to the airport.

That FBI woman was on again. The one who'd said she was close to Nina Guerrera. She was quite attractive but obviously much older than Nina. He read the name at the bottom of the screen. RETIRED FBI EXECUTIVE ASSISTANT DIRECTOR SHAWNA JACKSON. A very high-ranking official in the Bureau. Perhaps Nina looked up to her. Admired her. Wanted to be like her. An idea began to take shape. He used his phone to google her, found her Instagram profile, and clicked on it. Shawna lived in the suburbs of DC. Like Nina. Interesting. He scrolled through her posts.

In less than sixty seconds, his plan veered in a new direction. Shawna appeared in a photograph taken at a ceremony with Nina, who was receiving a community action award for mentoring an at-risk foster girl named Bianca Babbage. The petite teen was in the picture as well, her young face framed by long dark hair with a streak of blue.

He thumb-typed Bianca's name so fast he almost dropped the phone. He found her Instagram account first. He scrolled back a month and spotted her getting ready to start the fall semester at GW. Nina was standing with her, all smiles, in front of an apartment building. This girl was clearly very important to Nina. Someone she cared deeply about. He shoved the phone back into his pocket as his predatory instincts uncoiled. He had caught a scent.

Target acquired.

Chapter 44

Instead of her accustomed seat at the small table with Wade, Kent, and Buxton, Nina opted for the chair next to Breck's as the Gulfstream climbed to cruising altitude. She instinctively sought out a comforting feminine presence in Breck, who provided refuge from the testosterone-laden environment across the cabin. Phoenix was behind them, but the fallout from what the Cipher had done hung in the plane like a toxic cloud.

Nina was fully aware that millions had watched the video. They had seen the monster break her, crush her spirit, blight her soul as he slowly, methodically, and thoroughly destroyed every ounce of dignity she possessed. Now that she had some private space, Nina mustered the nerve to ask Breck what had been uppermost on her mind.

"Did it run all the way to the end?"

Thankfully, Breck understood the question without the need for further explanation. "Buxton gave the order and we made arrangements to shut the video down after only eleven minutes. Then we took all the Cipher's social media accounts back offline."

Next chance she got, she'd buy Breck a mint julep, or whatever they drank in Georgia. She cleared her throat, determined to hear the worst. "Did it get as far as the rape?"

Breck's pale skin grew pink, then crimson. "Yes."

Aware it was costing Breck to provide details, she still had to know exactly what the world had seen. And what was yet to come, because she was damn sure the Cipher wasn't finished with the show.

"Tell me."

Breck leaned so close their heads almost touched. "After you left, the video continued for a while with him choking you half to death, then slapping you until you were fully awake. Then he—" Breck put her hand to her mouth. "Oh, Nina, do you really want to hear this?"

"I do." Her heart was hammering, but she willed herself to listen.

Breck looked like she would rather be anywhere else. After a long pause, she squared her shoulders and looked Nina full in the face.

"He began to hit you," Breck said, her voice strained with emotion. "Really hard. All over. And he kept making you talk. Making you beg him for mercy." Her eyes welled with tears. "Then he stood with his back to the camera and opened the front of his cloak. His body was completely covered by the dark fabric, even his hood was still up over the back of his head. I couldn't see anything except his hands and feet. Then he climbed on top of the table and laid on your back and . . . and he kept choking you from behind and speaking in your ear while he raped you." Her last words came out as a breathless whisper. "That's what was happening when we shut the sonofabitch down."

Sweat prickled her hairline and dampened her palms. She tamped down her revulsion at the images rushing back to her to focus on something Breck had mentioned. The Cipher had spoken to her. She had forgotten that detail. "Could you hear what he was saying to me?"

Breck shook her head. "Too low for the mic to pick up. Do you remember what he told you? Is it important?"

"I'm not sure. Could Video Forensics enhance the sound?"

"Absolutely." Breck looked relieved to have something constructive to do as she pulled out her laptop and opened it on the armrest table attached to her seat. While it booted up, she turned to Nina and laid a gentle hand on her arm. "Do you want to go in the back and get some shut-eye? It's a long flight to Dulles."

Breck was offering her an out. A perfectly good excuse to retreat. No one would fault her for being jet lagged after so many cross-country trips and emotionally drained after the video had aired. She could easily say she needed rest, head back to the private lounge at the rear of the plane, and hide from the world for a few hours while she licked her wounds.

That may have been precisely what she *wanted* to do, but it was the opposite of what she *needed* to do. There were more girls like Trina out there, and if she was going to save them, she'd damned well better step up.

She covered Breck's hand with hers, giving it a brief squeeze before breaking the contact. "Actually, I'd rather get to work."

She stood and strode to the other table, surveying each of the men in turn. Kent had rushed out into the hall to find her after she'd left the Phoenix conference room and had remained at her side since that moment. When she went to the bathroom, he stood sentry outside the door. Wherever she walked, he'd been right on her heels, an overprotective, brooding shadow. Now, he regarded her silently from his chair.

Wade had spoken with her briefly, offering himself as a sounding board, but had not pushed the issue when she declined. He hadn't seemed surprised or offended when she gravitated to Breck, who had no background in psychology.

Buxton was uncharacteristically quiet, keeping his own counsel. She had no doubt the boss had spoken with his superiors about this new development. Excitement over Trina's rescue had been fleeting, and the Cipher's retribution had been swift and devastating for the whole team. And for the Bureau.

They had stopped talking when she got to her feet, watching her as she approached. "I'm ready," she said without preamble.

Wade eyed her. "For what?"

She had spent years shoring up her internal walls. Her legal name change reflected the fact that she no longer believed in hope.

Throughout her childhood, no one had fought for her. When a broken system utterly failed her, she had decided to fight for herself. As an adult, she now fought for others. She had learned to trust only herself. Time to try something different.

"Ready to do what it takes to catch this bastard," she said. "It's clear the Cipher knew a lot about me before he took me. It's also clear there are details I don't recall. Details that might point us in the right direction." She gestured to Wade and Kent, prepared to do something she had never done. "I'm asking for your help. I need to remember."

The two profilers exchanged glances.

"Where would you like to start?" Wade asked her.

She considered for a moment, relieved they didn't ask her if she was sure or if she wanted to wait. Perhaps they also felt time pressing down on them. "I'm not sure. Sometime before the abduction."

"He was fascinated by the scars on your back," Kent said. "Why don't we start there?"

She plopped down next to Wade, opposite Kent and Buxton, who remained silent. She addressed Kent. "You want to know how I got them?"

Wade shifted uncomfortably, already aware of the particulars from her file. She was sure it was one of many reasons he had doubted her suitability for the Bureau. It wasn't a pretty story, nor did it cast her in the best light.

Kent nodded. "Due to the Cipher's comments to you about them, I believe it's the best place to start."

She had no better suggestions. She scrolled back mentally, bringing up long-buried pain, prepared to recount one of the worst incidents of her life. "I was sixteen," she began. "CPS put me in a foster home with a childless couple. They were a bit older, in their late forties, so the authorities gave them a high school kid to foster. I thought they were ancient at the time."

"What happened the day you got your injuries?" Kent asked, keeping her on track.

"When I came home from school, there was a strange man in the house. I'd never seen him before. He reeked like he hadn't showered in a week, his hair was long and greasy, and he was huge and hairy, like a grizzly bear. He was yelling at Denny, my foster father. Looked like he'd punched Denny a few times. My foster mother was out of the house. No idea where."

The memories became more vivid as she recounted the tale.

"Grizzly took one look at me and said he knew how Denny could pay off his debt."

Kent's eyes hardened into chips of blue ice.

"Denny told me to go into the bedroom with Grizzly. I refused. I tried to run, but they caught me. Grizzly said he'd teach me my place. Told Denny to hold me still, then he took out a knife and cut off my T-shirt and bra."

She noticed Buxton's hands clench before he slid them under the table.

"Denny held me tight with my bare back to Grizzly, who took off his belt. It was one of those braided leather types. He promised to beat me until I passed out or went with him willingly, but either way I'd be going to the bedroom. He started on me, but I didn't give in, so he turned the belt around and swung it buckle first. That's what made all the gashes."

Kent looked like he wanted to hit something, but he didn't interrupt her.

"Finally, I told him I'd do whatever he wanted," she went on, surprised at the calm in her own voice. "Before Grizzly could drag me away, I dug a hand in Denny's pocket, where I knew he kept a folding knife. I'd decided to stab that motherfucker in the throat once he got me alone. Unfortunately, I went into the wrong pocket, and I got Denny's lighter instead.

"Grizzly grabbed my wrist and yanked me down the hall and into the bedroom. I told him I was on my period. He didn't care. I told him I had to pee. He didn't care. I told him I was about to barf and started retching, so he let me go to the toilet."

Even at a young age, she had learned to think on her feet after fending off a lot of people much bigger than she was.

"I went in the bathroom and looked around for a weapon. No scissors. Nothing sharp. Then I saw a can of my foster mother's hair spray. I got in position, holding the nozzle toward the door. I flicked on Denny's lighter and held the flame right under the can's nozzle. When Grizzly opened the door, I pressed down and blasted the flaming spray straight into his disgusting, hairy face. His beard caught fire. While he ran in circles screaming and smacking his face trying to put out the fire, I beat feet."

She half smiled at the memory.

"Ran straight past Denny, who was coming down the hall to see what was going on. Kept going until I made it to the crosswalk down the street. The elementary school let out after I got home, so I knew a crossing guard would be there."

"What did the crossing guard do?" Kent said.

"She put her vest over me and called the police. I still didn't have a shirt on. Less than five minutes later, the cops showed up. So did an ambulance. Turns out she told the emergency dispatcher I was bleeding pretty bad."

"What did the police do?"

"The cops were asking a lot of questions. While I was telling them what happened, one of the paramedics put something on my back that burned like hell. Must have been an antiseptic. I didn't think, I just reacted. Spun around and socked the guy as hard as I could. He was big, so it didn't seem to hurt him, but he grabbed my wrist. I'm sure he just wanted to stop me from taking another swing, but when I felt his big hand around my wrist, I lost it. Started kicking him and hitting him with my free hand."

"What did he do?"

"He was strong as hell. Quick reflexes too. Grabbed both of my forearms and pulled me into him so I couldn't kick his balls, which is where I was aiming. The other paramedic and the two cops joined in. It took all four men to restrain me. They finally let up a bit, then the guy who put the antiseptic on my back told me to calm down. I absolutely freaked when he said that. He grabbed my arm tight enough to leave bruises, then he got right up in my face and ordered me to . . ."

Her body jerked upright. She turned to Wade, mouth forming words that would not come.

His brows furrowed. "What is it?"

"Trina," she managed.

"What about Trina?" Kent looked completely baffled.

A cascade of memories showered through her, washing away the fog and bringing clarity. "That EMT who came to the scene in Phoenix. He had to cut Trina's shackles to get her loose. She kept freaking out and he ended up grabbing her wrists." Nina glanced away, embarrassed at her overreaction. "I kind of lost it when he did that."

She didn't mention that she'd elbowed the paramedic. Buxton would read it in her 302 soon enough, and she would face whatever discipline the Bureau doled out.

"What was it about the EMT?" Kent asked.

"Something he said." She was pulling fragments from the corners of her mind, stitching them into a pattern. "He shouted at Trina. Told her we were trying to help her."

"I don't understand the significance," Kent said.

"That's why I reacted to him." She was practically vibrating with excitement. "When the Fairfax EMT got up in my face, he told me they were trying to help me. He said I should learn to master myself."

"Master yourself?" Kent picked up on it first. "Strange word choice."

She was relieved they were getting it now. "Exactly."

Wade's forehead creased in confusion. "What's the significance?"

It had all come back to her. The weight of his body crushing down on her back, pinning her to the table. The musky smell of his sweat. The feel of his hot breath against her ear as he spoke.

"That's what the Cipher kept whispering in my ear."

Chapter 45

Nina rushed across the Gulfstream's oversize aisle. Breck, who had apparently been engrossed in her computer, looked up in surprise.

Unable to contain her excitement, Nina plopped down in the empty seat next to Breck. "We've got a lead." When Breck merely continued to stare at her, she smacked her palm on the table. "An honest-to-god, real-as-shit, genuine lead."

She felt Wade's presence behind her.

"The paramedic who treated the injuries on her back eleven years ago," he said by way of explanation.

She and Wade spent the next ten minutes filling Breck in on her epiphany as the others listened, answering the whole team's questions as they came. She should have been mentally drained, but she felt completely energized, and her excitement proved contagious. The torpor that had engulfed the team a half hour ago was replaced by fervor.

Buxton pulled out his leather portfolio and picked up the onboard sat phone. "I'm calling the task force."

Their supervisor was in his element. Buxton allocated assignments to various teams of field agents and analysts. It was as if the largest law enforcement agency in the United States had been holding its collective breath, waiting for this moment. This was the second time they had a viable lead to pursue, and, like he had before, Buxton wasted no time bringing every resource at his disposal to bear.

Nina heard him task one of the teams with tracking down reports from police and rescue personnel who responded to the crossing guard's 9-1-1 call. This was the result she was most anxious to see.

"Things are clicking into place," Kent said. "Like the medical tape residue and a variable schedule with lots of time off between shifts."

"I'll make sure those shifts are cross-checked with the dates of kidnappings and murders," Buxton said with his fingers over the receiver before resuming his conversation.

Breck bent toward her laptop again. "A paramedic would have knowledge of crime scenes and how to cover his tracks from forensic analysis." Her fingers began a staccato rhythm on the keyboard. "He might have gotten access to municipal government computers to identify potential targets in the system too."

Wade eased into a chair across the aisle. "I'm still not sure how he chooses his victims, but that will become clearer going forward. He may vary his methods, which would make sense, given the apparent randomness of other aspects of the crimes."

Within fifteen minutes, Buxton interrupted their ongoing discussion with an update. "The team going through the records discovered the police didn't list the names of the paramedics in their report. However, because the call involved an injury to a juvenile who was a ward of the state, the Fairfax County Fire Department retained their records."

"Do we have a name?" Nina asked.

"The two EMTs who responded to the call were Halberd Falk and Brian Dagget, both still on the job. Falk transferred to a fire station in Franconia, but Dagget still works out of the firehouse in Springfield."

Two possible names. Team FBI was a hell of a lot closer than they had been that morning.

Buxton nodded to Breck. "They uploaded employee photos of both EMTs to the task force database. Why don't you access the file and let's take a look?"

Breck opened a link to the FBI's secure server and moused over to one of the folder icons created by the task force. Nina's heart pounded so hard she thought it might burst as she waited for the first image to load.

When the man's face appeared, she let out a breath she didn't realize she'd been holding.

Dagget was white with blond hair and blue eyes. The image was in the ballpark with the DNA predictive image program. Was it him? She couldn't be sure.

Breck swiped the touch screen, bringing up the next photo. This was the moment of truth. If Falk didn't match the predictive description at all, they would know it was Dagget.

The image of a man resolved itself on the screen, and Nina sucked in an audible gasp as she looked at another man with blond hair and blue eyes. Falk could have been Dagget's cousin. She drew closer, her nose almost touching the screen, paying special attention to the area around the eyes. The only part of the Cipher she had ever seen without a disguise.

"Well?" Kent said into the silence as everyone watched her reaction.

She had expected to have the same visceral response she'd had when she looked at the phenotype-generated image, but she didn't. Were the men too much alike?

"Dammit. I can't be sure." An idea surfaced. She snapped her eyes to Breck. "Do you have access to the list of names Sorrentino gave us?"

Breck's face split into a grin. "Stand by."

Everyone was back in a holding pattern as Breck moused around the desktop, opening various files.

"Got it," she said, swiveling the screen slightly so Nina could see. "I entered the names on an Excel spreadsheet so all I have to do is sort alphabetically."

Wade peered over Nina's shoulder. "I swear, if both of these guys fight at the club, I say we lock them up anyway and sort it out later."

"At this point, I wouldn't rule that out," Buxton said.

A few more clicks and the spreadsheet shifted, rearranging the columns. There was only one matching name. Only one suspect. Nina blew out a long breath.

Halberd Falk was their man.

Buxton, who had been gripping the sat phone with a hand over the receiver again, put it back to his ear and began firing off new instructions.

A large warm hand rested on her shoulder, and she glanced up to see Kent gazing intently at her.

"You okay?"

Surprising herself, she did not feel the need to shrink away from the contact. "I'm good, thanks."

And she truly was. She had faced her demons to find the missing piece they needed. She turned to Wade. "And thank you too."

She felt like his true partner. The man who she had thought was heartless. The man who had tried to block her entry into the Bureau. The man who she now considered an ally and a friend.

"You did all the heavy lifting." Wade colored slightly, then added, "Thank you for trusting me after what I did to you."

Kent glanced from one to the other, trying to read the subtext. "What did you do to her, Wade?"

Nina answered for Wade. "What he thought he had to . . . at the time." She gave Kent a look designed to communicate that, to her, the matter was closed.

Breck let out an excited squeak. "You guys are never going to believe this." She glanced up at them. "Guess what his fighting name is?"

Wade groaned. "If you tell me it's the Cipher, I'm going to—"

"Odin," Breck said. "As in the god from Norse mythology."

The connection hit Nina with a jolt. "Dr. Borr's son mentioned Odin."

"Borr was Odin's father," Wade said. "That makes perfect sense. Falk would have considered Dr. Borr to be his actual father. The man responsible for creating him, in a way. Hell, for all we know he might have been Falk's biological father if he decided to use his own DNA again."

Nina's mind whirled with the implications. "Falk probably also bought into all of Dr. Borr's eugenics philosophies. Even though Borr died before Falk would have been old enough to meet him, he could have read about him."

"Didn't Borr's son say Odin was a one-eyed god?" Kent asked no one in particular.

"He was," Wade said, apparently up on his Norse mythology. "He supposedly sacrificed one of his eyes so that he could see all, know all."

A chill swept through Nina. "My god's eye necklace," she breathed, her hand reflexively going to her throat where it had once hung. "And that comment he made when we were DM'ing about how he was always watching."

"I could write a dissertation on this guy," Wade muttered.

For the next twenty minutes, they huddled together to review the previous cases from a new perspective.

"We're getting reports back now," Buxton called out, interrupting them. "It's only preliminary at this point. By the time they're finished, we'll know this guy's preschool teacher's maiden name."

Scary how much information the Bureau could amass in one hour with those kinds of resources.

"The scores on his admissions tests into the EMT program were off the charts," Buxton began. "He's also a damned good fighter from what we've heard." His finger trailed down the page of notes. "He's a loner. Lives by himself in a single-family home on the western side of Fairfax County. We're getting a search warrant for the property now. Should be able to execute it tonight."

"Is he on duty today?" Kent asked.

"He's currently on a leave of absence from work," Buxton said. "Told his supervisor he needed to take care of an ailing aunt in Boise."

"Let me guess," Nina said, rolling her eyes. "No aunt?"

"Bingo."

"What's his shift schedule?" Breck asked.

"His squad works two days on, two days off, two days on, four days off." Buxton allowed a rare grin. "They've matched up the dates. All of the abductions occurred at the beginning of a two-day or four-day break."

"How far back did they check?" Wade asked. "Do we know about the time around Guerrera's abduction?"

"He had just returned to duty after a disciplinary suspension," Buxton said. "Got into a scuffle with a firefighter in the locker room at the station house. Broke the guy's nose."

Wade nodded. "That would count as a precipitating stressor. His career was in jeopardy, which would cause him to feel pressure."

"I'll bet that's when he started cage fighting," Kent said. "Consciously or not, he was trying to find an outlet for his aggression."

Nina felt a rush as another piece fell neatly into place. "That would explain the trace evidence found in my case. If he started at the club during his suspension, he would have needed to buy MMA gloves. I'm sure Sorrentino would have sold him a pair."

She recognized the sensation of momentum. The case was building.

"Anything more on his personal life?" Wade asked.

Buxton consulted his notes. "Never married, no children that we know of. Parents are both deceased. His mother died of an aneurysm when he was five years old, and his father fell down the stairs at the family home when Falk was twenty-one." Buxton quirked a brow. "Only the two of them were there when it happened. Ruled an accident."

Wade spoke with absolute certainty. "I have no doubt his old man abused him. Falk pushed him down those stairs."

"He inherited the house," Buxton said. "But he bought a home closer to his work."

Nina held up a finger. "Hold on a sec." Something about the time-line triggered a thought. "If Falk is thirty-two now, then he would have been twenty-one eleven years ago."

"Depending on the date," Buxton said. "What's your point, Agent Guerrera?"

"When exactly did his father die?"

Buxton glanced down again. "September twenty-eighth."

"Falk treated my injury from the belt six days later," she said, heart thudding. "Probably his first day back after the burial." She glanced at Wade. "And his disciplinary suspension, which must have been why he was at home with his father. That's when everything happened."

"Another precipitating stressor," Wade said, voice kicking up a notch as he grew animated. "If his first murder was his father, Falk would be on edge, wondering if anyone would figure out what he'd done."

"And once a predator acts on his fantasies the first time, everything changes," Kent said, picking up where Wade left off. "He scratches the itch, but then he can't stop because the itch keeps coming back. I'm guessing he fantasized about murdering his father for years before he finally did it."

Wade's gray eyes were locked on Nina's. "He's under extreme pressure in his job and his personal life when he meets you. He sees that you've been abused, and he slots you into the category of victim. Then you fight him as he's trying to treat your injuries, and something snaps. He cannot tolerate disrespect from someone he views as inferior."

She tried to see it from Falk's perspective. "Then I escape from him, and he can't take it. He's superior in every way, I shouldn't have been able to defy him."

Wade nodded. "It's a challenge to his entire belief system. To set things right, he must put you in your place, control every aspect of your life, including your death."

Her mind came to a sickening conclusion. "So all of those other girls . . ."

"Were proxies," Wade finished for her. "Until he found you again."

She wanted to scream, to rage against the injustice of it. She could not possibly have known what she had set in motion the day she escaped from one kind of hell only to enter another, but she felt the weight of it on her soul. So many lives destroyed. So much pain and suffering.

"We have to find this bastard," she said. "We have to stop him." She was concerned about the depth of the information they had gathered in such a short period of time. "All these feelers going out, word might get back to him. I don't want to spook him."

"They're keeping the questions low key," Buxton said. "No reason to believe he knows we're onto him yet."

"Do we have enough to arrest him right now?" Breck asked.

Buxton shook his head. "The US Attorney wants a DNA match."

"Which means we'll need a search warrant for a buccal swab," Nina said.

"Agents on the task force are writing an affidavit now," Buxton said. "Even rushing, it'll take a couple of hours to complete the paperwork. Then they'll need to get a federal judge to issue the search warrant. Realistically, it will be about three or four hours until we have it in hand."

"If we're lucky." Nina groaned. "Otherwise we'll have to wait until morning."

"I won't let that happen," Buxton said. "And while we're waiting, I've contacted HRT. They'll deploy a team to execute the warrant."

She was impressed. The Hostage Rescue Team, colocated with them at the academy in Quantico, executed high-risk arrests and surveillance operations among many other tactical duties and assignments. The fact that they were being brought in at this critical stage demonstrated the Bureau's commitment to capturing the Cipher. Clearly, Buxton wasn't taking any chances. For the first time, she appreciated the impact this case was having on his career. Everyone from the Director down would be watching. No wonder his features showed signs of strain and fatigue.

"We hope to catch him at home tonight when we serve the search warrant," Buxton continued. "Then we can take him in for questioning and get a buccal swab for his DNA."

"Do we alert the public?" Wade said. "We can't let him kidnap another girl."

"As soon as we get a fix on his location, HRT will put him under constant surveillance until we're ready to go." Buxton lifted a shoulder. "I don't like it, but it's the best we can do before we have a warrant."

"And we have no idea where he is now?" Kent asked.

Buxton shook his head. "Not due back at work for two days. Not at the fight club. There's no aunt in Boise." He slid off his readers and rubbed the bridge of his nose. "He's a ghost."

Nina fumed in silence. She could finally put a name to her nemesis but couldn't lay hands on him. Where was he? More importantly, what was he doing?

"We'll be landing in under an hour," Buxton said, breaking into her reverie. "I want each of you to go home and put on your raid gear. As soon as the warrant's issued, I'll send out a blast text with the location of the command post, where you will report for a preop briefing with HRT. This is a full-court press, people. We're going to get this bastard tonight."

Despite the SSA's pronouncement, a sense of foreboding settled over Nina. Falk was out there somewhere, fueled by rage and whatever demons possessed him. And she had no doubt he was on the hunt. Would they be able to get to him before he found his next target?

Chapter 46

As soon as she arrived at her apartment, Nina had gone to her bed-
room to lay out her gear before taking a quick shower. With practiced
efficiency, she'd laid out a black tactical shirt, pants, boots, and her
FBI raid jacket on the bed beside her Glock and two extra magazines.
Prepped and ready, she could be out the door in two minutes once
Buxton texted.

She'd been sitting at her kitchen table while her hair dried, sipping
coffee with her laptop in front of her, when Bianca's signature knock
interrupted her. Tightening the sash on her short satin robe, she padded
to the door to find her young neighbor standing on the threshold. She
crossed her arms. "What took you so long?"

Bianca crossed her arms right back, then upped the ante with a
jutting hip. "I need an update on the investigation."

"The investigation is my problem," Nina said. "Not yours."

"It's everybody's problem." Bianca strode past her, pulled out one of
the kitchen chairs, and plopped herself down. "No one's safe as long as
that lunatic is out there, and from what I can tell, you guys are no closer
to catching him than you were a week ago." She traced a finger along
the FBI seal on the heavy ceramic mug. "You got any more coffee?"

"Bee, now's not a good time. I'm expecting a text from my boss.
When I get it, I'll have to leave."

"No problem. I'll go when you do. In the meantime, you can pour me a cup."

Nina relented. "You'll have to take it black, I'm all out of milk."

"Whatevs." Bianca waved a dismissive hand. "I just need caffeine."

Nina turned to the counter and slid the coffeepot from the brewing machine. She opened a cabinet, scanning for a mug.

"Since when do you watch MMA cage matches?" Bianca wanted to know.

She whirled around to see Bianca peering at her open laptop. Nina darted to the table and put her hand on the back cover, pushing it shut.

Bianca raised a pierced brow. "Who's Halberd Falk?"

Nina scrunched her eyes shut. The girl was nosy, and way too smart for her own good. "No one, Bee. Just forget you ever saw him."

The truth would come out later, and Bianca would soon know exactly who he was. But she wasn't going to hear it from her.

Bianca narrowed her eyes. "He's got something to do with this case, doesn't he?"

Bianca's oversize brain was working the facts around like a Rubik's Cube, and, as always, the pieces would soon fall neatly into place.

"Stay out of this, Bee."

Bianca straightened in her chair, eyes bright. "OMG. Halberd Falk is the Cipher." She put both hands to her mouth. "And you're heading out to arrest him, aren't you? That's why you have to leave. That's the text you're expecting from your boss."

Nina groaned. "I can neither confirm nor deny—"

"Yeah, right." Bianca made a shooing motion. "Go get dressed. I want to watch the video anyway." She opened the laptop again. "I promise I won't say shit about this to anyone." Bianca made a crossing-heart motion.

She could snatch the computer away and take it into her bedroom, but Bianca would just google Falk and watch it on her cell phone. Nina blew out a sigh, stalked into the bathroom, and began toweling off her hair.

"Holy shit, Nina," Bianca called out to her from the kitchen. "You have to see this."

Damp hair clinging to her forehead, Nina hung the towel on its rack before padding through the living room on bare feet to find Bianca wide eyed in front of the computer.

"What is it?"

"How much footage of this fight have you seen?"

"Only the first two seconds. You knocked before I could watch more."

Bianca's voice dropped in awe. "Look at his back."

She dropped into the other chair and motioned for the laptop. "Let me see."

The footage had obviously been bootlegged from someone in the audience who was sitting to one side of the metal enclosure. Bianca had stopped the video after the two opponents, who had been facing the crowd, rotated to square off. Falk's broad back was now to the camera.

His massive upper torso displayed unique body art. The design spanned his entire back down to his waist in a skillfully rendered geometric pattern.

"Three interlocking triangles," Nina said.

"That's not all," Bianca said, her voice trembling. "See what happens when I do this." She used her thumb and forefinger on the laptop's touch screen to expand the picture, zooming in on the tattooed shoulder blades.

Nina squinted as the picture went slightly out of focus.

Bianca tapped some keys. "Now look again."

When the image cleared, Nina felt her jaw slacken. In between the intricate black markings of the design, she made out circular scars.

"Cigarette burns," she breathed, unable to fully process what she was seeing. "Three of them." She tried to fit this into the mental picture she had of the monster. He had not done that to himself. The tattoo concealed the long-healed marks of torture.

"They form a triangle on his back," Bianca said. "The body art covers them, though."

"What does that symbol mean?" Nina muttered.

"Already on it." Bianca had her cell phone in hand, thumbs working the tiny keypad. "That's Odin's symbol. He's a Norse god."

"Of course," Nina said, mind racing. "That's why he made the shape of a triangle on my back. It's because he sees himself as Odin, son of Borr."

"It's because he's a freak." Bianca zoomed back out to normal focus. "Watch what he does next." She tapped the arrow icon in the center of the frame to start the video again.

Falk's opponent launched a brutal assault, the combination attack knocking him to the floor. Falk got to his feet and stood erect, bracing himself for another onslaught.

"He doesn't even try to avoid the hits," Nina said, frowning. "He wants to get pummeled."

"It's like he's baiting the other guy," Bianca said. "He stands there and lets him knock him down a couple of times. Doesn't even flinch or try to get out of the way. He just . . . takes it."

"Like punishment," Nina said, a theory taking shape. "When was this fight?"

"Four days ago."

"Right after the Boston murder," Nina said. "He was punishing himself for letting me get the drop on him. He showed weakness."

Bianca's eyes were still on the fight. "Now he gets up off the floor and destroys the other guy in about twenty seconds." She shook her head. "Dude is crazy as crackers, but he's a stone-cold badass."

Falk allowed a less skilled opponent to hurt him before fighting back. What did that tell her about the Cipher? Wade had guessed he had been punished severely by an authority figure—probably a father figure—as a young man. Someone had certainly tortured him years ago. The burns were evidence of that. So was his desire to identify with Dr. Borr, a man he could idolize and take on as a surrogate father.

She felt like she was getting a handle on his psyche, but true understanding was just out of reach. What would the profilers make of this?

"I've got to get dressed." She was suddenly anxious to get to Quantico well before the prewarrant prep. "You can stay here until I leave if you want."

"Hell yeah. I'm going to watch some of his other fights. The guy is beyond scary."

"You have no idea," she muttered under her breath.

She walked back to the bathroom and turned on the blow-dryer to finish her hair. The short locks did not need much styling to achieve the tousled look she favored. She switched off the dryer and put down her brush, surveying the results in the mirror.

Voices emanated from the kitchen, catching her attention. She made out the softer notes of Bianca's speech but could not place the male baritone conversing with her. It didn't sound like Jaime.

"Who's that with you, Bee?" she called out.

"Agent Taylor," Bianca said. "Says your boss sent him."

Nina walked to the living room, clutching her thin robe tightly together. A tall man dressed in Hoover blues stood in the kitchen. His neatly trimmed dark hair, clean-shaven face, and black-framed glasses were classic G-man. His entire demeanor screamed government issue, all the way down to his starched white collar.

"Who sent you?" she asked him.

"SSA Buxton," he said, pulling out his creds and flipping them open. He had an accent she couldn't quite place.

She approached and glanced at the federal ID. He was assigned to the Washington field office, but she didn't recognize him. Not overly surprising, since about seventeen hundred federal employees worked out of the WFO.

Still, something nagged at her. "Why wouldn't Buxton just text me?" she asked him. "I've been checking my phone for messages."

"He's been trying to reach you," Taylor said. "Must be something wrong with your cell. I was detailed to come and get you. There's been a major development in the Cipher case." He glanced at Bianca, who was too slow in concealing her look of avid interest, and added, "I'll brief you on the way."

"Bee, I'll catch up with you later," she said, then turned and extended her hand to Taylor, palm up. "Can I borrow your phone? I want to talk to Buxton."

"I left it in my car," Taylor said. "You can call him on the way."

The nagging feeling wouldn't go away. She tried to reconcile the facts. If Buxton couldn't reach her by text or phone and needed her for a critical operation, what would he do? She had no landline number for him to call, so he might send an agent from the closest FBI field office to check on her and give her the message. But why would he have the agent drive her to their meeting point? It didn't add up. She had to find a subtle way to test Taylor.

"I'd better get ready, then," she said smoothly. "Can't keep the SSA waiting. You know what they say, don't embarrass . . ." She deliberately trailed off, giving Taylor a significant look.

"The boss," he finished after a moment's hesitation.

"Exactly." She gave him a bright smile to conceal the fear that knifed into her, cutting to the bone. Every FBI agent knew the correct expression was "Don't embarrass the Bureau."

Taylor was an impostor.

Her focus shifted to Bianca, who still hadn't left. Nina couldn't let Taylor become suspicious that she was onto him, so she played along, buying time.

"Excuse me a moment while I get dressed."

First objective, get Bianca out. Second objective, get to her gun in the bedroom. She turned to Bianca. "Go back to your apartment, Bee."

293

"But I—"

"No," Nina said, a bit sterner than she'd intended.

Should she try to communicate a distress signal to Bianca somehow? The girl was a genius, and she loved codes. Would she take the hint and call for help when she got to her apartment?

Nina discounted the idea as soon as it fully formed in her mind. If the man standing in front of her was who she believed he was, Bianca's only chance was to leave immediately. If he suspected the girl had been tipped off, he wouldn't let her go. Nina pointed firmly at the door when Bianca gave her a beseeching look.

Bianca pouted her way out, closing the door behind her with a bit more force than necessary.

"What's this?" Taylor said from the kitchen.

He was bent over the open laptop on the kitchen table, staring at the screen.

"Nothing." She hurried from the foyer, pulse pounding. She had to go through the kitchen and the living room to get to her bedroom. Taylor was directly in her path.

His whole body tensed as he straightened. "You a fan of MMA?"

"Not really." She closed the distance between them in three long strides and snapped the computer firmly shut. "Just doing research."

He slid the black-rimmed glasses off his nose and gazed down at her with cold blue eyes. This time, when he spoke, there was no fake accent to obscure the voice she dreaded. "Liar."

Chapter 47

The thrill of combat sharpened Falk's reflexes. His hand whipped out before the bitch had time to react, fingers clamping on to her slender throat. His body thrummed in anticipation of a fight. She lashed out with her bare foot, aiming for the outer edge of his quadriceps. He easily anticipated the move, shifting position before the blow connected.

"No more of that." He squeezed, looking into her lovely brown eyes as they widened in panic. He read the terror in every jerk and spasm of her body as she thrashed.

She was no match for him, physically or mentally. She would fight him with all she had, but their dance had only one possible outcome. And they both knew it.

Ten minutes earlier, he'd come for Bianca, but fate had intervened, changing his plans. He'd accessed the Fairfax County municipal server through a back door as he had done for years, exploiting a vulnerability that gave him an avenue in from the Fire Department's system. Finding Bianca's address had taken him less than four minutes once he'd gotten to his home computer.

It had been obvious from Bianca's posts that she idolized Nina Guerrera. Another FBI agent would be someone the girl would easily trust. Someone she would willingly go with, especially if he told her Nina had sent him to pick her up. He'd planned to throw in something about Shawna Jackson to help sell the story. How hard could it be to deceive a seventeen-year-old girl? He had done it countless times before.

When he knocked at Bianca's door in his special agent disguise, Mrs. Gomez had informed him that Bianca was in the apartment next door with none other than Nina Guerrera.

Fate. Destiny. Whatever you wanted to call it. That moment had changed everything. The FBI was careful to conceal the home addresses of its agents, but Nina had dropped into his lap.

He thought about leaving to return in the middle of the night and take Nina by stealth, but he couldn't risk Bianca hearing from Mrs. Gomez that an agent had been looking for her. She might ask Nina about it, and the game would be up. He had to act now or miss this opportunity.

His new plan had been to take them both. He could easily overpower two females whose combined total weight was less than his. And he'd learned not to let the Warrior Girl get anywhere near his balls. He would disable her first, using the element of surprise, then little Bianca would be easy prey.

Again, fate had altered the trajectory of his path. Once inside the kitchen, he'd seen that damned computer. There was only one reason Nina would be watching a video of his fight.

The FBI had figured out who he was.

The information had not gone public—of that he was certain. Which meant he had to enact one of his contingency plans before the nationwide manhunt began. No more puzzles and clues. Now, it was time for the endgame. And that meant Nina Guerrera.

He no longer cared about Bianca. By the time the FBI realized their most famous agent was missing, it would make no difference if Bianca told her story of Agent Taylor coming to pick her up. Falk would be long gone. And he would have his prize all to himself.

But first, he had to end this fight. As much as he enjoyed playing with her, he was wasting valuable time.

Nina went limp in his choke hold. He loosened his grip a fraction, allowing air to reach her oxygen-deprived brain. It would not do to kill her now. He leaned close, anxious to hear and feel her breath against his ear.

Without warning, she aimed a palm strike at his Adam's apple. His reflexes kicked in, and he leaned back to lessen the impact of what should have been a devastating blow.

Taking full advantage of his momentary distraction, she thudded the heel of her other palm into his sternum. He lost his grip on her as she sidestepped and darted out of his reach.

He lurched after her, but she'd made it to the counter. He saw her yank a meat cleaver from the knife block and stopped in his tracks as she whirled around, swinging the blade in a wide arc around her.

"That won't help you, little one," he said. "You are only delaying the inevitable."

"Fuck you."

"So articulate. Exactly what I would expect from a throwaway."

Her eyes narrowed to slits, and he knew his taunts were having the desired effect. He wanted her furious beyond reason. Cage matches had taught him that opponents who were fueled by animal rage were not capable of higher thought processes involving such things as strategy, countermoves, and proper technique. Brute force would take you a long way, but cold logic and icy control would win the match.

"Remember our time together, Warrior Girl?" he said, ducking a vicious swipe of her blade. "I think about it every night. Sometimes I watch the video." He let a smile play across his lips. "And hearing you beg for mercy gets me off without even touching myself."

That did it. She surged forward, metal flashing as she swung the cleaver toward his head. He waited until the last moment, then brought his right hand up to catch her forearm while his left grabbed a handful of satin robe.

He twisted her wrist, and the knife clattered to the tile floor. She whipped her arm out of his grasp and spun her slight body in a tight circle. She careened away, leaving him holding the empty robe as she raced toward the bedroom, naked.

He had no doubt she was going for her gun, which was most likely on her nightstand. He charged after her, adrenaline coursing through him.

She flung the bedroom door closed behind her, and he crashed through it without breaking his stride. She had almost reached the nightstand when he launched himself at her. Momentum carried them both to the carpeted floor in a tangled heap beside the bed. He used his bulk to pin her to the ground, trapping her beneath him. She had made a tactical error. His superior size gave him a tremendous advantage in all forms of ground fighting.

Even though her defeat was imminent, she fought like a woman possessed. She had to know what awaited her if she failed, and she refused to surrender.

He moved over her body until he lay on top of her, their faces an inch apart, both of them breathing heavily.

"This is the best foreplay I've ever had," he whispered. "Thank you, Warrior Girl."

For the first time since their battle began, he read primal fear in her eyes. No longer focused solely on fighting him, she opened her mouth to call out for help. He could not have that.

He drew his hand back and slapped her across the face with all his strength. Her head snapped sideways, and she went still.

He reached into the breast pocket of his suit jacket and pulled out a hypodermic needle loaded with the concoction he had intended for Bianca. Fortunately, the two females were both petite. Injecting Nina with a dose for a normal-size woman could be fatal.

She began to struggle again, her uncoordinated movements telling him she was still stunned from the blow to the head. If he acted quickly, he would not have to risk concussing her with another strike.

The ketamine-based cocktail required an intramuscular injection. He sank the needle into her thigh and pressed the plunger down.

For a split second, her eyes flew open, then her thrashing stopped, and her lids fluttered closed. A deep sigh escaped her parted lips as she quieted underneath him.

He put his mouth to hers, tasting coppery blood. Her teeth must have cut the inside of her cheek when he hit her. He deepened the kiss, moaning with a heady mix of pleasure and anticipation. She was even more delicious than he remembered.

He forced himself to stop, slowly getting to his feet. He surveyed her as she lay supine at his feet, her caramel skin glistening with sweat. He wanted her right here, right now, but he would be patient. First, he had to take her away. Once they were secure in the hideout, he would have all the time he wanted to enjoy her.

And the world would have a new show to watch.

Chapter 48

Wade looked around the Suburban's dark interior. "Has anyone been able to contact Guerrera?"

He got the same negative response as before.

"I'm glad she sat this one out," Buxton said, goosing the gas to keep up with the phalanx of FBI vehicles making their way toward Falk's residence. "If she hadn't, I was probably going to pull her from the op anyway."

Guerrera had texted Buxton forty-five minutes ago to say she'd gotten food poisoning and wouldn't be in until further notice. No one had heard from her since.

Wade didn't like it. Nina Guerrera was the only person in the Bureau who wanted Falk more than he did. If he had food poisoning, he'd show up to serve the search warrant carrying a barf bag if he had to. He was certain she felt the same way.

"Can't we detail someone over to her apartment to check on her?"

Buxton shook his head. "This op is all hands on deck. There's no one to spare."

Kent was in the back seat next to him. "What about local PD?" he said. "Request a welfare check from a squad car in the area. She was a Fairfax County police officer until two years ago, I'm sure they'd be okay with that."

Buxton's dark eyes glanced at them in the rearview mirror. "We don't ask the police to check on an agent who has an upset stomach."

"Did you two ever stop to think that maybe she didn't want to come?" Breck said from the front passenger seat. "Maybe 'food poisoning'"—she made air quotes—"is her way out."

"Out of what?" Wade said.

"Were you watching the video with the rest of us?" Breck said. "She probably never wants to be in the same room with that bastard again." She shuddered. "And I don't blame her."

"So you think this is some sort of face-saving way for her to avoid Falk?" Kent said. "I don't buy it."

"We're almost at Falk's house," Buxton said. "If we don't get any more messages from her by the time we're finished here, I'll ask the locals to slide by her place." He shot Wade and Kent a hard look over his shoulder. "Satisfied?"

Not really, but it would have to do.

Buxton touched his earpiece. "When?" he said. "I'll notify the team." He angled the wheel, passing a slower car around a curve on the freeway. "No, we do not abort."

He tapped his earpiece, ending the communication, and turned to Breck. "Boot up your iPad. Falk's got a website now. He's getting ready to livestream a message."

Breck flipped open the tablet's cover. "What's the URL?"

"There's a link from his Twitter account," Buxton said. "It's up and running again."

"Is he at home?" Wade said. "Can we ping the location?"

"They're working on it," Buxton said.

Breck held the iPad in front of her and tapped the icon to go to full-screen mode. "Can you guys see?"

The question was directed at Wade and Kent. Buxton kept his eyes on the road. This warrant service would stop for nothing.

Wade nodded in response as he saw a masculine figure wearing a black cloak step in front of the camera.

"I'm the one you call the Cipher," he said. "Welcome to my sanctum."

"I really hope he's at home," Kent said. "I'd love for him to have an up-close-and-personal meeting with the HRT." His wistful look said he longed to be the team's door-banger for tonight's mission.

Wade was absorbed in watching Falk. The man's calm, self-assured manner was unsettling. Anytime a sociopath was relaxed and pleased, someone was suffering. Certain Falk would not have gone to the trouble of setting up a website unless he had something dramatic to show the world, Wade found himself holding his breath.

"Let me show you around," Falk said, picking up the camera from whatever stable platform it had been situated on. No longer in the frame, his muscular arm protruded from the wide sleeve to gesture toward the far wall. "I built this structure myself," he said. "It has everything I need."

The wall was covered in a pale green, textured foamy material. "Soundproof," Falk said, bringing the camera close enough to see more detail. "And there's more insulation behind the drywall. No interruptions tonight."

Fluorescent light spilled down from above, bathing the scene in an odd glow. Wade pictured a long industrial-style rectangular light fixture. The space resembled a prefabricated construction building, and the interior looked to be about the size of a two-car garage.

The cinema verité show continued as Falk rotated in a circle, showing all four plain walls. "And now, for the main attraction." He placed the camera back in its holder and angled the lens down for the first time.

"No!"

Wade heard Kent's guttural shout before his mind fully processed what he was seeing.

Nina Guerrera lay spread eagle on a wooden table in the center of the room. Unlike in the previous video, this time she was faceup. She was also either unconscious or dead.

"What's going on?" Buxton said as he maneuvered the SUV around a tractor trailer.

"Falk's got Guerrera." Wade barely managed to get the words out through his painfully constricted throat. As his boss cursed, Wade's fists clenched so hard he felt his nails dig into his palms.

Still addressing his unseen audience, Falk strode over to Guerrera. "I have a special visitor tonight." His voice was husky. "And when she wakes up, the world will watch what happens to the Warrior Girl."

"Step on it," he said to Buxton. "We need to get there before he starts in on her."

"But first, the big reveal." Falk reached up and pulled the hood of the cloak down to expose his scalp, which had a day's growth of blond stubble. As he continued to pull the fabric down, a pair of crystal-blue eyes in a chiseled angular face peered out at his spectators. "No more disguises." He let the thick garment drop to the floor. "My name is Halberd Falk." A feral smile crept across his face. "I am the future of the human race."

Stripped to the waist, his lower body encased in blue jeans, Falk's heavily muscled torso bore the marks of a recent scuffle. Guerrera had put up a fight.

"No more worries about DNA," Falk said, stepping closer to her. He bent down to lick her cheek with a languid stroke of his tongue.

Grateful she was still unconscious, Wade leaned in, making out the interlocking triangles spanning Falk's rippling lats. Photos of Falk at his MMA matches had been disseminated during the search warrant briefing. Wade had looked up the design, concluding that they had been right about Falk's god complex. His body art marked him as a powerful and divine being, far above petty mortal justice.

"No more nitrile gloves either," Falk went on. "This time, it's flesh on flesh." He edged around to the far side of the table so his massive body wouldn't block the view and reached out to touch the base of Guerrera's throat. His fingertip traced a leisurely trail down the center of her inert body. He paused at her narrow waist, splaying his palm and fingers wide to cover her entire abdomen from hip to hip. "So small," he breathed, before his big hand moved relentlessly toward the juncture of her spread legs.

"Get your filthy hands off her." Kent's words were filled with icy menace. He tore his gaze away from the screen to look directly at Wade. "I'm going to hunt that motherfucker until I find him," he said in a low voice meant for Wade's ears only. "And then I'm going to kill him. Slowly."

He understood exactly how Kent felt. Memories of the Chandra Brown case flooded his mind. This must have been what Chandra's last hours were like. If he had only listened, he could have prevented her death. And now, Guerrera would meet the same fate because he had failed to read the situation properly. Again. He was a trained profiler. He thought they had more time, thought they'd finally gotten the drop on him. He should have anticipated that Falk would move on Guerrera tonight. Should have insisted they check on her. He would never forgive himself.

He whispered his own vow to Kent. "I'll help you get rid of the body."

Chapter 49

Nina blinked, unable to fathom the torpor in her leaden limbs and the feeling of cotton in her mouth.

"Does the Warrior Girl awaken at last?"

That voice. A stream of images came to her, bringing with it a cascade of horror. Fighting in her apartment. Stars bursting in her head after a teeth-rattling slap across the face. A needle plunging into her thigh.

The monster had taken her.

Her eyes opened fully as adrenaline dumped into her bloodstream, dissipating the cobwebs. She tried to sit up. The logical component of her brain was finally coming online. Parts of her body began reporting in. She registered pain in her ankles and wrists. Tilting her head upward, she spotted the black plastic zip ties binding her to steel eye hooks drilled into the wooden surface of a crude workbench. She tried to flex her arm, but he had secured her so tightly she could barely move at all.

"You won't be getting away this time," Falk said, following her gaze. "Your fellow FBI agents will no doubt be breaking down my front door right about now. But that's not where we are. No one knows where we are." He crossed his arms, looked down at her with those cold, flat eyes, and whispered, "No one is coming to save you."

He loomed over her, eclipsing the fluorescent light above. "You defied me twice, little throwaway girl. You will suffer twice as long as the others." He rested a palm on her left breast. "Your heart is pounding." He moaned, closing his eyes as if to savor the feel. "You're absolutely terrified." He bent down, brushing her lips with his. "As you should be."

The contact felt like more of an assault than any beating she had ever taken. His breath was hot on her skin, smelling vaguely of mint. The scent of fresh soap clung to him. He had obviously showered, washing away the remnants of the FBI agent disguise, including the fake black hair.

Falk straightened and removed his hand. "I've waited so long to have you again." He lifted a brow. "Nothing to say to me?"

She gave him a hard stare. She would not play his game.

"What about your fans?" He gestured to his right. "Don't you have anything to say to them?"

She turned her head to see a small camera mounted on a tripod in the corner of the room. The lens was angled toward the table, and the little red light was on. She sucked in a breath. The monster was recording every second of whatever sick fantasy he was about to indulge.

"I'm livestreaming," he said. "The world will watch you cry out for my mercy. And I will show you none. After a while, you will beg for death. But death will not come until I am satisfied."

Fear crept through her, stealing her last vestiges of hope. Buxton and the rest of the task force would be at Falk's house, but he'd been too smart for that. He'd taken her someplace else. She was utterly alone. And she was in the hands of a madman.

"I'm in control, you understand me?" He thumped his bare chest with his fist. "I decide when you die. I decide how you die. I am your god."

She gazed up at him. He was huge, powerful, and determined to destroy her. He had been biologically engineered to be superior.

She, on the other hand, had not inherited any special traits. She had no pedigree. Sheer force of will and a willingness to bend the rules had seen her through. As she accepted the truth of her situation, resolve stole through her. She would not survive this night. Might not even survive the next hour. The only choice left to her was to die on her own terms.

The Cipher wanted her to grovel. Wanted to degrade her in every way possible. She would not give him that. He would take everything she had by the time he was finished with her, including her life. But he would not take her humanity.

Once she made this promise to herself, the situation became simpler. Her focus, clear. She would do everything in her power to escape. Keep her eyes open for even the slightest opportunity. Failing that, she would die fighting him, not begging.

Falk bent down to pick up a black toolbox from the floor. He rested it on the table beside her. She could only turn her head to watch his movements.

He popped the two latches. "Let me show you what I have in store for the next few hours." He lifted the lid and fished around inside. One by one, he began removing items and setting them in a neat row beside her. A pair of pliers, an awl, alligator clamps, a chisel, and a vise.

Each tool he laid on the table conjured increasingly horrific images until her stomach roiled. Whatever he had injected her with, combined with the abject terror rushing through her, sent a blast of bile up the back of her throat.

Her vision blurred slightly, then settled back into focus. "I'm going to be sick."

She felt her gorge rise and turned her head to the side. He had her pinned down so tightly she couldn't lift herself from the table. Holy shit. She was going to choke on her own puke.

At least she would not die by his hand. Fate had intervened to provide her with a way out. She did not fight it as the first wave of nausea hit.

Falk dropped the pliers. "Don't you dare vomit."

She heaved and her mouth filled with sour liquid.

His eyes narrowed. "Stop it."

Her body jerked as more fluid came up.

Cursing, he pawed through the toolbox until he pulled out a pair of tin snips. He leaned over her and clipped the tie on her right wrist, then reached around the back of her neck and pulled her forward, trying to elevate her head and turn it to the side.

Left arm still lashed down, she could only lift her body a couple of inches. Some liquid spattered the wooden surface beside her, but most of it stayed in her mouth.

"Stop it or you're going to aspirate."

Her only response was another convulsive heave.

"Shit." He reached across her and clipped the other tie. Once her arms were free, he yanked her upright into a sitting position and slammed her scarred back with his massive hand.

The remaining contents of her stomach spewed from her body as she coughed and sputtered. Her head cleared enough to realize Falk was automatically responding to his EMT training. She allowed him to tend to her body, freeing her mind to consider her situation. Both of her hands were loose, offering new options.

She only had a few seconds to formulate a plan, and she would only have one chance to act. Stalling for time, she forced out more coughs as she scanned her immediate vicinity. She refused to lie on this table and let the monster do whatever vile things he had planned for her.

She faked an enormous dry heave, doubling over and clutching at her belly. He had one hand on her thigh and the other on her back. She pretended to choke again, and, as she anticipated, he thumped her back hard. She went with the force of the blow, allowing it to drive her upper body down. She reached out as if to brace herself and grabbed the awl. Before he knew what she'd done, she thrust the sharp point into the center of his stomach.

He staggered back, cursing as he glanced down at the bleeding puncture wound. With preternatural speed, he snaked out a hand and latched on to her wrist.

She tried to pull her arm away, but she was no match for him.

"Fucking bitch," he said through gritted teeth. He flexed his powerful forearm, torquing her hand and forcing the tool from her grasp.

She needed to distract him, or he would body slam her to the table and bind her again. She recalled what Wade had told her when he profiled the Cipher before they learned his identity. She merged that with what she'd seen in the fight video.

"How often did your father beat you, Falk?"

He paused, still clutching her wrist, but made no response.

"Is that why you torture girls? Did Daddy mess you up so bad that you can't get it up without—"

"Shut up." Holding her in place with one hand, he clenched the other, pulling it back to smash into her face.

She maneuvered the cut piece of zip tie in her palm until its jagged edge protruded like the blade of a box cutter. Before his knuckles connected with her nose, she plunged the zip tie's sharp edge deep into one of those ice-blue eyes glaring down at her.

He howled and released her, clapping both hands over his injured eye. She grabbed the tin snips and quickly bent to cut both of her ankles free. As she scrambled off the opposite side of the table, he staggered around the room, bellowing like a wounded bull.

She held the sharp piece of plastic in one hand and the snips in the other, keeping the table between them. He reached out to grab for her, and she dodged backward.

"I'm going to spend the rest of the night skinning you alive," he said. "And then I'm going to fuck you while you die."

She scanned the room, spotting the door behind him. There were no windows or other avenues of escape. He was stronger, bigger, and smarter. But she would damn well use her substandard genes to keep fighting with everything she had.

She moved to the left, drawing him in her direction. She let him inch closer. Blood oozed between the fingers of the hand clamped tightly over his eye. He was every bit as dangerous as any wounded beast.

She waited until he was almost within striking distance and darted to her right as he lunged for her. Damn he was fast. MMA fighting had honed his reflexes to a razor's edge. She had misjudged him. If his depth perception hadn't been compromised by the loss of vision in one eye, he would have caught her arm. Instead, his hand closed on the air where she had just been.

He roared in frustration, hurling more expletives at her. She ignored his words and concentrated on his body movements. Every ripple of his taut muscles telegraphed his next move, allowing her the split-second advantage that made the difference between life and death. She kept edging around one side of the table, then rushing around to the other when he reached for her. Gradually, she ended up with the door behind her.

"It's locked," he said. "Don't even try it."

Her heart sank. She had worked so hard to get into position. All for nothing. How long could she keep up this dance? She flicked her eyes to the table. Now she was close enough to reach more tools. She eyed the one she thought would do her the most good.

"That body art doesn't hide those cigarette burns on your back, Falk. Did Daddy give you those? Was his genetically engineered son a disappointment?"

With a howling battle cry, Falk launched his body over the table. She snatched the chisel and held it upright, angling it toward him. His momentum kept his body coming down as he impaled his chest on the chisel's sharp edge.

They crashed to the ground, his bulk landing on her in a heavy thud. A guttural groan escaped his lips as the air left his body.

Clutched in her hand, the chisel's plastic handle jabbed into her. The rest of it had penetrated his upper torso just beneath the joint of his rib cage. She was having trouble breathing with Falk's tremendous bulk pressing on her. She couldn't fill her lungs.

She let go of the handle and tried to push him off. He didn't budge. Holy shit, she had managed to survive only to have him kill her by suffocation after he was dead.

No. Fucking. Way.

She pushed again. Nothing. The blood oozing from his chest formed a slick between their bodies. Maybe she could slide out from under him. She wriggled to smear the blood around and began inching sideways. She managed a few inches. She used her legs to gain leverage and pushed again. Slowly, her body slid out from under his.

She lay on the floor, sucking in great gulps of air.

Without warning, his brawny arm crashed down on her chest. He dragged her toward him.

"You . . . are . . . mine." The words came out as a guttural rasp.

She curled her legs up, planting the soles of her feet against his hip. "Never." She pushed herself away.

He rolled over and belly-crawled toward her. She scrambled backward, hands and feet slipping on the blood-soaked floor. He reached out, grabbing at her. She bent her knee, took careful aim, and directed her heel straight at his nose. With every remaining ounce of strength she possessed, she shot her foot toward its target. A loud crunch split the air as she connected, driving the bones of his septum into his brain.

The momentum of the blow drove his head back, and his body followed, slumping on the ground. He twitched, then he lay still.

She flopped on her back, gasping.

The door burst open and a column of black-clad HRT operators swarmed inside shouting commands. The cacophony of thundering boots and booming voices shattered the stillness that had filled the air only moments before. Fanning out, the tactical team secured the space in a matter of seconds.

One of the men aimed a rifle at Falk's head, while another kneeled beside him to check his vitals. Nina knew they would find no sign of life. If Falk had any breath in him, he would have made sure he killed her before he succumbed.

An operator crouched beside her. "Where are you injured, Agent Guerrera?"

She realized how she must look. "It's Falk's blood."

As she answered, a second man sank to his knees on her other side. "Nina," he said, voice thick with emotion.

She turned to see Kent surveying her, an expression she couldn't place pulling the hard lines of his rugged face taut.

"I'm okay, really." It was a lie, but she reveled in the pain.

It meant she was alive.

Chapter 50

Two days later
J. Edgar Hoover Building, Washington, DC

Nina sat at the gleaming round table in the far corner of the FBI Director's spacious office. She laced her fingers in her lap to avoid twisting them. She had only met Director Thomas Franklin once before, when she graduated from the academy in Quantico.

His expression was grave. Then again, he wasn't known for laughing. The rumor around the Bureau was that the man was total business. Even his pajamas were starched.

He leaned back in his black leather chair, a tinge of weariness hooding his eyes. "That was the longest news conference I've ever held." He shook his silvery head. "There were reporters from around the world. Seems everyone on the planet has been following this story."

She had no idea what to say, so she held her tongue. She had obviously cost him a lot of sleep and no small amount of resources.

"They were most interested in how we managed to track down the Cipher," he continued. "I was pleased at how quickly the team adapted when his house turned out to be empty."

The team had met with her after her medical exam to fill her in. After coming up empty at Falk's residence, they had decided to check on the house where he grew up. Satellite photos showed a shed on the far end of the property surrounded by trees.

"First and foremost, I am deeply impressed with your performance throughout this investigation. You had to deal with things no one should have to face, and you did it with the world watching you in real time."

She squirmed uncomfortably at the reminder. She still hadn't gotten used to people eyeing her when they thought she wasn't looking or having all conversation cease when she entered a room.

"You showed exemplary valor in facing Halberd Falk, especially considering what he had done to you in the past," Franklin continued.

"Thank you, sir."

"Your courage deserves special recognition," Franklin said. "I will be presenting you with the Shield of Bravery at an official ceremony next week."

She was stunned. Director Franklin had submitted her for one of the FBI's highest honors. The Shield of Bravery was awarded for courageous acts in the line of duty involving a task force, undercover operation, grave situation, or crisis confrontation associated with the Bureau's highest-priority cases. This case probably fit every part of that description.

Still, she didn't feel worthy. "Sir, I did what was necessary to survive. Any other agent would have done the same."

"You did more than survive," he said. "You overcame great personal trauma under extreme duress and used your training and your wits to stop a killer who would have continued to take lives." Concern wrinkled his brow. "No, Agent Guerrera, no other agent could have solved this case. It had to be you."

A hot flush stole up her neck as she smoothed the crease in her slacks, giving herself an excuse to look away from his piercing gaze.

"There's another reason I wanted to speak to you," he said, mercifully changing the subject. "Supervisory Special Agent Buxton has requested an extension to your temp assignment in the Behavioral Analysis Unit."

Her head came back up. "How could I help the BAU, sir?"

"There have been a series of abductions in the DC metro area for a number of months. The Washington field office has the lead. I believe you are familiar with the particulars?"

She was intimately familiar with them. "My team is running point on the investigation."

"There hasn't been much headway," Franklin said. "SSA Buxton believes the four of you could look at it with fresh eyes, applying some of the same techniques you did in the Falk case."

"The four of us?"

"You, Kent, Wade, and Breck." He steepled his fingers. "If things go well, the team might even become permanent."

The possibility intrigued her. Supervisory Special Agent Conner, her current boss at the Washington field office, was not a fan of her unorthodox methods of investigation. Buxton, on the other hand, seemed to take her previous law enforcement and life experience into account rather than viewing her as merely the most junior member of the team.

Franklin interrupted her musing. "I didn't want to mention this in front of anyone within your chain of command because of what you have recently endured. Given everything that has happened, I could also transfer you to something less . . . stressful instead. Something that would keep you out of the public eye."

"You think I need to come out of the field?"

"Not at all," he said. "I'm offering you a choice."

She could assist with the abduction investigation out of Quantico, return to her previous assignment at the WFO, or request a transfer to a desk job. Yeah, right.

She straightened. "Please let SSA Buxton know I'll report to Quantico first thing in the morning."

Franklin regarded her for a long moment. He gave her a slight nod before the corners of his mouth quirked up.

Maybe the rumors weren't true after all. That looked like an actual smile.

"I have one final order of business," he said, growing serious again. "The task force collected a tremendous amount of data about your background. Once we knew Falk was aware of the circumstances of your birth, Buxton sent teams down every possible investigative avenue. Task force members obtained statements from the trash collector who found you as an infant, the social worker who named you, each of your living foster family members, most of your teachers, and every ER doc who treated you each time you went to the hospital throughout your childhood."

She sat, transfixed, imagining scores of her fellow agents fanning out all over Fairfax County, tracking down everyone who had impacted her life. "Sounds like they were very thorough."

"Some of this information was not included in any official reports," Franklin said. "I suspect much of it is completely unknown to you." He paused as if choosing his next words carefully. "I believe that it is your right to see what we gathered. It is, after all, the story of your life until the date of your emancipation at seventeen."

The story of her life. Not exactly the kind you would read to kids at bedtime.

"Here is a copy of the entire file," Franklin said, pushing the thick manila folder that had been on the table next to him over to her. "It's for you to keep."

"Thank you, sir." She picked up the dense file, clutching it to her chest.

"Good luck, Agent Guerrera."

She stood, understanding herself to be dismissed, and headed out the door. The administrative assistant gave her a curt nod as she passed by the outer waiting area.

She walked down the wide corridor, footsteps echoing on the tile floor. The area was uncharacteristically deserted, giving her the opportunity to consider what the Director had told her about the file. The manila folder felt enormously heavy. Its contents weighed on her mind as well as her arms.

Inside were the details of her childhood. Every bit of pain, humiliation, and abuse carefully documented in plain clinical text. The reports inside followed her trajectory from throwaway to Warrior Girl. She'd traversed a dark path to reach the light. She could walk that same path now from the perspective of her adult self, learning new things about the people who had previously controlled her life. What had been their motives, their hidden agendas, their secrets? Why had they tormented her? Answers she had longed for as a child were contained in the trove of documents now in her possession.

She strode past the copying room and paused. She took a few steps back and went inside, finding what she was looking for next to the copying machine. Nobody was around.

She hesitated a long moment. Coming to a decision, she crossed the room and turned her back to the copying machine. She laid the manila folder on the small table to her left. Opening it, she picked up the first few sheets of paper and straightened them. This would take a while.

Drawing in a deep breath, she began to feed the pages into the shredder, finally putting her past where it belonged.

Chapter 51

The Yellow Brick Road
FBI Academy, Quantico

The morning after her meeting with the Director, Nina's feet pounded the uneven earth along the winding trail. Early-morning sun dappled the ground through the tall Virginia trees. She should have waited. Should have given her body a chance to recover from the trauma Falk had inflicted. But this journey was not for her body. It was for her soul. This time, she would complete her journey along the Yellow Brick Road.

She had come early to be sure there was enough time to finish the course, shower off in the locker room, and report to Buxton for her first briefing. A couple of miles in, however, she'd begun to have second thoughts. Covered in bruises, her body ached with every step.

She arrived at the next obstacle and paused. The trench was about twenty-five feet long and six feet wide. Just to keep it interesting, the instructors always kept it filled with muddy water. A series of logs braced against each other formed a low overhead barrier designed to force runners to crawl through. In order to go forward, she had to be willing to sink down into the muck.

"Ladies first."

She lifted her gaze to see Wade jogging toward her from the opposite direction.

"What are you doing here?"

"Heard from one of the instructors that you were out here this morning. Figured we never got a chance to complete the course last time, so I decided to join you."

He had run from the finish line like he had before, skipping the obstacles, to meet up with her.

"That doesn't answer my question."

"We're going to be partners," he said. "Partners have each other's backs."

"You don't have to do this."

"Yes, I do."

Giving her head a small shake, she stepped into the trench, the chilly water shocking her system. The slimy bottom sucked at her feet as she picked them up to move forward. She took another step, then lowered herself down onto her hands and knees. Body half-submerged in sludge, she low-crawled.

Wade splashed down beside her, the filthy water sloshing up onto his face and dribbling into his mouth. He spat it out and kept going.

Her body trembled with chill and fatigue as they made it to the other side and climbed out. He grinned down at her, teeth stark white against the mud on his face.

She had emerged from the muck but had not come out unscathed. She was sullied, tainted, but not alone. Wade had gone through it with her.

She gathered herself and forced her legs to run, determined to keep going. After the ordeal, a shower would be her reward. She would scrub her body from head to toe. And maybe she would feel clean again.

And then she saw the wall ahead, blocking her path.

The wall was her biggest challenge on the course. She was short, barely five feet tall. Nina had been the smallest one in her police recruit class as well as the FBI trainee class. Her size had always been a burden until she had learned to fight and compensate in other ways.

Despite all her training, all her skill, Falk had nearly butchered her. She could not have overpowered him. Only quick thinking had saved her.

She considered the obstacle before her.

"Are you going to stand there and stare at it all morning?"

She whipped around to see Kent several yards behind her, catching up to them at a full run. With Kent's background in Special Forces, she figured he could run the course twice in the amount of time it took her to complete it once.

She spun back to confront Wade. "Did you invite the whole damn unit?"

He didn't look remotely apologetic. "I might have sent a text or two."

She rolled her eyes and returned her attention to the wall without answering Kent. Putting the two men out of her mind, she jumped up. Her fingers clutched the top of the barrier. Then slid off. She fell straight down, landing right on her ass in the dirt.

"You've got this," Kent said, smiling down at her. "Next time back up and get a running start, plant your foot on the wall, and launch your body up. Let me show you." He loped toward the barrier and leaped up, planting a foot on the side to propel his body upward. His hands clasped the top, and he flexed his powerful arms as he pulled his upper body over. His legs followed, and in one fluid motion, he disappeared to the other side.

He walked around and gestured toward the towering barrier. "It's all about technique."

"Being six-foot-four doesn't hurt," she said.

"Come on, Guerrera," Kent said. "Show me what you've got."

It was going to be ugly. She sprinted toward the wall, planted her foot, and managed to get a good grip on the top this time. She heaved her body upward and flung an arm over, struggling to keep from falling back.

She felt the barrier shake, and suddenly Kent was hanging beside her, holding himself in a pull-up position so he could coach her from a few inches away. "Use your feet."

She kicked at the wall with her sneakers until the rubber tips got enough purchase to propel her higher. Muscles burning, she managed to heave herself up just enough to get her upper body over. After that, she used gravity to finish the job.

She landed heavily on the other side. A second later, Kent thudded down neatly beside her. Wade followed next.

Only a few obstacles left to go. They continued through the course. While Wade and Kent chatted, she saved her breath for the next challenge.

Breck's bright red hair stood out as she ran toward them. She had obviously come from the end of the course, as Wade had.

Nina looked up at her new partner. "Seriously, Wade?"

"Nice of you to show up for the last *two* miles," Wade called out to Breck in a teasing voice.

Ignoring the barb, Breck fell into step beside Nina, matching her stride. "How's my girl?"

She must have looked every bit the charity case she was at that point in the run. Every muscle in her body screamed for her to stop. She was bruised, sore, and exhausted. "I feel great."

Breck shot her a dubious look. "Sugar, you look like ten miles of bad road."

Wade cataloged a litany of observations. "You're favoring your left leg, you wince every time you use your right arm, and you're sucking wind."

"Doesn't matter," she said. "I'm going to finish."

"And we're with you all the way," Kent said.

She realized they needed her to accept their help. If she was going to be part of this ad hoc unit, she would have to change her way of doing things. Over the years, she'd learned not to depend on anyone but herself. Others had let her down too many times. Now she had to figure out how to be part of a team.

She considered the three people flanking her as they drew close to the end of the course. A new feeling she couldn't identify surged through her, renewing her strength. Together, they were all going to make it. When they crossed the finish line, she realized what the feeling was.

Trust.

She thought about what the judge had told her at her emancipation hearing all those years ago. The hearing that had not only changed her name but the trajectory of her life. *"Circumstances have made you very independent at an early age, Ms. Esperanza, but you must allow others to help you when you need it. Remember that."*

She had remembered his words, but only now did she finally understand what the judge had been trying to tell her. The same lesson she had learned on the Yellow Brick Road.

She had become a warrior who no longer had to fight her battles alone.

ACKNOWLEDGMENTS

My husband, Mike, has been unstintingly supportive through all my endeavors. The best partner and friend anyone could want, he is my rock.

For my son, Max, who shows me the world through the eyes of a child every day. How blessed I am.

To my family, whether related by blood or the bonds of friendship, I am forever grateful for your understanding and patience over the years.

To my agent, Liza Fleissig, who shares my vision and makes miracles happen. Her advice, support, and outstanding professionalism have helped me navigate many unexpected bumps in the road. And there have been some bumps . . .

To my other agent, Ginger Harris-Dontzin, whose sharp eyes and equally sharp mind have been tremendously helpful as rough ideas struggle to take shape.

To the men and women of the FBI, who dedicate themselves to upholding their motto, "Fidelity, Bravery, Integrity." A special thanks goes out to Ret. Assistant Director Jana Monroe, Ret. Special Agent John Iannarelli, and Ret. Special Agent Jerri Williams.

To Megha Parekh, my acquiring editor with Thomas & Mercer, for her guidance through every part of the process. I am humbled and blessed by her support and willingness to take a chance on a fresh voice.

My developmental editor, Charlotte Herscher, put her considerable talent toward making this story better. Her incisive observations and keen eye for details were invaluable.

To the amazing team of marketing, editing, and artwork professionals at Thomas & Mercer, I am incredibly blessed to have such talented professionals by my side.

ABOUT THE AUTHOR

Photo © 2016 Skip Feinstein

Award-winning author Isabella Maldonado wore a gun and badge in real life before writing crime fiction. A graduate of the FBI National Academy in Quantico and the first Latina in her department to attain the rank of captain, she served as a patrol officer, hostage negotiator, spokesperson, recruit instructor, patrol supervisor, gang council coordinator, and district station commander. Her final assignment was as the commander of the Special Investigations and Forensics Division before retiring after twenty-two years on the force. Ms. Maldonado is a member of the FBI National Academy Associates, Fairfax County Police Association, International Thriller Writers, Mystery Writers of America, International Society of Latino Authors, and Sisters in Crime, where she served as president of the Phoenix Metro Chapter in 2015 and sat on the board until 2019. The author of the Detective Cruz series, she lives in the Phoenix area with her family. For more information, visit www.isabellamaldonado.com.